"Real" Indians and Others

Mixed-Blood Urban Native Peoples and Indigenous Nationhood

Bonita Lawrence

UBCPress · Vancouver · Toronto

Published in Canada by
UBC Press
2029 West Mall
The University of British Columbia
Vancouver, BC V6T 1Z2
www.ubcpress.ca

National Library of Canada
Cataloguing in Publication
Lawrence, Bonita
"Real" Indians and others :
mixed-blood urban Native peoples
and indigenous nationhood /
Bonita Lawrence.
Includes bibliographical
references and index.
ISBN 0-7748-1102-1 (bound);
ISBN 0-7748-1103-x (pbk.)
1. Indians of North America—Urban
residence—Canada. 2. Indians of
North America—Mixed descent—
Canada. 3. Indians of North Ameri-
ca—Tribal citizenship—Canada.
4. Indians of North America—Canada
—Ethnic identity. 5. Indians of North
America—Canada—Government rela-
tions. 6. Indians of North America—
Legal status, laws, etc.—Canada.
I. Title.
E78.C2L378 2004   305.897'071'091732
C2004-900849-8

To my mother
Eveline Marie Anida Mélanson Lawrence
September 1916–February 1999
Who was the primary inspiration for this work.
Merci, ma mère.

And in memory of the late Rose Cunha,
whose vision, strength, and kindness
were so important to so many people.

Contents

Acknowledgments

I want to thank my family for helping me to keep my balance, so far from home. There are also many friends who helped to make this journey possible. I want to thank my Ph.D. supervisor, Sherene Razack, for her assistance in shaping the thesis that became this book, and to acknowledge the encouragement of Lise LaFrance, Kim Anderson, Zainab Amadahy, Lorraine Le Camp, Peter Kohnke, Noulmook Sutdhibhasilp and Gail Maurice. I also want to recognize the support of people from the Four Directions Aboriginal Students' Centre at Queen's University—Robert Lovelace, Peter Cole, Pat O'Riley, and Carl Fernandez. *Chi Meegwetch* to the women I sang with while I was writing the thesis—Zainab Amadahy and Isabel Saez (and Shandra Spears!)—and to those I sing with now—Laura Schwager, Kelly Maracle, Alison Ferrant, and Stephanie Lovelace. And finally, to the people whose stories shaped this work—*Chi Meegwetch!*

I also wish to acknowledge the support of the Social Sciences and Humanities Research Council of Canada in writing the thesis that became this book.

Preface

This study grew from the awareness, as I looked around me, that many individuals in the Toronto Native community were visibly mixed-blood. While everybody simply professed a Native identity, some of us, it seemed, purely on the basis of appearance, were "more Indian" than others. Occasionally, I would be aware of tensions that were manifested around appearance, between dark-skinned Native people who denied the Nativeness of white-looking people and light-skinned people who maintained silence about the subject of their visible difference. Focusing on this issue seemed an effective way of addressing what lay behind the silence and tensions within the Toronto Native community about differences in appearance and what it signified. That this subject is close to my own heart, as an individual who has wrestled with her own ambiguity about her Native identity, only made this project all the more compelling to undertake. By way of explanation, I offer my own story.

I grew up in a family that identified itself, for the first few years of my life, as expatriate British. "We" (my father's story) were one of a handful of working-class British families who settled on the South Shore of Montreal at the end of World War II. In the tiny community I was born into, our family existed uneasily, nurtured on my father's tales of the Royal family, and anticipating the day when "we" would be returning to England. Silent in this version of who we were was my

mother, who took no part in the life of this little British community—
nor in the life of the equally tiny French-Canadian hamlet, which the
English immigrants had descended upon after the war. The extent to
which my mother—dark, French-speaking, Catholic—was ostracized
by the people around us, English *and* French, is something that was always there, so taken for granted as to be almost a nonissue. Mahogany-
skinned uncles, and aunts with Native features but French accents,
had visited us throughout our childhood—but they were simply part
of my mother's family, the silenced side of our family identity. They
did not fit with our "Britishness," but no explanations were offered.
In any case, I was quite young when my mother left my father, and
that chapter of our life as an (almost) British family came to an end.

Always told by my mother that "there's Indian in us," there was
nevertheless no language to describe who we were, on the South Shore
of Montreal in the early 1960s. By the time I was seven, family survival outweighed all other considerations. The frugal security of the
postwar white working-class existence we had enjoyed while my father was around had given way to an outright struggle for survival.
We were a desperately poor single-parent family—six of us subsisting
on the minimum-wage salaries of my mother and one sister, living in
French communities as outsiders, and moving continuously in search
of cheap accommodation. My mother lived in fear of having her children taken away from her. This imposed severe constraints on us,
as she did not dare to appeal to social assistance and always insisted
that rent and bills had to be paid first, so that we would not appear to
be in crisis, even if that left almost nothing for food. Her hard work
paid off in that she was able to maintain us as a family in the face of
tremendous odds. But the price of this struggle for survival has been
an absolute ruthlessness on her part about abandoning anything—
including any identification with Native people—which might stand
in the way of our survival as a family. The social stability that whiteness represents has been something that has been fought for, tooth
and nail, in my family.

So even as we gave up on attempts to explain our family as British,
in common-sense ways my siblings and I were not taught to identify
with the Native part of our heritage. Instead the rising nationalist
movement that gradually engulfed Quebec society weighed heavily
on our sense of who we were, as we struggled to situate ourselves, a
French-speaking mother and English-speaking children, on different
sides of the widening linguistic divide around us. By the time I was

a teenager, Englishness and whiteness had become common-sense
definitions of who my generation of our family was, even if a heritage
of chaotic poverty still marked us and set us apart from the working-
class white Anglo kids we went to school with. The wave of Native
militancy that sprang up during the early 1970s passed over us un-
touched, except for my mother's occasional expressions of a sense of
vindication. On a number of occasions in my young adulthood, during those intervals when I had spent any time outdoors and acquired a
tan, I was (as I thought it at the time) "mistaken" for Indian. Living in
all-white communities in Eastern Canada, where Native people have
been rendered largely invisible, I had little opportunity to socialize
with Native people.

My young adulthood was marked by self-destructive behavior,
manifested through drug and alcohol abuse and through abusive
relationships. I was almost thirty by the time I first attempted to
take control of my life and began my healing process. When I entered
university at the age of thirty-one, I quickly realized how poor the
fit was between who I was and the "real" Canadians (middle-class,
white, and Anglo) who surrounded me. This precipitated intensive
self-exploration in an attempt to explain my obvious differences. And
yet it was not until I received a student grant and spent two months
in the Cree community of Moose Factory, Ontario, that my mother
finally began to talk about her family to me—over the phone, long
distance, in short anecdotal accounts of childhood experiences. For
the first time, I began to struggle with an "in-between" feeling, which
was no longer linguistic, or class based, but racial. With the eyes of
the white society, I had learned to see the Native people around me
as "Other." But with my mother's stories in my ears—and with the
numbers of Cree Métis women I met in Moose Factory who looked
like her—and treated me like one of their own—I began to feel a
confused sense of connection between myself and these "others."
This sensation left me feeling increasingly at sea, hemmed in by
negatives—for if I gradually began to realize that my Native heritage
was real, and had had a tangible effect on my family's life, there was
certainly no way that I, with my years of light-skin privilege and my
unexamined notions of who or what was "Indian," could understand
myself to be a Native person. The following year I accompanied my
mother back to the Maritimes, in an attempt to recover our Mi'kmaq
family history—a process that has, in some ways, created more questions than answers about who we are as Native people.

I am left with piecing together an Aboriginal heritage out of family history as my remaining relatives remember it, from fragments gleaned from genealogical records maintained in two different Maritime Provinces, and from elders' accounts, weaving together bits of information about a time period almost a century earlier, among profound silences. Central to this process has been reinterpretation—taking accounts from family members that continually position our Nativeness as inconsequential or marginal and refiguring them to understand our Native identity in contemporary Native terms.

Identity, for my mother, was a complex issue. Around strangers, she would acknowledge that she was "part Indian" only reluctantly. She endured racist treatment from nuns at school as a child, being called "sauvagess" by Acadian boys, and other forms of denigration throughout her life. But what kind of name described her? She was brown-skinned but blue-eyed; she grew up off-reserve, nonstatus, and not speaking Mi'kmaq, with only periodic visits with Mi'kmaq relatives. There has been no tradition of "Métisness" in the Maritime Provinces. You were Indian or white—or you simply had no name for yourself. My mother, like most of her brothers and sisters, grew up calling herself "Acadian." They all left the Maritimes and married white. Most of her siblings settled in the United States, but my mother and one brother and sister stayed in Canada.

Before her death, my mother, like her one remaining sister, routinely distanced herself from her Native identity—acknowledging it primarily by deprecating it. On the one hand, she was not comfortable with being identified as Native. On the other hand, she also did not feel that she was a "real" Indian, since she did not grow up in a Native community and did not learn Mi'kmaq. Like her siblings, she had long since learned to see her Native identity as irrelevant. She had also learned, over the years, how to fit in so that her visible difference seemed irrelevant. Our generation in my family now lives with the repercussions of having been brought up to consider our Native heritage, at very deep levels, to be meaningless. And yet, like a tough weed whose roots are pervasively anchored everywhere in the soil of this land, and which therefore *cannot* be uprooted, our Native identity continues to manifest its presence in my family, even after a generation of silencing.

It is out of these experiences of belonging and not belonging, that I felt the need to seek out other mixed-blood Aboriginal people, from all walks of urban Native life, to discuss issues of Native identity. And yet, for me, it is impossible to pretend to be able to write objectively and dispassionately about this subject without taking into account what it was like to interview thirty other mixed-blood Native people on the difficult subject of their identities. There were the occasions when I would arrive in an exhausted and vulnerable state for an interview with a participant whom I had been introduced to through friends and did not know very well. I would find myself suddenly struggling with the worry that they might be so much "more Indian" than I was that my own identity claims might seem meaningless. On some occasions, the depth and solidity of participants' connections to community as revealed through their stories *did* have this effect, and I would go home in a state of upheaval, convinced that my claims to a Native identity were so minimal as to be, in a sense, fraudulent. On other occasions, I worried that other participants might not be "Indian enough" to be valid subjects for the thesis, from a vantage point that felt comfortably (if shallowly) grounded in my own Mi'kmaq heritage. My own sense of entitlement to a Native identity thus fluctuated wildly throughout the interview process.[1]

Gradually, however, through a year of exhaustive interviewing and another year of intensive discussion with other individuals within the Toronto Native community, the parameters of urban mixed-blood identity in Toronto gradually became clearer. Mixed-blood urban Native people may or may not look Native. They may or may not have Indian status. They may or may not have come from a reserve. In many, perhaps most, cases they do not speak their Native language. For many of them, by far the majority of their time is spent surrounded by white people. And yet, mixed-blood urban Native people are Native people for one clear reason: they come from Native families, that is, from families that carry specific histories, Native histories. In urban contexts, where other bonds of identity (language, band, territory, or clan) may no longer apply, family becomes all the more important for grounding a person as Aboriginal.

At the same time, many urban mixed-bloods have described how their families, which are the sources of their pride in their own identity, are also the sites where they have been most frequently discouraged from expressing any pride in that identity, or even from learning about it. The reasons are myriad and complex. Some were abjured to be silent about their identity as children, for their own protection in the face of racism, while others were told nothing about their heritage to make it easier for them to assimilate into a white identity. Some individuals come from families so disintegrated by alcohol and cycles of abuse that Nativeness has become too associated with pain and shame to be discussed. But for probably the majority of urban mixed-bloods, their parents and grandparents were silent about Nativeness simply because lifetime habits of silence, learned in childhood at residential school, or in negotiating a racist society, have been almost impossible to break. The multiple and sometimes paradoxical responses of Native families to the violence and loss that colonization has represented include silence, adaptation, and resistance.

A recurrent theme in the family histories of urban mixed-bloods is loss of relationship to their communities of origin. Government policies of deliberate interference in Native family life, such as residential school, loss of Indian status, and the forced adoption of Native children, as well as termination and relocation policies (in the United States) have resulted in individuals being permanently exiled from what was once home. The implications of this rupturing of ties to community, for peoples whose identities are rooted in a connection to land and other people, are profound. One individual referred to her family's experiences of loss of community as resulting in "generations of loneliness, isolation, and alienation."

The participants frequently wrestled with the reality of deliberate government misinformation. On a seemingly routine basis, officials erased all record of Native heritage on adoption forms. Census takers refused to categorise individuals as Native, listing them (in Canada) as French or (in the United States and Latin America) as black or Spanish instead. Priests changed the names of individuals or their families on residential school admission records and listed Native wives as "French" on marriage registries. Indian agents removed the names of orphans from their band lists after they were deposited, presumably for good, at residential school. Nativeness was erased, however and whenever possible, on many of the official documents that today are used to determine an individual's identity and heritage. In many cases this deliberate misinformation has made it almost impossible for individuals to recoup any knowledge of their own histories, as family stories and official records do not match. Finally, for some of the families, Christianization, slavery, or alcoholism have wreaked their particular havoc, cutting off the transmission of language, culture, and history at the root.

In the face of this organized obliteration of Indigenous presence, the contemporary generation of urban mixed-blood Native people has been reconstructing Native histories around the once-silenced voices of their parents and grandparents. In the process, they have been re-shaping their own lives to challenge assumptions that their families' Native identities are going to vanish. At the same time, as urban mixed-bloods, they have to negotiate multiple affirmations and denials of their Indianness (including denials from white family members) according to the extent to which they conform to hegemonic standards of what constitutes a Native person. Moreover they are negotiating these profoundly contradictory realities from a position of real weakness—in an urban setting where, despite significant numbers, the collective "clout" of an impoverished and deeply damaged community is minimal and where possibly the majority of the population lacks any legal recognition as Native people at all. Urban mixed-bloods in Toronto therefore struggle with the realities of both invisibility and placelessness, situated in the heart of a colonizing culture still predicated on the "vanishing Native," being eclipsed by the struggles of dozens of "multicultural" communities for survival and advancement, and facing First Nations leaders who disown and undermine their very existence. Despite this, the resilience, strength, and pride in heritage of urban mixed-blood Native people resound throughout their narratives.

The legacy of oppression they carry is tangible, however. No discussion about the people I interviewed is possible without some reference to the violence, dispossession, and sense of homelessness that marks most of their family experiences. For almost all of the participants in the study, their families left their home communities either through state-organized policies that forced them to leave or under the threat of other kinds of violence. Experiences of alienation and loss resonated through most of their histories, as did the choices of many of their families to be silent about their Native identity, in the interest of survival.

Indeed as participant after participant in this study related stories of their families' struggles, the continuous recurrence of histories of oppression and repression gradually began to form a metanarrative about encounters with genocide. This metanarrative has become the underlying premise shaping this book: that urban mixed-blood Native identity cannot be adequately understood except as shaped by a legacy of genocide. The meaning of the term genocide, as coined by Raphael Lemkin in 1944, during the discussions leading to the United Nations Genocide Convention, was given as follows:

> Generally speaking, genocide does not necessarily mean the immediate destruction of a nation, *except* when accomplished by mass killing of all the members of a nation. It is intended rather to signify a coordinated plan of different actions aimed at destruction of the essential foundations of the life of national groups, with the aim of annihilating the groups themselves. The objective of such a plan would be disintegration of the political and social institutions, of culture, language, national feelings, religion, and the economic existence of national groups, and the destruction of personal security, liberty, health, dignity, and the lives of individuals belonging to such groups. . . . Genocide has two phases: one, destruction of the national pattern of the oppressed group; the other, the imposition of the national pattern of the oppressor. (Lemkin 1944, quoted in Churchill 1994: 12–13)

I did not arrive at this way of looking at mixed-blood urban Native identity lightly, or casually, and certainly not through rhetoric, but rather because of a recognition that no other perspective encompassed the realities of the stories told to me. The fact that the participants unanimously agreed with this interpretation of their stories highlighted my sense that this premise is absolutely true to the realities of the people I interviewed. Because of this, in appendix 3, "Narratives of Encounters with Genocide," I have gathered together a handful of peoples' family histories as told in their own words. These stories provide a sense of how colonial control of Native identity has been lived "on the ground."

And yet the lives revealed to me also attest to the tremendous resiliency of Native people and Native cultures. Survival and regeneration, in a sense, are the common themes that bind urban mixed-blood Native peoples' lives together. It is my hope that this work can do justice to the family histories so kindly shared with me, can give them the kind of care and attention they deserve, and can situate them, as narratives of mixed-blood urban Native identity, no longer seen as marginal to the histories of Indigenous nations but recognized as crucial to our survival into the future.

We'lalioq! Um sed nogumak.
(Thank you! All my relations).

"Real" Indians and Others

Introduction
Mixed-Blood Native
Identity in the Americas

Identity, for Native people, can never be a neutral issue. With definitions of Indianness deeply embedded within systems of colonial power, Native identity is inevitably highly political, with ramifications for how contemporary and historical collective experience is understood. For Native people, individual identity is always being negotiated in relation to collective identity, and in the face of an external, colonizing society. In both Canada and the United States, bodies of law defining and controlling Indianness have for years distorted and disrupted older Indigenous ways of identifying the self in relation not only to collective identity, but to the land. This book engages both processes—how mixed-blood urban Native people understand and negotiate their own identities in relation to community and how external definitions and controls on Indianness have impacted their identities.

For many years traditional academic understandings of Native identity have been couched in terms of *primordiality*, a state of existence in contradistinction to modernity, whereby language, ways of living, and cultural knowledge as manifested by distinct beliefs, traits, and practices, transmitted in relatively unbroken lines from a distant past, and generally combined with "racial" purity, have defined membership in a specific tribal group. In recent years far more sophisticated understandings of ethnic identity have been developed, whereby such identity is no longer viewed as a static given transmitted from the past but is, rather, seen as socially constructed and mediated by contact with nation states and with other ethnic groups (Gould 1998, 13–14). James Clifford, for example, has described the manner in which Indigenous peoples, in the face of violent colonial assault, find powerful, distinctive ways to live as tribal people in an invasive world. He suggests that in the interests of survival, peoples such as the Mashpee Wampanoag Nation in New England have for years been engaged in "reviving and inventing ways to live as Indians in the twentieth century" (Clifford 1988, 9).

However, in the context of the Indigenous peoples of Guatemala, the constructionist approach has been articulated by Kay Warren as follows: "The constructionist approach notes that the Guatemalan categories *indigena*, *natural*, or *maya*, may be contrasted with *ladino*. But in practice, both the significance of the contrast and the labels used to mark 'self' and 'other' are tremendously variable over events, lifetimes, and recent history. From this viewpoint, there is no Mayan or Ladino, except as these identities are constructed, contested, negotiated, imposed, imputed, resisted, and redefined in action" (Warren 1992, 205).

This constructionist viewpoint, while in some respects very useful, is also deeply troubling to many Native people. What is missing, in such a viewpoint, is an awareness of how deeply colonialist perspectives have permeated virtually all aspects of any settler society built on Indigenous peoples' lands, including the academic institutions that construct these viewpoints. It is not only a matter of the "violence, curiosity, pity, and desire" that frequently accompanies the Western intellectual's gaze at those, such as Native people, who have been silenced in the bourgeois West (Clifford 1988, 5). It is the fact that the knowledge base at the core of Indigenous societies continues to be devalued within precisely those academic contexts that are busily theorizing Nativeness as merely contingent and negotiated. What Cree scholar Lorraine Le Camp referred to as the "terranullism" of critical theory—the habit on the part of academics from all backgrounds to adopt a postconquest set of assumptions, that the Americas are originally empty lands, devoid of any valid Indigenous presence (Le Camp 1998)—means that the fundamental questions about land and sovereignty in the Americas have yet to be raised in any meaningful way within most disciplinary discourses.

Native scholars who have engaged in these discourses are all too frequently challenged as to their ability to authentically represent Native peoples. Vine Deloria Jr.'s review of *The Invented Indian: Cultural Fictions and Government Policies* by James Clifton succinctly explores how the apparent modernity of contemporary Native American life is used as a tool of disenfranchisement by those such as Clifton who are characterized by Deloria as being angry and disappointed at Indians for not living up to their childhood fantasies. Deloria notes that these attacks are often part of a struggle for turf, whereby white academics are invested in maintaining an authoritative voice for themselves as "Indian experts" by demanding that their authority to determine who or what is authentically Indigenous be maintained, even at the cost of challenging the ability of Native scholars to represent Native people (V. Deloria 1998).[1] Meanwhile, there is a profound gap between the increasingly exclusive enclaves of the universities, where most critical theory is produced, and the lived experiences of the majority of Native people, who overwhelmingly are not in the universities—a contrast that is perhaps best characterized by Philip Deloria as "a self-focused world of playful cultural hybridity and a social world of struggle, hatred, winners, and losers (with Indians usually numbered among the losers)" (1998, 176). This reality continues to resonate for Native academics, artists, and others who are attempting to explore complex and nuanced notions of Native identity.

In the context of ongoing colonization, to theorize Native identity not as an authentic essence but as something negotiated and continuously evolving can have dangerous repercussions for Native people in terms of asserting Aboriginal rights. James Clifford has explored the example of the Wampanoag Indians of Mashpee who in 1977 were required to prove their identities as Native people in order to pursue their land claim:

> To establish a legal right to sue for lost lands these citizens of modern Massachusetts were asked to demonstrate continuous tribal existence since the seventeenth century. Life in Mashpee had changed dramatically, however, since the first contacts between English Pilgrims at Plymouth and the Massachusett-speaking peoples of the region. Were the plaintiffs of 1977 the "same" Indians? Were they something more than a collection of individuals with

varying degrees of Native American ancestry? If they were different from their neighbours, how was their "tribal" difference manifested? During a long, well-publicized trial scores of Indians and whites testified about life in Mashpee. Professional historians, anthropologists, and sociologists took the stand as expert witnesses. The bitter story of New England Indians was told in minute detail and vehemently debated. In the conflict of interpretations, concepts such as "tribe," culture," "identity," "assimilation," "ethnicity," "politics," and "community" were themselves on trial. (Clifford 1988, 7–8)

In his account of this trial (which the residents of Mashpee lost) Clifford points out that a central issue that the Mashpee Indians faced was the white need for certainty about the parameters of Indian "difference." To be recognized as a group within the Wampanoag Nation, the Mashpee community had to be capable of demonstrating to white people the primordial nature of their claims to Indianness.[2]

The experience of the Wampanoag people at Mashpee is not unique. Most disputes over Indigenous land title anywhere within the Americas hinge on the requirement that Indigenous people prove their primordiality. For example, when the Gitksan and Wet'suwet'en peoples went to court in the 1980s to assert their ancestral claim to fifty-eight thousand square miles of territory in Northern British Columbia, the elaborately detailed oral histories that elders presented in courts over the space of a year, establishing unbroken governance and land use for the past twelve thousand years, were rendered invalid by the manner in which the plaintiffs were continuously presented as contemporary interlopers whose claims to Indigenous land title were invalid because they were not the same people as their ancestors were—because they held paying jobs, lived in houses, consumed pizza and other European foods, and in general lived contemporary lives (Monet and Skanu'u 1992, 141–69). Indeed in the Supreme Court decision of the appeal launched by the Gitksan and Wet'suwet'en peoples for this case— Delgamuukw—the court took it upon itself to define the nature and extent of Aboriginal title in Canada, in ways that demand that Aboriginal people maintain primordiality. The court decision makes Aboriginal title contingent upon Aboriginal peoples not engaging in practices "which would sever their special relationship to the land" (as defined by the courts) and continues the trend within recent Supreme Court decisions, such as Van der Peet, Smokehouse, and Gladstone, to limit the Aboriginal rights named in the Canadian constitution to precontact practices (Mainville 2001, 26–33). Nor are "progressive" non-Natives necessarily our allies here. Many theorists on racial identity and antiracism appear to have accepted notions of Native identity that are based on primordiality—so that, for example, in the United States, whole communities of mixed-race Native people who do not look Native are dismissed as being "really" white or black.[3] And attacks on the authenticity of contemporary Aboriginal existence continue to come from white environmentalists who disparage the modernity of contemporary Native existence and use their arguments to campaign for new restrictions on emergent Native land rights.[4] In such contestations of identity (which are always on white terms), Native people who are revealed as transgressing the boundaries of so-called authenticity through their modernity can be dismissed as fakes, or severely restricted in their abilities to develop their communities in contemporary ways. Given such high demands from all quarters, including those who consider themselves our allies, for primordial Nativeness, to theorize Native identity *solely* as negotiated and shifting demolishes the boundaries that colonial governments demand as fundamental to Nativeness.

And yet, ironically, it is precisely because of the embattled aspect of Native identity—how it is constantly being negotiated in a context of domination—that engaging in ongoing struggles to challenge the demand for primordiality is necessary work that Native academics must do. Canadian court decisions continue to restrict Aboriginal rights to precontact activities. The Western imagination continues to paint the world as populated by "endangered authenticities," always juxtaposed to modernity, always going crazy in the face of the inescapable momentum of progress and change (Clifford 1988, 4–5). There is no future for Native people within these frameworks, other than as "the Vanishing Race." However, Mohawk scholar Taiaiake Alfred has pointed out that the choices currently offered for Native people in contemporary academic discourse—between primordialism (the Indigenous identity consisting of unbroken tradition and continuity) and the constructionist approach, which Alfred calls instrumentalism (Indigenous identity based solely on a conscious manipulation of traditions and cultural inventions as part of the emergence of nationalist ideologies)—are both part of an essentialist (and I might add colonialist) fallacy. He notes that there is no simple answer to whether peoples or nations or cultures change or stay the same, as aspects of both inevitably occur (Alfred 1995, 88). What is unspoken among these "choices" is the question of who sets the terms to evaluate Indigenous identities. Identity, in this sense, is primarily about how history is interpreted and negotiated and about who has the authority to determine a group's identity or authenticity (Clifford 1988, 8). The central focus of this book is urban mixed-blood Native identity in Canadian contexts. It explores the tensions and complexities of Native identity when one is mixed-blood, urban, and either possessing or lacking legal "Indian" status or band membership. Throughout this work, Native identity is explored as a negotiated and highly contested set of realities. At the same time, as many of the participants of the case study that comprises the core of this work have discussed, identity is also lived as a deeply embodied reality, to the extent that a number of individuals speak in terms of "blood memory," even in the face of the overwhelmingly diasporic nature of urban Native life. For, as the case study documents, the lives of urban mixed-bloods, both in Canada and the United States, are indelibly stamped by processes of diaspora created by government policies designed to sever Native peoples from their communities, such as forced removal from lands in the face of settler encroachment, displacement through residential schooling and adoption, and termination of tribal status.

While this book focuses primarily on Canada, a basic issue that resonates throughout it is the broader North American context in which Indigenous identities are negotiated. For Native people in Canada to take the presence of the United States seriously is perhaps not as difficult a task as for American Indians to consider Native perspectives from Canada important. Nevertheless both sets of perspectives are necessary—not only in the sense that settler-state boundaries are irrelevant to Native people and that Canadian and American colonization histories have been deeply interwoven, but because each country has maintained distinctly different ways of regulating Native identity. Taking the larger picture into account enables a much deeper understanding of the issues shaping mixed-blood Native identity in Anglo-dominated North America. A very different discourse on mixed-blood status and Indian identity, which developed in the United States, is gaining an increasing foothold in Canada. And yet this discourse is inevitably overlaid on top of another one, that which was created by Canada's Indian Act.

A crucial issue emphasized in this book is that these very different discourses must be understood within the contexts where they developed—the respective colonization histories of Canada and the United States. The fact that Native identity in Canada has primarily been shaped by a system of regulation and control that Britain developed as a global imperial power, while the peculiarities of the United States' origin as a settler colony in rebellion from the same network of imperial power prevented the American government from implementing direct legislative control over tribal identity until much later in the process of Manifest Destiny, has meant that distinctly different ways of controlling Indianness have developed in two otherwise very similar settler states. Because of this, although colonial authorities within Canada often worked in tandem with American authorities, and at other times "piggybacked" off of American Manifest Destiny (so that military violence south of the border enabled Canadian authorities to pacify and subordinate Native peoples north of the border primarily through the *threat* of military violence), distinctly different settlement histories and colonization policies have led to certain divergences in how Native identity is conceptualized in the different countries.

In the United States, the inability of the new republic to openly assert direct colonial control over Native communities from its inception has meant that the United States pursued other policies—notably the deployment of settler violence and warfare, later supplemented by legislation and government policies, all of which focused on directly removing whole communities from their land base and gradually destroying tribal sovereignty, rather than controlling Indianness through identity legislation from the start. In Canada, by contrast, the direct colonial control exerted by a settler state maintained by a global imperial power enabled Canada to create the Indian Act's legal status system and its highly divisive manner of externalizing "half-breeds" and creating patriarchal divisions within Native communities, which automatically and continuously "bled off" people from their communities without the need for other policies of removal.

Along with these differences in colonization history are contemporary differences in circumstances between Native peoples in Canada and the United States. Generally speaking, American Indians have a much larger land base but a much smaller population relative to the size of the settler population than Native people in Canada.[5] They face a colonizing nation-state that is immensely more powerful and whose underlying premise of Manifest Destiny now encompasses much of the globe. They also face a New Age movement the sheer size and predatory scale of which is difficult to comprehend in Canadian terms. Because of these and other differences, American Indian ways of conceptualizing mixed-blood Native identity are highly distinct from those of Native people in Canada. Therefore in the early chapters of this book I focus, in a comparative manner, on some of the differences between identity legislation and colonization histories in Canada and the United States.

This book moves back and forth from examining some of the broad implications of Indian legislation to exploring specific aspects of urban community realities. One of the first points that must be made, given that urban mixed-blood Native people by definition do *not* live in those few sites recognized by the federal government as Indian land, is that the kinds of life experiences that shape urban mixed-blood Native identity are highly contingent on the kinds of urban spaces that constitute their homes—and that in many respects these differences cross Canadian-U.S. lines. In particular, because of the historical progression of colonial domination across North America, urban mixed-blood Native people face different realities in different regions of the continent, especially in Canada. In western Canada, all but the most light-skinned urban Native people must negotiate a society that is fundamentally still actively colonialist, where rigidly segregated spaces, a regime of tacitly organized police violence, and one of the highest rates of imprisonment in the world ensure that Nativeness, particularly in urban centers, is contained in zones of fundamental illegality where universality does not apply.[6] In the western United States, the everyday settler violence of a fundamentally Indian-hating society contributes to a similar set of realities as those facing the more nakedly colonial regime that shapes life for urban mixed-bloods in western Canada.

By comparison, in the large cities of eastern Canada, and possibly even more in the cities of the eastern United States, urban mixed-bloods face the triumphant and globally powerful face of North American white supremacy, which hides its colonizing roots under a cosmopolitan and liberal façade. The power that this society has gained from establishing itself on the appropriation and devastation of a continent now enables it to proclaim itself as the seat of Western liberal humanist values, even as it draws in and transforms most of the world into its global market. Urban mixed-blood Native people in the large eastern cities must therefore wrestle with the logic of this apparently all-powerful dominant culture every day, where "the Indian wars" have been declared won, where Nativeness is considered extinct and is recognized only as a fleeting, primordial essence, and where an Otherness that is mixed-blood or urban *cannot* be recognized. Urban mixed-bloods in these regions therefore routinely face demands that they "perform Indianness" in order to have their Aboriginality recognized at all. Accompanying these realities is the other face of the dominant society—the most privileged sectors of the society who are confronting a postmodern collapse of meaning and its accompanying angst and who are aggressively asserting their need—and in some cases their *right*—to consume Otherness. Often it is these people who are most disappointed in the multifaceted and at times ambiguous Otherness of urban mixed-bloods and who routinely set themselves up as arbiters of who has the right to claim an Aboriginal identity.

It is also impossible to examine mixed-blood Native identity without taking into account the historical legacy of Native-white liaisons that still shapes contemporary realities. Across the Americas, two very different nation-building discourses have shaped Native-white intermarriage—the strongly white supremacist abhorrence of miscegenation common to settler societies with a large white population, such as Canada and the United States, and the practice of *mestizaje* promoted within those Latin American countries with only a small white settler population. In western Canada a counterdiscourse rupturing concepts of miscegenation, that of *métissage*, also arose during a specific set of social relations in the mid-nineteenth century. These nation-building discourses have been crucial in teaching large numbers of the detribalized and mixed-blood children and grandchildren of Indigenous people to see themselves primarily as citizens of the settler states, for whom any real Indigenous identity is permanently lost. Although this is an important aspect of mixed-race urban Native reality, I have not explored this process in detail. Instead I have chosen to emphasize the importance of legal regulation of identity for Native people. Nevertheless it is important to note that in many respects a deeper look at mixed-race identity across the Americas needs to take into account the different perspectives that mixed-blood peoples in different regions of the Americas have adopted toward their Indigeneity, largely as a result of the different nation-building discourses that shape the contexts they are forced to negotiate.

In a very real sense, this study is about multigenerational experiences of urbanity—about an urban population that has grown up in cities, whose members are well-adapted to city life, and who have found new ways to express Aboriginal identities as urban people. In a sense it is necessary to address urbanity, and the diversity in Aboriginal experience that it suggests, in order to be able to even introduce the subject of being mixed-blood. It is impossible to talk about being a mixed-blood urban Native person without first challenging the stereotypes rampant throughout North American society, which suggest that being Aboriginal and being urban and mixed-blood are mutually exclusive categories. Outside of such stereotypes, however, the implications of urbanity for Native identity in general, when cultural heritage is closely linked to a strong connection to the land, are considerable. The implications of urbanity for mixed-race Native people, in a context where considerable pressures to assimilate have strongly impacted their families, are even more important to consider.

For urban mixed-bloods across different regions of Canada and the United States, the complex realities referred to earlier are often negotiated simultaneously with a different set of tensions—histories of internalized racism and the fears that haunt many urban mixed-blood Native families that Nativeness, like any space of racialized Otherness, is a deeply dangerous place. Many urban mixed-bloods, accordingly, frequently wrestle with assimilatory desires that might run very deep in their families, desires to reject the unsafety of Nativeness and embrace and be part of triumphant white culture. Nor must the deep structural effects of racism be ignored. Despite the fact that light-skin privilege is always mediated by class, gender, and location, the reality, across Indian Country, is that there is almost always a nexus of increasing access to wealth and privilege that accompanies increasing whiteness. This must be taken into account in understanding the at-times contradictory nature of mixed-blood identity in Anglo North America, with its different spaces of marginality and privilege. Clearly, to exist as a mixed-blood urban Native person in Canada or the United States is to negotiate profound strains and ambiguities as daily existence.

Many Native people are troubled that the price of emphasizing a mixed-blood identity is a devaluing of tribal identity, as Creek-Cherokee academic Craig Womack writes:

> I'm somewhat ambivalent about the whole notion of celebrating mixedblood identity . . . emphasizing a generic identity over tribal specificity. It's not the issue of mixedblood identity that bothers me since, for better or worse or a combination of the two, this is

a contemporary reality for many Indian people, including myself. What bothers me is making mixedblood identity the primary focus of one's identification or one's writing. I'm wondering if identifying as mixedblood, rather than as part of a tribal nation, diminishes sovereignty? . . . What might be called for is a view of identity in terms of the larger picture—the tribal nation—rather than in terms of the (individual) fragmented mixedblood. (Womack 1997, 32)

And yet, even as mixed-blood Native people insist on the primacy of a tribal identity, being legally disqualified from the life of their Indigenous nation through loss of Indian status makes a thorough reclaiming of a tribal identity very difficult. Furthermore, in some cases, the lives of urban mixed-bloods do not necessarily correspond to the tight boundaries dividing Native and white, either with respect to appearance, or in the sense of feeling entirely at home in the Native world or in non-Native settings. For these reasons, the case study that informs this book explores the struggles of the participants to negotiate sometimes highly contradictory circumstances.

On the other hand, flying in the face of any preoccupation with being "mixed" are the feelings expressed by a number of the individuals I interviewed, about ancestral memory, about being the conduit through which the silenced voices of their families must now be heard. This speaks to a notion of an undivided Native identity existing in a "racially mixed" body. It is clear that identity, particularly in contexts where the effects of a legacy of genocide continue to unfold, is far more complex than any neat categories can suggest.

It is important to recognize the extent to which identity is dependent on social milieu. One cannot live out a certain identity in the abstract. The existence of such an identity must be recognized by other individuals before it can be lived as real. For most mixed-blood Native people, a crucial issue in their ability to identify as Native people has been the expansion of the category of Native to include them. In eastern Canada, the opening up of the category of Native to include mixed-blood people is a relatively recent development, coming from a number of directions, both internal and externally imposed—including the growing numbers of mixed marriages in urban contexts, the refiguring of categories of Indianness under Bill C-31, and a conscious attempt to reject colonial divisions among Native people.[7] In western Canada, however, an entirely different set of historical conditions existed in the nineteenth century, where mixed-blood Native people who had been created as a social group because of the fur trade were cut out of the treaties negotiated with western tribes and were therefore forced to struggle for recognition of political nationhood *as* mixed-blood people in the face of the ascendant Canadian settler state. As a result, in western Canada the existence of mixed-blood Native people—the Métis—has always been recognized.

On the other hand, because of the extent to which the Indian Act has tied Nativeness to Indian status, whether an individual even identifies as *being* mixed-blood is highly dependent on whether they are a status Indian and whether they come from a reserve. This was continuously manifested in the case study, where those individuals who had grown up on-reserve or who had spent considerable time in their home communities throughout their lives, even if they were blond-haired and blue-eyed, did not conceive of themselves as being mixed-bloods but simply as being Indian. Between those who have been legally excluded from Indianness, for whom being mixed-blood appears problematic, and those whose Indianness has been legally assured and who therefore do not see themselves as *being* mixed-blood, the effect of legal categories of "Indianness" on mixed-blood Native identity is central to this study.

In speaking of urban mixed-blood Native identity, what can never be forgotten is the context in which such identity issues are being articulated—within settler states whose claims to the land depend on the ongoing obliteration of Indigenous presence. It is therefore important to take into consideration some of the potential strengths and weaknesses, for urban and First Nations or tribal communities, when urban individuals of Native heritage make choices that take seriously their Indigenous heritage. In a sense, when urban mixed-bloods begin to take their Native heritage seriously, what is really meant is that they are taking cultural genocide seriously—both in terms of the phenomenal pressures that most urban mixed-blood families have faced historically to minimize, deny, and in every way virtually eradicate their Indianness and the absolutely unchallenged everyday assumptions permeating the dominant culture that Indianness will *continue* to die with mixed-bloodedness and urbanity—that the thousands and thousands of individuals across North America who each generation become mixed-blood through intermarriage and who grow up outside their communities will inevitably leave their Nativeness behind.

And yet because of the ongoing colonial context in which Native identity is negotiated, the moment when individuals who are both urban and mixed-blood, particularly if they do not have tribal membership, begin to take their Aboriginal heritage seriously appears as a moment of both power and danger for Aboriginal communities. The dangers may be less immediately apparent, but need to be reiterated. One problem is the trend across North America for white people, often those centrally involved in the colonization process, to pretend to be mixed-blood Indians—as Ward Churchill puts it, cloaking themselves in the identity of their victims (Churchill 1994, 228). Another worst-case scenario is for *virtually* white people to resurrect an extremely distant Native ancestor whose existence has no other tangible implications for an otherwise white family than to enable that individual to "boundary cross" in the name of that ancestor and therefore have access to otherwise forbidden Native spaces, usually for some form of personal gratification—including claiming (with dominant culture authority) the right to speak with a Native voice. At its most extreme, such individuals not only invade urban Native spaces, but colonize and profit from them—not only taking jobs but setting agendas.

It is important not to view situations too simplistically, to assume that any light-skinned person involved in the urban Native community is "fooling genocide" (Forbes 1987)—invoking a distant Native ancestor for the personal satisfaction of being able to claim to be "both the victor and the vanquished."[8] The generations of intermarriage with whites that have taken place in many Native communities, particularly in eastern North America, have created many light-skinned or white-looking Native people with solid claims to an Indigenous identity. And yet these realities inevitably raise the thorny question of limits to Indianness—issues of legal entitlement, cultural protection, the closures that are continuously being invoked by some Native people against others with at least some claims to a Native identity, and the implications of not invoking closure. It is no accident that in Canada, where colonial rules governing Native identity have been recently changed, Native communities are often highly concerned with setting boundaries as to membership.

In some respects this concern for boundary setting is based on the need to maintain Native land in Native hands and to control who will have access to community resources. There is the ever-present, pressing need to protect the cultural knowledge that the colonizing culture for over a century has targeted for extinction and a determination that only those who have shared a colonized people's history should participate in shaping its destiny. And there are also the scarring experiences of racism that darker Native people have experienced and the strengths and comforts of shared collective knowledge and values, which outsiders to reserve communities cannot share. Nevertheless, in the context of a colonizing culture, any concern with setting boundaries to Indianness is inevitably shot through with legal definitions and notions of Indianness originating in the dominant culture.

For tribal communities, the moment of danger that mixed-blood urban Native people represent lies in their potential ability to create a counterdiscourse on Indianness that affects the contemporary status quo of tribal societies in unpredictable ways. This appears particularly dangerous if survival in Indian Country is premised solely on protecting fragile and endangered reservation communities from outsiders—with the accompanying belief that urban-based Native people have nothing tangible to offer in terms of Indigenous empowerment.

And yet I believe that any of the dangers articulated earlier are considerably overshadowed by the potential power of this moment. First of all, urban mixed-blood Native people are *not* extraneous to Indigenous communities. As this book hopes to demonstrate, they represent the other half of a history of colonization, the children and grandchildren of people removed, dispersed, and continuously bled off from Native communities as a result of ongoing colonization policies—residential schooling, termination and relocation, the theft of Native children into the child welfare system, and a century of removing Indian status from Native women and their descendents. For urban mixed-bloods and tribal people to meet, from different current locations but with an acknowledgement of historic connections and to find ways of working together across current differences, could represent another stage of rebuilding the shattered hoops of different nations, a powerful process of decolonization.

The second strength that urban mixed-bloods can bring to Native people as a whole is demographic. As this book will touch upon, in Canada the presence of large numbers of mixed-blood, nonstatus, and detribalized Native people—the by-product of centuries of fur trade—has always been seen as a threat to a settler society that, due to its colonial nature, has been inherently white supremacist. The tremendous demographic increase in total numbers of Native people, which happens when nonstatus urban people of mixed heritage identify as, and are recognized as, Aboriginal, can force a change in the relationship between Aboriginal peoples and the settler society. In this respect, if urban people of Native heritage begin to take seriously the cultural genocide that is central to this heritage—and can find ways to work with contemporary tribal communities in ways that strengthen both urban and reserve-based communities—then Native people can enter into much more powerful relations with the dominant society.

To date there is a conflicting discourse coming out of Indian Country on the issue of mixed-blood identity. While contemporary Native fiction writers, many of whom are mixed-bloods, frequently explore mixed-blood themes in their work, some Native American academics have profoundly rejected mixed-bloodedness as a viable Native identity. Elizabeth Cook-Lynn, for example, unequivocally states that intermarriage and the presence of the Métis were as devastating to Plains Indian life as the destruction of the buffalo, because of the manner in which the extended family system, which held together Lakota/Dakota societies, was destroyed by unregulated intermarriage (Cook-Lynn 1996, 35–36). In contemporary Native contexts, Cook-Lynn criticizes the individualism and cultural hybridity that mixed-bloodedness appears to signify and the inability or unwillingness of many mixed-bloods to consider tribal realities as viable in the contemporary world (Cook-Lynn 1998). In such perspectives, the role of government regulation in shaping Indianness historically, both for urban mixed-bloods *and* for tribal citizens, drops out of the picture.

Indeed the role that legal control of Native identity has played in shaping the lives of urban mixed-blood Native people—and the identities of all Native people—is an issue with which this book begins and will return to again and again. In Canada federal Indian legislation has shaped who among Native people even considers themselves to be mixed-blood and who does not. And finally, simply being urban—which itself is shaped no less by identity legislation than any other aspect of urban mixed-blood reality—is a site of deep divisions over who is a "real" Indian and who is not. Because of this, the legacy of how colonial regulation of Native identity has shaped self-definition as Native people—between those whose Indianness is assured by federal regulation and those whose Indianness is not—is central to this book. The continued influence of colonial regulation of Native identity still defines who has been legally recognized as Indian and who has been classified as nonstatus or Métis, those whose "blood quantum" lies below a fairly arbitrary cutoff point for definitions of Indian-

ness and those with "sufficient" blood quantum, and those who have
been legally "allowed" to remain band members or on tribal rolls and
those who have not.

The question of who is an Indian, which lurks beneath the surface
of many of the issues that contemporary Native communities are
struggling with, is much larger than that of personal or even group
identity—it goes directly to the heart of the colonization process and
to the genocidal policies of settler governments across the Americas
toward Indigenous peoples. The question Who is an Indian? in North
America begins with the colonial project of land theft and regulation
of Native identity, either through direct legislation such as the Indian
Act (in Canada) or as part of the process of privatization and selling
off of reservation land, both before and during the allotment era in
the United States. At present formal regulation of Native identity in
Canada and the United States must be seen as having an overarching
primary goal: to set the legal parameters by which Indigenousness
can be said to be eliminated. Once these parameters have been set,
policies can be put into place to continuously restrict and diminish
membership in Indigenous societies, until the "final conclusion"—
the elimination of Indigenous peoples *as* peoples, according to these
parameters—is reached. These bodies of legislation have had powerful
effects on how Indianness is seen in common-sense ways; as a result,
a central issue in terms of Native empowerment in both Canada and
the United States must involve a careful deconstruction of the ways
in which federal regulation has shaped who is considered to be Indian.
This book will hopefully contribute something to a growing dialogue
that is beginning such a process of deconstruction.

It is important to be clear that this book, while exploring how legislation has shaped Native peoples' understandings of Indianness, is
not suggesting that traditional understandings of Indigenous identity
no longer exist. Nor does it suggest that legislation or nation-building
myths were the sole, or even the primary, means by which Indigenous
peoples were colonized, dispossessed, and murdered (although nation-
building myths continue to be a primary means by which the histories
of Indigenous presence—and the violence of colonization—are routinely erased). The regulation of Native identity by settler states can
only be effective once Native peoples have been dispossessed of their
lands to the extent that they must rely on some form of negotiated coexistence with settler governments, coexistence that always demands
that Native peoples conform to government legislation about who is

Indian. In the same way, national mythologies that erase Indigenous presence while absorbing detribalized people into a fundamentally Indian-hating body politic cannot be effected unless a settler society has the power to demand external conformance with settler dictates, particularly in terms of language use and other open expressions of Indigenous culture. The legislative and discursive means by which Indigenous identities are assaulted and erased—and the process given a patina of legality—are therefore only the current expression of a vast range of destructive processes that have been utilized to destroy Native people. These processes have included deliberately introduced diseases and alcoholism, wholesale land expropriation, resource plundering practices, the deliberate use of starvation tactics, settler violence and organized military violence to subjugate communities and suppress resistance, centuries of widespread and concerted attacks on Indigenous spiritual and ceremonial life, and finally the theft of Native children, first into residential schools and then into the foster care system.

Seen against such a backdrop of violence and destruction, the regulation of Native identity by government legislation and the erasure of Native presence and historical memories of the colonization process by foundational nation-building myths may appear relatively innocuous. And yet, when backed by the possibility of state violence or loss of access to government monies if one does not comply with government agendas, controlling Native identity becomes central to subverting or suppressing Native resistance. Viewed hemispherically, or even in terms of the individual settler state, the question of who is an Indian begins to loom larger and larger, both in terms of the land theft it has enabled (and continues to enable) and in terms of its contemporary implications for Indigenous empowerment. It becomes visible as an issue running far deeper than the individual concerns of urbanized and mixed-blood individuals, to the heart of the genocidal agendas of settler states across the Americas.

This book begins at this point—with an exploration of how federal regulation of Native identity, policies of diaspora, and mythologies that render Indianness extinct or invisible, affect the lives and identities of Aboriginal peoples. Its primary focus is Canada, and indeed much of it is highly specific to eastern Canada. It includes a c study of how the afore-mentioned laws, policies, and mythol have shaped the lives and identities of the Native people, m them mixed-bloods, who form an urban Native communit enty thousand people in Toronto, Ontario. And yet it also engages generally with the range of ways in which Native identity has been controlled and regulated in different contexts, taking into account the different histories and local conditions faced by Native people in other parts of Canada and exploring, in a preliminary manner, the system of blood quantum regulation utilized in the United States. The goal here is to give a sense of the different pressures shaping, distorting, and marginalizing Indigenous identities in different places and the nuanced and local complexities of urban mixed-blood Native experience stemming from these different histories. Indeed it is only possible to deeply understand the particular issues facing urban mixed-bloods in eastern Canada by taking the larger view.

The manner in which the Canadian government's regulation of Native identity has become deeply internalized, by Aboriginal people as well as by members of the dominant culture, severely restricts the kind of future we are capable of imagining. It is equally obvious that the growing obsession with blood quantum in the United States (and invading some reserve communities in Canada) has many Native communities south (and north) of the border stymied and deadlocked. By situating the issues facing one urban community in eastern Canada within the range of ways in which Indigenous identities are under assault in different contexts, I hope to destabilize the common-sense notions of Indianness created by the colonizer and in this way to throw open new possibilities for creating a future where not only Indigenous survival but Indigenous empowerment is assured. It is also hoped that by taking this broad approach, the dilemmas and solutions embraced by urban mixed-bloods in one city in eastern Canada might be useful for Native people elsewhere in rethinking how their ways of conceptualizing Native identity have been shaped by the regulatory regimes and foundational myths of the colonial order in their homelands.

In the Canadian context, Toronto was chosen as a site to explore how an urban community understands mixed-blood Native identity for a number of reasons. First of all, while I no longer live in Toronto, it is the community that for many years I considered to be home. Because of this I have been grounded enough in the issues and have a wide enough range of relationships within the urban Native community to ensure that this research expresses the concerns of a wide cross-section of the community, in a relatively accurate and concise manner. But Toronto was chosen for another reason as well. In the

Canadian context, Toronto is relatively unique in that it usually represents the final stage of a process of urbanization that might begin with an Aboriginal family being relocated from their community of origin—by various policies of removal or loss of land through resource development—to small adjacent towns. From there they may be relocated to regional centers such as Thunder Bay, Sarnia, or Windsor, and then eventually to Toronto (although large urban centers such as Vancouver and Toronto are also sites of direct migration by people from nearby reserves). Furthermore Toronto's location in eastern Canada, where policies of genocide have been in place much longer than in western Canada, ensures that many more of its Aboriginal residents are the products of multiple generations of intermarriages, dislocations, and removals. In addition to this, as a primary area of immigration, the urban Native community in Toronto is also host to a number of Indigenous migrants from the United States and various Latin American countries.

Finally, because Toronto is located in eastern Canada, where Aboriginal peoples on the whole are far less visible than in western Canada and where the presence of large numbers of people of color ensures that the racialized Other in Toronto is not Aboriginal, urban Native people in Toronto suffer from a certain invisibility. The presence of 70,000 Native people in a city with a population of approximately 2.4 million has generally made little impression on the city as a whole. For all of these reasons Toronto in many respects represents the end point for urban mixed-blood Native people, the setting where the most extreme levels of dislocation exist among its Aboriginal population, and the site where Native people as a whole are the most invisible. For an urban and mixed-blood Aboriginal population to survive at all under such circumstances is itself a testament to one of the ongoing themes in this book—the impossibility of in fact "legislating away" or otherwise destroying a culture and the enduring nature of Indigenous identity despite continuous assaults.

A major concern articulated throughout the book is the question of the future—what forms of nation-rebuilding can reconcile the almost insurmountable differences in experience, and the highly distinct agendas of, urban and reserve-based communities? From intense discussion with some of the urban Native people who have undertaken leadership roles in the Toronto community, this book will attempt to explore what directions can be taken to begin to overcome this colonial legacy of ongoing limitation, distortion, and extinction of Indigenous identities and the divisions among Native people that these processes have created.

The first chapter of the book presents an overview of colonization processes in Canada and introduces the different regulatory regimes to control Native people that developed respectively in Canada and the United States. The next three chapters present an in-depth examination of how the Indian Act has categorized Nativeness by gender and race, exploring the extent to which this legislation has shaped how Native people in Canada understand who they are.

Chapters 5 to 8 focus on tracing the effects of laws, policies, and mythologies on mixed-blood families within the Toronto Native community. From information gathered in intensive interviews with twenty-nine urban mixed-blood individuals, as well as through long-term discussions with different individuals within the community on the subject of Native identity spanning much of the past five years, I have sought to draw a picture of this community and its concerns. These chapters are fashioned from oral histories—exploring both the participants' family histories and the historical processes that have shaped their experiences. A central feature of this section is an exploration of the issues that caused families to leave their Native communities behind and the circumstances they faced in coming to the city. These histories are explored in detail in an effort to make sense of the tremendous silence about Native identity that has been a feature of much of urban Native family life in the past forty years. This silence has rendered Native heritage ambiguous for a number of the participants, as well as for the author. In a sense these chapters are about how the participants have come to understand themselves as Native people, flowing from their family histories.

Chapters 9 to 11 focus on how the hegemonic images and definitions of Indianness flowing from identity legislation and Canadian nation-building myths affect the participants' views of themselves and their identities. The issues raised in this section—whether one looks Indian, whether a person has band or tribal membership and grew up on a reserve or in the city, and whether one is legally defined as Indian—are at the heart of many of the confusions that urban mixed-bloods have had to negotiate around their identities. In these chapters I attempt to understand how the images and definitions of Indianness created by the colonizer to control Native people have become so central to Native peoples' own self-images.

The final chapter of the book looks to the future, at ways to overcome the phenomenal divisions that have been created among Native peoples through the regulation of Native identity. Rather than denying or de-emphasizing the differences between urban mixed-bloods and on-reserve Native people, I attempt to focus on these differences as a first step in considering what we have in common. At the same time, if the case study demonstrates anything it is that facile assumptions about full-bloodedness and mixed-bloodedness, about urbanity and Indian status and tribal membership, are revealed to be false and stereotypic. This chapter explores how urban mixed-blood Aboriginal people see their roles in the rebuilding of their nations and the forms of nation-building that could accommodate our diverse realities and concerns. In doing this I have deliberately attempted to dream— to refuse to be limited by what is currently considered realistic. As Ward Churchill has suggested, we have to imagine the unimaginable in order to make any kind of viable anticolonial resistance in contemporary North American society.[9]

Throughout this work I use the terms *Indian* (which is not as commonly used by Native people in Canada as it is in the United States), *Native*, *Indigenous*, and *Aboriginal* in a fairly interchangeable manner, reflecting the diversity of terms that different Native people in Canada now use to refer to themselves. In a similar manner, the terms *half-breed*, *mixed-race*, and *mixed-blood* are used interchangeably to refer to individuals who define themselves as being of mixed Native and non-Native heritage. The term *half-breed*, while considered pejorative and outdated by many scholars in the United States, has historical significance as the legal category used to classify mixed-bloods in Canada, under the Indian Act. For this reason, and because some mixed-blood individuals have reclaimed the term *half-breed* as part of their history, I have chosen to retain it, particularly when referring to historical and legal issues pertaining to mixed-bloods in Canada. I use the term *Métis* (sometimes further defined as western Métis) primarily to refer to those individuals who are mixed-race and nonstatus from western Canada. Finally in certain contexts I use the term *Indian*, *status Indian*, or *treaty Indian* to differentiate those Native people who have Indian status from those who do not. Generally speaking when the term *Indian* refers only to status Indians, it is reflected in the text.

The term *Indigeneity* is primarily utilized to signify a more decolonized understanding of what could otherwise be termed *Nativeness* (or *Indianness*). It refers less to precolonial states of existence and identity than to a future, postcolonial refashioning of Indigenous identities that are truer to Indigenous histories and cultures than those identities shaped by the colonial realities that continue to surround Native people at present.

PART I. THE REGULATION OF NATIVE IDENTITY

1

From Sovereign Nations to "A Vanishing Race"

This study of urban mixed-blood Native realities engages closely with how legislation such as the Indian Act has shaped contemporary Native identity. In this work colonial legislation governing Indianness is seen as a discourse, in something of the sense that Foucault used the term—as a way of seeing life that is produced and reproduced by various rules, systems, and procedures, creating an entire conceptual territory on which knowledge is formed and produced (Loomba 1998, 38). The Indian Act, in this respect, is much more than a body of laws that for over a century has controlled every aspect of status Indian life. It provides a conceptual framework that has organized contemporary First Nations life in ways that have been almost entirely naturalized, and that governs ways of thinking about Native identity. To date few individuals appear to have recognized the depth of the problem that the Indian Act represents—its overarching nature as a discourse of classification and regulation, which has *produced* the subjects it purports to control, and which has therefore indelibly ordered how Native people think of things "Indian."

To treat the Indian Act merely as a set of policies to be repealed, or even as a genocidal scheme that we can simply choose not to believe in, belies how a classificatory system produces a way of thinking—a grammar—which embeds itself in every attempt to change it. The different Indigenous subjects produced by the Indian Act and other Canadian legislation—the designation of some Indigenous bodies as Indians, some as Métis, and some as Inuit—have been naturalized as distinct groups of Native people with entirely different histories, whose difference the Indian Act, and other Canadian legislation such as the Constitution Act, now merely acknowledge. What is lost is the history of how these different kinds of Indigenous subjects have been *created* by legislation—for example the manner in which Native women have for over a century lost Indian status if they married men without Indian status and how those Native people designated by whites as "half-breeds" (now called Métis) have been continuously, legally externalized from Indianness.[1] As a result these different categories dividing Indigenous people are continuously reproduced as "natural" and are attributed to *inherent* cultural differences. Inevitably struggles for self-determination that follow the logic of such classification will end up reproducing its categories—and exclusions—in new contexts.

To speak of how pervasively the Indian Act—and identity legislation in the United States—has permeated the ways in which Native people understand their own identities is not to deny us the agency to move beyond its logic, or to suggest that we have lost all access to traditional cultural ways of understanding the relationships between people, their communities, and the land. It does, however, suggest that we have to think very carefully about how concepts of self and community have been violated by generations of living under colonial laws. It means we have to carefully deconstruct the various categories that have been created by the Indian Act, such as *status Indian*, and *Métis*, and consider the possibility of choosing new paths that might create common goals, rather than the separate—and competing—roads that each group at present has had to take toward empowerment.

Understanding how the Indian Act has shaped Native identity will not change the fact that different kinds of Indigenous subjects have been indelibly created by this legislation. Denying differences or simply exhorting people to disbelieve difference will not remove the very real multiple legal and structural divisions that this history of regulation has created between groups. However it is possible for distinct communities to explore what real historical connections exist between them and to organize in ways that specifically challenge Indian Act logic. These ways include returning to more traditional frameworks, or, when necessary, creating new frameworks of organization more accurately grounded in the identities and ways of living that preceded this colonial dismembering and reordering of Indigenous peoples' identities. Unpacking the history of identity legislation in the Indian Act is a central step in this process. However, given the extent to which systems of identity regulation developed by the United States government—particularly the notion of blood quantum—have begun to invade communities in Canada already fragmented by the Indian Act, it is also important to understand the differences in the regimes of regulation that have shaped Native identity in Canada and the United States and how each needs to be understood according to their historical specificity. It is not only that identity legislation works in different ways in each country, but that the means chosen to regulate Native identity in Canada and the United States arose from distinctly different histories—histories that are deeply linked (in ways that neither settler state currently acknowledges).

COLONIZATION AND IDENTITY REGULATION

I believe it is important to think of the enactment of legislation naming or categorizing individuals or groups as "Indian" as crucial moments when the governments of the ascendant settler nations of Canada and the United States—agencies that until that point had had no legislative authority over any member or citizen of an Indigenous nation—asserted such authority. In Canada that moment was first seized in 1850 when the government of what was then the colony of Canada, anxious to assert its nation-building capacity at a time of impending devolution of direct British rule, passed the first law arrogating to itself the authority to define who was or was not a member of an Indigenous nation—designated in generic terms as "Indian." These first laws concerning Indians would grow into a massive body of repressive legislation upholding a legal form of apartheid that still exists in Canada.

A centralized body of legislation controlling Native identity in openly colonial fashion did not develop in the United States. As a newly independent republic in the process of establishing itself under revolutionary legal principles, a major concern, articulated primarily through the judiciary, was how to reconcile essentially illegal territorial expansion within the framework of law. In the process of territorial expansion, the United States government negotiated over 370 treaties with separate tribes, treaties that upheld the rights of specific tribal groups in ways that could not initially be nullified simply by colonial fiat. Decisions about Indians were therefore made largely through the judiciary, as well as through a prodigious volume of governmental statutes and regulations. The result was an immense body of Indian law, where relatively little attention was focused on defining Indian identity; rather the focus of much judiciary opinion was to erode the power of Indian tribes as a whole.

Two early and definitive court decisions in this respect were *Johnson v McIntosh*, which invoked the Doctrine of Discovery with respect to the question of the nature of tribal property rights, characterizing tribal lands as part of the land mass of the United States, and *Cherokee Nation v Georgia*, which maintained that tribes were "domestic, dependent nations," immune from the regulatory authority of individual states, but subject to the ultimate authority of the federal government (Barsh and Henderson 1980, 50–54). It was not until the 1880s, when the triumph of Manifest Destiny had been achieved through the military "pacification" of many of the western tribes that government policy began to focus, in a concerted manner, on breaking the collective basis of tribally owned land by dividing reservations into individual allotments. From this point, a series of U.S. Supreme Court decisions narrowed and restricted the limits of tribal sovereignty, until by 1902, in *Lone Wolf v Hitchcock*, the Supreme Court upheld the notion that Congress had virtually unlimited plenary power to control the lives of its Indian "wards," that the rampant corruption and abuse of power involved in the confiscation of Indian lands was "a political process" outside of the power of the judiciary to intervene, and that the United States government could violate the terms of treaties at will (Clark 1994, 107–11). Almost hidden in this juggernaut of rampant theft of Indigenous lands and destruction of the authority of tribal governments was the gradual assumption of governmental control over tribal rolls, the categorization of tribal members according to their percentages of Indian blood, and the distortion of traditional views of tribal identity that this entailed. In all cases, in both countries, the primary reason for the categorization and regulation of Indigenous populations was to ensure not only that the bulk of their lands were smoothly transferred to whites with a patina of legality but that the process of dismembering and recasting

Indigenous identities would permanently subordinate captured populations.

The framework through which the United States as a newly independent republic dealt with tribal nations was embedded in the ferment of struggle to encode ideas of political or civil liberty within a body of law and a structural framework of governance. The Constitution was the written manifestation of the beliefs of its authors, embodying an avowed commitment to the universal potential of human liberty as the basis of organized society. And yet, given the racialized framework in which "universality" was conceptualized, relations with Indian tribes tested American idealism to the limit and attracted the most critical European scrutiny. If the American government expected recognition from the international community on the basis of their *sui generis* political sovereignty, they would, in turn, have to recognize the ancient sovereignty of Indian peoples, or discover some profound political distinction between white and Indian societies not yet accounted for (Barsh and Henderson 1980, 31–32).

The contradictions arising from this stance, particularly on the part of European powers such as Britain, involved not only the fact that the charters of many of the colonies that Britain had founded on the East Coast of North America, which later became the United States, had explicitly been based on an exterminationist relationship to the Indigenous nations (whose lands were being claimed). It was also the case that Britain, by the end of the eighteenth century, had already been engaged for a considerable interval in global colonial ventures premised on racial hierarchy and the notion that Britain had the duty to govern inferior races and to impregnate them with reason, progress, and the rule of law (Mahmud 1999, 1223). Britain, after over a century of warfare with East Coast Native nations and anxious not to repeat the experience, affirmed through the Royal Proclamation of 1763 that a nation-to-nation relationship must govern the process of land acquisition in British North America and insisted that the American government abide by these terms as conditions of peace both after the Revolutionary War and the War of 1812. But it did so largely because the specter of unfettered territorial expansion south of the border threatened Britain's Canadian colonies to the north (Barsh and Henderson 1980, 43–44). Britain (and the international arena that it represented) therefore policed the United States' obligation to deal with tribal nations as sovereign entities, where any territorial acquisition on the part of the United States had to be capable of being legally framed in a manner consistent with that of a republic concerned with political rights and liberties. Meanwhile, in its Canadian colonies to the north, Britain embarked on a process of openly colonial occupation and expansion, where "the native was only the object who furnished the body on which colonial power was to be inscribed" (Mahmud 1999, 1227). The powerful discourses classifying colonized peoples and their attributes, which Britain was developing in the process of subjugating the nonwhite peoples of the world (Mahmud 1999, 1227), were from the start utilized to control "the Indian" in Canada, while in the United States, under the glare of European scrutiny, such a colonial framework could not be openly manifested. As a result, the development of a body of Indian law was central to the development of the United States itself—as the only means through which colonial control could progressively be imposed on the tribal nations. It is perhaps not surprising that most developments in terms of a body of doctrine in U.S. Indian law did not occur until after the violent and illegal conquest of the tribes, which was nevertheless maintained as a legal process because U.S. government policymakers chose to keep it beyond the reach of the law (Harring 1994, 5).

Looking north of the border, the fact that Canada was able to pacify the Indigenous peoples of half a continent on a virtually nonexistent military budget cannot be understood without taking into account how British officials have *always* used the threat of warfare and its attendant starvation south of the border to control Native populations in Canada. In a sense Canada piggybacked off of American Manifest Destiny, using the starvation and territorial limitation brought about by the destruction of the buffalo and the Indian wars to the south to force treaties on captured populations in the north, all the while maintaining a posture of innocence and denial about the fundamentally violent nature of the colonial process in Canada.

Control of Native people in Canada has thus been maintained largely through the creation of an extremely repressive body of colonial law known as the Indian Act, upheld always by the threat of direct military violence. Through this legislation, the only level of Indigenous governance recognized by Canada has been the elected government imposed at the local reserve or band level. Initially implemented on populations in eastern Canada demoralized by disease and alcoholism after two centuries of fur trade and Christianization, these "governments" were forced on the western nations after the selective use of policies of deliberate starvation, premised on the destruction of the buffalo, had forced them to enter into treaties and settle on reserves. Definitions of Indianness almost from the start controlled who was recognized as an Indian band, who could get any land under the treaties, and who could live on this land. Side by side with this policy of carefully controlled segregation was another one, that of carefully controlled assimilation, which was the primary means by which Canada sought to destroy its pacified Indian population.

Enfranchisement, the removal of Indian status from an individual, thereby creating a Canadian citizen of Aboriginal heritage who has relinquished his collective ties to his Native community and any claims to Aboriginal rights, has been a central part of the Canadian government's assimilation policy since the Gradual Civilization Act of 1857.[2] This act proposed voluntary enfranchisement as a "privilege." Initially an Indian had to be schooled, debt free, and of "good moral character" before he could be enfranchised—at which point he would receive twenty hectares of land, freehold tenure, from his former reserve. This last provision violated the terms of the Royal Proclamation, by asserting that colonial governments could parcel out reserve land to individuals without band permission (Miller 1989, 110–11). The Indian Act later proclaimed this process legal.

Through various changes in the legislation over the years, Native people could be enfranchised for acquiring an education, for serving in the armed forces, or for leaving their reserves for long periods of time to maintain employment. In 1880, the compulsory enfranchisement of those Indians who were university educated or had entered a profession was stopped. However, at that point, entire bands were allowed to enfranchise. Voluntary enfranchisement, in any case, was a tremendous failure—between 1857 and 1918 only 102 persons enfranchised. In 1920 compulsory enfranchisement, at the discretion of a board of examiners and with two years' notice, was instituted. While this policy was stopped in 1922, it was reintroduced into the Indian Act in 1933 and remained on the books until the 1951 Indian Act. This legislation was openly aimed at the elimination of Indigenous peoples as a legal and social fact. The deputy minister of Indian Affairs, Duncan Campbell Scott, wrote in 1920:

> I want to get rid of the Indian problem. . . . After one hundred years of being in close contact with civilisation it is enervating to the individual or to a band to continue in that state of tutelage, when

he or they are able to take their positions as British citizens or Canadian citizens, to support themselves and stand alone. That has been the whole purpose of Indian education and advancement since the earliest times. . . . Our object is to continue until there is not a single Indian in Canada that has not been absorbed into the body politic, and there is no Indian question, and no Indian Department. (Scott, quoted in Miller 1989, 207)

On a daily basis, enfranchisement provided formidable opportunities for Indian agents to control resistance in Native communities, by pushing for the enfranchisement (and therefore the removal from their communities) of anybody empowered by education or a secure income. War veterans were also often enfranchised, thereby removing many of the men who had experienced relative social equality overseas, as well as men who were accustomed to fighting, from reserve communities.[3] Wives and children were enfranchised automatically along with their husbands, but no provision for land was made for wives.

The first legislation defining Indianness was passed in 1850. In lower Canada this legislation, created to define who should be granted reserve land, was the first in Canada to establish a definition of an Indian, albeit loosely, so that Indian status thus depended on Indian descent or marriage to a male Indian.[4] In Upper Canada, by comparison, legislation passed in 1850 to protect the property of Indians simply contained the statement that the act was applied to "Indians, and those who may be inter-married with Indians."[5] While the Gradual Civilization Act of 1857 focused on enfranchisement, the definition of an Indian contained in the act was still along the lines of the more inclusive definition in the 1850 legislation in Upper Canada. In fact by the time the British North America Act of 1867, which created Canada as a nation, was passed, the term *Indian* was still not officially defined.

In 1869, however, the Gradual Enfranchisement Act was passed.[6] This legislation gave the superintendent of Indian Affairs (or his agent) extremely wide powers. He had the right to determine who could use Indian lands. He had the power to stop or divert Indian funds and annuities. Less than one-quarter Indian blood was to be a disqualification for "annuity interest or rent." Those "intermarried with Indians settling on these lands . . . without license" were liable to be "summarily ejected." Prison terms and fines were to be levied on those who supplied liquor to Indians (Jamieson 1978, 29).

This legislation contained the framework to undermine and replace Indigenous governments with a municipal-style elected system of band governance. Chiefs and councils were elected, to replace traditional forms of governance; these officials could be disposed of at will at the discretion of the Indian agent. Band councils were given authority over only minor matters—public health, property maintenance, maintaining public order, and so on. Most important, although these bands were referred to in the legislation as the "Tribe in Council," the legislation deliberately bypassed the national or tribal governments recognized in the Royal Proclamation of 1763 (Monture-Angus 1999, 34), and instead dealt only at the band level, with individual communities and their inhabitants, typically one hundred to two hundred people. There was no provision for traditional groupings going beyond the band level; this was done deliberately to undermine existing traditional governments at the level of the individual nation and to bypass the power of the confederacies, the large geopolitical and spiritual units that had for centuries asserted their jurisdiction over different regions of what is now Canada (RCAP 1996, 1:275–6). This act also comprised a central attack on the collective nature of landholding, by forcing the subdivision of reserves into private lots, with location tickets allotted to men and women. As the next chapter will explore, the 1869 Act was also crucial in beginning the process of removing the Indian status of Native women who married non-Natives and indeed of forcing Native women to become members of their husbands' communities upon marriage, reversing the matrifocal practices common in many of the eastern nations.

After the 1869 Act, Indian legislation became even more punitive and restrictive. The 1874 legislation, which brought Indigenous people in Manitoba and British Columbia under its control, was primarily taken up with criminalizing those western Native people who were facing the first onslaught of colonization. Indians convicted of being found in a state of intoxication, for example, could be imprisoned for up to one month under this legislation (Jamieson 1978, 43). In 1876 the first Indian Act collected all previous legislation pertaining to Indians into a body of law comprising over a hundred sections.[7] As chapter 4 will explore more closely, almost immediately a series of modifications were introduced to the act that differentiated between

"Indians" and "half-breeds"; meanwhile, the act also introduced more patriarchal definitions of Indianness.

The 1880 modifications to the Indian Act clearly targeted western nations for the same destruction of their collective land base and social organization as eastern nations had encountered in 1869. This legislation provided for the removal as trespassers of any Indian and his family not of the band who "settled or hunted" on band land (Jamieson 1978, 45). The Department of Indian Affairs was formally established to maintain greater control of Indian reserves.

Although Canada had negotiated treaties with the Plains Cree and Blackfoot peoples throughout the course of their westward expansion, they had continuously refused to deal with Métis communities. In 1870, under Louis Riel, Métis people in the Red River Valley declared a provisional government and demanded entry into the confederation *as* Métis people. Canada responded by admitting them as the Province of Manitoba, but then sent police and settlers to harass and persecute local Métis. Many of them fled west. By 1885, with Canada once again encroaching on Métis settlements, this time in Saskatchewan and Alberta, the Métis rallied again under Louis Riel. Two or three small battles were fought between local garrisons of police before Canada responded by sending large numbers of troops from the East to crush the so-called uprising. The Métis leadership was arrested, and Louis Riel was hung. Canada then persecuted and starved out local Cree communities, hanged Cree leaders, and imprisoned the crucial Cree strategists involved in resisting the reserve process—Big Bear and Poundmaker—until their health was broken and they died. The 1885 Rebellion (also known as the Riel Rebellion or the Northwest Rebellion) broke the long Cree resistance to Canada's westward expansion and shattered Métis resistance entirely.

As a result of the 1885 Rebellion in western Canada, changes to the Indian Act were introduced that codified extremely harsh measures to suppress resistance in Native communities. All Plains bands were classified as "loyal" or "disloyal" (in a context where almost unanimously the various Plains bands had struggled to remain neutral during an essentially Métis rebellion, despite incipient starvation, hoping to mount a widespread movement for renegotiation of treaties rather than take up arms). In addition to the hangings of eight Cree men and the lengthy jail terms served by approximately fifty other Cree individuals, there was widespread persecution of members of bands labeled "disloyal"—including withholding of monies and rations, confiscation of horses, and in some cases the breaking up of bands and their forced integration into other bands (Stonechild and Waiser 1997, 254–63). It was on this basis that many Cree people fled to the United States, where they remained until after the turn of the century, preferring to take their chances with the Indian wars to the south than to face the intense campaign of attrition being waged in western Canada.

Other repressive measures were introduced to Plains bands as well, to prevent any Native people from congregating together. For example all reserves were declared off-limits to anybody but band members after dark, and an informal system of passes was instituted, whereby Indians were not allowed off their reserves without written authorization from the Indian agent. The pass system was still utilized in some regions until after World War I, although Native resistance and police reluctance to enforce the practice hindered the Department of Indian Affairs' efforts at maintaining the system. Indian agents were also given powers to enforce anti-vagrancy laws, the primary legislative provisions governing prostitution in Canada until the 1970s, which provided Indian agents with the power to control Indian women through designating them as "common prostitutes." Cultural institutions and spiritual practices, such as the potlatch on the West Coast, and the Sun Dance on the Plains, were banned, although truncated versions of these ceremonies continued to be practiced, despite repression, in the decades afterward (Miller 1989, 191–95). The wearing of ceremonial regalia was gradually prohibited, until any kind of dancing involving regalia could only be done with prior written permission (Dickason 1992, 326). And finally residential schooling was made compulsory, to separate children from their culture and to break the strength of Native families (Miller 1989, 196–98).

The 1894 changes to the Indian Act created an additional, much more simplified and inclusive definition of an Indian solely for the purpose of the liquor section of the act. The definition of an Indian under the liquor section included any individual, male or female, with or without Indian status who was reputed to belong to a particular band, or who followed the Indian mode of life, or the child of such a person (Jamieson 1978, 48). Furthermore, in court cases where non-status Indians or Métis were involved, judges frequently reserved the right to punish them according to Indian Act stipulations.

Different provisions were continuously introduced into the Indian Act that weakened Native control over reserve lands. For example, in 1879, the Department of Indian Affairs was enabled to lease reserve lands without band consent. In 1894 bands lost the power to decide whether non-Indians could use reserve lands, and individual band members were permitted to lease their allotment tickets to non-Natives, regardless of the band's wishes. This was widened in 1918 to enable the Indian agent to lease any uncultivated land on the reserve to non-Natives without band approval. An 1898 statute allowed Native people to be forcibly removed from any reserves adjacent to or partly within towns of eight thousand inhabitants or more. Meanwhile, the department continued to sell off reserve lands near municipalities (Dickason 1992, 323). In 1911 a further act allowed public authorities to expropriate reserve lands for public works, without a surrender of lands; meanwhile judges were allowed to issue court orders to move reserves near municipalities of a certain size if it was "expedient" to do so. This provision, known as the Oliver Act, was passed so that Parliament would not have to pass special legislation every time it wished to expropriate reserves in the vicinity of smaller settler towns. In 1919 the governor-in-council was authorized to make regulations allowing leases for mining operations on reserves without band permission. Indeed in 1936, in a move that made the purpose of Indian administration in Canada nakedly clear, responsibility for Indian Affairs was transferred from the Department of the Interior to the Department of Mines and Resources (RCAP 1996, 1:285). In contrast to these changes that allowed the government and individual whites to have broad access to reserve lands, legislation in the 1920s ensured that Indian "squatters" on band lands, even those who only went there to fish, were to be evicted and jailed.

The Indian Act was revised ten times between 1910 and 1930, primarily in an effort to curb mounting political resistance by Native communities. For example, amendments in 1910 prohibited Native people from using band funds for land-claim actions without the approval of the superintendent of Indian Affairs, while in 1927 it was made a criminal offense to solicit or give money for pursuit of a land claim without similar permission (RCAP 1996, 1:296). The cumulative effect of these restrictions was to make it extremely difficult for Native people to hire lawyers or in any other ways engage in political organization to protect their lands.

The 1951 Indian Act has been hailed by many as a turning point for Native people. For the first time a number of provincial and national Native organizations were consulted. The laws hindering Native communities from engaging in legal actions or political resistance were removed, as were many of the more blatant discrepancies between the criminal code and the Indian Act; for example, the laws concerning intoxicants, the prohibition on Indian ceremonies and dances, and the requirement of obtaining permission from Indian agents to travel or sell produce. Native women were given the right to vote in band elections. Compulsory enfranchisement for Native men was stopped. And yet the discretionary powers of the minister of Indian Affairs or governor-in-council were actually increased. Furthermore, in a decision that would have far-reaching and devastating consequences for whole generations of Native children, their families, and the communities at large, Section 87 of the 1951 Indian Act made provincial laws applicable to reserve communities in cases where the Indian Act had traditionally been silent (Huntley and Blaney 1999, 7). It was this section that gave provincial child welfare agencies jurisdiction over Indian reserves, thus enabling them to apprehend Native children en masse. The result was the "sixties scoop," where large numbers of Native children were removed from their families and communities and placed in non-Native homes. Finally, as the next chapter will explore, in terms of Native women who married non-Natives, the 1951 Indian Act was devastating.

IDENTITY LEGISLATION AS A DISCOURSE OF DOMINATION

Understanding how Native identity has been shaped by the Indian Act requires an exploration of the actual legislation and the changes it brought about, as has been briefly introduced earlier. But it is also important to explore the meaning of having one's identity legally regulated. What happens when one moves from being part of a continent-wide network of nations to being a member of a subordinated "Indian race"? Janice Acoose has described how being classified by the Canadian government as a status Indian under the Indian Act represented a violation of the rights of her Cree/Métis and Saulteaux cultures to define her as *Nehiowe* or *Nahkawe*, which removed her, in common-sense ways, from any real sense of being part of the destinies of her own nation(s) and instead placed her as a powerless and racialized individual at the bottom of the hierarchy of Euro-Canadian society (Acoose 1995, 23). For Indigenous people, to be defined as "Indian" is synonymous with having our Indigenous Nations dismembered.

In many respects the regulation of Indigenous identities through legislation is part of a discourse through which crucial aspects of European race ideology were imparted as a world-view to Native people who were no longer in a position to resist such categorization.[8] Legislation regulating Native identity has been, both for Canada and the United States, a necessary means of unraveling social connections, which maintained the collective nature of most Indigenous societies, and therefore severing the ties between Native peoples and most of their former land base. Of course the only way in which Indigenous peoples can be permanently severed from their land base is when they no longer exist as peoples. The ongoing regulation of Indigenous peoples' identities is therefore no relic of a more openly colonial era—it is part of the way in which Canada and the United States continue to actively maintain physical control of the land base they claim, a claim which is still contested by the rightful owners of the land.

And yet, for colonized people, the discursive meaning of having one's identity regulated is central to understanding its impact, not only on who we think we are but on our relationship to the land. Within Indigenous traditions, land is central to the survival of the people *as* peoples. For most of the Indigenous nations, their languages are intricately linked to the land itself. Okanagan writer Jeannette Armstrong describes the relationship between land, identity, and her N'silxchn language:

> As I understand it from my Okanagan ancestors, language was given to us by the land we live within. . . . I have heard elders explain that the language changed as we moved and spread over the land through time. My own father told me that it was the land that changed the language because there is special knowledge in each different place. All my elders say that it is land that holds all knowledge of life and death and is a constant teacher. It is said in Okanagan that the land constantly speaks. It is constantly communicating. Not to learn its language is to die. We survived and thrived by listening intently to its teachings—to its language—and then inventing human words to retell its stories to our succeeding generations. It is the land that speaks N'silxchn through the generations of our ancestors to us. It is N'silxchn, the old land/mother spirit of the Okanagan People, which surrounds me in its primal wordless state. (Armstrong 1998, 175–76)

Meanwhile Laguna Pueblo writer Leslie Marmon Silko describes some aspects of the strength that comes when Indigenous peoples still live in the sites from which their cultural strength and historical memory devolve:

> A dinner-table conversation recalling a deer hunt forty years ago, when the largest mule deer ever was taken, inevitably stimulates similar memories in listeners. But hunting stories were not merely after-dinner entertainment. These accounts contained information of critical importance about the behavior and migration patterns of mule deer. Hunting stories carefully described key landmarks and locations of fresh water. Thus, a deer-hunt story might also serve as a map. Lost travelers, and lost pinon-nut gatherers, have been saved by sighting a rock formation they recognize only because they once heard a hunting story describing this rock formation. The importance of cliff formations and water holes does not end with hunting stories. As offspring of the Mother Earth, the ancient Pueblo people could not conceive of themselves within a specific landscape, but location, or place, nearly always plays a central role in the Pueblo oral narratives. (Silko 1998, 10)

From looking at different, tribally specific perspectives on the relationship between land and collective identity, we can get a sense of the extreme discursive warfare that colonization represents—the need of settler nations to attempt to erase the world-views of the Indigenous peoples whose territories they claim, not only by erasing knowledge of self through identity legislation, but through destroying access to the cultural and historical knowledge and knowledge of self contained in the land. In both Canada and the United States, shattering ancient Indigenous forms of self-organization and self-knowledge has been intrinsic to breaking the connections between Native communities and their land base.

For this reason land appropriation or privatization in both Canada and the United States has always been accompanied by specific attempts on the part of the colonizer to rewrite or further fragment how Native peoples conceptualize themselves. This is perhaps most graphically (and chillingly) illustrated in the United States, where the attempt to shatter the communal character of tribal land-holding through breaking up reservations into individual allotments involved the quantifying of degrees of Indian blood of each tribal member who received an allotment. In doing this, the new rationalist sciences of classification were utilized to categorize reservation residents. In order to determine who was "full-blooded" or not, in a context where European-style record-keeping did not exist, bizarre series of tests were devised by physical anthropologists, who determined that size of feet, degree of curl in hair, and the extent to which a scratch "reddened," as well as a host of other physical parameters, could determine how much Indian blood an individual possessed (Wilson 1992, 121).

The spaces of fundamental illegality where Native peoples were confined by law soon were the sites of far more extreme violations by white scientists, however, whose mission of confirming the superiority of European civilization could be accomplished only by the most violent and dehumanizing incursions into Native spaces. Samuel George Morton pioneered the "science" of phrenology in the United States, by asserting that racial traits could be correlated with skull capacity. Morton based his evidence primarily on his extensive collection of the skulls of six hundred Native people obtained from archaeological sites, from those who robbed Native American graves, and from the bones of those who died in the smallpox and other epidemics sweeping Indian country, as well as from lesser numbers of skulls of African Americans and poor whites (whose graves could also be dug up with relative impunity). By measuring the cranial capacity of large numbers of skulls, using lead shot, Morton argued for the scientific reliability of his claims. Native American skulls were examined with a view to determining whether degrees of "racial mixing" could be measured. Soon the dead bodies of those Native people killed in army massacres were being beheaded and their skulls shipped east to be used for "scientific studies":

In 1868 . . . the Surgeon General issued an order to Army medical doctors to procure as many Indian crania as possible. Under the order, 4,000 crania were obtained from the dead bodies of Native Americans. Indian men, women, and children, often those killed on a battlefield or massacre sites, were beheaded and their crania taken to the Army Medical Museum. There, doctors measured the crania, using pseudo-scientific assumptions to prove the intellectual and moral inferiority of Indians. These studies were used until the 1920s by federal officials as a measure of racial purity to

determine who was and who was not a full-blood Indian. . . . Tribal
enrollment lists from the early twentieth century based on such
racist biology continue to be the legal documents used to determine heirs in awarding land claim compensation. (Yellow Bird and
Milun 1994, 18)

These "scientific studies" to measure Native American intelligence
and establish blood quantum cannot be separated from the other use
made of Native American skulls and skeletons (not to mention other
body parts), particularly after military massacres, as trophies of conquest. Indeed these apparently disparate processes within a colonizing
society functioned together, as the U.S. Army increasingly took on
the scientific task of collecting the bodies of slain Native people, of
"processing them" (removing flesh from bone) in army hospitals, and
of shipping their bones eastward to museums, for display or simply for
categorization, tribe by tribe, on the premise that soon all that would
remain of Native Americans would be relics stored in museum cases
(Thomas 2000, 23, 57). By the turn of the century, thousands of Native
American skeletons filled museums across the country, right next
to "live specimen" exhibits, where captured, homeless, or displaced
Native Americans, who were brought to live in museums, rubbed
shoulders with other live "samples" of colonized peoples from Africa
and the Far East (Thomas 2000, 59–60).

The object of this brutal "science" of classification and control
must not be lost in the details of the horror it enacted. Nor should we
separate the brutality of how identity legislation was implemented in
the United States with how centrally it has shaped the colonization
process in Canada. Such methods of dehumanization were crucial to
the overall project, in both countries, of declaring "the Indian" irrelevant to their own history and indeed denying the Indian a history.
This is the logic of extermination—the discursive violence that is per-
petrated when colonized peoples have their identities reduced to mea-
surable physical traits or to a strict code of categorization. Through
such classification, the citizens of subordinated Indigenous nations
were not only to be legally dismembered from their own identities
and recast as "Indians," as part of the process of taking their lands,
but in the process they were to be dismembered from their pasts and
therefore from their futures.

By exploring identity legislation as a discourse aimed at the total
destruction of Indigenous ways of conceptualizing the self in relation

to nationhood and land, I am not suggesting that this total destruction has in fact taken place and that elders have lost their power to impart traditional Indigenous knowledge to their communities. Jeffrey Gould, in exploring the effect of the myth of *mestizaje* on Nicaraguan Indians, has noted that the relationship between colonization discourses (which includes government identity legislation) and Indigenous resistance is extremely complex. Two distinct approaches to hegemony have been articulated to describe such relationships: as a naturalized, invisible ideology, or as a shared discursive field of contestation. The first approach suggests that the world-view of the colonizer becomes entirely naturalized, that it appears "normal" and no longer seems to represent the ideology of a particular group. The second approach has been described as follows: "I propose that we use the concept [of hegemony] not to understand consent but to understand struggle, the ways in which the words, images, symbols, forms, organizations, institutions, and movements used by subordinate populations to talk about, understand, confront, accommodate themselves to, or resist their domination are shaped by the process of domination itself. What hegemony constructs, then, is not a shared ideology but a common material and meaningful framework for living through, talking about, and acting upon social orders characterized by domination" (Roseberry, in Gould 1998, 12).

I believe it is the second description that most accurately describes the effect of identity legislation on Native peoples in Canada and the United States. It is not that Native peoples have blindly internalized colonial frameworks so that they no longer are resisted as colonial. It is more that identity legislation has established the field in which Native peoples must situate themselves and the terms under which they must struggle to resist that legislation. The colonial discourse embedded in identity legislation has even invaded how resistance is conceptualized—for example, when the band governments created by the Indian Act, in order to bypass nation- or confederacy-level governments, in all earnestness don the label of "First Nations" in order to talk a form of self-government that has nothing to do with the traditional sovereignty of Indigenous nations.

At present a vital aspect of decolonization for Native people is cultural reclamation—what Winona LaDuke has referred to as "retraditionalization"—the recovery of one's own community's traditional practice (LaDuke, in Caldwell 1999, 102). If the Indian Act and identity legislation in the United States has for over a century shaped not only who we think we are but how we resist colonialism, then retraditionalization cannot be undertaken at a community level without deep attention being paid to who we think is a Native person and to what the boundaries are, both of our Nations and our territories—as well as the implications of the choices that are currently being made in the name of protecting sovereignty.

In Canada, Native peoples have survived a past where the heavy hands of Indian agents and priests enforced the multiple regulations that controlled where and how and under what terms they could live, while other legislation controlled who would be externalized from Indianness and therefore have their Indigenousness officially erased. Current Indian legislation is far less invasive and controlling in everyday terms; however laws controlling "Indian" identity still shape the routes that Native communities take in their struggles for empowerment in crucial ways, both in terms of gender and race.[9]

One example of how the naturalized divisions between those designated as Indian and those designated as Métis continue to invade even decolonization struggles at the community level are the different land claim efforts ongoing by descendants of the Pahpahstayo band. Representatives of the Pahpahstayo Reserve, which once covered forty square miles of land that is today a part of South Edmonton, first signed a treaty in 1877. Nine years afterward, however, the individuals residing on the reserve at that time were forcibly removed and discharged from the band as "half-breeds." The band and reserve ceased to exist at that point. In 1996 a group calling themselves the Pahpahstayo First Nation announced a land claim for part of South Edmonton, stating their intention to reclaim their treaty rights and obtain reserve status. Meanwhile another group, called the Pahpahstayo Band no. 136, has asserted that since all of its members are status Indians, they are eligible to have a land claim and receive compensation from the government.

Other individuals, following the logic of government categories of Indianness, dispute the whole claim, stating that the former Pahpahstayo Reserve was a Métis settlement, and not an Indian reserve, so that no claim is now possible. These individuals believe that members of Pahpahstayo Band no. 136 have treaty status only because their ancestors joined other reserves after Pahpahstayo Band no. 136 was disbanded as a "mixed-blood" community (Ziervogel 1996, 8). Thus, the question of past classification as "half-breed" or "Indian" is still shaping how contemporary Native people struggle to reclaim their ancestral land base. In this respect, as the next chapters will explore in more detail, colonial regulation of Native identity still controls the future of Indigenous nations.

2

Regulating Native Identity by Gender

For many Native people today, the common-sense nature of identity legislation may appear to be relatively innocuous. If they are band members (in Canada) whose Indian status has never been threatened with removal, or if they (and their children) have sufficient blood quantum or in other ways qualify for tribal membership in the United States, identity legislation can even appear to be serving a necessary function in protecting their communities from mixed-blood or Bill C-31 "outsiders." Identity legislation, like all Indian legislation, has set the terms under which Aboriginal peoples must organize their lives, and in a sense, the terms that people must use to resist domination. Native people have adapted accordingly.

It is primarily those who are mixed-blood, as well as others who have been removed from their communities by any number of colonialist policies, who often find themselves caught on the "wrong side" of identity legislation. It is for these individuals that identity legislation is rendered highly problematic, due to the arbitrariness of the various regulations, their utter indifference to traditional Indigenous ways of evaluating who was a member/citizen of the nation and who wasn't (which was precisely their purpose, in terms of reshaping Indigenous identities), and the inherent dehumanization of having one's identity regulated by (largely biological) standards of "Indianness." However, because of the individual nature of each set of circumstances, it inevitably appears as if "the problem" resides solely with mixed-bloodedness or urbanity, not with dehumanizing identity legislation. The role that identity legislation has played in *creating* mixed-bloodedness (and urbanity) as problems for one's Indianness falls out of the picture—as well as the role such laws have played in controlling and therefore, in a sense, creating on-reserve/tribal/full-blood identities.

In Canada a history of gender discrimination in the Indian Act has created an ongoing conflict within Native organizations and reserve communities around notions of individual and collective rights, organized along lines of gender. It is crucially important, then, to understand the central role that the subordination of Native women has played in the colonization process, in order to begin to see the violation of Native women's rights through loss of Indian status, not as the problems faced by individuals, but as a *collective* sovereignty issue.

GENDERING INDIANNESS IN THE COLONIAL ENCOUNTER

The nation-building process in Canada began to accelerate between 1781 and 1830, in what is now Southern Ontario, when the British began to realize the necessity of bringing in settlers on the lands where previously they had engaged in the fur trade, to secure the territory they claimed against the threat of American expansion. Settlement of the area was only made possible as individual Anishinaabe (Ojibway) bands were gradually induced to cede, in small packages, the land immediately north of Lake Ontario and Lake Erie to the British. Many of these land surrenders were framed as peace treaties, to ensure that the British would be allies to the Ojibway against the possible northern encroachment of American settler violence; on this basis, only male leaders or representatives were asked to participate in treaty negotiation and the signing away of land (Schmalz 1991, 120–22).

In negotiating only with men, the British deliberately cut out the stabilizing presence of older women and the general authority that was given to their voices in major decisions concerning the land. As Kim Anderson has written, traditional Native societies were often matrilineal in very balanced ways (2000, 66–68). Even in societies where men made the decisions about which lands to hunt on each year, clans organized along the female line frequently controlled land inheritance. To bypass older women in traditional societies effectively removed from the treaty process the people centrally responsible for regulating land access.

Moreover the British were confident in their knowledge that, as Major Gladwin articulated, "The free sale of rum will destroy them more effectively than fire and sword" (Schmalz 1991, 82). The "chemical warfare" of alcohol, deliberately introduced north of the Great Lakes after the Pontiac uprising of 1763, had an immediate and devastating effect on Ojibway communities in the Toronto and southwestern Ontario region, whose social disintegration and their resulting dependency on the British was devastating (Schmalz 1991, 87). In such circumstances, as the abilities of the men to make good choices for the future were increasingly destabilized by alcohol, it was frequently the women whose decision-making capabilities became crucial for the survival of the society as a whole. The fact that the women invariably spoke with the future of the children always in mind meant that "choices" being forced on the men, such as surrendering the lands they could no longer hunt or trap on in exchange for the promise of assistance in the transition to farming (or later, of jobs in resource development), were most strenuously resisted by the women, who saw holding on to the land base as the only way in which the social fabric of the society to nurture the next generation would survive at all.

Finally, as Kathleen Jamieson has noted, most of the early land treaties and Indian legislation were premised on the Indigenous peoples the English were most familiar with—the Anishinaabe (Ojibway) and Haudenosaunee (Iroquois) peoples. Especially in Haudenosaunee society, female-led clans held the collective land base for all of the nations of the confederacy. Removing women, then, was the key to privatizing the land base. For all of these reasons, a central aspect of the colonization process in Canada would be to break the power of Indigenous women within their nations (Jamieson 1978, 13).

It is also important to take into account not only the concerns of British colonial administrators, for whom Indian administration was but another post of the empire, but the fears of the growing body of white settlers, where colonial anxieties about white identity and who would control settler societies were rampant. As Ann Stoler has noted, the European settlements that developed on other peoples' lands have generally been obsessed with ways of maintaining colonial control and of rigidly asserting differences between Europeans and Native peoples to maintain white social solidarity and cohesion

(Stoler 1991, 53). Colonial societies have had to invent themselves as new groupings of individuals with no organic link to one another, in settings that are often radically different from their places of origin. They have had to invent the social institutions that will then define them as a society—and they have to be capable of rationalizing or justifying their existence on other people's lands and the brutality through which their presence is maintained. The very existence of white settler societies is therefore predicated on maintaining racial apartheid, on emphasizing racial difference, both white superiority and Native inferiority.

This flies in the face of the actual origins of many white settlements in Canada—which frequently began with displaced and often marginal white men, whose success with the fur trade or settlement, and often their very survival, depended on their ability to insinuate themselves into Indigenous societies through intermarriage. The early days of European-Native contact frequently involved negotiated alliances with local Indigenous communities, often cemented through marriage. This was particularly the case in French Canada, where early policy, particularly in the Maritimes, hinged on the notion of creating "one French race" in North America through the marriage of French men with Native women. While "frankifying" Native women may have been the goal of the French regime at the time, actual practices suggest that Acadian colonists, marginal men within Europe with relatively few loyalties to empire, tended to adapt to Native realities, as being much more suitable than European ways of living in the new land. In 1753 one French missionary predicted that within fifty years the Acadian colonists would be indistinguishable from Mi'kmaq and Maliseet communities (Dickason 1985, 21–26). Perhaps in response to this apparent cultural ambiguity on the part of the Acadians that troubled colonial authorities, racial categories began to be hardened by legislation throughout French Canada, particularly in Quebec.[1]

Meanwhile the entire structure of the fur trade, in both eastern and western Canada, involved "country marriages" between European men and the Native women that the traders depended on so heavily for their survival—and a growing reliance on the mixed-blood children of these marriages to fill specific niches in the fur trade—which meant that, as time went on, the boundaries between who should be considered European and who should be considered Native (and by what means) have not always been clear. By the mid-

nineteenth century, the presence of numerous mixed-blood communities in the Great Lakes area made it difficult for Anglo settlers to
maintain clear boundaries between colonizers and colonized.[2] Social
control was predicated on legally identifying who was white, who was
Indian, and which children were legitimate progeny—citizens rather
than subjugated Natives (Stoler 1991, 53). To render this issue even
more complicated was the precedent set by the case of *Johnstone et al.
v Connolly*, which upheld the rights of a customary marriage between
a fur trader and a Native woman over a later church marriage between
this same individual and a wealthy white Montreal woman.[3]

Moreover fur trade society in western Canada, in the years before
the 1885 Rebellion, was in many respects highly bicultural. Many settlements consisted primarily of white men married to Cree women,
raising Cree families. While the language spoken in public was English, the language spoken in many of the homes was Cree. Clearly, if a
white settler society modeled on British values was to be established,
white women had to take the place of Native women, and Native
women had to be driven out of the place they had occupied in fur
trade society, a process that would continue through successive waves
of white settlement, from the Great Lakes westward across the continent. The displacement of Native women from white society, and
the replacement of the bicultural white society that their marriages to
white men created to an openly white supremacist society populated
by all-white families, was accomplished largely through the introduction of punitive laws in the Indian Act concerning prostitution
and intoxication off-reserve. These laws targeted Aboriginal women
as responsible for the spread of venereal disease among the police and
officials in western Canada and therefore increasingly classified urban
Aboriginal women as prostitutes within the criminal code after 1892
(Carter 1997, 187).

The growing devaluation of mixed marriages in western Canada in
the 1880s was sharply highlighted by *Jones v Fraser* in 1886, wherein
the judge ruled that the court would not accept that "the cohabitation
of a civilized man and a savage woman, even for a long period of time,
gives rise to the presumption that they consented to be married in our
sense of marriage" (Carter 1997, 191). Mixed-blood children were also
targeted for removal from white society, often through court decisions
that made it impossible for them to inherit their fathers' property.[4]
Sarah Carter suggests, in fact, that forcing Native wives out of settler
society could only truly be effected by restricting the rights of all

wives in western Canada.[5] Therefore, in the process of driving Native women out of white settlements, serious restrictions were placed on the rights of white women.

GENDER DISCRIMINATION IN THE INDIAN ACT

Many of the legal disabilities for women in the Indian Act have existed as much by omission as by explicit statement, through the use of the constant masculine term in the legislation, even though a separate legal regime has existed for Indian women, with respect to marriage, childbirth, regulation of sexual conduct, exclusion from the right to vote or otherwise partake in band business, and rights to inherit and for a widow to administer her husband's estate. Because of the constant use of the masculine pronoun, confusion has existed at times in various communities as to whether Native women actually have any of the rights pertaining to men in much of the Indian Act legislation (Jamieson 1978, 56). Finally, definitions of Indianness have been asserted in such a patriarchal manner as to be fraught with discriminatory consequences for Indian women.

As the previous chapter mentioned, legislation in 1850 first defined Indianness in gendered terms, so that Indian status depended either on Indian descent or marriage to a male Indian. With the Gradual Enfranchisement Act of 1869, not only were wives removed from inheritance rights and automatically enfranchised with their husbands, but Section 6 began a process of escalating gender discrimination that would not be definitively changed until 1985. With this section, for the first time, Indian women were declared "no longer Indian" if they married anybody who lacked Indian status. On marrying an Indian from another "tribe, band, or body," she and her children now belonged to her husband's tribe only (Jamieson 1978, 29–30).

Prior to 1951 some recognition on a local basis was given to the needs of Indian women who were deserted or widowed. Indian women who lost their status were no longer legally Indian and no longer formal band members, but they were not considered to have the full rights that enfranchised women had. These women were often issued informal identity cards, known as "red tickets," which identified them as entitled to shares in treaty monies and recognized on an informal basis their band membership, to the extent that some of them were even able to live on the reserve. It was not until 1951 that women who lost their Indian status were also compulsorily enfranchised. This meant that they not only lost band membership, reserve residency, or any property they might have held on the reserve, but also access to any treaty monies or band assets (RCAP 1996, 19:301–02). Section 6, governing loss of status, was only one of the many aspects of the 1869 legislation that limited the power of Native women in their societies. Particularly in the context of matrilineal practices, this act ripped huge holes in the fabric of Native life. The clan system of the Iroquois was disrupted in particularly cruel ways. Not only was the matrilineal basis of the society (and therefore its framework of land tenure) threatened by legislation that forced Native women to become members of their husbands' communities, but the manner in which white women received the Indian status of their husbands resulted in the births of generations of clanless individuals within reserve communities, since clan inheritance passed through the mother. Finally, in addition to these processes, which subverted and bypassed the power of Native women in matrilineal societies and opened up their lands for privatization, Native women were formally denied any political role in the governance of their societies. For example when the 1869 legislation divided reserves into individual lots, married women could not inherit any portion of their husband's lots, and they lost their own allocations if they married non-Natives. After 1884 widows were allowed to inherit one-third of their husband's lot—if a widow was living with her husband at his time of death and was determined by the Indian agent to be "of good moral character" (RCAP 1996, 4:28–29). Meanwhile, in 1876, the Indian Act prevented Native women from voting in any decisions about surrender of reserve lands. The many ways in which Native women were rendered marginal in their communities by patriarchal colonial laws not only made it more difficult for them to challenge the tremendous disempowerment that loss of status represented—it made land theft much easier.

From the perspective of the colonial administration, the 1869 legislation had two primary goals—to remove as many individuals as possible from Indianness and, as part of this process, to enforce Indianness as being solely a state of "racial purity" by removing those children designated as "half-breed" from Indian communities. At the same time, however, if reserve residents were to grow increasingly mixed-blooded, it would facilitate their enfranchisement, as individuals who were "too civilized" to be Indians. In this respect it is, of course, important to note that when white women married Native men, they also produced "half-breed" children, who nevertheless were allowed to stay in Native communities as Indians. Because of patriarchal notions that children were solely the products of their fathers, these children were not recognized by colonial administrators as half-breed. However communities where there was a great deal of such intermarriage were often reported of approvingly, as when glowing comments were made about Caughnawaga (Kahnawake) in the 1830s that "there is scarcely a pure blooded Indian in the settlement" (Jamieson 1978, 23).

It is clear from the government debates at the time that this legislation was also aimed at undermining the collective nature of Native societies, where lands, monies, and other resources were shared in common. By restricting reserves only to those who were granted location tickets, by externalizing the Indian women who married white men and their children, and by forcing exogamy on Native women (where the custom in many communities was that Native men would join their wives' extended family, who controlled the land along clan lines), most of the collective aspects of Native society were to be subverted or suppressed.

In 1874, legislation altered and elaborated upon the definition of the term *Indian*, making Indian descent solely flowing from the male line. With this act, the status of the illegitimate children of Native women was also continuously subject to changing standards at the whim of the superintendent of Indian Affairs, depending on whether the father was known to be Native or not. The superintendent was also given the power to stop the payment of annuities and interest to any woman having no children, who deserted her husband, and "lived immorally with another man" (Jamieson 1978, 45). Other legislation criminalized Indian women further, targeting them as prostitutes and providing them with penalties of one hundred dollars and up to six months in jail. It should be noted that being externalized from Indianness through loss of status, and being therefore forced to leave their communities, did not free Native women from being subject to criminal restrictions under the Indian Act when they were off-reserve. Such criminalization continued because of the much looser definitions of Indianness created expressly for the liquor section of the act, and because of the custom followed by many judges at the time of punishing nonstatus Native women according to Indian Act stipulations.

The 1920s legislation that evicted or jailed Native "squatters" on band lands had severe implications for women who lost their status and were increasingly rendered homeless, especially if their husbands were not white but were, rather, nonstatus Indians or Métis, or if their marriages to white men failed, or they were widowed (Jamieson 1978, 51). Indeed throughout the 1930s, an ongoing issue for the Department of Indian Affairs involved the numbers of Native women who had lost their status through marriage and were still receiving annuities and who either continued to live on the reserve or squatted on its fringes with nonstatus Native husbands. Indian agents were given the authority to evict these families with impunity (Jamieson 1978, 53). While cutting down on welfare and medical expenses to Indians was continuously effected throughout the 1930s, one duty that was never neglected, regardless of the cost, was the relentless tracking down of the fathers of "illegitimate" children of Native women, which often involved having Indian agents travel across the country to find them. These fathers, whether Indian or white, were then asked to sign forms affirming paternity of the child (Jamieson 1978, 54).

While the 1951 Indian Act represents a lessening of colonial control for Indian men, it actually heightened colonial regulation for Indian women in general and especially for those women who married non-Natives. The membership section became even more elaborate, couched in almost unreadable bureaucratic language, which spelled out not only who was entitled to be registered as an Indian but who was not. The male line of descent was further emphasized as the major criterion for inclusion—in fact mention of "Indian blood" was altogether removed. The areas of the act that dictated who was not an Indian included Section 12(1)(b), which removed the status of any woman who married a non-Indian (which included American Indians and nonstatus Native men from Canada), and Section 12(1)(a)(iv), also known as the "double-mother" clause, which removed the status of any individual whose mother *and* paternal grandmother lacked Indian status prior to their marriages to Indian men. Section 12(2) also enabled the "illegitimate" child of an Indian woman to lose status if the father was known not to have Indian status. All band lists now had to be publicly posted, and an appeal process was put into place, so that the child's Indian status could be "protested" by the band within twelve months of the child's name being added to the band list, if the father's Indian status was in question. Because of this, large numbers of so-called illegitimate Indian children, in many cases with two Native parents (but with the father being nonstatus), were denied Indian status.

The major change for Native women who "married out" was that from the date of their marriages they were not only automatically deprived of their Indian status and band rights, but by order of the governor-in-council they were declared enfranchised. Enfranchisement for these Indian women, however, did not involve the same conditions as those that had been experienced by Indian men and their families either through voluntary or involuntary enfranchisement. Individuals who enfranchised, voluntarily or involuntarily, had to have sufficient resources to survive off-reserve. No such condition was considered necessary for Indian women compulsorily enfranchised, since they were assumed to be, effectively, "wards" of their husband. Their prior children were erroneously enfranchised with them until 1955; in 1967 these children were reinstated—when they could be traced. A federal government position of registrar was created to oversee the complex matter of who would be maintained on band lists and who would be struck off. In case Indian women attempted to hide their marriages to non-Indians by marrying in an urban center, at least some arrangements were effected between Statistics Canada and the Department of Indian Affairs in an effort to ensure that most, if not all, marriages of status Indians were eventually reported (Jamieson 1978, 65).

The financial losses experienced by Native women due to loss of status have been considerable. When enfranchised, the women were entitled to receive a per capita share of band capital and revenue, as well as the equivalent of twenty years' treaty money. Since the treaty money is either four or five dollars a year, depending on the treaty, the women were therefore entitled to receive either eighty or one hundred dollars. However, during the interval when large numbers of women were being enfranchised and "paid off," most Native communities had relatively few assets and revenue available to provide meaningful shares to the women. Many of those bands subsequently received significant monies from resource development, to which the enfranchised women and their children never had access.

Another series of financial losses that Native women experienced when they lost their Indian status included the lack of access to postsecondary-education funding, free day-care provisions in some communities, funding for school supplies and special schooling programs, housing policies that enabled on-reserve Indians to buy houses with assistance from the Central Mortgage and Housing Corporation and Indian Affairs, loans and grants from the Indian Economic Development Fund, health benefits, exemption from taxation and from provincial sales tax, hunting, fishing, animal grazing and trapping rights, cash distributions from sales of band assets, and the ability to be employed in the United States without a visa and to cross the border without restrictions (Jamieson 1978, 70–71). Finally, Indian women were generally denied access to personal property willed to them, evicted from their homes, often with small children and no money (especially when widowed or separated), and generally faced hostile band councils and indifferent Indian Affairs bureaucrats (Jamieson 1978, 72).

However it is the personal and cultural losses of losing status that Indian women have most frequently spoken about. Some of the costs have included being unable to participate with family and relatives in the life of their former communities, being rejected by their communities, being culturally different and often socially rejected within white society, being unable to access cultural programs for their children, and finally not even being able to be buried with other family members on the reserve. The extent of penalties and lack of compensation for losses suffered has made the forcible enfranchisement of Indian women "retribution, not restitution"; what Justice Bora Laskin, in his dissenting opinion in Lavell and Bedard, termed "statutory banishment" (Jamieson 1978, 72).

Finally, in terms of Native empowerment generally, it is important to note that this "bleeding off" of Native women and their children from their communities was in place for 116 years, from 1869 until 1985. The phenomenal cultural implication hidden in this legislation is the sheer numbers of Native people lost to their communities. Some sources have estimated that by far the majority of the twenty-five thousand Indians who lost status and were externalized from their communities between 1876 and 1985 (Holmes 1987, 8), did so because of ongoing gender discrimination in the Indian Act.[6] But it is not simply a matter of twenty-five thousand individuals. If one takes into account the fact that for every individual who lost status and had to leave her community, all of her descendants (many of them the products of nonstatus Indian fathers and Indian mothers) also lost status and for the most part were permanently alienated from Native culture, the numbers of individuals who ultimately were removed from Indian status and lost to their nations may, at the most conservative estimates, number between one and two million.

By comparison, in 1985, when Bill C-31 was passed, there were only 350,000 status Indians still listed on the Department of Indian Affair's Indian register (Holmes 1987, 54). In comparing the potential numbers of people lost to their Native communities because of loss of status with the numbers of individuals still considered Indian in 1985, the scale of cultural genocide caused by gender discrimination becomes visible. Because Bill C-31 allowed the most recent generation of individuals who had lost status to regain it, along with their children, approximately one hundred thousand individuals had regained their status by 1995 (Switzer 1997, 2). But the damage caused, demographically and culturally, by the loss of status of so many Native women for a century prior to 1985, whose grandchildren and great-grandchildren are now no longer recognized—and in many cases no longer identify—as Indian, remain incalculable.

THE STRUGGLE TO CHANGE THE INDIAN ACT

Given the accelerating gender discrimination in the Indian Act created by the modifications of 1951, Mohawk women in the 1960s created an organization known as Indian Rights for Indian Women, which attempted to address the disempowerment of Indian women, particularly with respect to loss of status. In 1971 Jeannette Corbiere Lavell and Yvonne Bedard, two Indian women who had lost status through their marriages, challenged the discriminatory sections of the Indian Act in the Canadian courts. In doing so they relied on a precedent set in 1969 in R. v Drybones, where an Indian man named Drybones, who had been convicted of being intoxicated off-reserve under Section 94(b) of the Indian Act, appealed his conviction to the Supreme Court on the basis that this section was in violation of the equality guarantee against racial discrimination set out in Section 1(b) of the Canadian Bill of Rights.[7]

With the success of Drybones, Lavell challenged the deletion of her name from her band list, while Bedard, in a separate case, challenged the fact that her reserve was evicting her and her children from the house which her mother had willed to her, even though she was no longer married to her husband. Both women lost at the federal court level, but were successful at winning appeals, and their cases were heard together in the Supreme Court. Their argument was based on the fact that the Indian Act discriminated against them on the basis of race and sex, and that the Bill of Rights should therefore override the discriminatory sections of the Indian Act with respect to membership, as *Drybones* had with Section 94(b).

In 1973 the Supreme Court, by a five to four decision, ruled against Lavell and Bedard. Among other reasons, the decision noted that since not all Indians were discriminated against, only Indian women who married non-Indians, then racial discrimination could not be said to exist; and since enfranchised Indian women gained the citizenship rights that made them equal (in law) to white women, then gender discrimination could not be said to exist. While this judgment clarified none of the issues, it did assert that the Bill of Rights could not take precedence over the Indian Act. Because of this decision, the Indian Act was exempt from the application of the Canadian Human Rights Act in 1977 (Holmes 1987, 5).

The Maliseet community of Tobique was the next focus of resistance. The women at Tobique began their struggle over the issue of homelessness—the manner in which their band council interpreted Indian Act legislation to suggest that Indian women had no right to own property on the reserve. As the women addressed the problems they faced, their struggle slowly broadened until their primary goal became changing the Indian Act (Silman 1987, 119–72). Since the decision in *Lavell and Bedard* had foreclosed any possibility of justice within Canada, the Tobique women decided to support Sandra Lovelace in an appeal to the United Nations Human Rights Committee. Lovelace argued that Section 12(1)(b) of the Indian Act was in violation of Article 27 of the International Covenant on Civil and Political Rights, which provides for the rights of individuals who belong to minorities to enjoy their culture, practice their religion, and use their language in community with others from the group (Beyefsky 1982, 244–66). In 1981 the United Nations determined that Sandra Lovelace had been denied her cultural rights under Article 27 because she was barred from living in her community. Canada, embarrassed at the international level, at this point stated its intention to amend the discriminatory sections of the Indian Act. After some degree of consultation and proposed changes, Bill C-31, An Act to Amend the Indian Act, was passed in 1985.[8]

The violence and resistance that Native women struggling for their rights faced, from male-dominated band councils and political organizations during this interval, cannot be ignored.[9] For example, when Mary Two-Axe Earley and sixty other Native women from Kahnawake (then known as the Caughnawaga band) chose to focus international attention on their plight by bringing their organization, Indian Rights for Indian Women, to the International Women's Year conference in Mexico City in 1975, they were all served with eviction notices in their absence by their band council (Jamieson 1979, 170). Meanwhile when the Tobique women, protesting homelessness in their communities, occupied the band office in order to have a roof over their heads and draw attention to their plight, they were threatened with arrest by the band administration, physically beaten up in the streets, and had to endure numerous threats against their families from other community members.[10]

It was with *Lavell and Bedard*, however, that the polarization between nonstatus women demanding their rights as Indians and status Indian organizations such as the National Indian Brotherhood (now the Assembly of First Nations) and the Association of Iroquois and Allied Indians came to a head. For example, the National Indian Brotherhood, which intervened *against* Lavell and Bedard, supported the argument that gender discrimination against Native women had been instituted in the 1869 legislation (and enshrined in every Indian Act since then) as a benevolent process to protect Indians from the white men who married Indian women.[11] And a position paper of the Association of Iroquois and Allied Indians (AIAI), which had asked the government to intervene in the Supreme Court, concurred with the Supreme Court that Section 12(1)(b) was "merely a legislative embodiment of Indian custom" (Jamieson 1978, 83).

More damningly, the widespread discrimination against Native women first introduced in 1869 continues to be upheld by some individuals as legislation designed to "protect" Native communities from the white husbands of Native women. The most recent example of this argument, which continues to be raised whenever it is politically expedient, is demonstrated by Taiaiake Alfred in *Windspeaker* (February 2000). Alfred, in comments that are curiously suggestive of a belief in the benevolence of the Canadian government toward its colonized subjects, states that gender discrimination in the Indian Act was put there to oblige Native people because "the Indians complained" about what would happen if white men were allowed to marry Native women and live in their communities. Alfred also asserts that gender discrimination was traditionally practiced in Native communities but that it should not be *seen* as gender discrimination, simply because, culturally, women had to bear a stronger responsibility for who they married than men did, as mothers of the nation. Because of this, the virtual banishment of these women and their children from Native communities for marrying nonstatus individuals has been justifiable and certainly does not require redress (Alfred, in Barnsley 2000, 6–7).

Kathleen Jamieson has demonstrated, however, that the various governmental debates that attended the passing of this legislation make clear that the intent of the act was *not* to prevent white men from living on the reserve—it was to prevent their mixed-blood children from having any rights to community assets and to limit the abilities of community residents to support nonband-member relatives and others who would normally be welcomed to share whatever resources the community had. [12] Other individuals in recent years have claimed that it was acceptable for the Indian Act to discriminate against Native women because "it was traditional" within Native societies. Jamieson refutes these arguments as well by documenting some of the objections raised by Native communities to this legislation at the time that it was passed. [13]

The federal government, moreover, with *Lavell and Bedard*, took the position that it could not alter any of the membership sections of the Indian Act until the entire act was revised, thus feeding status-Indian fears created by the White Paper. In 1969, in a document known as the White Paper, the federal government proposed to unilaterally terminate Indian status, thereby terminating its fiduciary responsibility and the various rights and exemptions accruing to individuals of Indian status, including reserve land holdings. This preemptive move, if successful, would not only have enabled remaining Indian reserves to be privatized and lost to Native people but it would have removed any legal framework for redress of lost land. It would have removed Native control over education and thereby invalidated efforts to address the massive loss of language brought about by residential school. Finally, the massive poverty and social problems of Native people—a result not only of loss of access to a resource base and tremendous structural racism within Canadian society but also through years of being denied, as Indians, the basic financial benefits accruing to Canadians and of having generations of Native people "imprisoned" in residential schools—would have become each individual's "fault," and it would have been up to the individual Native person to rectify the situation as best they could. Assimilation, rather than nation-building, would gradually become the only realistic or viable goal for Native people.

The response to the White Paper was immediate. A massive mobilization of Native people across Canada proceeded until the paper was shelved. There are repercussions, however, which have lasted until this day. First of all, the Canadian government continues to propose bills that reintroduce aspects of the White Paper in a more piecemeal fashion. Canada has, however, become far more expert at dividing opposition among status Indians in the process. Secondly, the emphasis that status Indian organizations now place on resisting changes to the Indian Act has effectively divided them from nonstatus Native people. Prior to the White Paper, throughout the 1960s, Native people across Canada were resisting their ongoing colonization in a relatively unified manner. After the White Paper, status Indian organizations became much more focused on protecting status Indian rights, while Native people who lacked Indian status were forced to begin to organize alone to acquire some rights as Native people.

Because of these many layers of fear engendered by the White Paper, and because Indian activists had already begun to see the Indian Act as a lever that could potentially embarrass Canada at the International level (as the Maliseet women in fact succeeded in doing in the Lovelace case) and that could therefore be a bargaining tool, many of the status Indian organizations supported the position of the federal government in refusing to alter any of the membership sections of the Indian Act without amending the act as a whole. Kathleen Jamieson has suggested that this was based on the erroneous assumption that the Canadian government was not also continuing to use the Indian Act as a lever against Native people, as it had been doing for a century already. She has also noted how, during the struggles over the White Paper and *Lavell and Bedard*, the Indian Act was somehow transformed from the legal instrument of oppression that it had been since its inception to "a repository of sacred rights for Indians" (Jamieson 1978, 2). And yet despite the extreme positions taken by some of the activists at the time (and since), other individuals clearly saw the gender discrimination in the Indian Act as deeply problematic, and so there was no consensus within the National Indian Brotherhood initially over *Lavell and Bedard*.

In 1980, perhaps in anticipation of the upcoming Lovelace decision, Canada created an interim policy that allowed Indian bands to request suspension of Sections 12(1)(b) and 12(1)(a)(iv). Fifty-three percent of all bands requested suspension of the "double-mother" clause (which affects adult Native men and women who live on reserves) while only nineteen percent chose to suspend Section 12(1)(b), which affects only Native women and their off-reserve male and female descendants. This tremendous discrepancy suggests that band governments in general at that point did not regard the rights of Indian women (and their off-reserve children) as important (Holmes 1987, 6). Indeed the multiple legacies for Native communities of having patriarchal relations enforced for over a century by the Indian Act continue to resonate throughout Indian Country.

After over a century of gender discrimination in the Indian Act, the idea that Native women should lose status for marrying nonstatus or non-Native men has become a normalized assumption in many communities. As a result, our basic understanding of who is mixed-blood and who is not is highly shaped by gender. The family histories of on-reserve Native people have routinely included the presence of white women married to Native men, as well as (in some cases) the children of Native women who had babies by white men but were not married to them, and whose status was not protested. These experiences have not been seen, or theorized, as mixed-blood experiences. These mixed-blood children have been allowed to have Indian status, they have been considered to be Indian and have never had to leave their communities. Indian reserves, particularly those adjacent to white settlements, may have grown progressively mixed-blooded under these circumstances—but they have not been *called* mixed-blood communities, and on-reserve mixed-blood families have therefore not been externalized *as* mixed-blood people.

It has been the children of Native mothers and white, nonstatus Indian or Métis fathers who have been forced to become urban Indians and who, in their Native communities of origin, are currently being regarded as outsiders because they *have* been labeled as "not Indian." Gender has thus been crucial in determining not only who has been able to stay in Native communities but who has been called mixed-blood and externalized as such. In this respect, gender discrimination in the Indian Act has shaped what we think about who is Native, who is mixed-blood, and who is entitled to access to Indian land. These beliefs are only rendered more powerful by the strongly protectionist attitudes toward preserving Native culture as it is lived on reserves at present, where outsiders may be seen as profoundly threatening to community identity.

This history has even deeper repercussions, however, for Native communities today. Because the subordination of Indigenous women has been a central nexus through which colonizers have sought to destroy Indigenous societies, contemporary gender divisions created by the colonizer continue to subvert sovereignty struggles in crucial ways. And yet, almost inevitably, when issues of particular concern to Native women arise, they are framed as "individual rights," while in many cases, those who oppose Native women's rights are held to represent "the collective." In a context where a return to traditional collective ways is viewed as essential to surviving the ravages of colonization, Native women are routinely asked to separate their womanness from their Nativeness, as if violations of Native women's rights are not violations of Native rights.

Even the American court decision most often cited as a positive example for Aboriginal governments in terms of exercising the right to control their own membership, *Santa Clara Pueblo v Martinez*, involved upholding the sovereign right of a tribal government to deny membership rights to the children of a female tribal member, as part of resisting the imposition of federal rights legislation within tribal territories. *Santa Clara Pueblo v Martinez* involved the case of Julia Martinez, a member of the Santa Clara Pueblo, who married a Navajo Indian two years after a tribal ordinance passed that clearly outlined that membership in the tribe was patrilineal, that nonmember husbands could not be adopted into the tribe while nonmember wives could. Martinez's children, who grew up at Santa Clara Pueblo and who are Tewa-speaking and culturally fully members of their community, could reside in the community only until the death of their mother and could not inherit her property.

Julia Martinez and her daughter Audrey therefore brought suit in federal court against the tribe and its governor, claiming that this membership rule discriminates on the basis of both sex and ancestry in violation of Title I of the Indian Civil Rights Act. This act, passed in 1968 with the goal of allowing the federal government to "protect Indians from their own governments" (as if the federal government is some neutral third party), was the first major federal legislation addressing the operation of tribal governments since the Indian Reorganization Act of 1934. Immediately after its enactment, the federal courts began to take jurisdiction in cases challenging the decisions of tribal courts and councils, assuming that the Indian Civil Rights Act waived tribal sovereign immunity from suit. In *Santa Clara Pueblo v Martinez*, however, it was held that without congressional authorization, tribes are exempt from suit and that waivers of sovereign immunity cannot be implied but must be expressed. Julia Martinez was therefore barred by Santa Clara Pueblo's immunity from suit from taking the tribe to court (Clinton et al. 1973, 384–89). For women such as Julia Martinez, then, her tribe's victory meant her children's disenfranchisement.

3

Reconfiguring Colonial
Gender Relations under Bill C-31

The 1985 Indian Act (generally known as Bill C-31) embodied three fundamental principles: (1) the removal of gender-based discrimination; (2) the restoration of status and membership rights to eligible individuals; and (3) the recognition of band control over membership (Huntley and Blaney 1999, 9). In doing so, Bill C-31 separated Indian status and band membership, created new divisions among Indians with respect to who can pass their status on to their children, and made it impossible for nonstatus women to regain status through marriage.[1]

As a result of the bill, approximately 127,000 individuals have regained their Indian status; however another 106,000 were denied reinstatement (Barnsley 2003c, 1, 14). Moreover, the ability of the reinstated women to pass their status on to their children is limited to one generation, known as the "second-generation cut-off." Perhaps more devastatingly, Bill C-31 not only continues but enlarges the "bleeding off" of individuals from legal recognition as Indians by extending new status restrictions to men as well: while nobody now loses status for marrying non-Natives, all Native people now face certain restrictions on their ability to pass status on to their children. Since the majority of nonstatus Indians and Métis people (estimated at about 600,000 people in the mid-1980s) were not made eligible for registration under the new Indian Act, the legal divisions between status

Indians and other Native people have been maintained (Holmes 1987, 13).

Furthermore, since most of the women who regained their status will not be able to pass it down further than their mixed-blood children, restoration of status to one generation of women who lost it has simply deferred Native families' experiences of gender discrimination for a generation, as the grandchildren of these women will once again lose their status. Other forms of gender discrimination have been created by the legislation as well. Finally, the desire of many of the reinstated women to return to their homes and to have their children made band members was bypassed by the bill, by the manner in which it changed band membership criteria to enable bands to develop their own membership codes. In this respect, Bill C-31 has managed to end formal gender discrimination in the Indian Act while still maintaining patriarchal divisions among Native people—largely through not addressing past injustices. Furthermore, it has succeeded in imposing new and crippling restrictions on maintaining Indian status, which, in a context where so much of contemporary Native community life depends on being legally defined as Indian, can be considered genocidal in scope.

Gender continues to shape definitions of Indianness under Bill C-31. There are a number of ways in which Indian women who are reinstated achieve only what is known as "partial" status (that is, status with restrictions on whether it can be passed on to one's children or not). The most common circumstance, the second-generation cut-off, is that women who lost status under Section 12(1)(b) of the 1951 Indian Act are only reinstated under Section 6(1)(c) of the new act; their children, unless they marry somebody with Indian status, are only entitled to be reinstated under Section 6(2); *their* children cannot inherit Indian status at all. The only exception to this is if an Indian woman had married somebody without Indian status after 1980. If her band had chosen to proclaim 12(1)(b) invalid, as they were given the option at that time, she could be reinstated under 6(1)(a). Individuals who never lost status, by comparison, are always registered under 6(1)(a); they can pass status on to their descendents without limit, although under Bill C-31, if they marry individuals who are nonstatus, the status of their descendants will face limitations, depending on the particular circumstances.

Many of the categories for reinstatement are highly time dependent and still encode gender differences into the categories. In particular, the reinstatement of the children of unmarried mothers is fraught with gender discrimination on deep levels. Under section 12(1)(c) of the 1951 Indian Act, Indianness was considered to flow only from the male line to male children. Because of this, the illegitimate male child of a male Indian born before Bill C-31 came into effect, even if his or her mother is white, is eligible for full status under 6(1)(a). Only one Indian parent is needed to establish full status if the child is male and if his father is Indian (Gilbert 1996, 54). This was established in 1983 in *Martin v Chapman*, where the Supreme Court of Canada stated that the registrar could not legally prevent the illegitimate son of a white woman and a male Indian from being registered as Indian. Meanwhile, this court ruling does not apply to the illegitimate *daughters* of white women and Indian men—these individuals are only entitled to be registered under 6(2)(Gilbert 1996, 53).[2]

On the other hand, the children of unmarried status Indian women must prove Indian paternity to be registered under 6(1)(a); otherwise they are reinstated under 6(1)(c) and their children receive only 6(2) status. In essence, two Indian parents are required for full Indian status if the child's *mother* is Indian.

If the child was born prior to the implementation of the 1951 Indian Act, entirely different sets of rules apply. The earlier Indian Acts allowed illegitimate children to "share in the distribution monies of the band" during the interval in which they were nurtured on reserve as babies, while their paternity was being established. If the father was found to be nonstatus, the child was not considered a member and cannot be reinstated under Bill C-31 at all. If, however, during that two year period, paternity could not be clarified, and the individual can offer proof that he or she "shared in the distribution monies of the band" for two years and a day, they are eligible for reinstatement under Section 6(1)(c) of the new act.

Other individuals can only receive certain types of status depending on which Indian Act was in effect when she or he was born. For example, if a person's parents enfranchised, their ability to be registered with full or partial status depends on whether the parents enfranchised before or after 1951. Prior to 1951, wives and children were automatically enfranchised without their names appearing on the order; the children of parents who enfranchised then (subject to proof of relationship with the enfranchised individual) can be reinstated with full status under 6(1)(a). However, if the parents enfranchised after 1951, the name of the wife appears on the enfranchisement notice, which means she was privy to the decision. This apparent complicity on the part of the wife toward enfranchisement for some reason is allowed to restrict ability to reclaim status; their children can only be registered under Section 6(1)(d), and their grandchildren will receive only partial status under Section 6(2).

As these details demonstrate, a central feature of Bill C-31 is its divisiveness. It has encoded multiple categories for reinstatement, resulting in a wide divergence in possible outcomes for individuals. This massively disempowers Native people, by forcing them to conform to multiple, almost incomprehensible, regulations for reinstatement, in an extremely time-consuming process that provides no guarantee that their status will be reinstated. By not addressing past gender discrimination, it has ensured that gender discrimination continues. And most damningly, it has made Indian status much harder to keep. Intermarriage now represents a "ticking time bomb" in Native communities, inexorably removing Indian status from the descendants of anybody who chooses to marry somebody without Indian status.

BAND MEMBERSHIP

During the process of amending the 1951 Indian Act, Aboriginal leaders demanded much greater autonomy in deciding First Nations membership. The clearest alternative to the open colonialism of the Indian Act was the approach to tribal membership that had been formally recognized throughout much of United States history, most clearly articulated during *Santa Clara Pueblo v Martinez*, that a tribe's right to control its membership is basic to its survival as a cultural and economic entity.[3] However, Canada, through Section 10 of the current Indian Act, recognizes only a very limited control by First Nations over determination of membership.

Prior to Bill C-31, most status Indians also had band membership.[4] Under the current act, Indians who regain their status may not qualify for band membership, while a person may be granted membership who lacks Indian status (such individuals will not, however, be included in funding arrangements by the federal government). It was mandatory, in the process of assuming control over membership, that all bands accept the four categories of individuals whose Indian status is secured through Section 6(1), which includes women who lost status under 12(1)(b) of the 1951 Indian Act (but not their children), individuals who lost status through the double-mother clause—

Section 12(1)(a)(iv), or through Section 12(2), illegitimacy—and those individuals whose grandparents enfranchised before 1951. Bands who assumed control over their membership after 28 June 1987 are also required to accept those individuals reinstated under 6(2), including the children of women who lost their status and individuals whose grandparents were enfranchised after 1951.

First Nations are free to design membership rules that reflect their unique cultures and customs. Some bands have made their membership codes as wide as "aboriginal ancestry and historic family ties to the traditional lands" of their people (with limited membership for those who have only one grandparent from the community, unless they are status Indians, wherein exceptions might be made). Other bands formulate their codes in terms of "citizenship," which is less dependent on specific amounts of ancestry than on ability to speak the language, and social and cultural ties to the community, with the stipulation that there will be a probationary period of five years during which the individual must acquire knowledge of the way of life of the community. Some bands demand familiarity with traditional clan structures or affiliation into traditional houses. Some bands depend less on ancestry than on individuals being nominated by existing community members. On the other hand, some bands fix blood quantum requirements—at 50 percent or 25 percent. In some cases, those who are "original" band members prior to Bill C-31 are deemed to have 100 percent blood quantum, even though Indian status is a very poor indicator of degree of Indian blood. Some bands impose residency requirements on non-Native spouses, others deny them access to the reserve, while still others simply accept them as band members. In some cases, bands demand prohibitive levels of documentation from individuals and request that they contribute some of their personal monies to the band capital fund. Other bands rely on more cultural or traditional factors. And yet despite the diversity of choices exercised by different bands, the fact that only band members with Indian status can receive government monies places significant constraints on bands who choose to disregard Indian status as a marker of Indigeneity.

It is important to note that the broad range of circumstances that bands face—from being urbanized and engulfed by white society for centuries, to facing the chaos of the first decades of violent contact and colonization—are reflected in the codes they choose, which have closely reflected their needs as a community. And yet it is impossible to speak of First Nations membership codes without referencing both a history of extreme government coercion over every aspect of band life and a century of colonial identity discourse that still shapes common-sense ways of seeing "Indianness," particularly in ways that are deeply gendered and yet see gender as absolutely irrelevant. This issue is particularly important with respect to those bands that have chosen to adopt membership codes based on blood quantum.

REPERCUSSIONS OF BILL C-31

The reaction of different bands to changes to the Indian Act under Bill C-31 has varied in the extreme. Some bands have devised codes that have successfully brought back to their communities people lost through past legislation. Others appear to have made this bill the occasion to assert their sovereignty primarily by closing down against perceived "outsiders." In the uproar, it is telling that many Native people regard Bill C-31, and not prior versions of the Indian Act, as the root of the problem.[5] Identity legislation in the Indian Act has functioned so completely—and yet so apparently invisibly—along gendered lines that at present the rewriting of Indian identity under Bill C-31 in ways that target men as well as women are viewed as intense violations of sovereignty, while the gendered violations of sovereignty that occurred in successive Indian Acts since 1869 have been virtually normalized as the problems of individual women. And all of this is being done in the politically charged atmosphere of communities that have long been under siege in terms of their very survival.

The effects of reinstatement have been drastic for some bands, in terms of severely straining their already overstretched and inadequate resources; however, the majority of bands have been only moderately affected:

Of the more than 600 bands in Canada, a total of 79, or 13 percent, face a potential population increase of more than 100 percent. The majority, 379 bands, or 62 percent, face membership increases of between 10 percent and 30 percent. The Native Council of Canada conducted a random survey of Indians affected by Bill C-31, and less than one-half of those surveyed wanted to return to the community. Of those, about 70 percent wanted band membership so they could regain some of their culture, not to go home to live on the reserve. ("Bill C-31" 1996, 7)

Maurice Switzer, a member of the Elders' Council of the Mississaugas of Rice Lake, has suggested that the preoccupation with the financial implications of Bill C-31 has obscured its cultural implications. He notes that many of the individuals who gained back their status under Bill C-31 have a wealth of expertise learned in the non-Native world that could contribute much to the well-being of their respective First Nations—and that the same bands who rejected these individuals have thought nothing of paying white consultants four hundred dollars an hour for legal or economic advice when it might have been obtained more reliably and cheaply from their own C-31 membership (Switzer 1997, 2).

Some C-31 women speak of their fears of exclusion due to nepotism and favoritism in their communities (Huntley and Blaney 1999, 15), of the manner in which they are treated like second-class citizens when they return home, and the fact that their communities refuse to accept the notion that inherent Indigenous title to the land must reflect the rights of newly reinstated members. Some of the daughters of these women have commented that their brothers' memberships were processed far more quickly by their bands than theirs were (Huntley and Blaney 1999, 15). On the other hand, in other communities, reinstated women were provided with housing, assistance in accessing educational funding, and generally, despite the limited resources, welcomed back to their communities of origin (Huntley and Blaney 1999, 27–36).

Indeed it is striking that, after the reversal of a century-old policy that allowed the numbers of status Indians in Canada to increase by approximately one-third, no thought was given by the First Nations to request funds for community education about the history of gender discrimination in the Indian Act, or about the fact that the so-called outsiders who now seek band membership are in fact merely the children of those forced to leave. Instead, community members have been left to make sense of the repercussions of C-31 on their own. In the process, a central issue shaping the response in many communities is the fact that it has long been accepted that if Native women marry white men they *should* forfeit their right, and their children's, to be band members and live in the community—while it is perfectly alright for Native men to have married white women for years without ever having their rights to band membership or community residency challenged. Even the language used by on-reserve Indians in referring to those individuals whose status was reinstated under Bill C-31—

terms such as "new Indians" (Switzer 1997, 2) rather than "Indians who have regained their status"—is telling. Even more serious are comments made by individuals who claim that the century-long double standard is acceptable, because of the high responsibilities traditionally placed on Native women to preserve the culture. While it is true that Native women have always been at the center of traditional societies, these statements that defend gender discrimination in the Indian Act as "traditional" never reference any of the continuous assaults on Native women's traditional practices that came with colonization. Indeed in the absence of such an analysis, what is left is a punitive attitude toward Native women, reminiscent of church biases, and a real unwillingness to enable those women who lost their status to pass on culture and tradition to their urban mixed-blood children. At the same time, most communities maintain a total silence about the generations of white women who were allowed to live in Native communities passing along European culture to *their* mixed-race children—or the fact that the ability of these white women to remain band members has never been challenged.

Three Alberta First Nations, the Sawridge First Nation in Northern Alberta, the Tsuu T'ina First Nation outside Calgary, and the Ermineskin First Nation of Hobbema, have challenged the constitutionality of Bill C-31 on the basis that it violated the Aboriginal rights of First Nations to determine their own membership and their Native traditions that stated that women should take on the citizenship of their husbands. In 1995 the courts upheld the rights of Bill C-31 Indians and ruled against the band's challenge. However, Justice Muldoon, who made the decision, did so by attacking the validity of Native traditions and Aboriginal rights.[6] The bands appealed this decision to the Supreme Court, and in June 1997 the Court overturned the 1995 ruling, citing bias on the part of Judge Muldoon. The Congress of Aboriginal People then filed for an appeal of the federal court's most recent ruling (McKinley 1997, 2).

Larry Gilbert, in discussing the Sawridge case, has noted that Muldoon's decision adopted the notion that the plaintiff's right to control their own membership had been extinguished by the 1876 Indian Act and, furthermore, that any infringement of the plaintiff's rights were justified by Sections 15 and 28 of the Charter of Rights and Freedoms. He suggested that the court was dismissing one of the most fundamental rights of self-government, the right to determine membership, and that if the decision stands, it could affect self-government negotia-tions, the treaty process in British Columbia, and future court cases on the existence and nature of self-government (Gilbert 1996, 209). What was missing in this extremely important argument was the fact that the right to determine membership only became a negotiated issue during Bill C-31—and that it is entirely consistent with government tactics of divide and conquer that this extremely important right was only offered First Nations so that they could choose to refuse any obligation to correct the legacy of government-imposed gender dis-crimination. Ironically, as with *Santa Clara Pueblo v Martinez* in the United States, the sovereign right of Native communities to deter-mine their own membership is being asserted primarily against the children of their female membership.

Catherine Twinn, who with her late husband Walter Twinn was a plaintiff for Sawridge First Nation, in an interview referred to Bill C-31 Indians as "strangers who would bring conflict, stress, and prob-lems" to the reserves. She stated that in time the "strangers" would destroy the land base of reserves (McKinley 1997, 4).[7] Regardless of the vested interests involved in much of the organized opposition to Bill C-31, given the extremely oil-rich nature of the three First Na-tions appealing expansion in their membership, Twinn's comments obviously resonate within some communities. It appears that the ex-istence of reinstated Native people who did not grow up in Native culture is capable of striking a chord of unease in many Native com-munities. It is worthwhile considering that it is this anxiety over the implications of opening up Native identity in unknown directions, rather than primarily an issue of sexism, which may be at the heart of the unwillingness of some on-reserve Indians to redress gender dis-crimination in reinstating Bill C-31 Indians as band members.

It cannot be denied, however, that it is primarily women (and their male and female children) who are facing the violence and hostility of some communities who are determined that they will never be rein-stated. In July 1997, for example, Gina Russell and Agnes Gendron led a contingent of more than thirty women from Cold Lake First Nation to protest the manner in which their band continues to discriminate not only against Bill C-31 Indians, whom they refuse to reinstate, but against women who married nonstatus Indians or non-Natives *after* 1985. In a sense, the band is continuing to penalize women who marry nonstatus or non-Native individuals, as if Section 12(1)(b) of the 1951 Indian Act still existed (Dumont and De Ryk 1997, 15). The Cold Lake band may be doing this as an assertion of sovereignty, in claiming their right to control band membership. However they are merely clinging to one Indian Act in preference to another—and doing it on the backs of the women who were formerly members of the community. Still, as Patricia Monture-Angus notes, strong resistance to the reinstatement of C-31 individuals probably represents a minority opinion in most Native communities (Monture-Angus 1999, 144). Furthermore, some of the reinstated women have found significant support in their communities and in some cases from chiefs and councils.

After Bill C-31, a number of bands, in drawing up new membership codes, have begun to emphasize blood quantum as the defining characteristic of who should be considered a member of their community. There is a profound difference between regulating identity by blood quantum and by Indian status; however this difference is obscured when bands begin by designating full Indian status as synonymous with full-bloodedness. It is therefore important to note the distinction between what Jamieson calls "Indian Act blood" and "Indian blood." With the exception of the 1869 legislation, which included a requirement of one-quarter Indian blood, the Indian Act has regulated Indianness virtually without reference to *actual* blood quantum, that is, on what a person's precise record or degree of Native and non-Native ancestry is.

Every aspect of the Indian Act relating to Indian blood begins with the notion that Indian status is equivalent to "pure-bloodedness," and that the contorted fragmentation of identity within Indian Act categories actually reflects an individual's real blood quantum. However, for over a century, the "Indian" in the Indian Act has primarily been a creation of the act itself and of Victorian notions that judged a person's heritage only by their descent along the male line (Jamieson 1978, 60). By comparison, it might be useful to briefly explore how blood quantum was implemented in the United States and how it regulates Native identity today.

BLOOD QUANTUM IN AMERICAN CONTEXTS

Under U.S. federal law, an Indian is what the law legislatively or judicially determines him to be.[8] At times this has been interpreted in terms of biology, while at other times tribal custom has been recognized.[9] Legislating Native identity has therefore taken place "on the ground," as specific cases arose, particularly around the subjects of tribal jurisdiction, criminal proceedings, or with respect to tribal membership as negotiated in different treaties. Until the 1850s, courts concentrated on defining—and eroding—the status of tribal governments and paid little attention to establishing definitive, centralized definitions of Indianness. Notably, tribes were never unilaterally deprived of their right to determine their own membership; by comparison, bands in Canada only *acquired* a limited form of that right in 1985.

At different intervals in the past, however, by insisting that certain groups were "no longer Indian," whites have been able to steal their land. Jack Forbes, for example, has described a number of instances in which Native Americans were classified as free people of color so that their land might be taken.[10] Furthermore, in some of the treaties signed between 1798 to the 1830s, specific reservations or individual allotments were set aside specifically for "half-breeds."[11]

The General Allotment Act of 1887, characterized by Felix Cohen as "an incident in the transfer of Indian lands to white ownership"(Cohen 1942, 206) and by Theodore Roosevelt as "a mighty pulverizing engine to break up the tribal mass," represented both an all-out attack on the collective nature of American Indian life which attempted to force Native people to adapt to concepts of private property, and a means of appropriating large amounts of the land set aside for reservations under various treaties.[12] The remaining "leftover" land after allotment on each reservation was considered freed up for white settlement. By the end of the allotment period, in 1934, one hundred thousand Indians were landless and detribalized, and Native Americans as a whole had lost 80 percent of the land value they had possessed in 1887. Over ninety million acres of former reservation land had been lost, only forty-eight million acres remained in Indian hands (Cohen 1942, 126), and an official discourse of racial classification had become permanently enshrined in Indian Country.

As tribes accepted allotment, their membership rolls were reviewed by the Bureau of Indian Affairs in order to determine individuals' blood quantum and who would therefore be eligible for allotment. The process was accelerated by legislation in 1919 that provided the Department of the Interior general power to determine tribal membership for the purpose of segregating tribal funds.[13] Full-blood and mixed-blood rolls were authorized, and membership in the tribe was evaluated accordingly. This legislation was repealed in 1938; however, the Department of the Interior has retained the authority to establish tribal rolls that list only those tribal members to whom it is legally required to provide funds. In 1934 the Indian Reorganization Act terminated the allotment policy and extended a relatively high level of power and responsibility to tribal governments. The primary effect of this act on urban Indians was that it established a national blood quantum level of 50 percent for individuals to be considered Indian by the federal government and to be eligible for its services (Deloria and Lytle 1984, 138). At present, the standard set by the federal government for "official" Indianness, particularly for the thousands of American Indians who are now urban after over a century of intensive assimilation policies, is 25 percent. While tribal governments retain the authority to determine their own membership, most accept the federal standard of 25 percent blood quantum

The other key aspect of Native identity discourse in the United States is the notion of federal recognition of tribes, with the corollary that those Indian nations that are not federally recognized are frequently seen as "extinct" within the dominant culture. Federal recognition of a tribe means that the U.S. government acknowledges that the tribal nation exists as a unique political entity with an acknowledged historic government-to-government relationship with the United States.

A significant aspect of federal recognition is the issue of blood quantum, particularly for the small eastern nations who survived settler encroachment and the forced relocation interval in the 1830s. Some tribes, like the Lumbee and the Wampanoag (many of whom have continuously intermarried with black and white settlers but have maintained an identity as Native peoples) are not federally recognized either because they were never at war with the United States or because they did not sign any treaties. Indeed many of the tribal groups in the eastern United States who evaded the army during the times of forced removal have avoided contact with the government since then but have retained their identity. Occasionally such groups are recognized by state governments but not the federal government. As Terry Wilson notes, few researchers have considered miscegenation as a means of maintaining Indian identity. Most scholars, instead, postulate that tribal extinction is an inevitable result of racial intermixing. However, the East Coast Native nations, dispossessed and overwhelmed by the sheer numbers of white and black people settling around them, had only three choices: assimilation, intermarriage, or migration. Many chose to remain in "marginal environments," clinging to an Indigenous identity and to small bits of land, while intermarriage and the acquisition of the majority population's material culture traits often gave them the appearance of non-Indians (Wilson 1992, 113). Contemporary concerns of these communities usually focus on classification as Indian and recognition by the federal government.

The other tribes most concerned with obtaining federal recognition are those who had their relationship with the federal government ended through a policy in the 1950s known as termination, in which the tribal status of a number of Indian tribes was arbitrarily removed, their lands sold, and state control extended over their affairs. In 1978 a Federal Acknowledgment Project was created, to deal with the forty-odd tribal groups petitioning for recognition (and a reserve). In some cases, such as the Tunica-Biloxi of Louisiana, the petition was first mounted in 1826 and was finally granted in 1981. As of March 1992 there were 132 groups seeking federal recognition (Hirschfelder and Kreipe de Montano 1993, 39–40).

As Wilson notes, much of contemporary Native American concern about identity, with its mixed-blood/full-blood connotations, stems from attitudes and ideas fostered by the majority white culture (Wilson 1992, 116), while the process of actually determining blood quantum is fraught with contradictions. "In areas such as Oklahoma, where there is much intertribal and interracial marriage, matters can get complicated. I have a friend who describes himself as a "mixed-blood full blood" because his four grandparents are all full bloods but members of different tribes. Record keeping not infrequently stumbles over quantum issues. In one case eight siblings were listed with five different Indian blood percentages, although all shared the same mother and father" (Wilson 1992, 121). A profound problem for American Indians, after over a century of having their identities determined by racial pedigree, is how blood quantum discourse enters even into attempts to critique its effects. Elizabeth Woody demonstrates this contradiction, as she challenges her mother's community's attempt to limit individuals whose blood quantum falls below specific levels from tribal membership, while at the same time using the discourse of blood quantum to identify herself: "I will remain enrolled at Warm Springs because for five generations my maternal ancestry has been part of the people there. Standards have been set by contemporary tribal governments that may fracture this lineage in the future. If descendants are ineligible for enrollment because of the fragmentation of blood quantum, who will receive the reserved rights of our sovereign status? I am 16/32 Navajo—which means my father was a full-blooded Navajo—12/32 Warm Springs, 3/32 other tribes and 1/32 European descent" (Woody 1998, 154). A final consideration is demographics. Creek/Cherokee Métis academic Ward Churchill has referred to the whole notion of blood quantum as "arithmetical genocide or statistical extermination." He notes that if blood quantum is set at 25 percent, and intermarriage is allowed to proceed as it has for centuries, then eventually Indians will simply be officially defined out of existence: "In 1900, about half of all Indians in this country were 'fullbloods.' By 1990, the proportion had shrunk to about twenty percent and is dropping steadily. Among certain populous peoples, such as the Chippewas of Minnesota and Wisconsin, only about five percent of all tribal members are full-bloods. A third of all recognized Indians are at the quarter-blood cut-off point. Cherokee demographer Russell Thornton estimates that, given continued imposition of purely racial definitions, Native America as a whole will have disappeared by the year 2080" (Churchill 1994, 193). Churchill also notes that when you take into account the members of the two-hundred-odd Indigenous Nations whose existence continues to be denied by the American government, the Native peoples who were terminated from the 1950s to the 1970s, and those individuals who now fall below blood quantum levels, the numbers of individuals with a legitimate claim to being American Indians by descent, by culture, or both, rises from the official number of 1.6 million to upward of 7 million (Churchill 1994, 194). It is obvious, then, that blood quantum discourse critically controls and shapes the directions American Indians take toward empowerment.

Given the specific history of how blood quantum standards developed (as a process enabling the destruction of collective land holdings and phenomenal land theft), the insidiousness of its quantification of racial pedigree, and the "statistical genocide" it forces in the advent of intermarriage, Native people in Canada should think twice about the implications of adopting blood quantum as a membership code. And yet this is precisely what some Native communities have chosen to do, in the wake of Bill C-31.

BLOOD QUANTUM IN CANADIAN CONTEXTS

The Mohawk community of Kahnawake, on the South Shore of Montreal, is perhaps the clearest example of a community situated in

Canada that has adopted a code for the reinstatement of membership based on a full-blown blood quantum requirement, combined with regulations restricting intermarriage. This membership code, which has been in effect for over a decade now, has two stipulations:

> *Moratorium on Mixed Marriages*: Any Mohawk who married a non-Native after 22 May 1981 loses the right to residency, land holding, voting, and office-holding in Kahnawake.

> *Kahnawake Mohawk Law*: As of 11 December 1984, a biological criterion for *future* registrations requires a "blood quantum" of 50 percent or more Native blood. (Alfred 1995, 165)

Kahnawake has been one of the earliest communities in Canada to adopt a blood quantum standard and has been the boldest in its membership restrictions. It has, therefore, frequently been labeled "racist" by white people and by Native people who uphold the system organized by the Indian Act. And yet, in examining the position taken by the federal government with respect to First Nations membership in different contexts, it is obvious that Canada routinely enforces blood quantum restrictions on communities involved in land claims settlements, while penalizing other communities as racist if they enforce blood quantum restrictions as part of their own self-determination mandate.

Peter and Trudy Jacobs, for example, were residents of Kahnawake who had been denied certain services as nonmembers. Peter Jacobs, a black man adopted as a child by Mohawk parents, grew up in the community but is not considered to be Mohawk, according to current membership criteria. His wife Trudy, a Kahnawake Mohawk, lost her membership when she married him. The couple brought a case against Kahnawake to the Canadian Human Rights Commission, the tribunal ruled in favor of the couple, and ordered the Mohawk Council of Kahnawake to stop racially discriminating against the couple and to provide them with the rights available to other members of the community ("Tribunal" 1998, 2). At the same time as the Canadian Human Rights Commission has been monitoring racial discrimination in Native communities, however, Canada has been forcing a 25 percent blood quantum requirement on Inuit people in Labrador in order for them to be eligible for a land claim (McKinley 1998c, 9). Moreover, Canada and the government of British Columbia, during self-government talks with the Sechelt Indian band, have also demanded that the band limit its membership to people of Sechelt ancestry, excluding their non-Native spouses, even though the Sechelt people have *specifically* refused to make this distinction between categories of membership. For Canada to elevate a branch of its government as a watchdog for human rights violations in Native communities is extremely ironic, given its history as a colonizing power, which has for over a century maintained a body of racist and sexist legislation controlling every aspect of Native life in Canada.

For all that, however, the blood quantum system remains a flawed and contradictory attempt to control boundaries between the dominant society and the community. Controversial issues continue to arise in the community with respect to the membership code. In 1995, for example, the Kahnawake Band Council barred students not on the Mohawk registry from Kahnawake's schools, an edict the school board refused to enforce. The Mohawk students who are ineligible for membership, by virtue of having less than 50 percent blood quantum, had initially been allowed into the community schools following the Oka crisis,[14] because of the community's concern for the safety of these children in off-reserve schools ("School Board" 1995, 1). The firing of Kahnawake peacekeeper Kyle Cross Briseboise after he was ruled to have only 47 percent Native blood is another problem that the community has had to deal with ("Kahnawake Excludes Students" 1995, 1), as is the barring of Carl "Bo" Curotte from running for chief of Kahnawake on the basis of having only 46 percent Native blood ("How Indian Is Indian?" 1996, 12). Enforcing blood quantum rules has continuously forced the band council to make decisions that fragment and objectify Native identity and that demands that band members externalize some members of the community in order to "protect community." Meanwhile, the community continues to actualize the notion that "Indianness" is purely a matter of blood, even as they attempt to validate the reality that culture also determines Indianness.

Taiaiake Alfred, in writing about his community's decision to adopt these restrictions, has asserted that the standard that the community would have chosen to adopt would have been cultural, rather than a matter of Indian blood, had not years of colonization created significant confusion as to what constituted tradition in his community (Alfred 1995, 174). While these are valid concerns, Alfred, in this work, chose to foreclose any further discussion of this issue by simply stating that anybody who questions the automatic right of the band to maintain its own membership is de facto challenging Indigenous nationhood. While it is undeniable that Native communities should have the right to control their own membership, if they choose to do so without reference to a history of colonization and the government's role in selectively externalizing some members but not others, it is inevitable that the children of those former band members who the government arbitrarily chose to exclude will continue to see the process as unjust.

Perhaps more important, in the changeover between defining Indianness by status and defining Indianness by blood quantum, the sexism of the old system is being replicated in the new system. Overwhelmingly, the individuals who are seeking to be reinstated as Mohawks of Kahnawake are Native women who lost their status and their children. These individuals must submit to blood quantum measurement, while individuals who never lost their status do not have to and can remain silent about the generations of intermarriage between Native men and white women that took place on reserve, which has diluted the blood quantum of those whose membership is not in question. Any purely racial means of determining Indianness in Canada will continue to affect women (and their children) differently from men (and their children) because of the unacknowledged history of sexism in the Indian Act. The imposition of blood quantum standards therefore cannot be treated as a gender-neutral process.

Enumerating the flaws in membership codes, however, does not answer the huge question: How are tiny communities constantly facing a society determined to destroy them, and retaining the only land still recognized as Indian territory, to maintain standards between insiders and outsiders? While this question is one that all reserve communities must wrestle with (and must struggle among themselves to find the answer that fits their community best), the answer becomes much starker and more negative if reserve communities are posited as being the only remaining sites where "real" Native people still exist. Taiaiake Alfred is one individual who has taken this position quite openly. Not only does he regard the reserves as the only places left in which Indigenous cultures can be maintained, he suggests that those who are not eligible for band membership in a First Nation should consider themselves to be no longer members of their Indigenous nation of origin.[15] Alfred and other theorists who adopt the notion that the only sites where Nativeness still exists are the reserves, such as Elizabeth Cook-Lynn (1998), essentially consider the Indigeneity of all nonstatus urban mixed-bloods to be terminated.

By declaring the Nativeness of urban mixed-bloods to be terminated, these theorists simply add to the messages that urban Native people already receive from the dominant culture, that Nativeness and modernity are inherently contradictory. The question then arises: What happens to Indigeneity in the face of mixed-bloodedness (and urbanity)? Does it cease to exist or does it merely change? And are those changes so definitive that no meeting place can be found?

4

Métis Identity, the Indian Act, and the Numbered Treaties

While loss of Indian status, for whom and under what terms, has been the focus of the previous chapters, there is another, entirely different relationship between status Indians and nonstatus Native people in Canada, both historically and in contemporary times. There are whole communities of Native people, across Canada, who are not the products of loss of status but, rather, have never received Indian status at all.

The 1876 Indian Act contained a new way of limiting the numbers of communities acknowledged as Indian in eastern Canada. This legislation narrowed federal recognition of Indianness to those Native people who already lived on recognized reserves or belonged to recognized Indian bands (Gilbert 1996, 15). All other Native people in eastern Canada were considered nonexistent; the government did not recognize any obligation to them. It was this narrowing of the scope of Indianness that has enabled the government to refuse to recognize a number of Native communities in eastern Canada who have not been signatory to any of the treaties covering their land base and who therefore remain unrecognized and nonstatus.

In western Canada, however, communities of nonstatus Native people have been created by another process—by arbitrarily externalizing from Indianness an entire category of Indigenous people, designated as "half-breeds" and now called "Métis." This category of Nativeness will be the primary focus of this chapter.

DEFINING MÉTISNESS

The origins of those who are now known as Métis are extremely diverse. The fur trade, as it expanded into the Great Lakes region and then into western Canada, relied heavily on Native women, whose marriages to white men were negotiated as part of trade agreements and who used their skills to supply fur-trade posts with the food, clothing, moccasins, and snowshoes they needed to survive. They also traded other goods with them, paddled their canoes, and acted as guides and translators in their journeys. Mixed-blood settlements were therefore inevitable by-products of the expansion of the fur trade, as the children of these Native women gradually filled a wide range of occupations under the fur trade, which ranged from direct employment as voyageurs paddling huge canoes loaded with skins thousands of miles, to more autonomous positions as traders providing the fur trade network with food and supplies.

Their communities were extremely diverse, from the urbanized neighborhoods of those mixed-bloods whose marriages had ultimately brought them to cities such as Montreal, to the distinct semi-migratory trading communities in the Great Lakes regions, to the farming communities of the Red River district, to the migratory bands who hunted buffalo commercially to supply the pemmican trade.[1] Peterson and Brown, in their study of the diverse origins of Métis people, conclude: "The history of the métis peoples runs deeper and more broadly across the North American landscape than has previously been acknowledged. . . . The processes and conditions which caused the métis to coalesce at Red River as a self-conscious ethnic group were rooted in both an historic past and a wider geographical frame, just as the processes of ethnic formation or 'métisation' continued after 1885, often independent of the Red River métis" (Peterson and Brown 1985, 4–5).

The unique circumstances that caused specific groups of mixed-bloods in the Red River settlement to declare themselves a Métis nation in the face of the encroachment of Canada and to attempt, both in 1870 and in 1885, to create a place for themselves within Canada as Métis people, the violent military suppression of the rebellion that ensued, and the subsequent dispersal and marginalization of mixed-bloods in western Canada, are all a part of the history of Métis people. However, another aspect of Métis history relates to the legal process of how individuals designated as "half-breeds" were cut out, or chose to opt out, of treaty relationships with the promise of receiving "half-breed" scrip, representing a cash payment or a piece of land, but without any recognition on the part of Canada of their collective Indigeneity.

From this diverse history, and from the legal regulation of Native identity, a multitude of contemporary uses of the terms *Métis* and *mixed-blood* have developed. The cultural/historical use of the term Métis has been its most common form of usage, referring broadly to the descendants of those mixed-bloods who identified as Métis in the Red River settlement during the mid-nineteenth century, with the recognition that this included all western Métis people. The use of this term to denote a common cultural heritage to some extent masks the tremendous diversity of experiences subsumed under the Métis label in western Canada. Like the category "Indian," which homogenizes the identities of dozens of distinct Indigenous nations in Canada, the category of "Métis" currently encapsulates not only the different historical experiences of being mixed-blood that existed under the fur trade but also the tremendous differences that exist among *contemporary* Métis. These different groups range from northern nonstatus Cree-speaking people who still, to some extent, live off the land, to those who still live in historic Métis communities, including those in eastern Canada, to those whose ancestors are Métis but speak only English and have been urban for decades.

Individuals who claim a historic Métis heritage in western Canada make a strong distinction between being *Métis* and being *mixed-blood*. The term *mixed-blood* (or frequently the term *mixed-race*, in Canada) generally refers to individuals who are the products of recent intermarriages between status Indians and non-Natives, with no connection to historic mixed-blood communities, although such hard-and-fast categories often fall short of the real experiences of nonstatus individuals whose heritage includes both status Indian *and* Métis ancestors. In recent years, western Métis organizations have continuously attempted to restrict Métisness to western Canada, as the heartland of historic Métis experience. Despite this, the descendants of the historic mixed-blood communities that existed under the fur trade in eastern Canada have made claims for redress as Métis as well. Finally, to render the situation even more complex, since the inclusion of the Métis category in the Constitution Act of 1982, mixed-blood individuals in eastern Canada who cannot get their Indian status back are increasingly being encouraged to join local Métis organizations, whatever their ancestral Indigenous heritage.

In September 2002, the Métis National Council (MNC), which Canada recognizes as the primary organization for Métis people in Canada, through its provision of core programs for Métis people, adopted a new definition of Métiseness, which restricted membership in the Métis Nation solely to individuals who could claim descent from the historic Red River community. This not only excluded former member groups such as the Métis Nation of British Columbia and the Métis Nation of Ontario, it excluded a sizeable number of nonstatus individuals in western Canada whose diverse histories are not from the Red River but who identify strongly (and receive services) as Métis.

It is striking that, in doing this, the Métis National Council has made strong statements distancing themselves from their former constituency, calling them "wannabees" (in much the same way that status Indian organizations currently dismiss Métis people). It has not yet been clarified how many people are excluded from the government funding that the Métis National Council controls, based on their new tightened membership restrictions. However, the Métis Nation of British Columbia has launched a lawsuit against Human Resources Development Canada for funding the Métis National Council's employment and training programs, which are no longer delivered to the excluded BC Métis. Newer, more inclusive, Métis organizations are now forming to represent the various individuals now excluded from the MNC. These organizations have invited the descendants of Bill C-31 individuals, who cannot get their status back, to join them, stating that they are "really" Métis (Barnsley 2003b, 15).

For all of these reasons, regardless of the exclusive ownership of the term claimed by western Métis organizations, and the manner in which the Métis National Council has recently narrowed the definition of Métis to a far more extreme extent even within western Canada, definitions of Métisness now affect all nonstatus mixed-blood Native people, whether they are from western Canada, from historic Métis communities, from eastern nonstatus communities, or are simply urban mixed-bloods.

The crucial complexity for Métis and mixed-blood people is that it is impossible to accurately disconnect the cultural and historical mixed-blood meanings of Métisness with the legal issue of being nonstatus. As I noted in the introduction to this book, in contemporary times, many mixed-bloods are status Indians, but because they have Indian status they conceptualize themselves solely as "Indians," no matter how mixed-blooded they are. The mixed-blood category is reserved solely for nonstatus Indians, in Canada. Meanwhile, in western Canada, any nonstatus Native individual, no matter what their Indigenous heritage, is commonly referred to by others and refers to himself or herself in everyday terms as Métis. At the same time, Métis people from northern, Cree-speaking communities who are phenotypically Native-looking often consider themselves to be simply "Indians without status cards." What this means is that how Indianness is regulated in Canada has a central effect on how Métisness is understood, regardless of the various definitions adopted by Métis organizations in western Canada.

At present, it is the practice when looking at history to name any historical group of mixed-bloods as Métis, with the implication that they always self-identified as such. I believe we have to be more careful in this respect. Some mixed-blood communities have had long histories of separation and cultural distinctiveness from their ancestral Indigenous nations. In other instances, however, the differences between tribally based so-called full-bloods and mixed-bloods are not as cut-and-dried, and the distinctions between them have been created quite arbitrarily by government regulation of Native identity, which categorizes one group as Indian and the other as half-breed. In any case, given the fluid and highly adaptable nature of mixed-blood identities historically, it would seem that once the fur trade, which provided many mixed-bloods with specific niches for distinct livelihoods, had given way to white encroachment, then large numbers of those individuals who still maintained close contact with their relations would have merged back into more distinctly Cree or Saulteaux or Dakota forms of existence (which in any case were themselves being changed by colonization). However, for the most part, this was not allowed to happen—instead, the Indian Act expressly disallowed it, by creating "Indian" and "half-breed" as two entirely distinct categories of Indigeneity, and by not allowing those classified as "half-breed" to enter into treaties or to live on the newly created reserves.[2]

In stating this, it is important to be clear that a sizeable group of Red River mixed-bloods might have chosen to retain distinctly Métis identities, no matter how Canada chose to classify them. And it is their right to do so. Métis people, then as now, should be free to embrace their hybrid distinctiveness as "New Peoples" if they choose to. However, in this work, I contend that the very existence of the label *Métis* today for such a wide range of nonstatus people in western Canada owes more to the creation of the legal category of "half-breed" during the signing of the numbered treaties than from a desire by all of the ancestors of the people who are today called Métis to remain permanently defined by a specific historic interval of mixed-blood experience under the fur trade.

Without denying the nationhood claims by individuals who today have no choice but to struggle for empowerment as Métis, I believe that Métisness as a category of existence today should be seen as a product of having a history of intermarriage with non-Natives and of embracing culturally hybrid forms of existence that were frozen by government legislation into the defining feature of a Nativeness that the government did not consider to be Indian. In this chapter, therefore, I hope to examine the assumption that there has *always* and *everywhere* been an inherent and immutable difference between all Métis and all Indian identities—or indeed, that there are singular identities *as* Métis or Indian—through exploring the role of the Indian Act in shaping these identities.

EXTERNALIZING THE "HALF-BREED"

It is to be noted, however, that it is practically impossible in instructing the Commissioners to draw a hard and fast line between the Half-breeds and the Indians, and some of them are so closely allied in manners and customs to the latter that they will desire to be treated as Indians . . . and hence, [the undersigned] is of the opinion that it should be left to the judgment of the Commissioners to determine what Half-breeds, if any, should be dealt with as Indians. (Sifton, in Bartko 2000, 268)

When Canada began its expansion into the western regions of the continent, definitions of Indianness in eastern Canada had been set at one-quarter blood quantum. However, officials in the Indian Department, in negotiating treaties with the new Indigenous nations they encountered, began the practice of exerting much more stringent controls over who would be accepted as Indian. When the Indian Act was created in 1876, these practices were made explicit. The act contained a provision that for the first time excluded anybody who was not considered to be "pure Indian" from Indianness. It stated that, "No half-breed head of a family (except the widow of an Indian, or a half-breed who has already been admitted into a treaty) shall . . . be accounted an Indian, or entitled to be admitted into any Indian treaty" (1876 Indian Act, in Waldram 1986, 281).

But who was "Indian" and who was "half-breed"? Coates and Morrison (1986) have suggested that these distinctions, to a tremendous extent, have been *created* by colonial categories. The fifty-year interval in which Treaties 1 to 11 were signed across western Canada and the north, and the changes to the Indian Act that accompanied it, have been crucial in dividing the Indigenous peoples the Europeans encountered into categories foreign to their own self-image—one group becoming "Indian," the other becoming "half-breed." At times Native people resisted these divisions and, depending on who negotiated the treaty, some flexibility was shown as to who would enter into which category. In some instances, different members of the same family chose different categories, so that half the family "became" half-breed while the other half "became" Indian. In any case, however, those designated as half-breed were categorically denied the right to sign treaties and therefore to live on what was designated as Indian land, while those designated as Indian were denied the right to claim individual scrip for cash or freehold land.

Treaties 1 and 2, encompassing southern and central Manitoba, which were signed in 1871 with the Saulteaux, Cree, and other nations of the region, explicitly excluded half-breeds. However, Lieutenant Governor Simpson, who negotiated these treaties, allowed individuals to make the choice to identify as Indian or half-breed; most chose to be classified as Indian (Jamieson 1978, 41). Treaty 3, signed in 1873 with the Ojibway of the Lake of the Woods district of northwestern Ontario, was negotiated at significantly better terms than the first two treaties. When Lieutenant Governor Morris, who negotiated this treaty, attempted to segregate mixed-bloods from full bloods, the Ojibway leader Mawedopenais insisted that both categories of his people should be included in the treaty. As a result, the descendants of those designated as half-breeds by the Europeans now have treaty land in the Rainy River district as status Indians.

Based on the success of the signatories of Treaty 3, some of the Cree bands involved in the signing of Treaties 4 and 6 attempted to have mixed-bloods included in these treaties. The response of Lieutenant Governor Morris, in emphasizing the difference between half-breeds and Indians (and the notion of an essential sameness among all Indians), during the signing of both treaties, is instructive: "We have here Crees, Saulteaux, Assiniboines and other Indians, they are all one, and we have another people, the half-breeds, that are of your blood and my blood. . . . We did not come as messengers to the Half-breeds, but to the Indians. I have heard some Half-breeds want to take lands at Red River and join the Indians there, but they cannot take with both hands. The Half-breeds of the North West cannot come into the Treaty" (Morris 1880, 198, 222). In any case, in 1880, the Canadian government modified the Indian Act to specifically exclude "half-breeds" from coming under the provisions of the act, and from any of the treaties (Dickason 1992, 279).

According to James Waldram, the process of differentiating between Indians and half-breeds did not necessarily conform either to actual racial blood quantum or to individual self-identification. In a context where racial mixing was frequently difficult to determine, factors such as lifestyle, language, and residence were employed (Waldram 1986, 281). Individuals who were considered to be "living like Indians" were taken into treaty, while those who had worked hauling supplies for the Hudson Bay Company and as a result knew some English, were registered as half-breeds, in each case regardless of ancestry.

This standard used to distinguish Indians from half-breeds in western Canada has in fact been virtually meaningless since its inception, given the fact that at the end of the nineteenth century most individuals categorized as Indian in eastern Canada had already been forced into some sort of transition to farming life or seasonal wage labor. In the context of over two centuries of colonial contact, so-called authentic Indianness was a rare commodity. And yet it was a commodity that Europeans craved and which colonial governments clearly demanded in order to acknowledge Indianness. As this account of treaty negotiations in the Northwest Territories suggests, any adulteration of popular stereotypes of Indianness was interpreted as evidence of mixed-blood: "I have not seen an Indian as he is popularly known or depicted since I left Calgary. These so-called Indians of the north are all half-breeds . . . If they choose 'treaty' then they are written down Indians, if they select 'scrip' then they are called half-breeds" (Leonard and Whalen 1999, 53). In any case, whether individuals were categorized as Indian or half-breed, these European labels were irrevocable. If classified as Indian, one's name was included on the band list as someone who came under the treaty; if classified as half-breed, one was (after 1885 and in theory) given scrip for fee simple title of up to 160 acres of land, or money scrip to the value of up to $160.

Many Native families who were not present when registration was first carried out never made treaty lists and thereafter were considered half-breeds. Indeed, whole bands that were absent during treaty signing similarly lost any chance of acquiring Indian status and became, de facto, half-breed communities (Holmes 1987, 4).

The later numbered treaties perhaps demonstrate the most glaring contradictions between the government's rigid classifications of "half-breed" and "Indian" and how people actually saw themselves. According to Coates and Morrison (1986), mixed-bloods who lived along the northern Mackenzie River and in the Yukon had never differentiated themselves from their Native communities of origin prior to the signing of treaties.[3] However, the flurry of prospecting in the Mackenzie valley during the Klondike gold rush convinced the government to negotiate Treaty 8 in 1899 with the Native peoples of the southern Mackenzie Basin. At that point, anybody deemed to be half-breed was separated out and offered scrip rather than treaty.

Patricia Bartko's exploration of the signing of Treaty 8 supports Coates and Morrison's notion that the assignation of Indianness or mixed-bloodedness during this treaty was quite arbitrary and suggests that white stereotypes about the primitiveness of Indians are at the root of the problem. Treaty commissioners, for example, expressed considerable disappointment at their first sight of Lesser Slave Lake Indigenous people:

The crowd of Indians ranged before the marquee had lost all semblance of wildness of the true type. . . . It was plain that these people had achieved, without any treaty at all, a stage of civilization distinctly in advance of many of our treaty Indians to the south after twenty-five years of education. Instead of paint and feathers, the scalp-lock, the breech-clout, and the buffalo robe, there presented itself a body of respectable-looking men, as well-dressed and evidently quite as independent in their feelings as any like number of average pioneers in the East . . . One was prepared, in this wild region of forest, to behold some savage types of men; indeed, I craved to renew the vanished scenes of old. But, alas! One beheld, instead, men with well-washed, unpainted faces. . . . It was not what was expected. (Mair, in Bartko 2000: 264)

Bartko notes that these stereotypes informed who was classified as half-breed or Indian during the signing of the treaty—those individuals who had successful, even leadership, characteristics and charisma were considered to be half-breeds, while those who seemed to require charitable assistance, such as the families of widows, were considered to be Indian (Bartko 2000, 265–66).

It is important to acknowledge that some communities in the Treaty 8 area were more mixed-blood than others—however, Reddekopp and Bartko suggest that, on the whole, it is probably accurate to state that most of the people in the region were of relatively common ancestry. They also note that even after the signing of Treaty 8 (which heightened the differences between Indian and half-breed communities) the distinctions between the two groups were certainly not static. Because of the provision in the Indian Act wherein women gained or lost Indian status through marriage, and because most of the Aboriginal population in the area, Indian or Métis, married within both communities, there has been considerable two-way traffic in and out of Indianness and Métisness over the years, on both sides (Reddekopp and Bartko 2000, 228).

The discovery of oil at Norman Wells made the government begin negotiating Treaty 11 with Native communities in 1921. A similar effect happened as with Treaty 8, in that communities who had essentially not differentiated among their membership were suddenly forced into two distinct categories. The numbered treaties have thus been crucial to the project of forcibly identifying and segregating half-breeds from Indians, regardless of how individuals saw themselves.

And yet it is also true that in some areas of western Canada, differences between mixed-bloods, who self-designated as Métis, and local Indian bands have been quite tangible—and have also been the source of considerable animosity between groups. For members of the Blackfoot Confederacy, the manner in which Métis buffalo-hunters invaded their territories to hunt commercially for the pemmican trade was a constant source of hardship, particularly as the buffalo declined. For example, during the signing of Treaty 7, it was clear that the Métis as a group were entirely extraneous to the process—at Blackfoot Crossing, the Métis were camped with the white traders, both groups being there primarily to sell goods to signatories who would therefore have cash to spend (Treaty 7 Elders et al. 1997, xx). Indeed, Métis incursions into Blackfoot territory were a central reason why a number of their leaders were interested in meeting with treaty commissioners in the first place.

And yet, even in Blackfoot territory, there were other mixed-bloods than those who identified as Métis—the children of Blackfoot women and the white men who increasingly invaded their territories. It was probably impossible for their nations to externalize these individuals, even though their presence may have been highly problematic for communities who already faced multiple colonial incursions—including white whiskey traders, an occupying military force (the Northwest Mounted Police), and the presence of other Native people encroaching into their hunting territories—always with the threat of eminent starvation to contend with.

The life of Jerry Potts, a mixed-race man born of a Blood mother and a white trader father, is an example of the difficult and problematic nature of mixed-race identity *within* Blood society at this time. Potts lived in his father's world as a child, during the chaotic and lawless days of the whiskey trade in Blackfoot country. At his father's death, he was put into the custody of a violent and abusive trader who eventually abandoned him; he finally was raised by a trader who taught him to read and write. As a youth he joined his mother's tribe and afterward constantly moved between his mother's world and his father's. As an adult Potts hunted to supply whiskey traders, fought with the Bloods against the Cree, and avenged his mother's death by shooting her killer. A heavy drinker who reportedly spoke a number of Native languages but whose English was poor, Potts was asked to translate during the signing of Treaty 7, until his alcoholism made it impossible for him to function adequately. In his later years, ill with tuberculosis and severely alcoholic, he nevertheless worked for the police until he died (Treaty 7 Elders et al. 1997, 60).

Another area of conflict between Indians and those mixed-bloods who self-designated as Métis was their differential roles in the 1885 Rebellion. It is undeniable that this rebellion, organized by the Métis without significant Cree participation, was the occasion used by the

Canadian government to crush the powerful resistance that the Cree presence had signified during the treaty-signing process on the Plains (Stonechild and Waiser 1997) and that this probably represented a significant rift between treaty Indians and the Métis.

Aside from these very real, historically documented differences between specific Indigenous nations and those who self-identified as Métis, however, it seems undeniable that there is another story about mixed-bloodedness in western Canada that also needs to be told— which is that in some Native contexts (such as in the areas covered by Treaties 8 and 11), mixed-bloodedness and full-bloodedness were virtually indistinguishable (and entirely irrelevant) among a local Indigenous population, while in other Native contexts (such as some regions covered by Treaties 4 and 6), "Creeness" and "Métisness" were mutable categories. Meanwhile, in still other areas, such as within Treaty 7, mixed-blood tribal members of the Blackfoot Confederacy moved uneasily in the margins between the white world and the Indian world, while bands of those buffalo hunters who self-designated as Métis were regarded as enemies by the Blackfoot. To gather all these historically different experiences into one homogeneous Métis identity obscures more than it clarifies. Perhaps more to the point, however, it is the European determination to separate the half-breed from the Indian that has allowed Canada to deny its fiduciary obligation to any community that lacks Indian status and that has forced these individuals to rally themselves, in contemporary times, as Métis in order to survive as Indigenous people at all.

Even while the numbered treaties were being negotiated, Canada showed an implacable determination to continuously winnow out from Indianness all those who could be designated as half-breed. In 1879, the Indian Act was amended to enable individuals who were "really" half-breeds to withdraw from treaty (Hatt 1986, 197), while in 1885 and 1886, scrip first became available (Reddekopp and Bartko 2000, 214). To demonstrate the meaninglessness of such categories to Native people, as well as the widespread destitution on most reserves (in a context where half-breed money scrip could immediately be cashed), in just two years over a thousand persons, regardless of ancestry, discharged from treaty to apply for half-breed scrip and three Treaty 6 First Nations in Alberta ceased to exist as a result.[4] At this point, new regulations were created ensuring that individuals who "led the mode of life of Indians" were not to be granted discharge from treaty (Hatt 1986, 197).

When the northern boundary of the province of Ontario was set at the Albany River in 1899, it bisected the territory covered by Treaty 3, so that part of Treaty 3 territory fell within what became Ontario, and the remainder fell within the Keewatin district of the Northwest Territories. At this time, Indian Affairs decided that only Treaty 3 half-breeds living outside the new boundaries of Ontario were to be allowed to take scrip. Because of this, when the time came for negotiating Treaty 9 in 1905, the treaty commissioner, J. A. McKenna, advised against including the Keewatin district into this treaty, to prevent Ontario Cree and Ojibway people from claiming to be Keewatin half-breeds in order to receive scrip rather than coming under the treaty (Long 1978, 1).

Those labeled as half-breed, in Ontario, were not offered scrip. Most of the mixed-blood families who for generations had kept the fur-trading posts on James Bay supplied with food were brought into treaty, with the exception of Moose Factory half-breeds. These individuals, who were arbitrarily excluded from the treaty but offered no scrip, have petitioned for years for recognition and compensation. In recent years their organization has also included nonstatus Indians whose families lost status over the years because of gender discrimination in the Indian Act (Long 1985).

In rare cases, individuals who were known to be half or three-quarters Indian and were said to be following "an Indian way of life," who were destitute and prevented by hunting restrictions from living off the land, were allowed to be taken into treaty. This was the case particularly during the 1930s in areas of Treaty 8 and Treaty 11, when over 160 individuals, formerly counted as half-breeds, became treaty Indians (Coates and Morrison 1986, 259).

In the Yukon, meanwhile, where no treaties were signed, fewer distinctions existed between those who were mixed-race and those who were not. The churches, however, attempted to separate mixed-blood Native people from Native communities and categorize them as whites, regardless of how the white society ostracized and rejected them. For example, until World War II, mixed-blood children were generally unwelcome in white schools; however, they were barred from Indian day schools, thus preventing them from receiving any education at all. After the 1940s, however, these policies shifted and most mixed-blood youths were sent to Indian schools. The white father's identity defined the child—if he acknowledged the child, he or she was declared to be white, while if he did not, the child was considered Indian and raised as such (Coates and Morrison 1986, 265–67). The introduction of the welfare state after World War II forced a more standardized classification of race on families in the north. Family allowances in the Yukon and Northwest Territories initially were paid to Inuit and "all people living the Native way" in kind, while whites and "mixed bloods not living like Indians" were paid in cash (Coates and Morrison 1986, 269).

At the time that most of the treaties were negotiated, those who either were arbitrarily excluded from the treaties as half-breeds (especially in the years before scrip was offered) or who chose scrip instead of treaty, could not have conceived of the landlessness and desperation that would be the lot of most half-breeds (now called Métis) in the years after 1885. Those who fled white encroachment to live in the north struggled to survive, without a land base and with the basic source of their livelihoods—hunting and fishing—unprotected by treaty rights. Over the years, as status Indians organized to demand the rights to health care and education promised in the treaties, the contrasts grew even greater, as Métis people were denied these services, even though in many cases they lived in communities as remote as reserve communities, miles from hospitals or schools. Finally, the reality of landlessness meant that many Métis were reduced to a semi-squatting existence on marginal lands, always on the move, with the only alternative being the violence, poverty, and racism of the segregated spaces reserved for Native people in the cities of western Canada.

Generations of Métis people have worked as activists, not only to ensure the survival of Métis communities, but to speak up for the rights of all Aboriginal people. In 1982, when Canada repatriated its constitution from Britain, the Métis were finally officially recognized as Aboriginal people, in Section 35 of the Constitution Act (RCAP 1996, 1:207). With this recognition, however, Canada has taken no responsibility either to secure a land base or assume any fiduciary obligation for those who identify as Métis (or for any nonstatus Native people). Perhaps more important, this recognition has indelibly separated "Métis" from "Indian" as coherent and distinctly separate entities in the minds of the public (and many Indigenous people), as if there had always been, forever, hard and fast physical and cultural distinctions between all Indians and all Métis.

RETHINKING INDIAN AND MÉTIS IDENTITIES

If the preceding history clarifies anything, it is that both Indian and Métis identities have been shaped to a phenomenal extent by the racism inherent in the Indian Act. In this sense, to view these groups as the products of entirely different histories and the bearers of entirely different destinies belies the common origins of all Native people in the West, as members of different Indigenous nations who faced colonization pressures in different ways or who were classified in different ways by colonial legislation. Focusing solely on contemporary differences between treaty Indians and the Métis, without any exploration of what both groups have in common (as well as the diversity *within* each group masked by such colonial terms as *Indian* and *Métis*), at this point seems to conform too closely to the logic of the Indian Act.

It would seem more useful to understand contemporary Métis identity less as an issue of *inherent* cultural difference due to racial mixing and being the product of a "Red River" heritage than as a result of being nonstatus and historically excluded from legal rights and access to land because of the relentless rigidity with which racial categories were both created and maintained under the Indian Act. This statement should not be interpreted as challenging the nationhood claims of those whose realities are accurately and genuinely represented as Red River Métis. It is to suggest, however, that the categories "treaty Indians" and "Métis"—like status and nonstatus Indians in general—do not accurately represent either the citizens of Indigenous nations misnamed as Indian, nor the detribalized and nonstatus Native people misnamed as Métis. Certainly the original fur-trade distinction of Métisness, as signifying mixed-bloodedness and biculturality, is not an accurate distinction given the levels of mixed-bloodedness (and the necessary bicultural adaptation) currently prevalent among so many status Indian communities.

The fact remains, however, that while many of the divisions between these groups were created and imposed by the Indian Act in a relatively artificial manner, they have in many regions become very real differences in experiences of Nativeness. Even in subarctic communities, where cultural differences between Métis and Indian populations have been relatively minor, the superimposition of a legal definition of Indian status has effectively divided populations. When individuals on either side of the legal boundary are treated differently in most of the daily aspects of life, being treaty Indian or Métis begins to signify increasingly different identities (Waldram 1986, 286–87). Métis and treaty Indian communities, which often exist side by side in northern regions, are required to access different sources of funding and to organize from different constituent bases in order to improve the quality of life in their communities.

These organizational differences, then, take on a life of their own and force communities that once saw themselves as one unit (or at least as closely related) into different paths of development (Waldram 1986, 290–93). Far worse divisions have developed in regions where Métis and Indian communities have been defined as separate and different for well over a century, or in areas where hostilities historically existed between groups as a result of the Métis role in the fur trade, or in the 1885 Rebellion. These divisions can truly be said to have been naturalized, to the extent that contemporary struggles to renegotiate Native identity still rigidly maintain these distinctions.

The approach taken by the descendants of Chief Papasschase in their efforts to reconstitute their band are an example of this. The descendents of those individuals formerly in the Papasschase Band are appealing only to status Indian descendants to come forward to make their claim for band status, ignoring those descendants who are now considered Métis. It is unclear, from the outside, whether Métis descendants are being ignored because they are seen as "not Indian" or because their presence could complicate the process of acquiring a reserve and treaty rights according to Indian Act regulations, if the new band has members who are not status Indians (Paul 1997, 4). What is not being addressed, in this attempt at grassroots organizing to counteract Canadian colonial history, is the way in which the Métis descendants would have now been status Indians if their ancestors had not intermarried with those Native people who opted out of treaty status in 1888.

It is important to emphasize that real, tangible benefits—including an increased chance of a community's cultural survival—accrue to those communities who are able to prove their eligibility to be classified as a reserve under the Indian Act. The access to funding and programs that reserve status brings enables rural or northern communities to *physically* survive in a colonized world that has destroyed their traditional livelihoods. It is for this reason that other rural Native communities—such as those of the Mi'kmaq and Innu people of Newfoundland who currently do not come under the Indian Act—are struggling for recognition as reserves, even at the cost of accepting colonial definitions of their identities.[5] In this light, the fact that Métis people are overwhelmingly urban as compared to status Indians—in 1991 65 percent of Métis people lived in urban centers, as compared to slightly less than half of status Indians (Normand 1996, 11)—speaks volumes about how the Métis have had no access to programs and services that would preserve their rural communities. Only 1 percent of Métis people live on lands designated for Aboriginal peoples, as compared to the 36 percent of status Indians, who live on land designated as reserves or settlements (Normand 1996, 11–13).[6] It is clear that, in the interests of sheer survival, colonial frameworks continue, in gross or subtle ways, to shape how Native people struggle to resist colonialism.

For Métis people, the route that they have been forced to take toward empowerment, because of their legal exclusion from Indianness, has involved proving the Aboriginality of Métis people through the recognition of the Indigenous nature of historic Métis societies and demanding recognition of the existence of the Métis Nation. Because of the need to reference specific intervals when the Métis were recognized in historical documents, Métis empowerment has deliberately been linked to specific nation-building moments. In 1816, for example, after a winter of near starvation, a group of Métis voyageurs and buffalo hunters seized a shipment of pemmican from the Hudson Bay Company and captured and ransacked one of the HBC trading posts. They were challenged at Seven Oaks by the Red River governor; however, they fought back and killed twenty-one settlers in the process. This form of resistance to the territorial governor and the HBC, known as the Battle of Seven Oaks, was instrumental for local Métis people in developing a sense of agency and identity as "a people" (Dickason 1992, 263). Later, in 1870, in response to Canadian encroachment in what is now Manitoba, Louis Riel proclaimed the desire of the Métis to govern themselves. Both such historical moments served as inspiration for a contemporary Métis nation.

The nation-building process, however, encourages Métis people to continuously assert, often in negation of local realities, that they simply have a *different* kind of Aboriginality than Indians. This involves treating the Indian roots of all Métis people as "ancient ancestry" (ignoring the fact that many contemporary Métis may speak Cree and have Cree status Indians in their recent family) and maintaining a narrow focus on a relatively brief interval of history, which has been described as follows: "What developed [at Red River] between 1820 and 1870 represented a florescence of distinct culture. . . . The new nation was not simply a population that happened to be of mixed European/Aboriginal ancestry; the Métis Nation was a population with its own language, Michif (though many dialects), a distinctive mode of dress, cuisine, vehicles of transport, modes of celebration in music and dance, and a completely democratic though quasi-military political organization, complete with national flag, bardic tradition, and vibrant folklore of national history" (RCAP 1996, 1:151).

In a similar manner, the attitude taken in the Royal Commission Report about Michif reflects the current trend toward presenting the Métis as entirely different from treaty Indians, particularly with respect to language use. The report continuously asserts that an example of the distinctiveness of Métis culture is the fact that Métis people speak Michif (RCAP 1996, 1:151), even though the majority of Métis who are fluent in a Native language speak Cree (70 percent), while another 16 percent of individuals speak Ojibway, and 11 percent speak other Aboriginal languages. Only 6 percent of Métis who speak a Native language speak Michif (Normand 1996, 22). Through their languages, it appears that many Métis people are still linked as much to their "ancestral" Indigenous nations as they are to Métisness.

As another aspect of asserting their distinctiveness from treaty Indians, Métis organizations seem to be engaging in what Benedict Anderson has referred to as creating an "imagined community" (B. Anderson 1991), wherein one historical experience of mixed-bloodedness (that of the Red River settlement for a fifty-year interval) is held up as the history of all mixed-blood and nonstatus people in western Canada. This deliberate invoking of pride in a specific historical experience not only overlooks the broad range of experiences of mixed-bloodedness that existed across Canada during the fur trade but also the tremendous contradictions of Native-white contact, which were managed but not eliminated in historic Métis communities. Although many Métis communities developed at a time when power differences between Native and white societies were markedly less than at present, and while Native wives undoubtedly struggled to maintain Native cultural values in Métis settlements, it is impossible to ignore the steady marginalization of Native realities as settlements developed. This included the imposition of religious conversion and European dress and mannerisms on Native wives, the gradual loss of Native languages, and other manifestations of white dominance that confronted Native women and their mixed-blood descendants as part of their intermarriage with European men.

In many cases, this process of asserting the existence of a distinct Métisness—which is always separate from Indianness, anywhere that mixed-race Native people exist—is also spreading to eastern Canada and takes on many forms. For example, in the Report of the Royal Commission on Aboriginal Peoples, the testimony of Bernard Heard, of the Labrador Métis Association, speaks of the way in which Labrador Métis "lived on the coast . . . in complete harmony with the land and sea, much the same as their Inuit and Indian neighbours." However, writers of the section entitled "Métis Perspectives" comment upon Heard's testimony as follows: "The statement that the Labrador Métis are essentially no different from Inuit should not be misunderstood. It may be true that it is only geography and the attitude of outsiders that separates these two groups, but those two factors have been significant in isolating and shaping Métis cultures everywhere" (RCAP 1996, 4:255–56). Labrador Métis are thus not allowed to be indistinguishable from their Indian or Inuit neighbors. In the interests of asserting Métisness, their apparent differences from Indianness and Inuitness must be emphasized.

Particularly with recent attempts by the Métis National Council to drastically restrict definitions of Métisness, many Métis organizations across Canada are asserting this broad distinctive Métisness out of the best of intentions—in order to be inclusive to all individuals denied Indian status and to acquire numerical "clout." Currently, the numbers of individuals identifying as Métis have increased by 43 percent, now accounting for a third of all Aboriginal peoples in Canada (Taylor 2003, 5). This reflects not only a reclaiming of heritage by individuals of Métis ancestry, but the sizeable numbers of individuals who continue to lose Indian status because of Bill C-31 and therefore have nowhere to go but the Métis organizations. However, to unify as nonstatus Native people regardless of different Indigenous heritages or degrees of mixed-bloodedness solely to seek funding and legal clout under contemporary Canadian regulation of Native identity is one thing. To *identify* as Métis and to embrace a distinct identity apart from "Indians" simply because of lacking Indian status is something entirely different. Ultimately, it only feeds the Canadian-enforced divisions among all Indigenous peoples and represents a real loss to our traditional Nations of origin—whether they currently want us as members of their Nations or not.

With this in mind, it is important to consider that the form of nationhood that developed at Red River, with its military and European parliamentary orientations, is not the only direction mixed-bloods have historically taken to empower themselves. The mixed-blood population of northwestern Ontario, for example, sought to protect their rights as Aboriginal people by being included in the signing of Treaty 3. This option could be considered today, particularly with Treaties 4 and 6, where Cree leaders originally sought to have Métis people included.

Larry Gilbert has asserted that the granting of scrip should be recognized as proof of Indianness and that Bill C-31 demonstrated a significant double standard when it prevented individuals whose ancestors had accepted scrip from being reinstated as Indians, but left the white wives of status Indians with their Indian status intact (Gilbert 1996, 39, 62). In any case, the manner in which treaty Indian organizations routinely disregard and distance themselves from Métis people appears to be forcing the Métis into increasingly narrow options, of pursuing a Métisness that is always seen as highly distinct from Indianness and that can only create further divisions among different groups of Native people.

It is almost impossible to avoid profound intergroup conflicts while everybody is struggling with a colonial government to access rights for their community under government legislation, rather than attempting to develop lateral relationships among Aboriginal communities that diminish colonial control. Beginning to see the differences between contemporary Indian and Métis communities as distinct branches of the same root might bring about the possibility of working together for common goals as Indigenous communities.

PART 2. MIXED-BLOOD IDENTITY IN THE TORONTO NATIVE COMMUNITY

5

Killing the Indian to Save the Child

Like all Native people, the families of participants in this study faced phenomenal pressures to abandon their identities. Residential schooling and other government assimilation policies such as the apprehension of Native children by the child welfare system, and loss of Indian status, all represent forms of violence that worked on each individual's sense of who they were and how their Indianness was valued. What was particular to these families, as urban Native people, is that these policies overwhelmingly separated them from their communities of origin. These issues will be explored later, in terms of the three sets of experiences most commonly mentioned in the family histories of the study participants—residential schooling, loss of Indian status, and adoption.

RESIDENTIAL SCHOOLS

The Canadian residential school system was in operation from the 1890s until the late 1960s. Plans were first developed in 1879 to study the American experience of residential institutions and to develop a corresponding system in Canada, by expanding the network of religious schools and institutions already developed through the missionary efforts of the Roman Catholic, Anglican, and Methodist Churches (Miller 1996, 89–101). In the face of the growing resistance of Native people to their children's voluntary attendance at these institutions, the Indian Act was amended to make attendance compulsory in 1894 (Miller 1996, 129). However, Ottawa's constant cost-cutting resulted in overcrowded, poorly heated buildings where undernourished students frequently sickened and died. By the turn of the century, epidemics such as tuberculosis had taken so many lives that the deputy superintendent of Indian Affairs, Duncan Campbell Scott, admitted that fully 50 percent of the children who entered residential schools did not survive the experience (Scott, in Miller 1996, 133); in many places, these conditions continued unchecked until after World War II. The introduction of family allowances in 1944 provided bureaucrats with another means of enforcing residential school attendance, by withholding monies from parents who were noncompliant in relinquishing their children (Miller 1996, 385). Prior to the 1950s, approximately one-third of all status Indians and Inuit were in the schools (Miller 1996, 411); the numbers rose considerably during the 1950s, even as the system began to wind down in the 1960s.

The avowed goal of the residential school system was to effect the total assimilation of Native people into the body politic of Canadian society, through policies of removing children from their parents and societies, suppressing their language, and systematically negating the value of Native cultures (Grant 1996, 23–24). The schools were notorious for the damages wrought to generations of Native students by the indifference, insensitivity, hostility, and downright sadism of its administrators and teachers (Miller 1996, 309). Agnes Grant, in her research, describes the estimates from individuals she interviewed that fully 90 percent of their classmates are alcoholic, with many dying violently. She also reports that patterns of family violence in contemporary Native communities can clearly be traced back to the residential school experience (Grant 1996. 26). Grant notes that the suppression of Native languages resulted in the suppression of the oral tradition, which had been the primary vehicle for intergenerational transmission of Native values, culture, and identity (Grant 1996, 193). Chrisjohn and Young state unequivocally that the residential schools represent a Holocaust for Native people, both in terms of the suffering and in many cases the virtual destruction not only of individuals but of whole communities, and in terms of the cumulative effects of generations of loss of language and knowledge of culture on Indigenous nations today (Chrisjohn and Young 1997, 110).

Perhaps not surprisingly, residential schools represented the single greatest assimilation pressure reported in the interviews. Fifteen of the twenty-nine participants had grandparents or parents who had attended residential schools. None of the participants had lived at residential school themselves, although one woman, a northern Saskatchewan Métis, attended the residential school in her community while living at home.

Many of the participants had been told very little about their parents or grandparents' experiences at the schools, or the circumstances under which they had entered them. Four individuals, however, did know that their mothers or grandmothers had been "dumped" into the schools after losing one or more of their own parents. One person connected this directly to the epidemics—in this case tuberculosis—which had ravaged her community. Another spoke of the neglect her orphaned mother had experienced before entering the school, until the priest had her sent south to the residential school. In two cases, children went into the schools after their fathers died violent deaths. It appears that, particularly in eastern Canada, the schools functioned as a sort of "catchment basin" for Native children, as their communities were devastated by colonization. For small children whose families were torn apart by epidemics or alcoholism, in communities where all traditional institutions that might have protected orphaned children were being broken up and invalidated by the Church, there was no cohesive "safety net" left to shelter them, and so these children were left to be raised at residential school in inordinate numbers.

Most of the other children who attended the schools, particularly those from northern Ontario or western Canada, were removed from their families by Indian Agents or priests and sent to schools that were often a great distance from their homes, where maintaining contact with their families was almost impossible. The participants spoke of the bitterness of their parents or grandparents at spending most of their youth—in one case fifteen years—institutionalized, without any connections to home. In this respect, based on the experiences of the participants' families, the mandate of the schools—to remove Native children from any access to Native culture—appears to have been highly successful. In the group I interviewed, almost none of the family members who attended residential schools returned to their communities afterward. For most of the participants, their uncles and aunts had also left their communities behind after residential school.

Having immediate relatives left on the reserve was the exception, rather than the rule, for most of the participants.

In only one case, a participant reported that the experience of residential school could not cut the strong ties that bound her father to his community:

> When he was six, my father was taken away to the residential school, where he spent most of the year—I guess with the exception of Christmas and summers. And I should explain to you that, coming from a West Coast background, our cultures are very class-oriented, and my father comes from a very high-class background. He's also the oldest son, so there's a considerable amount of responsibility placed on him, within the community and in terms of being the person who'd hand down information, and names, and things like that. So he dropped out of school when he was in grade ten, to help take care of the family. With him, going away to residential school did have a big impact, but I think because the community invested so much in him, in terms of passing down knowledge, that there was always a really strong connection. The community was always thought of as home, and I think in the back of his mind he always imagined that he would go back.

In this case, however, the local minister in the community appears to have made a second try to sever this individual from his culture, by encouraging him and advocating for him to leave the community for divinity school. In this respect, he was successful—the individual stayed away from his community for much of his adult life. Eventually, on returning home, the skills he had acquired through his involvement in the Church as well as the National Indian Brotherhood were useful in facilitating his activities as a band manager. However, the sexual abuse this individual had suffered as a child within residential school ultimately was turned against his own children, and so the political skills he had learned at such a high cost were virtually useless in healing his troubled community.

Three individuals from southern Ontario reserves said that their parents had lost the use of their language in residential school, while their grandparents who had been to the schools still spoke it, but not in front of their families. Those whose parents were from more northern communities or from western Canada, reported that in most cases their parents still spoke the language after residential school, but they did not teach it to their children. Only one individual, a Métis woman from northern Saskatchewan, spoke her Cree language fluently. She reported being an exception in her community, because she had been raised traditionally by her grandparents; in most cases her contemporaries were losing the use of Cree.

One individual whose grandmother had been to a residential school spoke of how officials had changed the names of her grandmother's parents on the school records during the years when she attended the school and removed the name of her band as well. In this respect, the school functioned not only to remove Cree culture from the individual but also to remove any record of her connection to her family or community. Meanwhile, another individual described how her orphaned mother's name had been removed from the band list after she was sent to residential school; this hindered the participant in getting her Indian status back and made establishing community connections very difficult, so that ultimately her band denied her membership when she did get Indian status.

While vital knowledge about their relationship to their reserves was obscured through misinformation, the afore-mentioned participants experienced other forms of family disruption in the schools as well. Two individuals reported that their parents' siblings, uncles, and aunts were all sent to different residential schools; this entirely severed their familial relationships. In one instance, the individual did not even know that her mother had a brother until after her mother died.

Several of the participants described damage to their sense of self-esteem from the intergenerational alcoholism, sexual abuse, and other kinds of violence that had wracked their families since residential school. They spoke of how parents had been sexually abused in the schools or had come out without parenting skills or the ability to be close to anybody. Some described families where every relative was alcoholic and where physical violence and sexual abuse stalked the lives of close family members.

The participants also made it clear that the devastation of family ties caused by experiences at residential school affected how they valued their Nativeness. For example, one individual described how, after her father sexually abused her, she deliberately isolated herself from other Native people until she was eighteen or nineteen. A number of the other participants described more subtle ways in which residential schooling had affected how Nativeness was viewed in their family. For example, one woman mentioned how her mother would scold her in Cree whenever she grew her hair long—telling her that she looked like "a big, thick Indian!"

This woman also spoke of the vast space that residential schooling had occupied in her grandmother's life, and the complex mixture of painful and nostalgic childhood memories it triggered:

> When my grandmother was about eight, there was a big fire in the residential school. The school was made of wood at the time. At night, the nuns would lock the boys in their room. The girls weren't locked in, but the boys were. So then there was a huge fire—I forget what year it was, but to this day the old people still talk about it. There were thirty little boys killed, locked in there. And they were pounding and pounding on the door—they couldn't get out. So after that, the school was torn down. The townspeople made their own bricks and built a brick school. And my mom's generation didn't go into the residence, because they lived right there. They went to the school, but they didn't live in the residence.
>
> The school just got torn down last year, after all these years. It used to be on a hill above town, with a huge cross that shone at night. Whenever you went to my village, you could see it, just like a beacon up on the hill, shining. When it got torn down, my grandmother was really upset. Because that's where she spent her whole childhood. Like most of the elders in this community, she was sent here to go to the residential school and never went home again afterward. That's where she grew up, that was her only childhood home. It was very hard for her. I took her there when they were going to tear it down. She walked through the halls, and she just cried and cried.

Residential schooling represented a profound violence to the participants' families. The schools deprived their parents and grandparents of most opportunities to transmit language, customs, or knowledge of living on the land to their children, because this knowledge was taken from them as part of the schooling process. Moreover, the habit of silence imprinted on most survivors, about passing on language, culture, or even family information, has meant that many of the participants had been told very little about their family backgrounds. The alcoholism and cycles of abuse that a number of the participants have struggled with, and the devaluation of Indianness that such devastation brought, continue to manifest themselves in the next generation. Finally, the residential schools severed links between the survivors and their communities so thoroughly that most of the survivors did not return to their communities afterward. Urbanity, for half of the participants, *began* with this process, with their mothers and fathers leaving their communities for residential school.

LOSS OF INDIAN STATUS

Having or lacking Indian status has been an extremely significant issue in the lives of all of the participants in this study. Out of twenty-nine individuals, twelve are status Indians through their own lineage; however, only five are legally able to pass their status on to their children. Six western Métis participants, however, had status Indian grandmothers who lost status for marrying Métis men. One individual is an enrolled member of a small northeastern tribe in the United States, a stone's throw from the Canadian border.[1] Six participants are western Métis whose families have never had Indian status, and four individuals, all from the United States or Latin America, identify as nonstatus Indians. Two individuals had family members who either voluntarily or involuntarily enfranchised; both individuals, however, also had mothers who had lost status through Section 12(1)(b) and could thus be said to have been twice deprived of Indian status.

In many respects, this entire study has been shaped by the gender discrimination in the Indian Act that for over a century forced Native women out of their communities. Any work that deals with urban mixed-bloods will of necessity involve those who grew up urban and nonstatus with Native mothers more than those who grew up on reserve with Native fathers. This gendered history has underpinned this project—eight of the twelve status Indians I interviewed are the children of white fathers and Native mothers, while only four individuals have Native fathers and white mothers. When the six individuals whose grandmothers lost status are taken into account, we can see that almost half of the families interviewed—fourteen out of twenty-nine individuals—come from families that have had no choice about being urban at all—their mothers or grandmothers were removed from their communities solely because of gendered policies of removal in the Indian Act.

Two things became clear in this process. Within this study group, loss of status because of gender discrimination in the Indian Act has

had as assimilatory an effect on Native families as residential schooling, albeit in a different way. While some individuals have family
members who eventually returned to their reserves after years of dealing with the devastation of residential schooling, loss of status is a
central reason why significant numbers of Native people are *permanently* urban. The second issue, of perhaps even greater importance,
is the extent to which gender discrimination in the Indian Act represented a process of "genocide by numbers"—since in this small
group alone, the number of individuals who had Indian status and
band membership had fallen from nineteen to twelve to five in two
generations.

By comparison, enfranchisement affected only two of the participants. One participant's mother was enfranchised against her will for
leaving the community to work.[2] However, this woman also married
a non-Native and so would have lost status due to gender discrimination anyway; she had her status reinstated under Bill C-31. Another
woman's grandfather chose to enfranchise after World War II, as a result of the limited opportunities he saw for himself on the reserve; in
doing so his wife and children also lost status. This woman's mother
also married a non-Native and therefore effectively was doubly deprived of status. However, because of the regulations contained in
the Indian Act at the time her grandparents enfranchised (which will
be explored more closely in chapter 11), the woman's mother has
only been able to receive partial status, and as a result her daughter
is deprived of status altogether.

THE CHILD WELFARE SYSTEM

Patrick Johnston's ground-breaking 1983 work coined the phrase "sixties scoop" to describe the massive removal of Native children from
reserve communities that developed after the 1951 Indian Act enabled provincial child welfare authorities to extend their operations
to Indian reserves. The subsequent funding agreements that the federal government entered into with provincial agencies established the
parameters of the "scoop," with devastating results. Johnston's report
demonstrated how, particularly in western Canada and northern Ontario, the numbers of Native children in care skyrocketed within a
decade from less than 1 percent to between one third and one-half of
all children in care.[3] The majority of these children were not adopted,
but instead spent years in foster care; whether adopted or fostered out,

70 to 90 percent of the children grew up in white homes (RCAP 1996, 3:26).

Another problem was the practice of adopting Native children out of province or out of Canada—not only to the United States but to Europe. In 1982, 25 percent of all Manitoba children adopted were placed outside the province, and virtually all of them were Native children (RCAP 1996, 3:28). The statistics collected by the Department of Indian Affairs from the 1960s to the 1990s indicate that almost seventeen thousand status Indian children were apprehended by the child welfare system in that interval (Assembly of First Nations Resolution 10/99); this represents almost 5 percent of all status Indians at the time. In British Columbia, the Spallumcheen Band, a community of 300 individuals, lost 150 children—an entire generation—to the foster care system (Johnston 1983, 107).

The decision of the federal government to expand its role in funding social welfare services after phasing out residential schools suggests that welfare services became the chosen vehicle to deal with Aboriginal children in social need in the 1960s. At the time, it had already been accepted in the professional community that apprehending children should be the last resort in protecting children from harm (RCAP 1996, 3:26). The removal of any child from his or her parents was seen as inherently damaging, while the effect of apprehension on Native children was understood to be more damaging because of the removal of the child from a tightly knit community of extended family members into a foreign, and often hostile culture; nevertheless, social workers removed Aboriginal children from their communities in droves.

Johnston, and other analysts, have noted that the interventions of social agencies reflected colonial attitudes—that they devalued Aboriginal culture by not recognizing and using traditional Aboriginal systems of child protection, made judgments about child care based on dominant Canadian norms that ignored Native practices in child rearing, overemphasized the importance of material wealth as part of the "best interests of the child," and persistently used non-Aboriginal foster and adoptive placements (RCAP 1996, 3:26). Other researchers have noted that Aboriginal families at the time were dealing with severe disruptions caused by social, economic, and cultural changes, from a legacy of residential schooling, and in some cases, with the stresses of relocation. The research presents strong evidence that the federal government's willingness to pay child-in-care costs, and their resistance to supporting preventative services, family counseling, or rehabilitation, made the permanent removal of Native children from their families the treatment most often applied in problem situations (RCAP 1996, 3:27).

The results for Native children and their families were devastating. Children removed from their families and communities, in the context of a racist white culture, were "dumped" in foster families where they were extraordinarily vulnerable to pedophiles, to those who targeted them for abuse or neglect within otherwise white families, or simply to those who wished to exploit their labor. Even when children were placed in "good" homes, they were raised in ignorance of their culture, with no knowledge of their own identity, and few defenses against the racism of outsiders—or foster family members. The practice of obscuring the Native heritage of adoptees appears to have been too common to be dismissed as a "mistake." Indeed, the fact that families were so frequently not informed that their child had a claim to Indian status means that adoptees were routinely deprived of the rights accruing to status Indians—including shares of trust funds, access to services, and property rights (Johnston 1983, 95). It is important to acknowledge, however, that Métis and other nonstatus and urban Native children have always been dealt with by provincial welfare agencies and thus for years have faced a similar devastation to that experienced by status Indian communities in the 1960s.

For Native families, the suffering and despair caused by loss of their children frequently resulted in extreme alcoholism and other self-destructive behaviors. For the adoptees themselves, the statistics from correctional institutions and psychiatric hospitals record the toll, in terms of suicide, substance abuse, and extreme overrepresentation in prison.

Efforts of Native communities to deal with this problem have been hampered, first of all, by jurisdictional difficulties. In Canada, the federal government generally assumes responsibility for status Indians while the provinces are expected to provide social services. Because each province and territory entered into different funding arrangements with the federal government, a situation resulted whereby twelve different systems of child welfare placement were in effect, and where both the provinces and the federal government frequently disclaimed responsibility. The fact that status Indians and Métis, covered by separate legal regimes, must organize separately to protect their children, creates another level of complexity. However, a significant problem has been the fact that Canada refuses to recognize any form of Native sovereignty. As a result, the solution that developed in the United States to a similar problem—the Indian Child Welfare Act of 1978, which transferred jurisdiction for the welfare of Indian children to tribal governments—could not be undertaken in Canada, where no system of tribal courts exists (Johnston 1983, 89).

In 1981 the first agreement was signed authorizing a First Nation agency to deliver child welfare services. Since then, responsibility for child welfare has increasingly been delegated to agencies administered by First Nations and Métis communities. Most of these agencies have adopted placement protocols specifying that children at risk be placed first of all with the extended family, secondly with Aboriginal members of the same cultural and linguistic community, thirdly with other Aboriginal caregivers, and only as a last resort, with non-Aboriginal caregivers (RCAP 1996, 3:29). These agencies are now also focusing on repatriation—on ways to facilitate adult adoptees to regain Indian status, find their communities, meet their birth families, reestablish community ties, and in some cases, relocate to their communities of origin (Native Child and Family Services et al. 1999).

The experience of adoption or being fostered out has shaped the lives of significant numbers of urban mixed-blood people—including six of the study participants. Two of the individuals I interviewed had been adopted, while two were the children of adoptees. One of the adoptees had been given up to Children's Aid by her white mother, while another had been apprehended from her Native mother. Both have been reconciled to their birth families, but in both cases, their Native parent died before reconciliation. One woman learned that her Ojibway father had been left to die unattended on a stretcher in a Toronto hospital because the workers assumed he was just "sleeping it off." The other woman learned that her Cree/Saulteaux mother had died in her early thirties of a drug and alcohol overdose after losing both of her children to the child welfare system.

Both individuals, when they were adopted, had their Native ancestry hidden or minimized on the Children's Aid records. One woman's "full-blood" Ojibway father was listed as being one-quarter Ojibway, while the other woman's Cree/Saulteaux mother was listed as "Irish/Scottish," and her Métis father was listed as "French." Despite this, both ultimately found their Native families, and one individual was reconciled to her community of origin.

Such a positive outcome was not the case for the individual whose Ojibway father and four aunts were apprehended by the Catholic Children's Aid Society in Toronto in the 1940s. The father, who spent years in foster homes, knows who his mother is and what her community was, but had little other opportunity to learn anything about his heritage. In any case, the violence and alcoholism that marked his adult life, and his inability to parent, caused him to be separated from his own wife and children. The individual I interviewed does not know much about his father's life, and virtually nothing about their heritage, other than the name of his grandmother's community. He never met his grandmother before she died. While he still has one or two relatives in that community, there has been no real reconciliation process.

One individual that I interviewed had been told little about her heritage by her mother, but had some access to her Navajo grandmother in her childhood. Her mother's absolute silence about her past, which was a constant feature of her childhood, recently has become more comprehensible when this individual learned that her mother and one of her aunts appear to have been sold from her Navajo community to a white family in Saskatchewan. As her immediate family has all passed on, this individual knows only that she is Navajo; she was never even told the name of her Native community.

One individual reported that Children's Aid had apprehended her as an infant when her white father was arrested for fraud. They detained her until her Native mother was cleared of any role in the fraud and then released her. She did not speak of any issues that might have arisen from having been apprehended.

However, the mother of one of the participants had her second child arbitrarily taken away by hospital nuns at birth because she was not married. The participant describes the complex string of repercussions this action had on her family:

> When she had my sister, the Catholic nuns at the hospital took her away from my mom the minute she was born. Because my mom was a Native woman, and she already had a child, and she wasn't married. They removed my sister from my mom, and said, "We'll give you a year to get married and get settled down and get your life together, and if you can do that, then you can come back to us in a year and we'll give you your child. But if not, you'll never see her." They let her know that it was a girl—that's all—then they

took the baby away to Children's Aid and gave her to a farm family in Saskatchewan.

So that's the reason why my mom decided to marry my dad. He had gone to Toronto to try and find a job, because he wanted to marry her. He wanted her to live with him in Saskatchewan, but it wouldn't have worked, because his whole family shunned her. After they took her baby, she made her decision to leave everything behind, leave the whole family behind, all the supports and everything else—because there was a chance to make it here with my dad. So she came here to marry him, and got settled down with him, but in the process she got pregnant with baby number three. She managed to get back to Saskatoon to get my sister, and brought her back here, and then two months later she gave birth to her third child. Meanwhile, she'd also brought my oldest brother to live with her in Toronto, who by that point was about five years old. Until then, he was used to being with Grandma and Grandpa in Saskatoon, so for him it was like he was suddenly living with a total stranger, my dad. And by the time my mother got my sister back from Saskatoon, she was already one year old. As she got older, she was constantly running away, because she had not bonded with my mom. There was always conflict, and fussing, and sibling rivalry with the first three kids, because there were so many family issues to deal with during those first years in Toronto, because of the nuns taking my sister away.

My sister that got taken away—she has had really bad eczema all her life. You can just see all the scars on her. And she had such health problems when she was a child. It was terrible—she was always sick. She had smallpox and nearly died a few times. She still has asthma. And when she wasn't sick, she was always unhappy. And even now—she's still not happy in her life. She's not fulfilled, and I think it's all related back to that experience of being taken away as a baby.

All of the adoptees, or children of adoptees, reported having had considerable problems with alcoholism, drug addiction, depression, suicidal behavior, and uncontrollable rages. For their families, the removal of their children added a new layer of violence and loss to the other problems that they faced. One adoptee described her adoption as part of a whole complex of intergenerational violence and oppression that has afflicted her family:

My Native family's been so screwed up since my grandmother left for residential school. In some way we're all reacting to that, or still dealing with that. And then there's the fact that I lost my father because he was unattended while he was dying, because they just looked at him and saw a Native guy who was passed out . . . Losing my father, I think, is a pretty big issue of racism. And there's the fact that I was placed with a white family instead of a Native family.

I have this whole feeling of them having power over all of us. Power over my grandmother, power over my father, power over me.

These problems are continuing into the next generation. The son of the man fostered out in the 1940s described his struggles as a young adult with alcoholism, with uncontrollable anger, with keeping jobs, and with staying in school. The daughter of the woman who had been sold at birth described the weight of intense silence in her home around the subject of their Native identity, because of the shame her mother felt about being Indian and its effect on her. An adoptee describes graphically the sense of powerlessness and violation that so many adoptees experienced:

I have a real strong feeling, of picturing myself as a little baby, with these white people just passing me around. You know—you can look at this whole other side of it, where they were trying to find the best care for me—and that's probably all still true. But there's this feeling that I was completely powerless, cut off from my family.

And the anger in me about that goes out to the Native community, as well as to the white community. Especially when people come up to me and tell me, "You should be this, or you should be that." I just tell them, "Fuck you, you weren't there! I had to get through that whole time alone. I got through everything alone. If I'd killed myself, way back then—I was suicidal by the age of nine or ten—you wouldn't have even known about me. I survived. I chose to be here. I set the rules for my life!"

Another adoptee summed up the "big picture" of the effect of adoption on individuals:

I don't know of one adopted person that hasn't been really affected by the adoption process. Everything from prostitution to drug and alcohol abuse, to crime, to self-abuse, to attempted suicide. All of us, all of us—there's not one of us that I know of that's been adopted out that hasn't abused themselves in some way, shape, or form because of a lack of knowing who we are and where we came from. The statistics down at Aboriginal Legal Services say that 65 or 70 percent of all Aboriginal criminal offenders who come through there have been adopted out.

There was one teaching that I remember. People who work in our communities were sitting around one day, and they all said, "Who do you think are the hardest people to work with—the people from the residential school system or the people who've been adopted out?" And clearly everybody said it was the people who'd been adopted out who were the hardest to work with. Because in the residential school system—and this is not to minimize the atrocities that happened in the residential school system—you still knew you were Indian, and you were with your brothers and your sisters and your aunts and your cousins. But when you were removed, you didn't have nothing.

For most of the families of the participants, not just one but multiple experiences of assimilatory institutions and policies marked their histories. It is a legacy that urban mixed-bloods share with all Native people. And yet for urban mixed-bloods, the most devastating effect of these experiences was the manner in which they had permanently alienated them from their communities of origin. In many cases, the effects of this loss of community, and of the relationship to the land that was intrinsic to it, are still being felt by their descendants two or more generations later.

Paul Gilroy has suggested that the identities of African diasporic peoples have been profoundly shaped by a legacy of racial terror in the face of New World slavery (Gilroy 1993). In looking at the histories of Native peoples in the Americas over the past five hundred years, it is probably safe to say that if any experience defines them, it is that of indescribable and harrowing loss—of lands, of children, and of culture and identity. The violence of these losses has been manifested, to a greater or lesser extent, in every Native family. For urban mixed-bloods, these losses are compounded by loss of community, which appears to have deeply shaped contemporary urban Native identity.

6

Urban Responses to a Heritage of Violence

Generations of Native people have faced genocidal violence through the multiple institutions of a society determined to erase their Nativeness. However, for those who lived outside of Native communities, in the highly racist environments that characterize white society, the only way to try to assert some control over a difficult and frequently dangerous situation was to try to avoid *acting* Native around whites. A crucial difference, then, between the experiences of urban Native families and those who grew up in Native communities is the need on the part of urban people to find some way of managing the intolerable pressures on their identities that come from being always surrounded by white people, in a society that has offered little protection for Native people in the face of white violence. In this chapter, I look at the experiences of racism that shape urban Native communities and the multiple—and sometimes contradictory—responses of urban mixed-bloods to the pressures of living in a white supremacist society.

RACISM AND URBAN NATIVE EXPERIENCE

Most of the study participants' families carried histories of racist violence. In western Canada in particular, organized military and settler violence against Cree and Métis people has been recent enough to have affected the great-grandparents and even the grandparents of some of the participants. Several individuals came from families who left their communities after the 1885 Rebellion and spent years in exile in the United States to escape the organized repression of the Canadian government. Others fled further west, or remained in violent environments, squatting on the margins of white society in Canada. In general, the stories of the participants from western Canada resonated with family and community breakdown and with the disintegration of communities in the face of settler racism.

> A lot of the breakdown that went on in Native communities in the forties, fifties, and sixties in Ontario happened in my family three generations ago. Alcohol, violence, a whole downward spiral, a lot of tragic deaths. That sort of breaking of the past happened very soon after the hanging of Riel, for my family. A lot of people just went underground. My family was one of them. They just survived. They sold their scrip land in Manitoba, and moved west, prior to Saskatchewan becoming a province.

Meanwhile, the two East Coast participants most clearly showed the effects of the long-term colonization processes endured by their peoples, in terms of a community-wide loss of language and lack of knowledge of cultural practices. One individual described the constant threat of white assault that her family had lived under while she was a child; the other spoke about the decimation of her entire tribe and their forced removal from their traditional territory into the United States; her family is the only remnant of her tribe who still lives in Canada.

The handful of participants who grew up in Native communities described how they did not have to face significant levels of racism until they moved to all-white environments, as this Northern Saskatchewan Métis woman describes:

> My grandma raised me until I was about eight. Now, in my community, everybody's the same, right? The only people that are different are the teachers, who are white. We used to think they were weird, and we wondered if they peed—stuff like that. They were so different, and so clean, and they lived behind this big high wire fence, you know, in a compound. They had a special place, you know—they had nice houses and running water. And here we had

our houses—no telephone, outdoor toilets, no water. So to me, the only white people had been those teachers.

And then my mom married, so we moved to Prince George. That's the first time I ever saw so many white people. In grade five, I spent the whole year in class with my face behind my hands. It's not an exaggeration—I spent the whole year like this. The kids would call me names. I was so shocked. I never told my mom what I was going through. I lived in Prince George for five years, from the time I was nine until I was fourteen, and that's the only place I ever experienced so much racism, and at such a young age.

Some urban participants, on the other hand, experienced this process in reverse. One woman, for example, contrasted the defensive silencing around Nativeness that had marked her family's life off-reserve with the sudden immersion in a Mohawk environment and a stronger sense of being Mohawk, which resulted when her family moved back to the reserve when she was seven years old:

When I was in grade one, a woman who said she was Native came in to speak with our class. Thinking back on it now, I don't even know if she was. But she had long hair, and a headband on, and she sat down, cross-legged, on the floor, and talked to us about being Native. And I thought it was the coolest thing I had ever heard. And I went home and said, "Mom, Dad—there was an Indian in the class today, and it was so cool." And they said, "Well, you're Indian."

And I said, "What?" And I got so mad that I couldn't share with the class that I was Native too—and that I'd never heard this before. I was totally pissed off at my parents. I think it was maybe one of the first times when you realize your parents aren't always truthful with you.

Being Native just wasn't brought up, in my family. It's because there was a lot of racism, and my dad was looking to move up in the ranks of his job. I think he knew enough not to talk about it at all. Especially when he had a family to feed. But when I was about seven, my father got early retirement. So he decided to retire on the reserve, and brought all of us back. I was called names at first, when I got there. But it didn't take long for me to feel at home. And then, all of us were bussed in to the local school, off-reserve. All of the Mohawk kids—we went there on the Mohawk bus.

Most of the participants commented that the racism they faced was inextricably connected with where they lived and whether they were perceived as educated or uneducated, wealthy or impoverished. This affected the women, in particular, in different ways. One Cree Métis woman, for example, described how white men treated her as an "Indian princess" while she was growing up middle-class in Ottawa:

> The men I've been with, often they're trying to consume the colonial exotica. I've had my share of that. I had somebody who once called me "My little Indian"—he was really excited about being with somebody who was of Native ancestry.

She described how differently she was treated the first time she traveled in western Canada:

> I had this incident when I was in Manitoba, with an elder, in a restaurant, and there was a hair in her salad. The waitress just treated us like crap and basically inferred that we'd put it in there, and wouldn't give us our meal for free and all this kind of thing. Now, I was coming from this situation where, first of all—the customer's always right—and that had a lot to do with the notion of "who's the right customer?" I had always been the right customer, before that, and had always been able to assert myself—but no amount of assertion in this case would get me anywhere. And I suddenly realized, because I couldn't quite figure out how this was happening—"Oh! They're doing this because we're Indians!" And it was really shocking to me.

This woman noted that the dangers for Native women in such environments shaped how openly she could express her Native identity:

> If I had to regularly go through situations like having to walk through a scary, redneck part of Regina or something at night, I would adopt a different persona, such as not wearing my hair in a long braid, to make myself less overtly Native-looking, just to protect myself.

Another woman concurred with this, noting that being middle-class could not protect her from attempts by white men to degrade her sexually, whenever she traveled on business trips to northern Ontario:

> I was in Fort Frances and coming out of a motel room one day, about ten o'clock in the morning, and this white guy came right up to me and grabbed my breast and assumed that he was just going to waltz me right back into the room—you know, a total stranger. I got mad! I slapped him right across the face. When I told people about it, nobody reacted. It was nothing new to the Native women around me. They just shrugged, like, "Oh, yeah."

On the other hand, for some of the men I interviewed, whether they are even seen as Native has been shaped by stereotypes that make Nativeness and poverty synonymous. A very dark-skinned, Native-looking individual describes his experience:

> I remember working in the bush in Sept Iles—there was one Native guy that came in with us into one of the bars. There was him, myself, and a bunch of white people there. They wouldn't serve him, but they served me! I couldn't understand that. I was darker than he was. Now, I don't know if it was that they didn't think I was Native, because I was working with the engineers and he was one of the laborers? I don't know. Maybe they thought I was from some other country, while he had a Native look about him, and not any education.

Contemporary responses to everyday racism usually take the form of some kind of resistance. But for many of the participants whose families have been urban for a generation, in an era where Native people had no protection at all against the violence of white racist assault, the overwhelming response of these families to being urban was silence about Native identity and culture.

SILENCE AS A COPING STRATEGY

Many of the participants came from families where attempting to hide their Nativeness from the dominant society was their "defense mechanism" in response to the many acts of violence that had shaped their lives. Individuals were taught to avoid speaking Native languages in front of whites, or to do anything that overtly differentiated them from the whites around them. For many urban Native people, this amounted to a permanent, lifelong alienation from Native traditions, with high levels of self-policing as a form of protection. One individual describes how it worked in his family:

> I can remember one time walking down the road with my brother. We were on our way to school, and I remember I got really excited and started talking in Cree, some of the words that I'd heard from my cousins up north that summer. My brother, who was four years older than me, said, "No, no—don't speak that language here." So that was the kind of a message that I got. If you tried to do anything Native, you'd get into some kind of trouble. That was the way of life, then.

For this individual, escaping oppression could only be accomplished by sacrificing knowledge of culture:

> There was a reserve right close to Portage, just south, about five miles away. And when I looked at the conditions that they were living in—and then seeing that it didn't seem that there was any ambition there to do anything else but to stay on the reserve—I began to believe that my father was right, in saying, "The only way that you're going to get educated or gain anything in this life is to follow the white man's way." And this is the route that we followed. I'd like to have followed the traditions that I'm sure that my mother knew. But . . . it wouldn't have happened at that time. Today it's different; but back then when I was growing up it never would have happened, because the Native was a downtrodden person.

To avoid being humiliated by the treatment he frequently received from whites around him, this individual was forced to constantly deny or minimize the extent of the racism he had to negotiate in daily life:

> I was a person—that's all that mattered. I could compete in sports, I could compete academically, and I was a person. All of our friends were white, except a couple of people that I knew were Métis, but they would never admit it. I got in a lot of fights at school, from people that I didn't know, but then, I just thought, "Well, this is the normal way a young guy grows up." They'd call me names, but again, that never bothered me.

The only time it did bother me was sometimes, in high school, when they'd have the dances and things like that. I wouldn't really get out and mingle, except with my male friends. I guess I never thought I'd ask any girls out. It was probably a combination of being a shy teenager and being brown. I can't definitely say it was one or the other, but it was a combination of the two. I did feel that part of it was because my skin was brown. But it didn't last very long. I'd just forget about it, and we'd go on. I had a lot of friends who were girls, but not any real girlfriends in my high school years. It was a combination of the two.

One Métis woman described the abuse her family suffered in urban settings, where lacking a reserve meant lacking a space free from the violence of white domination and internalized racism:

My mom had cousins who would beat her and her sisters because they wouldn't be prostitutes. It's like my family thought they were better than anybody else, in their neighborhood, because they wouldn't bootleg, or be prostitutes . . . And there was sexual abuse. My mom was sexually abused by a friend of her father when she was only six years old, and he threatened to kill her if she told. And her sister, my aunt, was raped more than once. That's what they grew up with. Everything to do with being dark and growing up in the city was bad, totally bad. If they could have washed the color of their skin right off, they would have jumped in the river and done it. I mean, everybody was so jealous of their cousins who had lighter skins. And they would all buy the lightest shade of face powder that they could possibly get away with and use it all the time, every day, trying to look whiter. But they had jet-black hair, dark, dark eyes, and dark skin—much darker than me—and it was pretty hard to hide.

This woman described how she grew up alienated from Plains Cree culture because her mother wanted to protect her from racism:

The reason that we grew up in the city of Toronto was because my mom wanted to keep us from being exposed to the kind of racism that was so predominant in Saskatchewan when she was growing up. When I think about it, I realize that as much as I want to have my connections to where I'm from, because I feel so good when I'm out there, and I know that's where I would love to live, my kids would then be exposed to a whole scenario of racism that they haven't been, here. In Toronto there's such a cosmopolitan mix. Nobody ever points at them and calls them anything. The instances of racism that we've experienced in this city have been very, very few. Nobody has ever, here, done anything to me because they thought I was an Indian.

The repercussions of internalized racism were deep in this family. The woman described how it interfered with her attempts to learn about her culture:

When I first came back from a pipe ceremony, I was eighteen, and still living at home. It was my first time, going to a pipe ceremony at the Native Centre, and it felt wonderful to me. But my mother made me get down on my knees and beg God for forgiveness for going to a pagan ceremony. And I could have cried, because I knew this was terrible.

Years later, when I was in my mid-thirties, she admitted to me for the first time that my grandma and grandpa used to always go to the sun dances. But of course all I ever heard about, and saw, growing up, was the holy water and everything like that. But yes—they went to sun dances!

Another Métis individual described his mother's anger at the violence of her heritage and her resulting refusal to teach her children anything about their background:

I was learning traditional teachings, and I was talking to my family about what I was learning from the elders—and it was one of the few times in my life I've seen Mom get really mad. She looked at me, and she said, "Don't talk to me about elders. I'll tell you what our elders gave us." And she started to list it. "Family violence. Rape. Syphilis. Child Abuse. Alcohol. Debt. That's what they gave us. Don't talk to me about the elders." These were the type of stories that she didn't want to pass on. If that is your sense of history—and it just hangs there—why would you want to pass it on? She said, "Isn't it best to just be thankful for what you've got, and to keep on going?"

And yet the line between internalized racism and shame around Nativeness or maintaining a strategic silence in the interests of safety or to protect the children is not always clear. One individual described the attitudes of her mother and other women as motivated mainly by the desire to nurture but suggests that the result was a denigration of Nativeness:

> My brother and I used to get angry at my mother for not teaching us anything about our culture—and then, when questioned, she would say, "I made that conscious decision to protect you. The less you know about being Native, the more you will survive in this world." And then I was struck, on meeting all those other older Native women, from The Pas and places like that, who said exactly the same thing: "I've only wanted the best for my kid—and being Native wasn't any good."

Another participant, however, in describing his family's silence about being Métis, is careful about not always equating silence around Nativeness with shame. He notes that in an everyday sense, many people live their lives paying relatively little attention to their identities. This individual, however, also noted that if the society's norm is to be white, even casual and common-sense ways of living for Native people in white society require adaptation to white ways, whether the individual is ashamed of being Native or not. A heritage of white supremacy, then, continues to exert pressure on Native people to assimilate, even in environments where there is relatively minimal overt racism or shaming over racial identity.

For a handful of participants, particularly the older ones, the manner in which their parents had deliberately separated them from Native environments has contributed to a permanent sense of alienation from their Native identity, even as they subscribe, quite wholeheartedly (in theory) to notions of Native pride. These individuals demonstrated a profound separation in their minds between how they see themselves, and the "real Indians" that they feel they should be.

> I think I would have been much more comfortable with my identity if I had grown up on the reserve, or if there had been some acceptance of Nativeness in my family. If they had even said, "Yes, we're Native." But instead, there was this negation of their identity. It was never spoken about. "We don't acknowledge Nativeness, we

don't take it up, and if it's mentioned, we reject it, reject it, reject
it." It's very hard to get over that conditioning as a child, when
you're taught, because it's your parents' teachings.

Another individual was extremely candid about her family's efforts
to separate her from the more negative aspects of being Native. Her
words describe her sense of alienation from Nativeness, while at the
same time acknowledging a deep connection that in some respects
she fears.

In a very calculated way, we didn't have a lot of association with
our relatives on the reserve. They were free to visit, so long as
nobody was drinking. And likewise, when we went to the reserve.
Both my uncles were alcoholic. My mother in particular was very
selective about which families we could visit. Looking back, I'm
surprised we even visited there at all. Of course, we had relatives
there. But the message was always "Don't stay over there. Don't
let anybody in the house that's drinking."
    And so you grow up ashamed. And you think "Why would I ever
want to be associated with those drunks in the ditch?" The big
difficulty for me now is that I don't belong anywhere. You know,
I'm perfectly clear about that. I guess I just stay on the outside.
I think I would be entirely submerged. I'd probably be out there
sitting in a ditch with a bottle, too, if I thought too deeply about
which side I really belong on.

Silence about identity, as a tactic of survival or as part of the shame
of internalized racism, appears to have deeply shaped urban mixed-
blood experience. The cost of this silence, however, particularly when
it has been accompanied by the removal of people from the communities that hold their history, has been the rupturing of knowledge
about the past, and in some cases a profound sense of alienation, or
deep levels of ambiguity and discomfort, about their Native identity.

ADAPTATION AND RESISTANCE

It would be a mistake, however, to view accounts of family silence as
absolute. Two of the participants were siblings, and both had different
recollections of what they learned about Nativeness from their father
during childhood. One participant was a woman, who has little rec-

ollection of hearing about their Native identity at home. Her brother, on the other hand, who is slightly older, recalls his father telling him, "Be proud of who you are—you're a Métis." This individual, who attended a local school in a working-class area where there were Native students, found it relatively easy to reach out to Native people in his adolescence. His sister, on the other hand, who attended an elite, cosmopolitan high school, where Nativeness was romanticized but there were no Native people present, held on to notions of coming from a "noble but dead" culture until university, when she began to challenge her own assumptions and become involved in the Native community.

Other participants have also confirmed the importance of position in the family, in particular, in determining how much children learn about their backgrounds from their parents. For a few of the participants, the older members of their parents' or grandparents' generation grew up speaking their Native language and associating freely with Native people. The younger members, however, born after the parents began to internalize lessons about the importance of speaking English, or who in other ways began to pull away from their Native heritage, had been taught nothing but English, and in some cases identified primarily as non-Native. It is important, therefore, to consider that the stories told by some individuals about their parents' silence about Nativeness, and about cultural loss in their family in general, may not accurately express the full range of the family's experience. Gender, class, age, and position in the family are only some of the factors that may have influenced what the participants were told about their identities, or learned about their culture, growing up.

It is also clear, from the participants, that many of them were also able to name incidences of covert resistance to the white status quo that their parents sometimes engaged in. One individual, with a white mother and Native father, describes such an incident:

> I remember being four or five, watching television and asking my parents why the cowboys always won. I remember the feelings in the room. My mother answered, "Well, because they had better weapons." But my Dad answered, "Well, they didn't ALWAYS win!"

It is also obvious that despite the silence about culture that several of the participants mentioned in their families, their parents had obviously passed down enough pride in Nativeness to enable their children to take up a Native identity for the next generation—when it became safer to do so. Several of the participants discussed the fact that their parents had passed traditional values on to them without overtly naming them as Native values:

> I think for anyone with a Native background who wants to learn about their culture and who hasn't had access to it—which is most of us, including a lot of people on reserves—there's some sense of loss. But you know, I don't think we ever really lost the culture. I remember my grandmother and different people in the family from the Native side—there was no overt teaching, or dogma or indoctrination or lesson plan or school to being Native. But I think the values were there, from the beginning, from birth. And I think it was just something that is unconscious, and subtle. And yes, a lot of it has been lost—even some of the values and the ways of behaving and thinking, to a certain extent, that are seen traditionally as, you know, precontact Indian behavior. But a lot of it is still there. No, you don't have the medicines and what have you. The pipe isn't coming out at a funeral or anything. But I remember going home once, and it struck me—how different they were, and how the values were different, and the ways of relating were different, and how easy it is for me to be comfortable in any kind of reserve setting. I don't know traditional life—the language or the ceremonies, or anything. But I don't feel like I got cheated out of it. Because I think that the people that came before me, they hung on, and they kept their values, and I think they were passed on.

The impossibility of "losing a culture" was also taken up by some individuals who challenged the notion that Christianity and residential schools could fundamentally erase who a people are. They conceded that, in their families, their heritage could be—and had been—irrevocably altered, but saw the notion that it could be "erased" as an example of wishful thinking on the part of the dominant culture.

Some of the participants have related that the silence around Indianness that they remember from their parents was obviously not all that was happening in their parents' lives. A few individuals have described how their mothers were active in the Toronto Native community, through organizations created in the 1950s such as the North American Indian Club. These mothers, paradoxically, played a part in sowing the early seeds of the contemporary resurgence of pride in Native identity, even as they were silent about Nativeness at home. For these mothers, the fledgling urban Native community (which they played a role in developing) provided them with a safe place for expressing themselves as Native people in ways that they apparently could not do at home.

Some of the participants had very different childhood experiences from those described earlier. Those whose parents were openly Native—often in defiance of intense pressures to silence them—spoke of the costs of what amounted to an ongoing war in defense of their right to be Native:

> My mother is very interesting! She is very proud to be Oneida. It might be a little bit dysfunctional and unhealthy the way that she expresses it. She'll be in relationships with non-Natives, and she calls them "white man." And she wanted to put a blockade up on her driveway when Oka happened. And she can drink any other Indian under the table. She believes that she can put spells on people. She believes in bearwalking. My mother is not afraid of anybody. She's not a gentle woman at all. She's a very hardened woman. She grew up as the only Native woman in her school and in her neighborhood. Somebody only had to throw rocks at her once, she'd fight right back. Her own dad told her to "Get the hell out there. Don't be coming in here crying—get out there and fight your battles."

A few of the younger participants had activist parents who succeeded in changing discriminatory laws and building the institutions that shape the Toronto urban Native community today. One woman described how her mother had cultivated a network of Native friends in Toronto that formed the core of her social life. This woman attributes her present leadership role in the community to her mother's influence. Another participant was estranged from her father for most of the time of his political activism; however, it provided her with a sense of pride in her identity. A third described the changes that his mother's activism, around Native women's rights, made in his family:

> We were a very political family, very aware of our rights, very aware of human rights in general, which is what the issue started out as, for our family. It subsequently turned into a focus on Aboriginal women's rights, and I guess largely in part because the Indian Act

was discriminatory toward women, very obviously. It was the late sixties, early seventies. It was a time of a lot of activism. But it has changed our lives.

It is impossible to understand the lives of urban mixed-bloods without an awareness of the extent to which their families have had to struggle to assert a Native identity in a hostile white environment. Often challenged by reserve Indians for their lack of knowledge of traditions, or for the fact that their families appear to have attempted to assimilate, mixed-blood urban Native people must be understood as coming from a legacy of violence and from being forced to adapt to urban circumstances from positions of extreme vulnerability. Their struggles to build a base for their families in urban settings may have involved apparent acquiescence to the ways of the white society in some ways, combined with covert or open resistance in others. Their experiences, however, must be understood to be Native experiences, and the lives they live in the cities to be new hybrids of older ways. The fact that members of the current generation of urban mixed-blood Native people are reclaiming their heritage is testament to the success of their families' survival strategies.

7

Negotiating an Urban
Mixed-Blood Native Identity

Mixed-blood urban Native people have another parameter to their identity apart from their Native heritage, one that is shaped to a large degree by their white family. This is not often taken into consideration when mixed-blood Native people discuss their identities. Particularly for those individuals who by appearance look "all Native," the presence of white family members is frequently dismissed as if irrelevant to an otherwise Native identity.

We should be clear that there is nothing inherently wrong with intermarriage across cultures. But given the colonial relationship underpinning Native-white interactions in this society, intermarriage inevitably brings a heightened exposure to dominant culture ideals into the heart of Native families. And this is in a context where the pressures on Native identity are already intense. Urban Native people living in large cities such as Toronto must daily negotiate an environment in which Nativeness is marginalized, and yet the dominant culture is heavily invested in an image of itself as race-neutral. Unlike the smaller cities in northern and western Canada where colonialism is openly manifested, and where Native-white relations are immediately and visibly shaped by racial domination, the big cities in eastern Canada are spaces that are assumed to have transcended racism. In such cities, the colonial relationship between Natives and whites is seen as a tragic, ugly, and yet somehow accidental blot on Canada's past history. And yet even a casual exploration of urban white attitudes suggests that white Canadians regularly engage in a vast number of "conversations" about Indianness. These range from a generalized tendency to believe that Native people have died out, to high levels of resentment when Native people assert their hunting and fishing rights, to the increasing prevalence of New Age desires to appropriate Indian realities. These assumptions about Indianness, fed by the deliberate ignoring of Native realities in the school system, and the daily bombardment of images of Native dysfunction and marginality in the media, form a potent discourse about Indianness that works on how white people view the Native people that they are related to through intermarriage.

It is not only whites who are affected here, however. This discourse has also been central in teaching urban mixed-bloods what Nativeness is and is not. In particular, the apparent consensus from all quarters within the dominant society that "real" Indians have vanished (or that the few that exist must manifest absolute authenticity—on white terms—to be believable as Indians) functions as a constant discipline on urban mixed-bloods, continuously proclaiming to them that urban mixed-blood Indigeneity is meaningless and that the Indianness of their families has been irrevocably lost. It is important to note that such myths about the meaninglessness of a "watered down" Indigenous heritage generally operate at precisely the same time that Nativeness is being actively suppressed in families, in order to escape nonwhite oppression and claim a space in triumphant white culture. The result is a real difficulty, especially on the part of younger urban mixed bloods, in seeing the value of their Native identity. For mixed-bloods who look white, the consensus from the non-Native society that for them to in any way actualize their Indigenous heritage would be "inauthentic" and false—or indeed, even "appropriative"—works as a constant drain on their sense of self-worth.

Most urban mixed-bloods have therefore had to contend, at some point in their lives, with the fact that they do not fit the models of what has been held up to them—by whites—as authentic Nativeness. The response of many individuals has been to struggle to measure up to the images before them and to feel their identities tainted and diminished because they cannot be the "real Indians" they feel they are supposed to be. One individual described this process, graphically:

When I went to university I was confronted with these various definitions of what an Indian is. "This is an Indian," according to Anthropology. "This is an Indian," according to Environmental Studies. "This is an Indian," in terms of Social Work. "This is an Indian," in terms of Political Science. "This is an Indian," in terms of Law. All these various concepts of Indianness kept hitting me. And I found myself reading these books, learning this stuff— and constantly spewing it back out to people whenever I had the opportunity—making corrections, and trying to prove to everybody around me that I was the authority on all things Indian. Because I was made to feel that I had to be the authority on Indians in order to prove that I was Indian at all. It got to the point where I knew, deep down, that I was putting on a show, right? I knew that I was putting on a show—like, "I'm the most Indian Indian," you know? And then one day I found myself saying to myself, "Hey! I AM just like an Indian!" You know? Sort of . . . all happy about it. Like I'd been so twisted around in my own head, that all of a sudden I was looking at myself and thinking "You know, geez, I'm just like the Indians!" Right? That's when I realized, "What am I doing? This is absolutely ridiculous. I AM Indian. I'm from an Indian family! Open your eyes! Look at it!" And it's only once I realized that, you know, that I stopped wearing the feathers to class, and I stopped being the expert in the class.

Thus, ideological racism—a war of images—is a constant issue to be reckoned with for urban mixed-blood Native people.

All of the factors described—the different white "conversations" about Indianness that non-Natives are taught, and the confusion, distortion, and negation of positive Native identities that these conversations create for urban mixed-blood Native people—are the context in which intermarriage between Natives and whites takes place. In the following section, I will explore the study participants' actual experiences with white family members.

WHITE FAMILY MEMBERS AND NATIVE IDENTITY

While the participants' experiences with white family members varied, a broad pattern was immediately apparent. Because of the different treatment of Native men and women under the Indian Act, a distinct set of differences in experience emerged along lines of gender, with significant implications as to whether Nativeness has been openly included or has been reduced to a covert identity in the participants' families.

Two individuals had white fathers who left their mothers when they were born. Four others had fathers who were racist and in some cases abusive both to their mothers and to them. In each case, these were white working-class men from England or Ireland, whose social positions and job prospects were generally insecure, and who clearly targeted their Native wives and children to take the brunt of their problems. One woman described her father's—and his family's—treatment of her family as follows:

My father's family is from the Orange Society—Presbyterian, from Ireland. My parents were only sixteen or seventeen when they got me. And his parents totally disapproved of their son being with an Indian woman. When my dad went to jail, my mum lived in Guelph with them for maybe a weekend or a week. They set my mother up. They gave her money to go out drinking while they were looking after me . . . all to prove that my mother was neglecting and abandoning her children, that she was a drunken Indian mother that was unfit to look after the kids. I think they even went as far as calling the police and Children's Aid.

My parents must have been together off and on for at least six years, to get the three of us kids. My mom left him because he went after my sister. She wasn't eating some meal, and that pissed him off, and he picked her up and threw her across the room, and knocked her unconscious. That was it. He only did it once, and that's when my mom left. My mom's rule was "You can hit me, but not the kids!" So she left.

All of these individuals described their white fathers as far less competent and resourceful than their mothers, and one described his father as very troubled:

My father couldn't really keep an occupation. He was an alcoholic, and he was a very mixed-up man. I mean, not all whites are mixed up, but he was; he was one of them. Very, very lost.

For all these participants, a kind of war had raged in their families, between mothers who would not be easily dominated and insecure fathers who used different kinds of violence, including racism, sexism, and/or physical and sexual assault, in efforts to assert domination, not only over their wives but also over their children.

Two women whose fathers were from non-Anglo backgrounds describe quite different family dynamics. One woman described positive attitudes toward Nativeness from her Italian father, who accompanied his wife to ceremonies. However, she noted that the rest of her Italian family was far more ambivalent about her Nativeness—resenting the so-called special treatment that Native people received, but still expecting her to purchase items for them tax-free with her status card. The other woman, whose father was Japanese, spoke at length about her father's efforts to support her family's land claim, while at the same time encouraging assimilation to the Anglo-Canadian norm. She saw his efforts to promote assimilation as motivated not by anti-Native sentiments, but by a racialized father's fear for his children's survival in a hostile white environment.

Two individuals described very positive relationships with their fathers. In each case, however, the participant's Native identity was something that was not discussed. A handful of other participants described this phenomenon with respect to other family members—that their relationships with white family members were close, but that the terms of this closeness seemed to involve a silence about Native identity. Expecting—or demanding—this silence from Native children or grandchildren allowed white family members who could not or would not negotiate racial differences to nevertheless retain close relationships with their Native children or grandchildren.

Two individuals had fathers who entered their wives' worlds, supporting their life choices and living near their Native communities. It is important to realize the extent to which the patriarchal attitudes that lay behind the behavior of most of the white fathers were enforced by law. The Indian Act, which denied Indian status to Native women who married white men, also prevented non-Native husbands from living in their wives' communities. The two instances where the husbands were able to enter into their wives' communities were highly anomalous, in that one husband was able to live on his wife's traditional land because the land had not been made part of the reserve, while the other husband decided to buy a farm adjacent to his wife's reserve so that their children could be brought up in touch with their mother's community even though they weren't able to live on-reserve.

The individuals with Native fathers and white mothers described entirely different sets of family dynamics. First of all, the same laws that had deprived the Native mothers of their status and forced them to live in their husband's white society enabled the white wives of status Indians to take on Indian status and enter Native society. The white society's beliefs around gender that shaped this legislation also shaped the attitudes of most of the white women, whether they gained Indian status through their marriages or not. Most of them had been brought up to assume that they would enter the worlds of their husbands. In this apparent willingness by white women to enter Native environments, however, both positive and negative dynamics ensued.

Some of the mothers, working-class white women married to heavily assimilated working-class Native men, saw Native culture far more positively than their husbands did and encouraged their children to be involved in learning about their culture. In some cases, the mothers actively intervened to protect their children from racism—and knew enough to stay out of the way when their presence, as white women, was unwanted. Two mothers, on the other hand, were described as "wannabees," drawn to appropriating their husband's cultural background because it was perceived as exotic. One woman described how this worked in her family:

> My birth mum is white, and she's a real "wannabee." It was she who first introduced me to the Native community, where she really wanted to be accepted as the mother of a Native child. Then I started meeting people, and that was the extent of our contact, because the Native community's attitude was like "Thanks for dropping her off—goodbye!" We had to fight it out about that, and we haven't been the same since.

Some mothers appeared to be attempting "personal empire building," making their husband's Native culture an arena where they could overcome their gender and class subordination in the white culture and do their life's work among Native people empowered by their whiteness. One mother groomed herself to become a teacher in her husband's community, becoming relatively fluent in her husband's language, until his abusiveness forced them to separate. Another mother attempted to play a strong leadership role in community organizations in her husband's community; however, she was frequently rejected because of her patronizing assumptions about Native people. In each case, despite their aspirations to the contrary, these women were forced to "walk the walk" and take on the difficulties of Native life as they encountered it in reserve communities.

Two of the participants grew up with white single mothers who had left their abusive Native husbands while they were children. One individual reported her mother being quite supportive of her Native identity, while the other, whose mother was attempting a political career, had to negotiate silencing on certain levels from his mother, because she did not want to be publicly identified as the mother of a Native child. Both individuals had to deal with racism from their white grandparents.

Three of the participants had grown up in families where their mothers were of elite Anglo-Canadian backgrounds and their fathers were upwardly mobile, highly successful Métis men. In these families, the customary gender dynamics of Native-white intermarriages were reversed—these mothers expected that their husbands would adapt to their Anglo-Canadian values. The participants all reported that attempts by Native family members to reassert Native identity were being taken up in negative ways by their mothers. Family holidays in particular were sites of conflict, where white mothers saw Native traditions as invading and taking over the space where they were accustomed to enjoying their own rituals.

Both of the female participants from these backgrounds reported having tremendous difficulty in being accepted as Native by their mothers. One woman, the whitest-looking member of her family, found that her mother tended to minimize her Nativeness and at times even dismiss her attempts to reclaim a Native identity. Another woman, more visibly Native, recalls being caught between her grandparents' racism and her mother's subtle denials of her Nativeness. The two issues that the female participants struggled with involved their white mothers' difficulty in negotiating racial difference across bonds of gender, combined with the levels of power their mothers were accustomed to enjoying. For white women from wealthy Anglo-Canadian families, accustomed to taking up space and seeing their values reflected everywhere, having to accept their daughters' participation in cultural traditions that they could not share was difficult for them.

As conversations with a number of participants revealed, denials of Nativeness from white family members are frequently highly strategic. Generally, white family members attempt, through the use of common-sense racism, to eliminate what they see as "the threat" of Nativeness, with its potential to upset the unspoken authority they claim in their families as whites. One light-skinned Métis man described how his father's family denied his Nativeness in a clear desire to maintain white authority as a core family value:

> My father's sisters just dismiss my Nativeness! They say, "Aw, we have as much Native blood as you do!" That's their response. And I say, "No, you don't." Because there's a pride in my life, in being Métis. And they don't want to acknowledge that pride, or validate our heritage, our history, our culture.

The adoptees spoke of how threatened their adoptive families were when they began to openly embrace their Native heritage. In both cases, their experiences suggest that for these families, Nativeness is only tolerable as a subordinated identity. One of the women described how, through intense efforts, she was able to challenge her family's efforts to silence her:

> After the reunion with my birth family, my mom started making little digs about how "we brought civilization to you." She had never talked like this when I was growing up. This was just in reaction and in resistance to what I was starting to learn. I'd go home, and they'd be putting little digs in about Native people, or they would just shut me down. I'd start to talk about something Native, and they'd go, "Oh well, I went shopping the other day . . ." They would change the subject. And this went on for a while. I finally said, "I'm not going to be able to come home anymore. Most adoptive families break down, and this one's about to. You're about to lose me." I told them, "If you want to see me, I'm in Toronto. And not to go to the CN Tower, but to come to Native events. I really fucking mean it. You guys don't have to be Native, but you're going to have to learn that this is a part-Native family, and this is the only way we're going to be able to make it work." They came to a Native Tae Kwon Do event, and they came to my Native Theater School graduation. It's always hard, though, because I have to be the one that sets all these conditions. I have to be willing to risk losing them, to get them to meet me half way, and that's really hard.

This individual also related how her mother was reluctantly drawn into defending her daughter's Nativeness in the presence of other whites, while still fighting her daughter's manifestations of Native identity at home.

The other adoptee, however, reported that her Nativeness will always in some ways be seen as a threat to her adoptive family:

> My parents are just really Eurocentric. I've come to understand that they really do see life from inside a bubble. The only thing they know about Indians is what they see on TV. This is my mother's line: "I am so sick to death of hearing Indian people whine about having a lost culture . . . You didn't even have a culture in the early sixties! You don't ever hear anything about the good white people that took all of you in!" That's what I had to live with, growing up. And it's only been recently that my mother said to me, "You know, I saw some Indian people on TV the other day. They were really doing something with their lives." That sort of sums up what they thought about Indian people. They told me I was Native when I was really young—but we never talked about it. I was just the little brown white kid. They were supportive of me finding my birth family—but they sure went through their white guilt when I started claiming a Native identity. They would never talk about it, until I started questioning things and then—oh, you bet, I just felt my mother's anger, her rage. My mother said to me, five years ago, that if she had to do it over again, she would never have adopted an Indian! I just don't think they're ever going to change. There's only certain ways that I can say things so that they'll hear it. Or I just won't talk about it anymore, because they're just not going to change.

Many of the participants described a fundamental impasse between themselves and white family members around their choosing to take seriously their Native identity. While a handful of the individuals had family members who were genuinely supportive, and a few others were able to win over their whole family after considerable struggle, for the most part, white family members demanded silence about Indianness, and a Native identity not subordinated was usually seen as a potential threat to the identities of white family members. It is precisely this "non-negotiable" aspect of Native-white relations—to generalize, the manner in which white Canadian identity *demands* the silencing or subordination of Nativeness as the only possible form of relationship—that forces many mixed-race Native people either to entirely embrace their Native identity or to leave it behind.

RECLAIMING A NATIVE HERITAGE

Given the histories of oppression and loss that the participants inherited from their Native families, and the frequent denial or subordination of their Nativeness from white family members, reclaiming a Native heritage has been an extremely important aspect of the participants' lives. Each of these individuals has made a conscious decision to attempt to challenge assimilatory pressures within their families, to learn the traditions of their heritage, and to assert pride in a Native identity.

Three of the participants grew up, or lived for many years, in their Native communities of origin. For these individuals, growing up around Native people gave them a relatively uncomplicated sense of their own identity. They knew they were Mohawk or Ojibway or western Métis and that their lineage and heritage was based in their community of origin. Many of the people around them were relatives, and although one white-looking individual was occasionally teased, nobody externalized these individuals from their community because of their appearance or bicultural identity. Everybody knew that they belonged there.

Six other individuals, although urban-based from birth, are dark-skinned and Native-looking enough to have always considered themselves Indian. Three of those individuals grew up with positive feelings about their Nativeness, through involvement with other Native people in the Toronto community since childhood and with periodic visits to their mothers' reserves. On the other hand, three of the participants grew up with shame about their Indianness, through their families' alcoholism, or through childhood exposure to racism and other forms of abuse. For these three individuals, reclaiming a Native identity has been a long and difficult process, involving extensive self-nurturing and adoption of a traditionalist lifestyle involving sobriety, fasting, ceremonial life, and other aspects of a Native spiritual path. Each has achieved pride in their Nativeness through this process.

For the individuals mentioned earlier, Native identity may not have always been embraced, but it was seldom seen as contradictory—the individuals always thought of themselves as unequivocally Native. For the remainder of the participants, however, identifying as Native has been a process that initially required some adaptation. These individuals are, for the most part, the children of one Native and one non-Native parent, who grew up off-reserve in environments where their families were silent about their Native identity. There are also two individuals who were adopted and had their Native identities obscured. Most of these individuals are Native enough in appearance that they always knew they were Indian, but they grew up so apart from other Native people that being Native was seen as something irrelevant to their identity.

In one instance, the participant's white father was clearly in denial about his daughter's Nativeness—in ways that strongly affected her identity:

> My father was one of the most racist people in my life. He loved me more than life itself. But he was very racist. He did not like Native people. When we were living in one northern community, he had a little dog, which he trained to bark at Indians. He'd say, "Look at the Indians, look at the Indians," and the dog would go up to the window, if an Indian was walking by, and bark. That dog was trained to hate Native people. And I remember participating with that, in some respects.
>
> I had a huge group of friends who were very multicultural— French, Italian, German. There were a lot of different nationalities. But I never had any Native friends. A lot of Native kids from further up north used to get taken down to that community to spend the school year. But I never really associated with them. Sometimes some of them would come to the house, because Mom knew them from her work—but I was always really uncomfortable around them. They were just so different from me! These Cree kids, they wouldn't say boo, they were so quiet and shy. Here I was, into New Wave, doing my hair up and dying it blue, all kinds of things— and here's these kids coming from up north, who weren't anything like me.

For another woman, alienation had less to do with family attitudes than with the cutting off of cultural knowledge in her family, coupled with stereotypes from the dominant culture:

> I guess when I was a child, nobody pretended my dad wasn't Native. And it was a source of pride, I guess, because it seemed romantic or heroic. We didn't grow up in an area where there were any Native people, so I think in the absence of Native people they become very romantic. As long as they've been removed, they are very romantic. If there's a community down the road, or if half your

school is a bunch of breeds, they're no longer the romantic Noble Savage. I grew up in a place where the Noble Savage still existed. In part, I was buying into the exotica of my heritage, as a kid. I didn't feel that there was anything I could connect to, because there was no Native community around. So it was just, sort of, the dead romantic Indian, and we were part of it. That's what we had to claim.

For this individual, beginning to identify as a Native person involved confronting a profound sense of loss and pain, of suddenly realizing that all of her life she had been cut off from her own roots, and of beginning to realize that Native people were *her* people.

For all of these individuals, a crucial process in their lives was how they came to understand themselves as Indian. It was particularly significant for the individuals who look unequivocally white, who have had to overcome what they see as significant contradictions to claiming their birthright as Native people. For this individual, an extremely fair-skinned, reddish-haired individual, the transition from a non-Native to a Native identity was quite traumatic:

I always knew my mother was Native, but I never understood that this meant that I was Indian, or part Indian, or nonstatus, or whatever. My mother is dark, she has dark hair, she has a very Indian nose, the hook nose, and she always expressed that she was Native. I guess everybody in our neighborhood knew that my mother was Indian. And when the extended family would visit us from the reserve, I knew that they were all Indians. But to me, that didn't mean that I was Indian. Because if you looked like me, how could you be Indian?

The changeover, for me, happened overnight. There was this ethnic, cultural day at school, and we invited parents from different countries to come to the school. Now, my principal at the time used to be my mother's teacher, long ago, so he knew my mum was Native. So he sent a request letter home, inviting my mother to come to the school and give some kind of dialogue or speech about being Indian. So that night, my mum taught me how to make corn soup. She went and got me a deer hide dress from one of my aunts who lived up here in Toronto, with some stupid thing that men actually wear, a bustle, and did my hair in braids. So she had me all dressed up—and I think she smoked up before she went to school, smoked a couple of joints, probably had a couple of drinks, for courage. And then, in front of the whole school, from kindergarten to grade five, everybody was assembled in the auditorium, and my mother came out, to all those kids as an Indian woman. I don't know what the hell she talked about. I can't even remember; it was such a traumatizing day for me.

And so my identity changed overnight. As soon as it got out that my mother was Indian, other kids identified me as being Indian—before I even identified myself as Indian. But they didn't call me Indian, they called me "half-breed"; they called me "squaw"—yeah, those two words were used the most, squaw and half-breed. They only identified me that way because they saw my mother. So that was my coming-out experience. And still, I didn't really feel that I was Native.

I didn't really start identifying that I was Native until I was about seventeen or eighteen. I got into a fight with this other Indian woman, who had come to town. She was probably about forty years old, and we'd all been drinking, and for some reason, she started calling up our place and giving us these harassing phone calls. She got on the phone and she said that word "squaw." I said, "That's fucking fighting words, man—I'll be right up!" So I went uptown, and marched up the stairs, and banged on the door, and she came out, and came downstairs, and we took it out on the street. My mum was there with me. My mum took on one woman, and I took the other woman. I ended up in jail, drunk and disorderly. They kept me in overnight. I'd had all this drink, and the cops slapped me across the face. They told my mom, "We would have let her out hours ago if she would've just shut up."

Up until I was seventeen, there were only those two incidents that identified me as Native. Both of them were totally bizarre and traumatic experiences. To me, it was like saying, "This is what it is like to be Indian!"

Adoptees in particular have described how confusing it is to undergo an often disorienting process of understanding themselves as Indian and beginning to work in the Native community as Indians. One participant, whose adopted parents had been told that she was one-eighth Indian, describes how she first heard from her birth mother, who was white, that her father was Ojibway, a mere two weeks after she first decided to find her birth parents—and at the start of the Oka crisis.[1]

I first got really involved in the Native community during the Oka crisis, and that was with my birth mum. She took me out to the first protest, and I started meeting people. Oka took over my whole life, and because of that, everything happened so fast. I had my first Native boyfriend, who was this asshole, and I ended up homeless. Then I started working at this Native agency, and on my first day, some guy came in and looked at me and said, "White people are taking right over." And the executive director at the time ran over and said, "No, no, that's your sister," and the guy kept apologizing to me for about four years after that.

It was awful. It was all too much. I was just this bratty little university student who had thought she was white, and was pretty shut down emotionally, and had been just partying a lot. And I'd had a breakdown just before all this happened. So I'd been through two major life changes—three, if you count Oka—and all within about two years. I think I'd already been dissociating slightly, and I just started splitting off more, to fit all these new roles. I think that's how I handled it. I probably would have taken it a bit more slowly, if it hadn't been for Oka, but that just overwhelmed me.

A significant aspect of coming home for this woman happened two years later, when she acquired her Indian status, found her father's band, and was reconnected with her Native family. Meanwhile, for the other adoptee, getting in touch with her birth family brought her her first sense of belonging as a Native person. However, she still found entering the Native community initially traumatic, although absolutely necessary for her own identity.

In general, while taking up a Native identity has been difficult for these participants, they have described their experiences in the urban community as a process of being welcomed home. Most of these individuals now feel extremely positive about their identities and feel very much at home in the urban Native community.

CONTRADICTORY NATIVE IDENTITIES

For about a third of the participants, however, there has been no magic resolution into an unproblematic Nativeness from a childhood alienated from Native contexts. While all of these individuals identify as Native, some of them do not feel that they will ever really be accepted or at home in the community, because of the profound silencing and separation from their Native identities that they experienced growing up, or because they come from families with more than one generation of intermarriage and assimilation. Other individuals claim hybrid Native identities because their ancestry is multiracial, or in other ways is too complex to be reduced to a narrow sense of Indianness.

One woman, whose parents split up after her father sexually abused her, and who was raised by her white mother, has described the difficulties in having connections to her heritage. Unable to live in her father's community because of his presence, she reported frequently feeling very alien around Native people:

> I have very little connection with any Native community at all. So if anything, I just feel a complete absence. You know, seeing a Native person is supposed to be a positive thing. If you're at an event or something, it's supposed to give you strength, even if you don't talk to them. Whereas for me, when I see a Native person, I don't necessarily feel that connection. I'm not always recognized by them as a Native person, and that's a problem. And I'm also not comfortable just walking up and talking to anyone under most circumstances, since I'm usually fairly shy, so that doesn't help. But the fact remains—I don't feel that connection.

Two individuals who grew up during the postwar years when assimilation was the socially expected norm, and who did not develop a strong awareness of, or pride in, their Native identities until they were approaching their fifties, have described how difficult it is for them to feel at home anywhere. One white-looking woman, who grew up off-reserve, described an aspect of her discomfort as follows:

> I don't belong anywhere. I don't know much about my Native background. And with my appearance, I have great difficulty wearing any jewelry or anything Native like that. Every time I do, I feel like a "wannabee."

Meanwhile, the other woman, who got her Indian status back in her fifties but whose parents never told her she was Native, described how aspects of asserting Nativeness feel false to her:

> I don't feel totally comfortable with identifying as Native—it's like taking up a burden. And there are times when I just want to be me. And "me" is not an Indian person, the me that I know. I'm working

through this, and it seems that my identity is not as a Native person, it never was—it's an artificial thing that I'm taking up now. And even though I'm conscious and working on it, I still feel false with this. I'm not saying, "Oh, I don't have Native ancestry," you know—I acknowledge that—but just because you have physical or genetic connections, the culture doesn't come along as a particular gene or chromosome, you know?

Further discussion with both individuals in fact revealed complex and contradictory ties to *both* Nativeness and whiteness. The problem for these individuals is less a matter of not belonging anywhere, than living in a polarized society where whiteness and Nativeness are not admitted as existing in the same person. This woman discussed some aspects of her "double identity":

I was so angry, going to Ottawa, and listening to the tourist spiel. I figure all the visitors coming to Canada hear about how the Native peoples are some . . . motif in the corner. You know—the lies, the glossing over. I remember going through the parliament buildings, this great stone edifice, and the carving, and the architecture, and everything—this huge monolith sitting there . . . squashing Native people. You know what I mean? You just want to bomb it! That really hit home. I thought, "This is the enemy." It's like at that point I stopped being a Canadian, you know? Seeing this righteous edifice, with these giant oil portraits of all these white people who have been members of parliament, and all that—it's just this mecca for whiteness!

And yet, at the same time, I see myself as white-identified! I can't get rid of it—I can't take that off! And I'm not pushing myself anymore—because I figure, I'll get myself all traumatized here. I can't deny or rewrite who I was, because I still am that person, with a new awareness, and a claiming of identity. But I know I won't make a full transition. You'll never see me walking around wearing feathers and beads. Although I have this idea that I will make a Native dress with the beadwork and all that, one day. Whether I ever get to do it—and if I do, whether I actually wear it—who knows?

Some individuals have made it clear that they continue to see themselves as Native—they simply do not feel at home either in the

Toronto urban community or in their home reserve. Others are more ambivalent—they acknowledge that they come from Native families, but deep down inside they do not *feel* that they are Native.

Three of the individuals who are very white-looking have parents whose connections with their Native communities were lost through adoption or through losing Indian status. For all three, the "double whammy" of having their knowledge of family history cut off at their parents' generation, combined with their own white appearance, has resulted in a clear sense of being outsiders. While all three of them need to be involved in the Native community to affirm their identities, they also find it stressful to be around groups of urban Native people because of the way in which they are usually taken for white and viewed with distrust in Native environments. All three of them have managed to assert some control over how they are treated by functioning only in carefully delineated spaces within the urban Native community—at specific agencies for example—where they are already known as Native. Each, however, mourns in different ways the fact that they have been separated from their home communities, as one participant explains:

> I grew up in a middle-class white neighborhood in Edmonton. We don't know what reserve my father's mother came from. On his father's side, they're Métis but very assimilated. He rarely told us about his early life. We were told, "Be proud of being Native," but then they didn't teach us anything about BEING Native, you know?
>
> I think the thing for me is—most of the time I'm trying to become comfortable around Native people. I know this sounds ridiculous to a lot of people, but when you are surrounded your whole life by whites, you understand the white world very well—but understanding the Native world is a different thing.

A handful of the participants insist on more complex notions of what constitutes Nativeness and understand their Native identities as being hybrid. These individuals, of multiracial and mixed cultural identities, consider themselves to be Native, but find that they have to step back at times from the relatively narrow views of Native identity that are common in the urban community, in order to be able to define themselves more fluidly—in a sense, more accurately—than in dualistic ways. For the remaining participants, however, the only way to manage the contradictions of having a mixed-race identity—

something in between the rigid poles of "Indian" and "white"—has been to force their lives into the categories available and to use brutal clarity, silence, denial, and humor to deal with the ways in which they do not fit these categories.

As the participants struggle to maintain their Native identities, it is clear that each individual has had to negotiate a series of internal assumptions around what Native identity is—as well as external standards in the urban community about who is Native.

8

Maintaining an Urban Native Community

As this study has revealed, the label "urban mixed-bloods" spans a wide range of experiences—from those individuals who have grown up in Native communities and only came to the city as adults, to those whose families have been urban and intermarrying with non-Natives for two generations. Each participant that I interviewed, however, has been involved, to a greater or lesser extent, in the daily activities of the urban Native community, and as such is shaped by and maintains its standards. In this chapter, the study participants discuss the boundaries of Indianness in the Toronto Native community and what they see as central aspects of an urban Native identity. As part of this, they also discuss the central role that traditional spirituality is playing in empowering urban Native people and building a strong sense of identity and community.

THE PARAMETERS OF URBAN NATIVE IDENTITY

One third of the study participants, although personally Native-oriented, come from families where assimilatory agendas are still being actively pursued—where Nativeness is viewed as relatively unimportant to the family's identity. For these individuals, claiming an Aboriginal identity has involved challenging a history of family indifference (and sometimes active resistance) to their heritage. In a culture where family connections define one's Native heritage, having to assert Indianness in defiance of family preference has meant that major aspects of Native identity have been shot through with contradictions for these individuals. Most of them married white people and have had white-looking children. These individuals worried that Native identity might be problematic for their children. They saw it as important that their children feel they had a right to attend events in the Native community, as a person of Native heritage, but believed that their children would have to work out for themselves how they identified, as adults.

The remaining two-thirds of the participants had more extensive Native identification in their families. For some of these individuals, marrying Native partners had been a natural course of development for adulthoods deliberately spent primarily among Native people. For others, their partners were non-Native; however, all were making efforts, through bringing their children with them to Native events, and enrolling them in Native programs, to ensure that their children identified as Native in strong ways.

For all but two of the participants, "Indian blood" was seen as a necessary prerequisite for an individual to be considered Native. Most individuals, however, refused to specify how much blood was necessary, maintaining that Native people were divided enough without instituting blood quantum measurements. One individual considered it important that people have at minimum one Native grandparent in order to be considered Native. Others simply stated that there had to be something in an individual's life experience or family experience that made Nativeness relevant for the individual and that this was really the only valid determinant as to whether a person's Native heritage was sufficient for them to call themselves Native. Most agreed that they tended to accept others' self-definitions, although doubt and suspicion tended to accrue to nonstatus individuals who looked white and who did not have family connections in the community or who could not otherwise demonstrate that they came from Native families. Most of the participants rejected any form of externally bestowed rules about Nativeness, whether in terms of Indian status or blood quantum.

While most individuals explicitly stated that the amount of Indian blood that an individual possessed should not be important, a few participants felt that some aspects of being white-looking are problematic for the Native community, as one individual clarified:

> I've worked in community development now for about six years. And for a lot of Native people that really look Native, who are coming to Native organizations in search of some kind of help, I think it's really important for them to be helped, or work with, people who look Native, because there's a whole trust factor. And it's not just about shared experience—it's all about role modeling.

The fact of racism, the way it "works" on dark-skinned individuals and empowers white-looking individuals at their expense, thus militates against the tendency of many of the participants to accept individuals with any amount of Indian blood as unproblematically Native.

Throughout the interviews an unspoken assumption seemed to be operating that a history of genocide was what made it most important that Native identity require Indian blood—that membership in Indigenous nations (in the broadest sense) should accrue only to those who were descendants of those who had survived the colonization process. Paradoxically, however, it is also because of that history of genocide—in particular, policies of assimilation and colonial regulation of Native identity—that most individuals felt that this requirement of Indian blood should be interpreted as broadly as possible.

All of the participants were concerned with "wannabees"—white people who claim to be Native. Some individuals considered this to be a serious problem, while others felt that the price of having the kind of flexible boundaries on Nativeness that an urban community requires might be that a few "wannabees" might slip through the cracks—but that the cumulative effect of this problem on the community as a whole was minimal.

Two individuals, on the other hand, did not see Native ancestry as a requirement for taking up a Native identity. One suggested that if a non-Native person had been adopted by a Native family and had been raised within a Native environment as a Native person, then they should be considered Native. The other, who closely follows the spiritual guidance of traditional elders of the Haudenosaunee Confederacy, suggested that if white people wanted to learn the spiritual traditions *and live by them*, they should be accepted as members of a Native community. Both felt strongly, however, that individuals should be honest about their lack of blood ties and that something distinctly different was at stake when a person pretended Indianness or when individuals asked to participate in an Indigenous culture *as* white people.

About one-third of the participants felt that it was important to have Native partners, in the interest of maintaining a strong Native identity. For these individuals, having Native partners was important not only so that their children's sense of Nativeness would be stronger, but to reverse a trend in their families, toward marrying white. For one woman, who had regained her status under Bill C-31, it was important that her partner be a status Indian. Because of the second-generation cut-off, this woman could not hand her status down to a child unless she married a status Indian—and she was determined that her child be able to have Indian status, so that Nativeness was not lost in her family. Other individuals spoke more generally about the bigger picture—they felt that at this stage of Native-white relations, Native people needed to marry other Native people to keep Native culture alive.

For one individual, the pressure to have a Native partner stemmed from the strong responsibility she felt to her community, as a member of an important family within her West Coast culture:

It's always been in the back of my mind that I should be with a Native person. In part, I feel this way because of my family's status in our community—the fact that I'm the only child of a person who holds such a high position, who's supposed to be giving out all this information. It gives me a very high position within the community, as well, and so I feel a certain amount of responsibility. Even though I haven't really been raised at this point to fill this position, I still feel that there is some sort of responsibility to the community in that way.

On the other hand, three individuals, two of whom were from reserves, were comfortable with the notion that both they and their children would be Indians no matter what their blood quantum. They thought it was irrelevant whether their children had two Native parents or not and saw no problem with intermarriage. They all reported, however, that as they began to get older they wanted partners who would be comfortable with Native culture in the long run, so that they didn't have to constantly negotiate attending Native cultural events with a non-Native partner.

In general, the participants saw it as much more important that their children knew who they were as Native people than that they looked Native. A few indicated through their comments, however, that looking Native would ensure that the children felt more resonance toward their Native heritage. A couple of participants said that they had found it odd, initially, to have such white-looking children, or that they did not want to have children who looked really white. Several tended to be constantly evaluating, on the basis of looks, whether their children really belonged in the Native community—which suggests that at a gut level, looking Indian is seen as far more important to an individual's entitlement to participate in the Native community than individuals are willing to admit. The strategic denials of the importance of appearance to Indianness do not remove common-sense assumptions that those who choose to identify as Native should *look* Native. Despite this, however, none of the participants—even those who wanted Native partners to ensure that their children were more grounded in Native identity—saw it as important to make sure their children had high blood quantum. The Native partners did not have to be full-bloods—they simply had to be Native, so that their children would have an unequivocally Native identity.

In the urban context, where so many Native people have grown up in silence about the past, and where knowledge of heritage has been severed, the participants all felt that Native cultural identity is something that needs to be actively encouraged. Most felt that self-identifying was important, that individuals should assert their heritage and make attempts to learn about and develop pride in it. Involvement in the Native community was held to be important by a number of individuals, in that Native identity involves a strong collective element.

In speaking of the collective nature of most Native communities, a few individuals spoke of class differences in the urban community. One individual described his perspective:

> The Native community in Toronto is not so much a community as a series of circles. And the thing about the circle that I sort of run in . . . I wouldn't say it's part of a nation or community so much as a certain class of Native people. I mean, probably those who, once

they finish working, go home to a relatively stable environment, as opposed to a lot of our people, who are not so lucky. Toronto has a lot of people who are really in a bad place. But, you know, I always feel welcome with them. I mean, I can walk into Council Fire. It's a rough place, if you've ever been there. I can walk in there and sit down with a bunch of people—and sometimes there'll be some angry young man who won't like you because you've got dress shoes on, or something. But for the most part, I feel comfortable with them.

Another participant, however, spoke of how the economic benefits accruing from her white upbringing enabled her to protect herself from the more negative aspects of urban Native life:

I think I grew up with a lot of privilege, from being with white parents and having access to education and access to lots of other different opportunities. So I know how to protect myself. I take care of myself. I don't get involved in the politics, and that's how I always take care of myself. I don't live at the housing cooperative that I work at. I wouldn't live there for a million dollars, right? I don't need to listen to the gossip. I don't need all that stuff. I do my work, I go home, I have another life. And that's what's always been really important to me. So I can get involved as much as I want—and I can also remove myself.

These perspectives encapsulate a growing contradiction that many urban mixed-bloods are negotiating. On the one hand, they are heavily involved in work that addresses the social problems of the community. On the other hand, for a number of them, the privileges of having an education and a steady income (from those jobs) is used to remove themselves from the daily stresses of Native life—so they will not have to regularly negotiate the devastated circumstances that, on a fundamental level, are still the lot of so many urban Native people in Toronto.

In discussion with many individuals, the question of goals, of what kind of goals the urban Native community ultimately is aiming for, kept coming up. One individual encapsulated his concerns succinctly:

The worst-case scenario for an urban setting is to have a permanent underclass of Native people who are anomic—they are not allowed into the mainstream, and they are estranged from their traditional selves. That's the worst case. One tendency that could challenge that is the emergence of an Aboriginal middle class, a middle class that is promoting cultural pride. But the problem is, are they promoting values that are really Aboriginal? We've got lots of artifacts. Everybody's got an Indian name. We've got the tikinagan in the corner and the beaver pelt on the wall—but, you know, how much depth does that really have? Do we have the collective values anymore?

I mean, class is the great cultural equalizer. I can sit at my kitchen table, which is a middle-class kitchen table. It's not altogether different from a middle-class kitchen table in Tokyo or Bombay, or at my white neighbor's. We're speaking some different languages, eating some different foods, but what do we aspire to? A bigger house, a bigger car, a better school for my kids. These are the things that concern me. So we're not really making community, because we've got some vested interest in maintaining a certain standard of living, which becomes a higher priority.

I think a lot of successful, middle-class Aboriginal people distance themselves from other Aboriginal people because there are a lot of problems in Indian Country. I have had opportunities to take jobs in the north, and I've chosen not to, because I don't want my children to have to deal with a lot of the stresses that go on in northern communities. And I want them to be able to enjoy the kind of benefits that are available in Toronto.

In a sense we're doing what our parents did with us. The only difference is that our parents were closer to the hardships than we are. I mean, my parents were drinkers, and had no education, and all that shit. I wasn't middle class growing up. But I've become middle class now.

Class differences, in this respect, are problematic for Native people insofar as individuals take up an individualistic, consumerist approach, rather than using the social power that class privilege gives them to promote real cultural renewal.

From the experiences of the study participants, it is clear that for urban mixed-bloods, maintaining a strong Native family identity is not easy. A handful of the participants have only come to understand themselves as Native after years of struggling against hegemonic ways of thinking that denied or minimized the validity of their Native identities. In the meantime, they had families with white people and raised white-identified children who fit only uncomfortably or marginally into the urban Native community. Others are uncertain as to whether their children, who by that generation have only marginal Native heritage, should be expected to identify entirely as Native, or whether they should not simply see this as a viable choice for part of their identity. On the one hand, then, the urban community is struggling with the issue of intermarriage and its implications.

On the other hand, however, is the issue of growing class differences and the changes that this often brings to the collective nature of traditional Native life. While class differences are an issue in all Native communities, the pressures of urban life, with its intense culture of individualism, can far more easily push individuals to reject collective concerns for individual benefits. The urban Native leadership may therefore be at risk of growing increasingly divorced from the everyday experiences of poor urban Native people—and therefore unable to facilitate promoting the kind of cultural knowledge and pride that the community needs.

In some respects, it appears as if the concerns of theorists such as Elizabeth Cook-Lynn (1998, 124–31), about the individualistic aspects of urban mixed-blood identity and the negative effects of intermarriage on Native communities, may have some grounding in reality. The nature of urban life—where most work and home environments are organized in ways that ignore the demands of family or community, and where there are few all-Native spaces—encourages a growing individualism that only concerted struggle can challenge. Meanwhile, it is extremely difficult to overcome the assimilatory pressures of white-dominated urban environments. Intermarriage, in such contexts, cannot help but increase the pressures to ignore, or at least downplay, Native-centered perspectives. These problems suggest that although urban Native environments are profoundly strengthened by their flexibility in matters of appearance and intermarriage, there is a limit to the extent to which families can intermarry and still remain Native families. It also suggests that cultural values have to be promoted, particularly as a way of counterbalancing the individualistic pressures that accompany upward mobility in the city. In this respect, the traditional path that many individuals are struggling to follow, and the general investment in promoting Native cultural traditions that marks virtually all of the urban Native organizations in Toronto, bodes well for the future of urban Native people.

TRADITIONAL SPIRITUALITY IN AN URBAN CONTEXT

The participants in this study constantly emphasized the centrality of traditional knowledge and behavior to Native cultural identity. During discussions about this issue, it is perhaps not surprising, given the range of Indigenous nations represented in Toronto, that individuals called on a number of different sources of traditional knowledge.

For one woman, who had grown up in a northern Saskatchewan Métis community, being traditional clearly meant living off the land:

> I can say that I'm traditional, coming from being raised by my grandparents, having them raise me in their traditional ways—a Métis way. But it's not like traditional with the sweetgrass, or other things. We were traditional in that we were isolated. There were not a lot of white people we were exposed to. We didn't have electricity, or running water . . . I grew up with trapping. So for me, I've seen skinning, I've seen meat smoked, fish smoked. I grew up with fish and traditional meats, and they passed all that on. And the uses of certain teas, and bear fat, that are good for certain things.
>
> But it's also the way I was raised, right? The language was passed on, the way of raising children—I grew up in an extended family, where children are never hit; you are taught by example. You don't realize, until you're an adult, the values you've been raised with. My grandmother would teach me things. Like, if I did something bad, she would say, "You shouldn't do that—think about how that person is feeling!" Right? So we were taught to put ourselves in the other person's position, so that we would not do something to hurt somebody. And we were taught by example. They gave us verbal examples. That's the way our morality was taught. So they taught me a lot of things, even though I didn't realize it until I was an adult.

The Passamaquoddy participant called on her memories of childhood teachings from the elders, as well as her family's long association with the land in the community she grew up in, for her sense of tradition and what was important as a Native person, despite her own urbanization and the assimilation she and her family had experienced:

> Living in an extended family was important—like in my early days, when the elders were around and told people things. They taught

you how to set the traps—practical things too, like putting them on a matchbook, so you'd remember where you set them, you know? My uncle used these terrible leg-hold traps, raccoon traps, that clamp the legs. We used to set the traps, but he'd always have a book of matches, and we'd keep track of where the traps were by writing it down on the matchbook—so when you went out the next day you wouldn't be stepping on them. And then we used different roots. It's blurry now, in my mind, because there's nobody to talk to about it. For tonsillitis, we used the root of the skunk spruce. You'd drink that black tea made from the root, and it tasted terrible. You had to gargle with it. But I did it. I was the only person who ever had her tonsils removed in our family, and that's probably because I didn't keep up with the gargling! My mother knew some of those things, and I guess I learned when I was young, so every once in a while I get a snatch of it back.

The part I like about having Native roots, or whatever, is that— when I think back—we were here in the beginning. And it is the natural side, in our family . . . I know that when any one of us is ill, or that sort of thing, that the others of us are there, spiritually. It's not that you're able to move outside your body, or anything like that, but I just think that you can focus. I don't think it's the same with the Christian religion. I think that there's a powerfulness that comes with praying, but I don't think you can do the same thing, with Christianity. It's from my Native side. I don't understand a lot of it. But there's a natural association with the earth, to us—the earth, air, fire, and water.

There is something to it, the valuing of the land. I mean, we've fought for the land, when the town tried to take it away from us. And I remember my older brother saying, "Don't get too excited. We've had this land for two hundred years . . . and we're not going anywhere." I mean, you know, two hundred years—that's a lot of ancestors! I've never had visions, and I don't really feel the power, you know—some people really do feel the power from the earth. For me, it's more that I gain comfort from it. I gain great comfort, sitting on the rocks in my community, watching the ocean, touching the ground.

An Oneida woman, whose mother grew up off-reserve in a small-town environment, described how she learned what she knows about

Native traditions from teachings she has received both from urban elders in Toronto and at ceremonies in the United States and Mexico:

> I think what's important for Native identity is the way of life, and the medicines, and the ceremonies, and the connection with the Creator, and everything that the Creator has given to Aboriginal people. I believe that this has not been lost . . . I don't know what the prophecies say, but I know that we're physically living in a way that's much higher than I can grasp. I guess the most . . . authentic experience, for me, has been in ceremonies with my brothers and sisters in Mexico. And their medicine people have done ceremonies over here. I don't know that I would have gotten this far, in life, if I hadn't gone through the things that I went through in their ceremonies. I went through some major breakthroughs. I've gone through stuff that therapy wouldn't have touched, in some of those ceremonies.
>
> Being traditional, for me, means being kind. It means respect. I think it means helping and caring—working really hard. I really believe in visiting and spending time together, no matter where I am, wherever I am at the time. I love having people over. I think that's something that was always practiced and always done. You didn't visit for a day, you visited for a month.
>
> The loneliness is so deep, and I think it's been in my generation, and my mother's generation, and my grandmother's generation, and further back. There's a lot of work to be done, getting past the loneliness, and working and sharing together again.

For these individuals and others, choosing to follow a traditional life was a way of reclaiming what had been taken from them, through having been adopted, or taught little about their heritage. A number of women spoke about how the traditions provided them with balance and helped uncover suppressed family histories.

One Métis man, who had grown up in eastern Canada, described the tremendous difficulty of following traditions while living in a busy, contemporary middle-class urban world:

> For me—you can cut your hair, put on a suit, you know, sell insurance, and look completely blond and blue-eyed—and still be traditional. It took me a while to realize that fact. I do try to understand and respect traditional teachings. I've been trying to understand

and learn about them for more than ten years now, with sweat lodges, and that. It's been something that has given me so much strength. I think, especially for modern people, being traditional is an internal state, more than anything. It's not a perfect state— it's an ability to be able to slow down a bit and see things very clearly and carefully. To try to respect everything that is in my path, and try to see things as clearly as I possibly can, and to have some sense of trust developed, or an emotional relationship developed, to whatever I am encountering in my environment, before I really open my mouth. To me that's what it means to have traditional values. I mean, there are obviously traditional economies and traditional ways of living—and those are disappearing for a lot of people. But the values, I think, are still there.

Another individual, from an historic Manitoba Métis community, discussed his difficulties with a "traditional" spirituality that included Catholicism:

The traditional Métis spirituality is fairly orthodox Catholicism. But I'm not living that tradition. I go to sweats. I guess I'm pursuing my grandfathers—or grandmothers, I guess, in my case—through Aboriginal spirituality.

To me, the tradition was rural, and I'm urban. I'm the first generation off the farm, off the subsistence farm, and where you went to church. It's impossible to live that life. But in the Native traditions, I see myself as a visitor. Because that's maybe part of this whole question of legitimacy, right? The tradition I grew up in was strongly Catholic. The tradition of my Dakota Indian grandmothers before that? I don't know what it was. What were the Dakota doing in 1842? Were they in sweat lodges? Probably—I don't know.

For a handful of individuals, including those who grew up on-reserve or had maintained the closest ties to their community, their sense of themselves as Native people was not premised on learning about Native traditions. In general, they demonstrated great respect for traditional people, but did not think that this was the route they would follow in life.

A few individuals questioned whether urban Native people are learning what they need to know to uphold and further the cultural traditions of their own specific nations. One Ojibway participant expressed this succinctly:

> If what we're saying makes you Indian is a connection to the community, and a connection to family, and a connection to place—which is what I see as Indian—then the notion of there being an all-encompassing, continent-wide, Indian religion that I have to conform to if I'm going to be an Indian is a ludicrous thing—it's ridiculous. Especially with the people that are touting these pan-Indian ideas. Maybe it is an urban thing that's gone back to the reserve. Because it's on the reserve now, too.
>
> I see some elements in there that may be good. I'm not suggesting that there was never a connection of information or sharing between various Native groups. I think that's a positive thing. And I see it as being of benefit to some people, in the sense that maybe somebody is Indian but doesn't have those connections. Maybe that's what's going to give them the strength and the sense of who they are. But I think urban traditionalism should be used as a stepping stone. It will give you the strength to realize who you are. But use that to find out where you're from. Use that, you know, to find out who you REALLY are.

Others engaged more positively with notions of "pan-Indian" spirituality, viewing the conscious choices made by individuals to embrace and recreate certain aspects of different teachings as an inevitable process in the rebirth of culture and identity. Most individuals spoke of the need for communities—including the urban community—to decide for themselves what traditions and values they wanted to preserve, and noted that this choice was fundamentally all about nationhood.

Three women, however, demonstrated considerable impatience with the emphasis on "traditions" that they had encountered in the urban Native community. They spoke of teachings that were restrictive, too rigidly ritual-bound, and ultimately denying of their own life experiences. They felt that adopting uncritical attitudes toward the notion of "women's traditional roles" was dangerous in its attempt to adhere to precontact concepts of gender relations, without considering the implications for contemporary women of being forced to adhere to roles that may not be appropriate in the highly sexist and racist environment in which we live today.

For example, several women challenged the exclusion of menstruating women from urban ceremonies, from a number of different perspectives. One woman questioned how "traditional" this was, noting that in her northern Saskatchewan Métis communities, it was impossible for menstruating women to ever stop being involved in most activities, since so much depended on their labor. Another spoke of the need for women to challenge where "traditionalism" often situates them:

> You know, there's a real movement down in the States—I don't know about here—but a lot of the Native women are going to sun dance and sweats on their moon time. They say it's misogynous to take women out of these things when they're menstruating. There's one woman that I know, from down in Arizona—she holds sweats and sun dances. And she lets women who are on their time go into the sweat. She says, "I don't believe that political bullshit. That's all it is." She always causes a big stir, wherever she goes. I think it's great, because it gets people thinking: "Was it always like this?"

At the same time, many of the women who commented on how menstrual exclusion fit poorly into the realities of contemporary urban life were very interested in revitalizing certain ceremonial practices, such as the menstrual lodge, so that they would be able to practice ceremonies appropriate to menstruation, rather than simply being excluded. They saw the menstrual lodge as being important in acknowledging the power of women to give life.

Meanwhile, a few individuals raised the issue of homophobia in the Native community. One woman spoke of her need to be vigilant, to ensure that in embracing traditional teachings she was not subscribing to her own marginalization, emphasizing that for two-spirited women, teachings about women's roles were not enough.[1]

NEGOTIATING URBAN TRADITIONALISM

In reflecting on the words of the study participants, it appears that the pursuit of Native traditions and spirituality is playing a significant role in enabling them to maintain or develop an Aboriginal identity in the urban setting of Toronto, where Native people are so marginalized as to be virtually invisible in the mainstream. And yet what is meant by traditional spirituality varied widely among the individuals I spoke with. Those who grew up on the land see traditionalism as a land-based process, which can only be adopted into urban settings with extreme difficulty. Others, who are urban-based but who have been able to learn about their ancestors' practices, feel strongly that the traditions they participate in should be those that their immediate ancestors actually practiced, be it Catholicism or the Sun Dance. Still others partake of local ceremonies different from their own because they are a long way from their own land base and there is no other way in this city to practice any form of Native traditions. With this range of perspectives, it is obvious that in some form or another, revitalization and practice of traditions is important throughout the urban community. At the same time, these accounts raise a number of issues around the validity of urban traditionalism and how "tradition" is being applied, by whom, and to whom.

For example, a few individuals raised concerns about the kind of real grounding in Aboriginal culture that urban traditional teachings were actually providing. In this respect, a schism was immediately obvious, between those who were raised in Native communities and those whose families had been urban for more than one generation. Reserve-based or northern participants were more focused on the role that land-based collective living—hunting, fishing, trapping, gathering berries and medicines—played in the maintenance of their traditions, as opposed to the more abstract or ritualized aspects of traditionalism that a number of urban participants were involved in. This is only to be expected, given that for urban Native people, access to the land is usually restricted to walking in a park, observing the flourishing of weeds in an alley, or cultivating a small garden. In such contexts, it is inevitable that the bulk of cultural practices related to living on the land are simply unavailable to urban Indians. Nevertheless, the fact remains that the strength of Indigenous spirituality lies precisely in its rootedness to the physical world we live in. For urban Native people, an index of their alienation from the land might well be expressed in the extent to which a spirituality of abstract ritual becomes their mode of traditional cultural activity.

And yet, in discussions with individuals, it seems that it is precisely the *range* of practices of urban spirituality (all of which are practiced collectively, but in diverse places and from different cultural traditions) that gives Indigenous spirituality its power as a living practice in urban settings. This flies in the face of the notion of tradition as something to be rigidly preserved or dogmatically maintained as static.

A serious issue, however, related to this concern about the validity of urban spirituality, is the relative lack of emphasis in most urban settings toward relearning Indigenous languages. Individuals described how they sporadically attended language classes and stopped after learning only a few phrases, generally enough to allow them to identify themselves in traditional terms. This approach to traditional values is highly individualistic, enabling individuals to adopt the trappings that can help them to create an Indian identity for themselves, while ignoring the much more daunting (but necessary) task of attempting to learn about the cultural world-view encoded in their language—which is vital to any deeper understanding of what it means to be a member of an Indigenous culture, rather than simply an Indian.

Another problem concerns how women, as well as gays and lesbians, are situated within urban traditional life. It is perhaps useful to consider the words of Cree academic Madeleine Dion Stout:

> The spiritual and material tug-of-war that tradition enacts on Native women touches on our mothering and cultural roles in real ways since women leaders also solicit the support of Elders when we celebrate the continuity of our traditions in their political efforts. However, where men use Elders to reinforce their power and voices, women are often used by Elders to replicate the way in which women have always been expected to practice tradition: going through the necessary passages to bear and care for children. The danger here is that reactionary Elders will hold back progressive women. (Dion Stout 1994, 10)

Dion Stout, in commenting on the rampant levels of wife abuse in many Native communities, has noted that in many settings, Native women are systematically exploited and abused by Native men even as rhetorical statements are made about women being the "backbone of the Indian Nation." She asserts that women must look at notions of the "traditional" with clear eyes and take structural issues into account when considering the position of women. She also insists that traditionalists must become more comfortable with the notion of critical thinking.

It is significant that in the women's experiences, despite teachings that assert the power and centrality of Native women, none of the women could recall any instances of *proactive* spaces for women being made in urban Native traditional circles. Instead, the participants who had received teachings about "women's roles" for the most part described a fairly proscriptive and simplistic set of teachings dictating what they should wear, how they should sit, whether or not they could sing traditionally or play drums, and what they could not do when they were menstruating. Nor was it common, despite this high level of attention paid to the behavior of women in traditional culture, for the presence of women elders to be considered mandatory at traditional events. In speaking with the women participants, the most curious aspect of the gendered world-view that was being imparted to them as urban women was that the maleness of male elders was generally ignored. Because of this, the empowerment that female elders could provide to women, in imparting positive teachings and affirming female authority, was generally not seen as necessary. It was therefore relatively common for the women to attend spiritual gatherings and other events, where few Native women were available to teach the women, and be lectured to by men about what they could not or should not do. By comparison, men's traditional roles appeared to demand few restrictions on male activities within the community—and were always imparted to men by male elders.

Criticism of the changes that urbanization brings to traditional culture—as well as resistance to challenging homophobia, or the place of women within the traditions—is, at the deepest levels, triggered by a long-standing concern in Native communities about the need to protect Indigenous traditions in the face of a history of colonial subordination and forced cultural change. The question troubling Native communities in general, but which is even more relevant in urban contexts, is always, How much change can traditions accommodate and still be maintained as valid cultural practices?

Judith Plaskow, exploring this question with respect to Jewish realities, notes that the nature of fundamental spiritual change is both slower and less subject to conscious manipulation than the question of limits assumes. She suggests that a living spirituality is constantly created and recreated by a people who shape it in ways consonant with their needs (Plaskow 1990, xvi, xvii). Meanwhile, William S. Penn suggests that it is particularly important for Native people to reject notions of the traditional as being part of a more authentic past and to refuse to memorialize images, stories, and meanings of the past as if they were dead—because the dominant culture is highly invested in memorializing "dead Indians" and denying the existence of viable *living* Native cultures (Penn 1997, 107).

Following this logic, the differences between urban traditionalism and the practices in land-based communities should not be seen as evidence that urban traditions are not valid—provided that the urban traditions are filling the needs of the individuals who live by them. In a related manner, Aboriginal women, and two-spirited people, should feel free to challenge the traditions that are irrelevant, contradictory, or damaging to the contemporary lives they must lead, without fear that they are damaging the survival of their nations by asking tradition to change too much.

The Toronto Native community, then, is in many respects highly unique. Community members struggle with the issues of social marginalization and poverty that are faced by so many urban Native people across Canada; however, one powerful strength that the Toronto Native community has in its favor is the existence of a developing middle class capable of building institutions to support Native culture. And yet, this middle class is struggling with the individualism and consumerism that is rampant in urban middle-class white environments. Furthermore, in urban settings, it is clear that being mixed-blood is not *intrinsically* problematic and that, in fact, one of the strengths of the urban community is its flexibility over boundaries, where appearance, status, and urbanity are all (in theory at least) negotiable aspects of Native identity. However, given the fact that urban Native people must live entirely surrounded by white society, there are certain constraints as to how much intermarriage Native families can engage in and still remain Native. This is less a function of "maintaining bloodlines" than a need to maintain Native-centered perspectives, given the overwhelming power of the dominant society that engulfs urban Native people.

It is clear that the institutions that individuals have labored to build and nurture function as replacements for the land base to which urban Native people lack access, in terms of providing environments where Native identity can be nurtured and freely expressed. On the other hand, it is urban traditionalism that appears to be playing a central role in the urban community, as the glue that maintains a cohesive sense of Aboriginal identity for people who at every turn face hegemonic images of Indianness that damage or negate their sense of their own identity.

Because of the highly specific circumstances that urban Native people face in the cities, in which they must negotiate daily coexistence with the oppressor, it is likely that urban spirituality will continue to be modified to fit contemporary conditions, in order to keep it viable in urban settings. The fact that most urban Native people have no land-based practices to inform their spirituality—as well as the issues that Native women, and gays and lesbians, face with how traditional roles are interpreted in contemporary urban settings—will continue to inform struggles around the practice of urban spirituality. In this respect, we can expect that urban traditionalism *will* vary significantly from the face of traditionalism in land-based Native communities and that this should not be seen as a sign that urban traditionalism is not "real" traditionalism—anymore than urban Native people should be dismissed as not being "real" Native people. But this also suggests that urban communities need to develop connections to on-reserve communities, to keep introducing an emphasis on collective values, and to address the realities of language loss. The somewhat daunting task ahead is to try to understand how links can be forged between urban and land-based communities *across* these different understandings (and experiences) of culture, tradition, and spirituality, to strengthen our nations in general—particularly in the face of the legal, experiential, and discursive differences that divide Native communities.

PART 3. COLONIAL REGULATION AND ENTITLEMENT TO NATIVENESS IN THE URBAN COMMUNITY

9

Racial Identity in White Society

Aboriginal peoples' racial identities are fraught with complexities hinging on legal definitions of Indianness, cultural knowledge, and connection to Indigenous land base. In everyday terms, however, Nativeness also depends on how you are defined by others—which, in the white society, depends to a phenomenal extent on how you look.

The white society has had a profound influence on the identities of the study participants. Of the light-skinned individuals, only the handful of those who had spent significant amounts of time in Native communities as they were growing up had an undivided sense of their identities as Native people. For the remaining light-skinned participants, all had been strongly affected, one way or another, by the white society's objectification and fragmentation of Native identity, which impinged on how they saw themselves as Native people.

For dark-skinned urban Native people, meanwhile, racial identity in a white supremacist society is so overdetermined that no "choice" of identities is possible. The hard reality of racial oppression has been, and continues to be, so intrinsic to the lived experiences of Indianness for many of the participants in such powerful common-sense ways that, from this perspective, the existence of light-skinned or white-looking Native people is almost inherently contradictory. White supremacist values must therefore be seen as "working" in numerous ways on the identities of urban Native people: devaluing the humanity and narrowing the options of the dark-skinned individuals and rendering "inauthentic" the Indianness of those with light skin.

RECONFIGURING THE COLONIAL
BOUNDARIES OF RACIAL DEFINITION

Urban Native people are, on a regular basis, surrounded by white people who routinely expect them to *look* Native—and who often challenge their Nativeness if they don't. In this context, a form of resistance for Native people is to look at Native identity solely from the framework of Indigenous nationhood, stating that appearance and blood quantum are irrelevant, and leaving it at that. This amounts to an attempt to decouple Native identity from skin color and blood quantum and to reassert Nativeness as a cultural, not a racial, identity. While this perspective challenges the colonial manner in which white people define Nativeness solely by appearance, it leaves little space for examination of light-skin privilege within the urban community. It leaves even less space for exploring whether the need for racial distinctiveness in a society invested in denying the existence of contemporary Native people is something that urban Native people need to be worrying about.

On a daily basis, the biggest reason for Native people to ignore the relationship between Native appearance and Native identity is pragmatism. In urban centers such as Toronto, there are such high levels of intermarriage that many Native people have children who identify as Native, but who look white, or black, or anything *but* Native. For the parents, light or dark, the manner in which the dominant culture quantifies and denies the Indianness of their children is enough to make them firmly insist that Nativeness has nothing to do with appearance. The reality that intermarriage continues to be a fact of life in urban settings suggests that flexibility around appearance will continue to be maintained in the future—if urban communities wish to survive *as* Native communities. Pragmatism thus suggests that the best option for the urban Native community is to strategically disregard the relevance of appearance to Native identity.

In this respect, the urban Native community in Toronto appears to be following a time-honored tradition of recasting a situation wherein "the Indian"—as defined strictly by blood and appearance—seems (yet again) about to vanish into a situation where survival is ensured. In urban communities such as Toronto, Nativeness is alive and well, if one simply adopts a flexibility around the relationship between race and Nativeness. Georges Sioui describes a traditional Huron-Wendat perspective on a contemporary dilemma:

> In the middle of the seventeenth century, when we became drastically depopulated through epidemics and wars, often caused by missionary interference, we were saved from complete extinction principally because we had matricentrist socio-political traditions. . . . Our wars, which we did wage just as cruelly as anyone, had as their primary purpose the replacement of lost members through capture of enemies . . . and ritually, through adoption, giving them a new life in our Nations. . . . Seeing those young captives, patricentrist leaders would have said, as they often say today about some of their own people: "We have no use for these children: they are white, they are black, they are not Indian. They do not have a proper quantum of Indian blood." And we and other very weakened, vulnerable nations would have soon disappeared. But as I am implying, our good fortune was that we lived within a matricentrist, circular system, where people and other species are not disqualified and destroyed because of not being what they are not. (Sioui 1997, 55–56)

This attempt to be strategically flexible about appearance in the interests of rejecting the white society's perspectives, however, runs headlong into the intensely white supremacist nature of Canadian society, where power and privilege are organized along lines of skin color. In view of the staying power of racial oppression in Canada, how it gets refigured and reborn with each generation, it is worthwhile to consider how well the strategic flexibility that many urban Native people are attempting to exercise around skin color actually works. Most of the darker-skinned participants, for example, manifested contradictory attitudes toward the issue of appearance. Although almost all of the individuals interviewed embraced the notion that "appearance really shouldn't matter," several made comments that revealed how important it was to them, on a gut level, to be able to communicate with other Native people in the street—to have the acknowledgment of other people who looked like them, as they went about their daily lives. From their remarks, it is obvious that on certain fundamental levels, particularly in urban centers, in the face of a history of being subordinated, culturally diminished, and outnumbered by whites, Nativeness and darkness are inseparable and signify, accurately or not, a sense of safety, a shared history of racial oppression, and a shared understanding of community. Because of this, an emotional investment in looking Indian appears to have affected all of the participants, no matter what their appearance.

All of the light-looking individuals were asked if they had ever wanted to look "more Indian." The responses were varied. One woman conceded that she wished she had darker skin but felt that her body type as well as her internal spiritual growth made her look more Native. Another, however, described her anger at people who choose to intermarry without any thought about the repercussions for their children, who will have to negotiate a Native identity with a white appearance and orientation:

> I still do crave to look more Native sometimes. I think part of that's the bitterness toward my mum sometimes, or my parents. It comes out whenever I get little comments from Native people. Like, for example, when I showed my friends' wedding pictures to my auntie, she said, "Wow, they look like pretty white Indians!" And I thought, "My aunt, my uncle, and my dad all married white people. How the fuck do they get off criticizing people for looking too white? Are they gonna turn around and do that to their own kids?" And that's been my bottom line with everybody. "No, don't ever criticize anybody for looking too white—look at you, you're snagging a white woman!"

Some of the participants indicated that their desire to look more Native had coincided with a real lack of knowledge about their own culture, so that "looking Indian" seemed the ultimate arbiter of a Native identity. With a deeper understanding of their heritage they rejected the idea that they could "possess Indianness" by looking Indian. In a related manner, a few individuals, light-skinned or dark, described how when a light-skinned person is fluent in their language, the relative importance of appearance diminishes:

> In my community, there's a lot of blond hair and blue eyes. There's one woman in particular—she's totally fair. If she was away from the community, you'd think she was white. But then her accent is exactly like mine. And because she speaks Cree all the time, I

don't even think twice that she's Native, even though she's blond and has blue eyes.

This participant's words highlighted the extent to which many urban Native people, whether they are mixed-race or not, are insecure about their identities primarily because of loss of language and culture.

In asking the darker-skinned Native people about their attitudes toward light-skinned Native people, some spoke openly about feelings of anger toward those who seemed to be acting as arrogant as whites sometimes did around them. Others found it amusing that light-skinned people should desire to look Indian, given the devaluation of an Indian appearance for so long. Still others mentioned their suspicions that these individuals were really white wannabees. And yet, most of the darker Native people agreed, at least in theory, that appearance was no indicator of who was Native or not.

LIGHT-SKIN PRIVILEGE

Most of the white-looking individuals in this study have had to deal with racist talk about Native people, spoken openly in their presence, under the assumption that they were white. Others spoke of how they have been targeted for asserting their Aboriginal rights or making antiracist interventions. It is clear that the "honorary whiteness" that light-skinned Native people can enjoy if they desire vanishes when these individuals "come out" as Native by challenging racism.

It is also clear, from some of the anecdotes the participants shared, that the racism that other, darker family members are exposed to strongly affects light-skinned family members, as one individual describes:

When that woman was murdered in Regina two years ago, by three white university kids—picked up, beaten to death, and left to die— that could have been my sister. There's a real threat of violence that impacts on my life. It might not impact on me directly, because of my skin color, my hair color, my eye color, but it impacts people that I love and who are very close to me. And because of that, it really affects me. It has implications for me, in my life.

And yet, light-skinned privilege, particularly for those who already enjoy class and gender privilege, cannot be ignored. Every one of the

white-looking participants had received some form of unacknowl-
edged benefit from NOT having to show up with a brown face when
looking for an apartment, in dealing with government bureaucracy,
or in trying for a job in the mainstream. One individual demonstrated
his sudden, visceral realization of his own privilege on moving out
west to attend university:

> I was in Saskatoon, at the Indigenous Bar Association, and there
> were about thirty people in this party. The hotel security raided the
> party and banged on the door and yelled, "Everybody out! Every-
> body out!" And they were giving us all this grief. I came walking
> out, with all these brown faces around me. I went up to the elevator,
> ready to go down, because I was in another hotel. But when a Métis
> woman tried to go back to get her purse, one of them grabbed her
> and radioed downstairs, "Call the police. That's it! We're charg-
> ing this girl." So I went over and said, "What are you doing?" And
> they said, "She's being arrested . . . she's here in this hotel and she's
> not registered as a guest, at this time of night, and she's causing
> trouble." I said, "Oh! Well, I'm not registered as a guest either.
> You better arrest me too." And because they saw me as a white
> onlooker, they let her go.

This story makes clear the extent to which, in some contexts, looking white, especially if the individual has class and gender privilege,
provides individuals with tremendous social authority and privilege,
relative to darker people.

Cherrie Moraga is perhaps best at describing how identity fluctu-
ates according to context for light-skinned Native people, when she
describes how Native people in the southern United States see her
as mixed-blood, while to Native people across the border in Mexico,
her light skin and North American privilege mark her unequivocally
as white (Moraga 1996, 234). Light-skin privilege, then, changes with
location. It is also mediated by class and gender. For the mothers on
welfare that I interviewed, for example, light skin may have provided
them with one less obstacle in negotiating a daily existence; however,
many of the benefits of their light-skin privilege were removed by gender and class marginality. By comparison, some of the white-looking,
university-educated men I interviewed who occupied leadership positions in the community obviously enjoyed tremendous levels of
privilege, utilizing skills and resources from both the mainstream and

Native communities to enhance their personal opportunities. These men, interestingly enough, saw no contradiction in wholeheartedly asserting a fully Indian identity—particularly if they possessed a status card.

NEGOTIATING DENIALS OF INDIANNESS

Light-looking mixed-race Native people, unlike dark people, have the choice to accept or reject a Native identity. Most of the lighter-looking participants have found, however, through their experiences within their own families, that there is no middle ground—they can either "make an issue" (as whites see it) out of their Nativeness or it will be routinely and constantly minimized or denied. The mixed-race people who can pass as white, and who decide that they do not want to participate in the obliteration of their Native heritage, are thus constantly forced to declare themselves as Native, regardless of their appearance. In doing this, they are bucking the tide of common-sense racial classification, one of the foundational aspects of a white supremacist society. All of these individuals face the reality that they cannot meet the expectations of Canadian society, with respect to Indian appearance. Furthermore, they have to negotiate their identities within the Native community, where entirely different sets of rules apply, and where some individuals reject them, others welcome them wholeheartedly, and others zealously police the boundaries of Indianness, carefully noting transgressions. As a result, it is not uncommon for light-skinned urban Native people to negotiate multiple experiences of acceptance and denial of their Nativeness in a single day.

Some of the participants in this study are genuinely ambiguous in appearance; they are sometimes taken for Native and sometimes for white. These individuals, for the most part, describe how this ambiguity makes it difficult for them to feel entirely comfortable either in Native or white environments, because they never know how they are being seen. However, those participants who look entirely white do not even encounter this kind of ambiguous identification with a nonwhite lineage—their Native identity cannot be reconciled to their appearance at all. For these individuals, it doesn't matter how extensive their knowledge of their lineage is, or how much family they have on the reserve, or how stark is the genocide their families have experienced, or how Native-identified they are in a political sense—on a basic level, when they look in the mirror and see a white person's face, it rings false to say "we Indians." These individuals simply live with the contradictions:

> I identified that I was Native through my mother. I was Native through her—I wasn't Native on my own. The first job I got at a Native agency, I brought my mother all the way from Woodstock, to show everybody that she was Indian, that I was Native because I'm her daughter. And I got a photocopy of her status card, so that I could prove any time to anybody that my mom was Indian. I identified that I was Native, but I wasn't identifying within myself, on my own. It was always through her. I was only Native through other Native people—through the partner that I was with, or through affairs with Indian men, or through my mother—because I didn't have that myself. It was always "them and me," not "us." It was never inclusive. I never included myself with everybody else. Like the language that I still use—it's a separation language, it's not an inclusive language. I still use it. I still catch myself doing that, because of my appearance. It's a real dividing line!

One white-looking individual, the only member of her family who did not look either Native or Japanese from their mixed heritage, described a highly contradictory sense of her own identity after a lifetime of receiving multiple labels from whites. This woman, raised in an era when Native people were silent about their identity, recognized herself as a Native woman in some respects, but at the same time frequently referred to herself as white, and commented a number of times that "she didn't belong anywhere":

> Because everybody knew my father was Japanese, and it was just after World War II, I'd get chased home from school, being called a Jap. I'd be on my own, coming home from school, and the kids would come after me with sticks, and yelling "Jap"—that sort of thing. But then one day I went and looked in the mirror and said to myself, "These people are nuts. I mean, look at me!" And after that, once I didn't run anymore, once you're not troubled about it, then they don't chase you any more.
>
> And then there's the thing about growing up with Native blood, that people had no expectations of us. Nobody ever expected that I'd finish high school, or anything like that. So when I got a language prize, in grade nine or ten, the principal's response was "YOU

got a language prize?" We knew all the families—there were twelve
hundred people in that town—but nobody ever expected that any
of us would succeed at anything. And then when I finished high
school, and got a Burke's medal for leadership, again, people didn't
expect anything of me. People just expected that you'd end up in a
ditch like your uncle, anyway.

In those days, you didn't discuss being Native. And when I went
away to university, nobody ever questioned me. I was friends with
the Mohawk students, and the students from West Africa. It's never
occurred to me, but I was probably one of the few . . . white people
who associated with them. Like, I didn't see them as any different.
I think that it was easier for me. Because so long as I didn't talk
much, I fit in anywhere.

The racial ambiguity of light-skinned individuals, who are unable
to wholeheartedly identify as Native because of a white appearance,
has been described by Cherrie Moraga: "We light-skinned breeds are
like chameleons, those *lagartijas* with the capacity to change the
color of their skin. We change not for lack of conviction, but lack
of definitive shade and shape" (Moraga 1996, 232). This condition of
racial ambiguity on the part of white-looking mixed-bloods is commonly interpreted, by darker Native people, as being ashamed to be
Native. However, no amount of Native pride can help white-looking
Native people overcome the basic problem that racial identity in a
racist society hinges to a tremendous extent on how you look. For
many of the participants, this works continually on their ideas about
who they are and the validity of their Native identity, particularly in
the face of the daily denials of Indianness that they face, both from
Native people and from non-Natives.

DENIALS OF INDIANNESS BY WHITES

All of the light-skinned individuals I interviewed described how white
people (as well as people of color) actively denied their Indianness,
sometimes quite insistently, and the amount of work it took to negotiate a Native identity on a daily basis in the face of such denial:

If I mention that I'm Native, white people always like to tell me—
or black people too—"Oh, you don't look Native." And I'll say,
"You know, I really don't like hearing that, so stop." But they'll

keep on saying it, "No, you really don't look Native." And I always have to tell them, "No, you didn't hear me. You have to stop. I don't like that. I'm Native; that's that." So there's always this little conflict, with cab drivers or whoever.

For others, the sheer weight of white supremacist assumptions that would have to be dislodged before white-looking Nativeness could even be seen to exist has resulted in continuous interactions with white people who are simply unable to see them as Native:

It always seems like some kind of trauma when I have to identify myself as being Native. I remember sitting in front of the police chief, up in Sudbury, after I'd spent the night in jail, probably for being drunk and disorderly. My partner and I got thrown in jail, and the only people in that cell that I was in were Native women. There were four or five of us, all Native, but they let me out first. My partner had to stay in for hours after they had let me go. So the chief of police decided to have this discussion with me. I don't know if he was playing father or what. He asked me something like, "What are you doing with an Indian?" It was that blunt; there was nothing hidden about what he was saying. He did not see me as being Native. He couldn't understand it. And I just looked at him, and I said, "You know what? I'm Indian!" And it just floored him.

Another individual described being caught between her own family's denial of their Indianness and white peoples' denial, in trying to assert a Native identity at an early age:

The very first time I dealt with the issue of being Native was in grade six, when I did a show-and-tell. I brought in this really nice red willow basket that my grandmother had made and all this other stuff that we had stored in a closet—this beautiful beadwork pillow, and this other buckskin pillow, and a couple of other things that were from the family. And so I traipsed off to school and showed all this stuff and said, "I'm Native and this is some of the stuff that we have in our home. This is where it comes from. This is who made it," and all this stuff. But after I did that, one of the boys in my class came up to me and said, "You're not an Indian!" And

I said, "Oh yes I am!" And he said, "No you're not," and I said, "Yes I am!" And I went home and told my Mom and she said, "No you're not!" My Mom was really upset because I went and talked about being Indian and brought all this stuff in to show people.

For most of the participants, denials of Indianness by non-Natives functioned as a constant irritant, a form of racism that was monotonously predictable, and only occasionally enraging. While these denials at times created surrealistic and disorienting situations, which the participants then had to negotiate as part of everyday living, for the most part the participants attempted not to take them too seriously. Those who had grown up identifying as white spoke of the years when they had wrestled with a powerful internalized logic that insisted that they could not be Native if they did not look Native; for these people, white peoples' denial of their Nativeness represented additional obstacles to negotiate. On the other hand, those individuals who grew up with a strong sense of Native identity were far more easily able to dismiss non-Natives' attitudes toward them as irrelevant. For all of the light-skinned participants, however, denials of Nativeness from Native people were another story.

DENIALS OF NATIVENESS FROM NATIVE PEOPLE

A number of white-looking or light-skinned individuals described the difficulty of negotiating a sense of Native identity in the face of denial by whites when Native people also made it clear they didn't belong. Many of the participants described multiple experiences of everyday rejection from Native people, as this participant demonstrates:

I remember standing in front of the Native Center, and one of the drummers from the group that was drumming came outside and was joking around with his other buddy there. He looked right at me and called me "Shoganosh." And by then I knew that that meant a white person. I was really insulted and really hurt, because by that time I was already working in the community and doing what I thought was really important work.

I remember, too, when I was seeking treatment for my alcoholism at one of the Native agencies, they had this really long intake process over there. I remember being so uncomfortable in my own skin, and in my own body, because my identity as a Native woman was being questioned—because I didn't look Indian.

One woman described painful incidents that occurred in her childhood, which taught her that she was not valuable to Native people except when they recognized her as her father's daughter:

> With my father being in such a high-profile situation, I would regularly go up to Native elders and start conversations and be dismissed or pushed aside until my Dad introduced me, in which case I was thought of as adorable and lovely. They thought I was white, until my dad showed up, and then suddenly I was So-and-So's daughter and therefore acceptable. I also remember going to conferences with him. One time we were in Ottawa and my dad was speaking, and I fell asleep on a chair—and an elderly Native woman came and pushed me onto the ground and just sat down on the chair. There have been quite a few very painful early memories like that. You know, now I can deal with it completely differently, but it was very painful, when I was younger.

Another woman described a childhood incident where the Native community victimized her. As the daughter of a white policeman, she believes that she was targeted because it was much easier to attack her, and that she therefore represented an easier target than her father for the community's anger. In this case, it was not so much denial of her Indianness that she faced, as the devastating denial of common bonds of humanity from other Native people, because of her association with white authority:

> When I was four or five, we moved to this village, which is a predominantly Native community. My father was a policeman, which meant we lived at the police station. Looking back now, I realize that I didn't have a lot of friends. The Native parents wouldn't let their kids play with me because my father was a police officer, and the white parents wouldn't let their kids play with me because my mother was Native. So it was really hard. I went into the community as this gregarious little outgoing girl, who was really bright, always eager to do things, wasn't afraid to talk to people, that kind of thing. And when we left, I was a shy girl who'd really turned inward—it was hard for me to make friends.

We were only in that community for about a year. I think there was a whole lot of animosity and violence geared toward me from the Native community. One day my mom overhead a couple of Native kids talking about how I was gonna get pushed in front of the train that day. Then an attempt was made on my life. Somebody from the Native community shot at me, in my backyard. Within a week, we were packed up and gone. Because of that, a precedent was set that no police officers with children would ever be transferred up there again.

This individual, however, was accepted and nurtured in the urban Native community as an adult, to the extent that she now feels fully as if she belongs among Native people.

For those individuals who look white, but who have all the other markers of Indianness—status, band membership, and knowledge of lineage and heritage—denials of Indianness by Native people are only occasionally traumatic. For those individuals who lack other markers of Indianness as well, however—such as being nonstatus or lacking extensive knowledge of lineage or heritage—denials of Indianness by Native people can represent a routine devastation marked by a no-win situation. If individuals attempt to manage the situation by not caring if other Native people externalize them, they risk gradually losing their sense of being part of a community, by ignoring the importance of group recognition. If individuals continue to demand to be recognized as members of their community, however, they will continue to routinely face sometimes devastating disappointments.

The violence of racism that darker Native people must negotiate on a daily basis must be seen as integral to the lateral hostility that their denials of lighter Native people's Indianness represents. On the other hand, some participants described experiences where denials of Indianness were clearly used simply to externalize dissent.

THE LIMITS OF NATIVENESS

With individuals who are very mixed-race, occasionally the conversation was brought around to concepts such as "the limits of Nativeness"—the extent to which a mixed-race person with very little "Indian blood," particularly if their families had almost ceased to identify as Native, should be considered to be Native. For some of the participants, such conversation brought the issue of racial ambiguity into the open in ways that made them visibly uncomfortable. Addressing this issue without simply dismissing the Indianness of marginal people demands a flexibility about notions of sameness and otherness that can violate firm beliefs about absolute difference between whites and Native people. The individuals who were most uncomfortable about such questions were not necessarily those who were very mixed-race. Instead, it was participants who had grown up extremely alienated from Nativeness, such as some of the adoptees, who felt it was extremely important to belong, and as a result found it difficult to address racial ambiguity. For a few of the participants, however, who were very mixed-race and knew very little of their histories, unstated anxieties about whether their bloodlines should be considered relevant—whether the point had been reached when they should no longer be considered Native—seemed to be perpetually hovering beneath the surface of the interview process.

Two important issues to consider when attempting to understand "marginal Indianness" are the divergent experiences of Nativeness that mark those Nations with vastly different experiences of colonization and the different types of bonds that tie individuals and families to those communities. A couple of the participants had a sense of being only marginally Native because they came from small East Coast nations that have struggled to maintain themselves against extinction through intermarriage and adaptation to a white norm, but then found themselves living among people with much shorter colonization histories with much more racial distinctiveness. Other participants come from marginal *families*, which have been externalized from Native communities by the Indian Act or other processes of colonization. And some of the participants are reclaiming a marginal Indianness *within* families that for the most part no longer really identify as Native. It is primarily individuals in the last category, whose families' cultural identities have been almost completely erased, for whom claiming a Native identity is often seen as problematic. What, if anything more than "a few drops of blood," separates these individuals from white wannabees?

This is a difficult question to ask, not in the least because the lives of actual individuals are concerned. One way of looking at this issue, however, is noting the extent to which Native culture, in the interests of survival in a genocidal environment, is premised on the notion of hard-and-fast distinctions between whiteness and Nativeness. Lived experience, however, is always far more complex. Even without taking intermarriage into account there are no hard-and-fast definitions of what constitutes Nativeness in a context where blood, culture, and dedication to the cause of Native people have all played a part in the survival of Native peoples. The issue is not that Nativeness is a constructed category, but that Aboriginal identity flows from a complex history of colonization and strategies of resistance, including a history of adopting captured whites into different nations to maintain cultural survival or of having your children abducted into schools where "the Indian" is killed but the (racially Native) person remains. It includes having Native identity carefully regulated according to various standards of blood quantum or "living like an Indian," while at the same time racial segregation ensures that mixed-bloods are treated like Native people, and many other contradictory experiences that makes Nativeness at times an issue of blood and at other times of culture.

It is the precariousness of Native survival under a regime that is still colonial that makes Native identity an extremely complex issue. James Clifford's notion that ambiguity in Native identity cannot be "solved" but must simply be recognized—that there will always be individuals and communities who are white if looked at from one perspective, but Native if looked at from another perspective—is extremely useful here (Clifford 1988). The fact remains that when the boundaries of Native identity are maintained as hard-and-fast but intermarriage continues to proceed, there will always be individuals whose lives fall on the margins of those categories, but who are pressed to identify simply as being one thing or the other. Because urban Native people for the most part reject most notions about the fluidity of boundaries and assert that mixed-bloods must decide whether they are Native or white and live by it, this kind of rigid classification will *inherently* create boundary problems—or, in real life, credibility problems—for those whose racial mixture tends toward the margins of Nativeness.

ASSERTING A HYBRID NATIVE IDENTITY

While engaging with the question of the limits of Indianness is relevant for those participants whose Native heritage is relatively marginal, a number of other participants face another kind of difficulty with the tendency to homogenize Native identity that is prevalent in the Toronto Native community. For these individuals, their central concern is not whether their Indianness is too marginal, but the fact that it is seen as "too different" from the norm. Asserting hybridity is extremely important to their abilities to identify as Native people.

The individuals who assert hybridity most proudly are often those who are multiracial, who refuse to abandon their black or Asian identities as the price of embracing their Native identities. In the context of the Toronto Native community, where fairly rigid notions of Native identity are maintained, these participants' affiliations with multiple communities occasionally cause them to be viewed with some distrust. The African Cherokee participant in this study, for example, described how she did not simply feel pride about her "Africanness" and "Cherokeeness," but also about being a "black Indian"; part of a historical tradition that has a considerable presence in the United States. In Canada, however, where the tradition of black Indianness lacks historical longevity (outside of the Maritimes), she finds the black and Native communities to be disparate and disconnected, each disowning part of her heritage.

On a practical basis, for individuals to see their identities as hybrid is to allow their individual identities their diversity and specificity without dismissing them as *Native* identities. One individual, for example, felt strongly that being mixed-blood was a strength, not a weakness:

> When I look at my circle of friends—most of them are half-breeds. Then there's the odd one that's—well, they may look more Native, but they're really not, they're only half. I find you've got the best of both worlds, but also the worst of both worlds. You can always go over to the white side and fit in, and vice versa. I think I'd rather be a half-breed than to be either side, full. I'm comfortable with it.

In general, those participants who saw their Native identities as hybrid seemed to find it far easier to accept their white appearance than those who believed that the only way to be Native was to conform to rigidly bounded notions of Indianness:

> I've certainly encountered people with attitudes. But right now, and I think probably for the past ten years, my attitude is, basically, if someone wants to call me white, well, that's fine. I'm okay—to

you, I'm white—that's fine. It's not a crime! And some people will call me Anishnaabe, and that's fine too. I think of myself as a bit of both, and something else besides. And I don't know—I guess at this point I'm comfortable with however people perceive me.

At the opposite end of the pole to these individuals were those participants who held views that Native identity was a relatively homogenous essence. This perspective was common among those Native people who had grown up feeling like outsiders, who had an acute desire to belong among Native people. These individuals brooked no ambiguity about Indianness; their struggle involved finding ways to conform to it. They were able to manage contradictions in their self-image primarily through adopting a traditionalist perspective that rejected the importance of appearance to Native identity. This enabled these individuals to be comfortable as white-looking Native people and, therefore, to be less concerned with how other Native people saw them.

For the most part, the uncomplicated notions of Nativeness that these individuals maintained made it hard for them to acknowledge their light-skin privilege. They did not, for example, see identity as context-dependent and therefore were left with no conceptual tools to acknowledge how in some contexts, white-looking Native people have the privileges of whites, compared to darker people (which does not in any way deny that, in other contexts, they face considerable oppression as Native people).

From discussions with the participants, it is obvious that there is a need for clearer thinking on the part of individuals in the Native community—particularly those with rigid perspectives on Nativeness that deny hybridity and the reality of multiple locations—about what it means to be a Native person who looks white, both in terms of the constant dismembering of their identities within both white and Native society and in terms of the privileges that white-looking individuals enjoy. It is imperative, however, to point out that in some contexts—particularly with light-skinned individuals who are low-income with little education—the concept of having any kind of privilege seems to fly in the face of their generally impoverished lives—which suggests the need to understand how gender, class, and location mediates light-skin privilege. The question also arises as to how we can discuss appearance critically without falling into the dominant culture's reduction of identity to appearance. One way or another, the Native community as a whole needs to open dialogue around the issue of appearance more succinctly—without closing down on the current acceptance of a broad range of appearances as Native, which appears at present to be a tremendous strength to the community.

10

Band Membership and Urban Identity

Connections to the land, for Native people, are important in different ways than for settlers in the Americas. For Native people, land is about community, culture, history, and ancestral connection. In that sense, being part of a land-based Native community is at the heart of what being Indigenous signifies.

This would suggest, then, that as urban people, mixed-bloods in Toronto have no grounding in any collective identity. However, this is far from the case. For urban Native people, band membership—even if they are members of communities where they have never lived— carries tremendous significance. In its absence, urban Native people struggle very hard to find ways of anchoring their Native identities in collective ways.

The individuals that I interviewed had many stories to tell with respect to band membership—about being reinstated as band members, about being denied membership in their parents' communities, or about what band membership meant to their families. Other individuals who lacked such connections spoke of the ways that they struggled as urban people to ground their identities in a sense of community. During the process, the participants also discussed the meaning of place to Native people.

BAND MEMBERSHIP IN THE CITY

As chapter 3 described, after the passing of Bill C-31, a fury of struggle erupted in a number of communities, along gendered lines, over entitlement to band membership. However, despite this, most of the individuals I interviewed had had positive experiences with their bands in terms of being accepted as band members.

Three individuals, who had visited their reserves regularly as children, had never had any doubt that this was their home, even before they got their status and band membership back. Two others, however, spoke of the warm feeling they got when they visited their mothers' communities for the first time after acquiring band membership—a feeling that this, finally, was home for them. It is obvious that to a phenomenal extent, band membership provides urban status Indians with a sense of community acceptance and a deep sense of entitlement to a Native identity.

Ties to community are not necessarily always experienced as pleasurable. One individual described the difficulty of reentering her father's community as an adult after a long interval of separation from him because of his sexual abuse. She faced considerable problems in living there, because her community is still dealing with a legacy of violence stemming from residential school:

> I tried to spend a summer in my father's community when I was twenty-four. My father was living in the community at the time. It was a very, very difficult summer. Part of the problem was the realization that I wasn't going to be able to have a father-daughter relationship with him—that if anything was going to develop between us in the future, it would have to be in terms of us as adults, and in a completely different setting. But it was also the politics of the community. It's a very small community. There are only about 100 or 120 people there in the winter. The kids only come back in the summer.
>
> There's such intense politics within the community, and it's not like you go to work and deal with the politics and escape them by coming home—it just follows you everywhere. Family politics, band politics—the two are interrelated. There are abuse issues that haven't been resolved and people that just hate each other as a result of that. And then you enter the community and people are saying, "You know, you really shouldn't talk to this person or that

person," and you're trying to say, "Well, I'm my own person. I have to make my own decisions." And I was trying to identify myself as my own person, rather than as a member of my father's family, and especially as his daughter, which came with its own stigma, even though I had been away for so long. Partly that was because everybody knew what he'd done to me, and partly it was because he was the main representative of a family that they might be at war with, the other main families in the community—and partly it was because he's a very political person, and they would or would not agree with his politics. From a number of different perspectives.

Despite the damage that colonization has done to the life of the community, for this individual, her visits to the community remain a real and grounding experience of collective bonds, which ties her to a Native identity that would otherwise be relatively abstract.

Of the seven individuals I interviewed whose status was reinstated under Bill C-31, only one person has not been accepted for membership by her band. In contrast to the tales of belonging and the sense of entitlement spoken of by the other participants, this individual described the alienation she feels:

I suppose I did at one point feel rejected. Now I don't even give it a thought. I keep trying to think about it from their point of view, so I say to myself, "It's not surprising, is it?" I might have felt differently, I might have felt more connected, if they had accepted me. I might have felt that maybe I should go up there and teach. It would have been good if they had been able to help me with my education. I think I would have felt different.

I've severed some emotional ties there now, whatever emotional ties that were there. I was curious, and I was kind of high on this for a while. I know now that that has worn off. It doesn't make sense for me to try and fight for membership, when the community is so far away. Now, if it was within a hundred miles, that would be different. But because of the work involved, I'm not willing to chase that down and fight for it. Maybe if I was younger, and thinking of moving up there to live, work, and teach, then maybe I'd try some more—but I've kind of resigned myself. I'm too old to relocate. I'm gonna start needing medical services soon. See, the only relatives I've got up there live in an adjacent town and they're not band members either. I have no living roots that I know of there—although it's hard to trace relatives, too, because our name was translated into English, and I'd have to work with translators, because everybody up there speaks the language. I've probably still got some relatives there, but I don't know who they are.

The participants who had been reinstated all discussed the issue of entitlement to band membership at length. The interesting feature of these discussions was the manner in which the participants, once their own reinstatement had been effected, usually situated themselves within the mainstream of their bands, as if their own entitlement to band membership had never been in question. They would judiciously discuss the predicaments of those individuals they knew of who had been rejected by their bands, as if they had nothing in common with these individuals. Two of the participants, in particular, who were themselves reinstated Bill C-31 Indians, engaged in some aspects of "blaming the victim," expressing some level of belief that if individuals did not get reinstated by their bands, they probably didn't deserve it.

In almost every instance, the dialogue around reinstatement focused on the *intent* of Bill C-31 Indians in asking for band membership. This only reinforced the sense that each individual had to prove themselves worthy of being reinstated before they should be accepted as band members. It is clear that the forced estrangement of so many children from their mothers' home communities has been individualized in the minds of most Native community members. In no way has Section 12(1)(b) been seen as a *collective* violation of the birthright of Native women and their children. While most of the participants expressed in an abstract manner that it was an injustice not to reinstate people to their bands, most of them implied that Bill C-31 Indians must demonstrate the *right* reasons for wanting reinstatement (selfless devotion to community) rather than the *wrong* reason (looking for education funding or other financial benefits from the band). And yet, all of the status Indian participants who had band membership expressed pleasure at the educational assistance their bands had provided them and showed no sign of any deep sense of obligation to the band in return. A selfless desire to put the wishes of the community before one's own educational or other needs is, in fact, demanded of nobody *but* individuals seeking reinstatement after Bill C-31.

Furthermore, the restrictive or suspicious attitudes that many have demonstrated, in particular toward the children of women who lost their status, with the notion that they are "outsiders" whose dedication to Native people must be proved (or at least brought into consideration) before they can enjoy their right to band membership, needs to be compared to the fact that white women who married Native men (including the white mothers of some of the participants) have for many years enjoyed the privileges of automatic band membership (and in many communities continue to do so) without the issue of their dedication to the community ever being raised.

For the most part, the participants' experiences suggest that communities are more open to reinstating Bill C-31 Indians than the controversy around Bill C-31 would lead us to expect. It is worth pointing out, however, that for each participant, the burden of proof has been on them to find relatives who can vouch for them and convince the band to let them in. In this respect, it is safe to say that bands have not seen the loss of Indian status and band membership for Native women who married non-Native or nonstatus men as a violation of a Native person's birthright. On a collective basis, the First Nations have not acted as if the Indian Act has violated their sovereignty by over the course of a century forcing a total of twenty-five thousand band members and possibly one to two million of their descendants to leave their communities.

On the other hand, it is clear that bands *have* viewed the massive— and more recent—theft of Native children from their communities by Children's Aid as a violation of their sovereignty, so that they generally make every effort to repatriate these children to their bands, as this individual's experience of repatriation demonstrates:

It took me four years to get Indian status. One of the first things I did, when I was looking for my father, was to register with DIA's adoption registry. But my birth father's name, which my birth mother told me about, had never been put on my birth certificate, so there was no paperwork to match it up. It took some trying, to find my father's band—but then when I did, they told me that he was deceased. But they have a family services association up there, which assists adoptees in getting reunited with their families. So I put together a little budget and they flew me out there to meet my birth family.

I told them, "I want the reunion to be on the reserve, at the traditional powwow." I didn't know at the time that my whole family had been off-reserve for the last three generations. But they were obliging. "Okay—I guess we'll go to the reserve for the powwow.

We never go to the powwow, but we'll do it for you." So I flew to
Winnipeg and met my auntie there. We stayed overnight, and then
she drove me out to Fort Frances, where my grandma lives. We
had a motel that they paid for, and we all stayed there, and had our
reunion. Then we went to the powwow for two days—so I got to
dance there at least once. They showed me the burial mounds, that
are eight thousand years old, and the rapids were just beautiful, and
there was an eagle flying over the top of the powwow. Everything
was amazing.

After I met my family, they vouched for me, and they went up
to the chief. The chief and my uncle were pretty good buddies in
business, so I guess they put it through. And my status comes from
my father so I'm not a Bill C-31 Indian or anything like that—I'm
just a plain old status Indian. The band council voted on it and made
me a full member. It all worked out after I had met my family.

These accounts clarify a couple of issues on the subject of band membership. First of all, it was obvious from the comments of individuals
whose bands had reinstated them that band membership, with its implication of community acceptance, is probably the primary means
through which Native people secure a sense of their Native identity.
Indigenous identity, despite years of state regulation, remains both
collective and highly place-specific. These two aspects are intimately
related—it is ties to place that enable people to maintain collective
ties.

And yet it is important to recognize that most of the individuals who see their reserves as "home" have not actually spent much
time there. Nor do they plan to do so. It is therefore obvious that the
significance of band membership for urban Native people is highly
symbolic, especially if they did not grow up around Native people, and
secures for these individuals a sense of being grounded in a collective,
place-based identity, even if that identity is in some sense an abstract
relationship. Having a reserve to point to as a homeland, where one's
family has been part of a web of relations within the community,
anchors these individuals in profound ways as Native people, even if
most of the actual connections they develop in their lives are within
the urban Native community. One individual has described the sense
of rootedness that comes from knowing that your ties to a region are
ancient:

My family's been living here ever since there WAS a here. And not living here like living on the planet. I mean, living here like pretty much in the same place they're living now. The Great Lakes area is where they've lived the whole, entire time.

NEGOTIATING PLACELESSNESS IN URBAN NATIVE LIFE

For Native families who lack concrete ties to specific places, there is little to ground them in a sense of collective identity. For the seventeen participants of this study who do not have band membership or other long-term collective ties to specific lands, a major problem that they face is that they are *truly* diasporic. These individuals, whose families have been uprooted and scattered and who therefore cannot point to a specific place and say, "This is where I still belong," all commented, in one way or another, about the problem of being a member of an Indigenous nation *in the abstract*.

> For me, what's even more important than the status issue is not having a homeland that I can point to and say, "This is where my people come from." Because for me, my family background is this nebulous territory in the middle of Manitoba somewhere. So if I say, "I'm a Cree from Manitoba," and then I meet another Manitoba Cree, they'll say to me "Who the hell are you?" I mean, I grew up in Ottawa. It's kind of a fictional tie. I don't have a homeland, I guess.

The participants have all developed different ways of anchoring their somewhat abstract identities, on a personal and familial level. One way of establishing longevity and ties to place was through tracing lineage. If individuals could trace their lineage for several generations within specific communities, even if they no longer had any direct connection to that community, they still felt themselves to be rooted in that place. One of the adoptees, for example, conducted extensive genealogical research going back several generations. Knowing that she has significant family roots in the territory around Rainy River connects her in deep ways with an Ojibway tradition that is ancient. This individual may not have the stories of her ancestors— but she knows that she carries that continuity through her lineage. In many ways, the solidity of this connection diminishes the importance of her individual experience of adoption and alienation, because the ties that bind her to her Ojibway heritage are much older and deeper—precisely because those ties are still rooted in the region of their origins.

This individual's experience highlights an important function that such ancestral ties to specific regions play for many urban Native people, in diminishing the significance of otherwise-devastated family histories, by countering their genocidal implications with the knowledge that the upheavals that they and their immediate families have experienced are by far not "the whole story." Ancestral ties to place have enabled urban Native people to survive colonization *as* Native people—the stories may be lost, but the connections to the land based on lineage are still there.

Language was another vehicle that the participants saw as important for grounding individuals in their culture. The one participant who was fluent in her language described how differently the world looks from within the Cree language. Because language shapes thought and custom, and therefore behavior, knowing one's Indigenous language is essential to a really strong grounding in one's culture. One woman, who has made repeated attempts to learn her language, and who still plans to develop a working knowledge of it, spoke about how she saw language as anchoring her to her heritage in bodily ways, despite being diasporic:

> For me, it feels like—language is where you draw your nationhood, your identity from. It's like, what language are you from—that's where you come from, that language. It's not just words. I feel that there's a physical presence of something.

This participant also spoke of the more ephemeral aspects of identity, including the linking of ancestry, embodied knowledge, and relationship to land that is often referred to as "blood memory." For a number of the participants, flashes of what seemed like memories linked them to the past in ways that seemed to physically ground them in their ancestral heritage:

> The other day, I was chopping some meat, and suddenly my body felt like this was something that we've been doing for years and years and years. There was just a flash where I thought . . . I was somebody from two hundred years ago and, you know, I knew that this person was here—and we're still doing these things; these

things don't change. So there's a sense of something else too, besides the language, which grounds us in our identities.

Another individual also spoke of the connections between land, embodied heritage, and ancestors, in ways that clearly—and yet spiritually—anchored his sense of *political* entitlement:

> This is our home. It's in our blood, eh, in our psyche. This is where our ancestors were—it's all here. They're all here, all the spirits are here. The spirits of our ancestors are here, in this continent—not in another country.

The adoptees, in particular, who have had to deal with extreme feelings of loss for having been taken from their families and communities, tended to feel even more strongly that Nativeness was "in the blood" and could not be erased:

> Because of the very difficult relationship I had with my parents, my adopted parents, I honestly believed that our breakdown in the adoption was so much about seeing the world from two completely different places. Because even though they raised me in their value system, I'm a really firm believer that you have blood memory, and you have . . . something . . . As a Native person you have something in there that they would never be able to relate to. And that was just always a struggle that I had, and I just really believed that I was really different, and they would never understand me because I was Indian.

Some of the participants who had grown up white-identified described the sense of belonging that they felt when they first encountered Native people. Being around Indian people "fit" their lives in ways that they hadn't known they were looking for:

> I dropped out of school real early and started that whole partying scene. And my first parties were with these two Indian brothers, all the way from Ingersoll—and I hitchhiked. I'd go to Ingersoll, and that's who I did my drinking with. It's interesting that you can always find your own people, in maybe the town over, or the city over. To have never met each other, and then you meet each other and it's like coming home. "Oh, finally! Let's hang out!"

Others referred to an emotional bond that they felt as Native people to a collective past:

> Okay, there're two levels that I base identity on. My more intellectual response would be, "People identify that way for solid reasons, like family. This gives them their sense of who they are." The more gut level part of it involves in some way . . . being confused about it. Being part of the "lost generations," I think. It's more of a feeling, that way, of being part of an historic process, even of loss and pain, which is significant somehow. Like getting a feeling from people . . . that it means something to them. There's an emotional identification. It's not just saying, "Well—this is who I grew up with, and this is where I'm from." It's definitely . . . emotional. A lot of people will talk about the first time they heard the drum. I think that that's central, that emotional connection. It's like family, almost.

Given the extent to which concepts like blood memory are used to explain an ephemeral feeling of connectedness to other Native people, it seems important to examine this concept. I do not wish to engage with sociological or other critical theory perspectives that would simply dismiss such a concept as "essentialist." Instead, I will consider what the idea of blood memory enables and secures for Native people (by way of making clear how a rationalist dismissal of blood memory in some sense disempowers Native people). In a country where a powerful body of white politicians and scholars have for years maintained a monopoly on defining Indianness, and where Native peoples do not control the discourse that controls our lives, the concept of blood memory cuts through the pronouncements of "Indian experts," insisting that we are Indigenous because our bodies link us to our Indigenous past. In a country where "authenticity" is always demanded of Indigenous subjects, we do not have to justify our mixed-bloodedness or lack of Indian status, or to wait for courts and legislation to decide who is Indian, who is entitled or unentitled, and to internalize that logic—our bodies tell us who we are.

The concept of blood memory also reassures us as to our cultural survival. For a people who have had much of their knowledge of the past severed, blood memory promises a direct link to the lives of our ancestors, made manifest in the flesh of their descendants. In a country where countless past generations have been educated to have "the Indian" removed from the person, where Native people are pinned down by those who control them, where urban Native people are anxiously trying to discover what remains of the cultures so apparently erased or abandoned in the interests of survival, blood memory promises us that we can claim our ancestors' experiences as our own, that we can recreate our cultures based on what we carry in our genes. For people damaged almost beyond recovery by oppression, it offers us the strength of our ancestors to survive and persist. Blood memory, therefore, is incredibly seductive, in this postcolonial moment for urban Native people, as our nations continue to be dismembered, as racism escalates, and the colonizer's logic reigns unchecked—as our colonization, in fact, continues unabated.

In many ways, blood memory is something that is also impossible to deny. In deep ways, our bodies *do* have a knowledge all their own, and the site of memory, of handed-down memory, and of ancient ties to place, cannot simply be dismissed as "socially constructed." As Cherokee theologian Jace Weaver comments, the importance of historical events to heritage and identity are passed down through story from generation to generation, until such cultural coding exists finally beyond conscious remembering, so deeply engrained and psychologically embedded that one can describe it as being "in the blood" (Weaver 1997, 7). The notion of blood memory has deep value in traditional thought, and for many of the participants, blood memory has been an important way in which their families "kept the faith" to an often ambivalent sense of collective identity, despite entire lifetimes spent placeless and almost invisible, in the heart of the dominant culture.

Some individuals have developed personal ties to specific reserves through networks of friendships, which they see as rooting them in some respects in a relationship to a land-based community. Others involve themselves in urban spirituality as a means of grounding themselves within nature even in an urban environment. Finally, many of the participants have developed strong community ties, through work or activism, within the Toronto Native community.

PERCEPTIONS OF URBAN AND ON-RESERVE LIFE

It is useful to ask those who have lived in Native communities most of their lives what becoming urban has meant to them. For a northern Métis woman, urbanization—even the process of embracing an urban Native cultural orientation—was described as acquiring white values:

> I've been noticing now when I go home—because I've been away for fifteen years—that I'm feeling disconnected with my culture. Especially being in the city. Because people in the city, young people, are trying so hard to find themselves and find their culture. In the city, we do things like traditional singing, using sweetgrass—and we try to have a cohesive Native community. You know, you go to the Native center—we do things like that. And then I go home, and I'm not quite fitting in now. It's like white values have come into my head a lot. So my friends treat me a little bit differently. They'll give me a clean cup. Whereas before, they'd say, "Get it yourself." But now they're treating me like I remember treating white people. You know? Not to that extreme. They don't run and hide in the bedroom.
>
> When I was growing up, if a white person came to the door, then everybody would go hide right away, so that there'd only be one person there who had to talk to them. That's exactly what happens. And it's not that bad, the way they treat me—but it's like I'm getting further away. And I hate it. It's very hard. Because I remember, when I was at home, and my aunts who had been away for a long time would come and I would be shy with them, because they were like strangers. They had married white men, so they brought their white husbands along for a visit. And it was just more formal.
>
> I feel that people are a little uncomfortable when I go to visit. It's because some of this urban stuff has rubbed off on me, right? Even the joking—the way you joke at home is you put each other down. But it's not really putting them down, the way we do it. But in the white society, it's putting somebody down. Like calling somebody a dirty spoon, it means "you dirty cunt," right? I used to whip out those comments like nothing—"Hello, you dirty spoon!" But now if I go home and say that, they'll look at me like I'm insulting them—because I don't have it any more.

Another individual, from a southern Ontario reserve, did not experience such extreme differences in values and lifestyle, which speaks to the heterogeneous, semi-urban nature of his community. For this

individual, leaving the reserve primarily meant a greater politiciza-
tion, through working as a journalist and having had the opportunity
to visit numerous other reserves and becoming more familiar with
the power structures of white society.

A few of the participants strongly felt that because they grew up
off-reserve, their Indianness was flawed or in some ways inferior to
that of on-reserve Native people, even though they also sometimes
expressed an awareness that there was very little actual difference
in the lived experiences of the people on the reserve, as compared to
their own lives, in some cases lived right next door to the reserve.

One woman, however, described how her own sense, growing up,
that she was not "Native enough" for being from off-reserve, has
changed:

> I could be branded here for saying this—but a lot of people who
> haven't grown up on-reserve have for some reason retained a lot,
> in some cases a lot more, Indian ways of thinking. I don't know
> what it is. But there's something there. It's in the blood. You can't
> just get rid of it by moving to the city. It keeps coming back.

Other individuals noted that being on a reserve was only an interval of Native experience, not a primeval state of being. One adoptee
was adamant about challenging Native people who claimed a superior
knowledge of Indianness through growing up on-reserve:

> I think on-reserve Indians might have the feeling that their link is
> stronger, through the generations, because they've not been taken
> away or whatever. But I've had people tell me that they grew up
> in Saskatchewan, like a real Indian with horse and buggy, and I
> tell them: "No, no, no—you did not have a pre-Columbian experi-
> ence." This is my bottom line. I tell them: "I went through major
> oppression as an adoptee. I survived it all alone. I could have killed
> myself way back then, and you'd never have even known about
> me. Fuck you."

Another woman concurred with this, that given the genocidal nature
of the experiences of forced urbanization and assimilation that so
many Native families come from, these diasporic experiences that
individuals and families carry must be seen as part of their nations'

history, rather than the individual "accidents" they are usually assumed to be:

> Being adopted is a Native experience! Being mixed-race is a Native experience!

One woman suggested that Native people had to rethink what was meant by "Indian land"—that when Native people agreed to limit "Indian land" to reserves, they were ignoring the fact that all the land had once been theirs. Meanwhile, several of the participants were careful to specify that while many reserve Indians clearly had greater access to cultural heritage than most urban Native people did, some reserves were so dysfunctional with alcoholism, or so permeated with fundamentalist Christianity, that they could not fill this function. Other individuals felt that each situation had its pros and cons—and noted that the divisions between on-reserve and off-reserve people—especially with respect to the southern reserves near urban centers—were not as hard-and-fast as some on-reserve people made them out to be. Nevertheless, these individuals also asserted that simply because reserve Indians interact more on a regular basis with other Indians, this made them "more Native" in their orientation than urban Native people are.

One individual, who had worked in both on-reserve and off-reserve settings, saw it as important that both sides work together, because both had strengths to offer each other. Another pointed out that to her, as an urban Native person, on-reserve people, particularly those from the north, had many gifts for her to learn from:

> My feeling is that we all have different experiences, but we're all Indian people. And so I know that some of the people that come from the northern communities are truly gifts for me, because they seem to have this wonderful . . . quietness, a quietness that I really have a lot to learn from. So I feel that every experience provides something to learn from. I see the urban Indians, and I see the First Nations communities in this area—and they're struggling with different things. And then the people from the north—they're more connected to the land. I'm much more attracted to that, because they have something to teach me. They've taught me about the importance of family. And the laughter, right? The laughter, the

food, the community—they're tremendous gifts to me. Because I never experienced that.

LIVING OFF-TERRITORY

A crucial issue with respect to being urban is whether the individual is living in the same territory as their Indigenous nation. The participants in this study are perhaps quite representative of the diversity of Native people within the Toronto community, in that they come from thirteen different Indigenous nations. However, one third of them are Mohawks, Oneidas, or Ojibways from reserves that are very close to Toronto. For the other twenty participants, living in Toronto entails living in Ojibway territory as a non-Ojibway person.

These participants' experiences ranged from those who had grown up in Toronto and had never been to their home territory to those who were closely linked to their communities of origin but had lived in Toronto for several years and so had a Toronto-based identity as well as a "home" identity. The majority of the off-territory participants, however, came from backgrounds where they had no remaining family on their traditional territory, or had grown up not knowing where their original community was, through forced dislocation. Their identification with their Indigenous nation was mainly in the abstract. For these people, the most concrete identity they had was as urban Native people, and for the most part, they saw adaptation to (or even absorption into) the local norm as the only way to live as a Native person. One individual, of Cree and Saulteaux heritages, describes her realization that there is no going back for her and how as a result she has chosen to become more involved in Ojibway culture:

At one time I wanted to go back and reclaim my Creeness. I wanted to move to the prairies, learn the language, and try to learn more about what it means to be Cree. But now that I'm probably going to be staying in this region for good, it has occurred to me that I feel an affiliation to Ojibway culture. So now I would like to learn that language and perhaps follow that spiritual tradition a bit more.

So as far as seeing myself as part of some kind of community, or how I trace myself, I guess I've taken the tack that I have to look forward. There's no going back—I can't really make those connections to who we were on the prairies. But I'm building a life here as part of this community instead. The culture I'm learning about may not be the one that I come from, but it's as close as I'm going to get, around here, anyway.

The African Cherokee participant also described how she has gradually become deeply involved in the Mohawk traditions. She feels clearly that because the Cherokee and Iroquois peoples have common linguistic and cultural roots, the fact that she is drawn to Mohawk culture is a natural affinity.

Those individuals who had had a deeper access to their own cultural background before coming to Toronto felt too grounded in their own cultures to attempt to grow toward an Ojibway or Mohawk norm. However, their attempts to continue to learn about their own particular cultures were hampered by the lack of elders from that culture in the community and the lack of access to instruction in their own language.

The participants' words seem to suggest that with respect to issues of territoriality and extraterritoriality, living far from your own territory is only an issue to those individuals who have been strongly exposed to their culture as children, or who grew up in their communities of origin. The rest of the participants tended to adopt an urban identity coupled with a somewhat abstract identity as "a member of a specific nation" (rather than a very concrete location-based identity). Those individuals who had been definitively severed from their own contexts frequently spent a number of years living in hope of some day being able to go home to their villages where they might somehow recreate themselves within their ancestors' identities. In many cases, however, these individuals eventually became pragmatic and gradually began to absorb cultural teachings either of the Mohawk or Ojibway Nations.

In discussing the various issues involved with being land-based, two sets of problems have arisen. On the one hand, there is the real connection between being land-based and maintaining collective ties to identity, which each participant engaged with from different locations. On the other hand are the hegemonic perceptions about Indianness—the immense body of stereotypes within the dominant society that link Nativeness inextricably to an on-reserve environment. For the most part, the participants were relatively clear that they did not subscribe to knee-jerk ideas that on-reserve Native people simply were "more Indian" than them because Indianness requires a reserve experience.

Their responses, rather, indicated a comprehensive awareness both of the strengths that being reserve-based brought to Native identity, and of the reality that a considerable amount of interaction and cross-fertilization is taking place at present between the more southern and urban reserves and urban centers like Toronto—and that these interactions are important for both urban and on-reserve communities.

Several participants saw a need for on-reserve Native people to deconstruct the sense of "real Indianness" that being from a reserve generates. They suggested that Native people in general need to be clearer about what actual differences (and similarities) exist between on- and off-reserve Native people, rather than simply asserting in a blanket manner a sense of absolute difference. To continue to assert this notion of absolute difference is to promote the idea of reserves as culturally homogeneous communities, which ignores the real differences *between* First Nations, semiurban and rural, north and south, east and west.

On the other hand, the participants were also aware that being land-based was vitally important to maintaining a viable Indigenous culture, and that in this respect, for urban Indians, asserting a Native identity can be a highly contradictory enterprise—one that might continue to require unique and fresh approaches both in understanding what constitutes an Native identity, in building bridges with land-based communities, and in finding ways to deal with the issue of extraterritoriality and, in particular, with loss of language.

11

Indian Status and Entitlement

Urban Native communities are diasporic environments, composed of families and individuals who migrated to the cities from their home communities. Many individuals came to the cities because residential school alienated them from their homes; others came to find work after resource development made it impossible for their families to live off the land. Others continue to come because their reserves are economically unviable or to escape violence in their communities. But to a phenomenal extent, urban centers also represent the places that Native people migrated to because they lost their Indian status or never had it in the first place and therefore had nowhere else to go. From this perspective, urban Native communities are to a tremendous extent composed of the fallout from government regulation of Native identity.

Urban Native communities are unique in other ways, in that these are the only environments where status Indians and nonstatus Native people are able to work together in the same organizations, because these organizations are not funded on the basis of strict status distinctions, as they are on reserves. In this respect, Indian status in urban settings does not have to signify what it generally stands for in reserve environments. And indeed, for many urban Native people, their experiences with government regulation of Indianness have highlighted the racism and sexism of the Indian Act, and its utter inappropriateness as a vehicle for determining who is a Native person. Not having Indian status, or having it unequally granted for different members of the same family has impinged on their families' livelihoods, on their access to culture, and has affected, in deep ways, how they see their Native identities. It is perhaps not surprising then that for many nonstatus Native people, deconstructing the meaning of Indian status is central.

This, however, is frequently not the case for those individuals who have Indian status, particularly if they have never lost it. Many of these individuals have a highly politicized understanding of Indian status and see it as central to the survival of Native people. In this chapter, I will explore these perspectives in more detail, by beginning with those who are excluded from status.

MÉTIS PEOPLE AND INDIAN STATUS

If government categories of Indianness represent a war of jurisdiction over who has the right to define an Aboriginal identity—Native people or the government—then one group of casualties in this war have been the generations of Métis who have lived traditional lives out on the land, as well as experiencing tremendous marginalization and racism in the cities, but who have internalized the government's logic that disqualifies them from Indigeneity.

One very dark-skinned, Native-looking participant described how growing up off-reserve as Métis meant that he would forever feel the need to qualify calling himself Cree or even Native:

When I was about twenty-one or twenty-two, I started defining myself as a Native person. Not a Métis, because when somebody would look at me, they'd say, "No, you're not a Métis You're Native"—you know, that type of thing, because of the color of my skin and because of my features, because some of the Natives were lighter colored than I was. So I started defining myself as Cree, which wasn't exactly true, because both my mother and father came from Métis families. Now maybe one was more predominantly Native than the other, but they were both from Métis families. So how I define myself now is as Native, but still it's not the truth. I don't really come from a Native community—I was brought up in the white society and always participated in the white activities, went to the white school, and the whole bit.

The only real inkling that I got that I was Native was when I'd go up to my mother's community and I'd hear a different kind of language and then look at some of my cousins, and whatnot, and say, "Oh yeah, they're the same as me," but they'd be Native. So it's not really the truth to call myself Cree or Native, because I never really did live in the Native community.

Another participant described how her mother also could not see herself as a "real Indian," despite her Native appearance:

In the last few years, I've continually said to my mother, "Mom, you don't know how many people that I have met that have blue eyes and blond hair, but they think of themselves as Indian!" And maybe they're not full-blood, but they're Indians, as far as they're concerned. So I ask her, "How come those people have no problem with it but you do?" And that makes her stop and think. If these people claim to be Indians and they don't even look it, then maybe she should think of herself as Indian as well. But it's hard for her. When she was growing up, they never talked about their identity at all.

The reality of namelessness was constantly raised by those Métis people who had grown up urban, as well as by mixed-blood nonstatus Indians from other parts of Canada. For their parents, lacking entitlement to Indian status and a reserve and forced to adopt the standards of the mainstream meant that their Nativeness could not even be called "Indian." Western Métis people sometimes referred to themselves as "breeds"; however, for East Coast Native people, without a tradition of Métisness, being urban, mixed-blood nonstatus Native people often involved having no real name for themselves at all. These individuals simply struggled all their lives from a marginal position within the mainstream.

One participant from a northern Saskatchewan Métis community related how the logic of the Indian Act, which shaped the signing of the numbered treaties, is reflected in the Cree language (but is resisted as well):

In Saskatchewan, there're a lot of northern communities that are all Métis. The word for Métis in Cree means, "half sons." And the word for treaty Indians in Cree means, "full-bloods." There's nothing racist in it; it's just the way it is. But then the Cree treaty Indians have a word for us, which is "Mitisse"—they play on the word "Métis," right? So they call you "mitisse," which means, "my ass." But it's like a little teasing going on between the Métis and the treaty Indians.

In talking about cultural revival, this woman describes how her grandmother, who has lived a traditional life on the land as the wife of a trapper all her life, is not in a sense able to acknowledge her skills with medicines—but rather, sees them as Indian skills that she can only dabble in.

My grandpa's mom was a medicine woman, so she knew medicine. And my grandfather knew medicines, where to go and pick herbs. But it wasn't passed on. And my grandmother still uses traditional medicines. But she calls them, in Cree "the Indian medicines"— like its something that "the Indians" do, rather than the Métis. Even though, to me, we're all Indian, right? But up there, because our communities are separated, the treaty Indians and the Métis are apart. All the reserves usually have Métis communities right next door to them, so we live separate.

This individual also describes the meaningless of the distinctions between Indian and Métis in northern communities, from a child's perspective.

One time, when I was in grade eight, there was an announcement over the intercom. It singled out all the Native kids and raised our anxieties about racial tensions, because there weren't a lot of Native people in our school. Anyway, the announcement said something like: "All the status Indians come and register with your numbers." I said, "What number?" I had no idea of what they were talking about. So I went to the principal's office, and I asked them what number they were talking about. I said, "I'm Indian, but I don't have a number." And they said, "Don't you have a status number?" And I just said, "No." So I went home after school, and I talked to my mom about it, and she said that number was just for Indians. And I said, "But we're Indians!" And she said, "No, we're not Indians. We're half. We're Métis. We don't have a number." I was so confused. I have my culture, and I speak my language. I look Native. To me, all this time, I was an Indian. That's all I was. I didn't know about half-breeds. But that's the day I found out, that day, in grade eight, that I was not an Indian.

While these differences on one level are meaningless, an issue of crucial importance to contemporary Native empowerment is the manner in which the Indian Act—by separating Métis and treaty Indians into different communities and by providing one group with both benefits *and* constraints that the other did not face—has structured real divisions between Métis and treaty Indian communities. For Métis in remote northern communities, lack of access to treaty health benefits, in communities where being ill may mean having to be flown out by air ambulance and then having to pay for it, is a major problem for the elderly. Another problem for those communities where individuals still rely to a considerable extent on country food is that, for many years, harvesting rights have been denied to Métis hunters (although recently a number of court challenges, decisions, and reversals of those decisions have continuously affected Métis rights to hunt in different regions). This northern Saskatchewan Métis woman, for example, commented that in order for her family members to be able to hunt all year round they have always had to bring a treaty Indian along! This woman also described how tensions between her community and the adjacent reserve escalated during an interval when the band began pursuing a land claim:

> There's a reserve that's two miles out from my community. When I was in grade ten, there was a lot of tension, because they came so close to our village. They were trying to extend a land claim to encompass our village. There was a lot of fear and tension in the village, because we were afraid they were going to take the town over. I mean, the Métis aren't allowed to live on the reserve, right? The band seemed to be taking over everything. Our village is surrounded by the reserve, and we can't go on their land at all.

There are deep implications to these structural divisions, particularly for regions that have witnessed years of separation between Indianness and Métisness, which still have great resonance today. One woman, for example, whose Métis mother was from southern Saskatchewan, described the complex relationship of identification, alienation, and fear that her mother still maintains toward treaty Indians:

> For all these years, I guess my mom has felt some wistfulness, maybe, but mostly bitterness, about treaty Indians, because she always used to feel jealous that some of her cousins that grew up on the reserve had shoes, but [her family] didn't have shoes—things like that. She felt that the Indians were better off. And yet, at the same time, she saw reserve life very negatively. She would say things like, "Those Indians, you know, from the reserve—they're always partying, always drunk." She felt that in their family, they worked harder because they had to get ahead—because they didn't have anything to rely on.
>
> And she was afraid of them too. All we heard, growing up, was, "Don't go and associate with those Indians. Don't go to powwows," and stuff like that. And it's because of the medicine. My mom grew up knowing that there was a lot of bad medicine and being exposed to some of it, too. She's told us stories about some pretty bad things that have happened to our family with medicine over the years. So that was the other reason that she grew up trying to keep us away from Indians—that fear, that something bad could happen to us as a result. So if you had Indian status, then you lived on-reserve, and you had all these benefits that her family didn't have. But then you also had all those other things to be afraid of.

Given this heritage of forced separation, it would be worthwhile exploring in more detail how contemporary relations between Métis people and those who identify as Indian are structured by the Indian Act. However, because of the highly context-dependent nature of Native identity, and because this study did not take place in western Canada, such in-depth explorations are beyond the scope of this study. Instead I will examine how Indian-Métis relations are manifested in the Toronto region.

MÉTISNESS IN THE TORONTO URBAN COMMUNITY

In eastern Canada, where the category of Métis has little resonance and where Métis people are therefore free to choose whether to define themselves as nonstatus Indians or Métis, the extent to which the participants identified as Métis seemed to depend on whether they had actually grown up in western Canada, or on the color of their skin. This was most obvious in one family group I interviewed, where of two siblings who had grown up in eastern Canada, the darker one tends to identify as Cree/Métis while the lighter one simply calls himself Métis. The father, meanwhile, feels very aware of himself as Métis and not Indian; however, since he is so dark he has called himself Native all his life because most Native people simply refuse to believe that he is Métis. Métisness, then, appears to have been historically linked to a notion of being light-skinned, with darker Métis people simply assumed to be Indian in common-sense ways. More tellingly, in western Canada, Métis has not been seen as Native.

Two of the participants, both visibly Native but from vastly different experiences of Métisness, spoke of the quandary they face in Toronto where their Métis identity is not understood. For the northern Saskatchewan Métis woman participant, a major problem is that none of her friends believe that she is not from a Cree First Nation. Because of her Native appearance and her fluency in Cree, they constantly expect her to produce an Indian card in stores, or will ask her what band she is from, and are puzzled and disbelieving when she insists she is Métis. Meanwhile, another individual, who defines himself as a historic Red River Métis, does not feel right defining himself as Native, which is considered synonymous with Indian where he comes from. In Toronto, however, where everybody is encouraged to just call themselves Native, he is constantly accused of being ashamed of being Native for rejecting the label Native in favor of Métis.

One of the participants, a nonstatus woman from western Canada, with a status Indian mother and a Métis father, has rejected the label Métis for herself. As an adoptee she has felt like she didn't belong for most of her life, so Indianness feels very important to her. She sees being Métis as signifying an inferior, "less Indian" identity, which she rejects.

> Okay, this might be warped but, to me, Métis means being not as much Indian as if I was to say I was Cree/Saulteaux. That's what it means to me. I'd much rather say mixed-race than Métis. I'm kind of using mixed-race a lot more lately. I guess it's because when you say you're mixed-race, it doesn't question the Nativeness of your Native part, it just says you're "Indian and other." Whereas saying you are Métis is different—it means you are all mixed up, that you are very mixed-race and probably white-looking. I'm always

amazed when I see dark-skinned people who are very proud, who identify themselves as Métis. For me, personally, it doesn't work. And you don't hear it in eastern Canada. I think it's all wrapped up in my whole struggle with getting Indian status—the fact that I do kind of look Indian, and I don't have status. But how come all those white people get to have status? It's all wrapped up together. I don't want to be called a Métis. Goddamn it, I'm an Indian and I want my status!

One individual pointed out that in Ontario, Métis identity at present is simply a matter of individuals having their Native heritage verified so that they could have access to resources. This individual asserts that Métis people need to rethink their ideas about what constitutes their nationhood:

This whole definition of Métis right now . . . What people seem to be really hanging onto are these pictures of Riel, and so forth. And let's face it—I mean, my ancestors were probably not too fond of Riel. They were English half-breeds, and they were not Catholic, they were Anglican, or Protestant. So what is all this?

Another participant identified strongly with the concept of a Métis nation because he saw his own family's history of silence and denial of heritage as closely linked to the repression that Métis people experienced as a result of the 1885 rebellion. On a daily basis, however, he sees his history as strongly interconnected with all Indigenous people. He does not differentiate strongly between Métis and Indian— and most important, he notes that the meanings of both terms are changing:

As Métis people, many people say that we're bridge-builders between cultures. Well, that's a bunch of bullshit. Bridges get walked on. Maybe once we had a real function that way. But what defined Métis life keeps changing. So the question, the very question of what does it mean to be Métis or what does it mean to be a Cree man or woman, it's changing. It's not a static thing.

For individuals who grew up in western Canada, it is obvious that a heritage of being forcibly separated from Indianness has deeply marked them. Whether the individuals adopt strategies of asserting

Métis difference or attempting to subvert differences by refusing to acknowledge them, the fact remains that a history of externalization from Indianness has manifested itself in the identities and choices of these participants and their families. Only the individual who spoke of how lived meanings of Métisness and Creeness are both changing appeared to have found a way to move beyond the history of separation from Indianness that shapes Métis identity.

The other Métis participants, however, all children of western Métis who had grown up in eastern Canada, tended to focus primarily on the Native part of their Métis identity as the foundation of their Nativeness. For these individuals, Métisness (as signifying lack of Indian status and a reserve) is simply another brush with genocide that their families have had to face as Native people. These individuals spoke primarily of the difficulties they faced as nonstatus urban Native people, in a context where lacking Indian status, even for dark-skinned people, overwhelmingly means not being Indian enough.

For the status Indian participants, Métisness seemed to signify lack of connection to place and a diminished sense of Indianness. It must be emphasized that most of the status Indian individuals who held to this view were at least as light-skinned and mixed-race as most of the Métis participants, while several of the Métis people I interviewed were much darker and more Native-looking than most of the status Indians. A few of the status Indians referenced the belief that to identify as being of hybrid lineage, as Métis people do, is the same as not knowing how to align one's self racially or politically. They attacked Métis people in the community as being ashamed of their Nativeness because they insisted on their Métisness. Others conceded that asserting pride in Métisness might be something that was good for Métis people out west; however, they emphasized that, in Toronto, the notion of Métisness was simply divisive. These individuals tended to believe that all people should simply "identify as Native people," thus ignoring the centrality of their Indian status to the in-group nature of Indianness and the way in which nonstatus people have their identities routinely invalidated by status Indians *because* they lack Indian status.

Even the nonstatus participants from eastern Canada indicated that they preferred to identify as nonstatus Indians rather than as Métis because of the association of Métisness with lacking an Aboriginal territory and having an "untraceable" lineage (from circumstances wherein mixed-race people may have been marrying other mixed-race people for generations). These individuals preferred to identify as Indian (even if nonstatus) rather than risk a sense of being further externalized from Indianness by embracing a Métis identity. The vehemence with which the majority of the participants asserted the importance of identifying as Indian, rather than Métis, suggests that, in Toronto, Indianness as a cohesive group identity is extremely important to the self-image of most of the participants and that Métisness signifies being outside of this group identity. In this respect, individuals in the Toronto Native community appear to have entirely accepted the Indian Act's externalization of "half-breeds" in common-sense ways, as a natural phenomenon, while entirely ignoring the extent to which, especially in eastern Canada, great numbers of status Indians are mixed-bloods.

Finally, it is worth taking into consideration the fact that increasingly, in eastern Canada, Métisness simply represents a second choice for individuals who cannot get their Indian status back, but who need a form of political affiliation. In a context where so many status Indians are mixed-blood, and where Métisness enables individuals at least to politically affiliate, many individuals who cannot get their status back are "becoming" Métis by default.

REGAINING INDIAN STATUS UNDER BILL C-31

If the previous section outlines the extent to which mixed-race individuals in the urban Native community yearn for a cohesive in-group identity *as Indians* within the community, and externalize Métis people in the process, the issues raised by the refiguring of Indian identity under Bill C-31 highlight the extent to which, in urban settings, this cohesive sense of Native identity hinges on having Indian status. And yet the participants' experiences with attempting to have their status reinstated, or to gain status, under Bill C-31, demonstrate the extent to which relying on the bureaucracy of a colonizing government to bestow the central determinant of one's identity can be extremely problematic. For many individuals, frustrating, dehumanizing, and sometimes bizarre issues have arisen in their attempts to get back their Indian status. Others, however, who do not share these problems, do not tend to see Indian status as deeply problematic—instead they tend to cling to a notion that Indian status must be protected, as literally the last bulwark against the absolute destruction of Native people as peoples. In this chapter I will explore this range of perspectives.

A number of participants were ineligible for status because of the second-generation cut-off in Bill C-31. One woman, whose mother had grown up nonstatus because *her* father enfranchised, now faces the restriction that her mother is considered as having only one "full Aboriginal" parent, because her Native grandmother's signature on the enfranchisement document allows her mother to only acquire "partial" status, which cannot be handed down to descendants whose other parent is non-Native. Another woman related how getting her status back involved four years of research and having two separate affidavits sworn about her mother's identity, since the Indian agent removed her mother's name from her band list after she was sent away to residential school. Another woman described how her mother mistakenly assumed her status had been removed when she married a non-Native, although through bureaucratic oversight it had not. When she went to Indian Affairs to be reinstated, they discovered the oversight—and promptly removed her status, only to immediately reinstate her under Bill C-31. This means that any children born after her marriage cannot pass status on to *their* children, while those born before her marriage, with the same father, can. Yet another participant talked about her grandmother's red ticket, which was issued to women who'd married out but had then been widowed, to identify them as eligible for treaty monies. These documents were widely seen as "phony Indian cards" because the women who possessed them didn't really have status—which suggests that the tendency to externalize Indian women who lost status as "not really Indian" goes much further back than the present.

Cross-border jurisdiction issues between Canada and the United States figured in the difficulties that other participants faced in getting their status. For example, one participant found that her mother's attempts to regain her status have been held back by the reluctance of the Department of Indian Affairs to conduct research in the United States, where her Cree Indian grandmother had fled for several years after the Riel Rebellion. Another individual whose Cree and Saulteaux family members also moved back and forth between Montana and Alberta in the wake of the 1885 Rebellion, and who has been denied Indian status in Canada because of a history of intermarriage with Métis people in her family, is attempting to be recognized as American Indian by the Bureau of Indian Affairs in the United

States. This individual, an adoptee, faced considerable difficulties in trying to acquire Indian status in Canada, caught between adoption laws that prohibit full disclosure of birth parents' identity and Indian Affairs' restrictive and demanding edicts.

On an individual basis, loss of status has had severe repercussions for some families. One woman described the poverty that her mother's family experienced when her grandmother lost status for marrying a Métis man. Other women spoke of their mothers' predicaments, cut off from their communities for marrying non-Natives and forced to live in a largely hostile white society. Despite their mothers' independent attitudes and resourcefulness, the fact remains that these women were rendered far more vulnerable to the whims and attitudes of—and sometimes abuse from—their white husbands than they should have been.

Growing up nonstatus also affected the participants' sense of their own identities. Several of the individuals, particularly those who looked white and/or had entirely lacked access to their Native communities growing up, had found that a status card was important to their sense of entitlement to a Native identity, while a few, whose parents had kept them connected to their reserves through constant visiting, saw the Indian card as largely irrelevant most of the time. All of the individuals who had regained their status under Bill C-31 found that their mother's efforts to regain Indian status were the focal point for a whole shift in consciousness, a sense that being Native was valuable and needed to be supported and reinforced. These individuals asserted that it was the change in attitude, rather than the legal recognition itself, which was important. However, while many of the individuals interviewed were quick to preface their comments about status with "of course, a card does not make me an Indian," each also made some reference to the manner in which their sense of their Native identity *had* been reinforced by this legal recognition of Indian status.

Indeed many of the discussions about status with the participants revealed that while the contemporary generation of urban mixedbloods may have relatively easily adopted the rhetoric of rejecting government classifications, Indian status as a category determining Indianness still has tremendous resonance for most urban Native people. For example, some of the nonstatus or Métis participants described how, as they were growing up, an invisible barrier existed in their minds between themselves and status Indians. They might be of Native heritage, and consider themselves to be Native people, but they could not consider themselves to be "real Indians," because this category was only for status Indians.

Many participants were aware of the contradictory nature of their opinions about Indian status—the manner in which they tended to deny its validity in theory but were bound to its logic in deep ways. Most were highly aware of the power of the government to regulate identity—in fact, they felt that status Indians were more Indian than those without status, *because* of the entire apparatus of government recognition of Indianness, which shapes status Indian lives in ways that it does not shape the experiences of nonstatus Indians or Métis people.

By comparison with the problems related to acquiring status that many of the participants described earlier, three individuals were re-instated under Bill C-31 in a relatively problem-free manner. These individuals revealed little awareness of the difficulties that individuals can face in regaining their status. They seemed generally to assume that anybody of Aboriginal heritage can now simply apply and get their status back and that individuals who don't do so are not proud enough of being Indian to want to get it back.

THE MEANINGS OF INDIAN STATUS TO THE PARTICIPANTS

Given the extent to which, in urban settings, having Indian status works to affirm a sense of Native identity in powerful but unacknowl-edged ways, I have attempted to deconstruct the various meanings that individuals give to having Indian status.

First of all, having Indian status means affiliation (if not member-ship) with a reserve. As I explored in chapter 10, the symbolic value of band membership for urban mixed-bloods is extremely important for grounding individuals in a sense of place. Being members of spe-cific First Nations, as compared to those who can merely claim to be a member of an Indigenous nation in the abstract, speaks to the concrete connections to place and community that are central to Na-tive life, connections that band membership secures for urban status Indians, if only in a symbolic manner. One individual described how it worked for her:

When I used to work at one of the provincial territorial organiza-tions, at our assemblies, everybody would go around and they'd have [a name tag with] their name and their nation underneath it—not like "Cree Nation," but like "Saugeen First Nation," or whatever. And, well, that's more a question of belonging to a certain band, I guess. But it is also part of the whole status thing.

Aside from the symbolic value that status provides in linking a person with a specific First Nation, in daily life in the city, being able to say you are a member of a specific First Nation is also a way of saying that you are part of a specific tribal heritage. Status then is equated quite openly with cultural knowledge or heritage. Nonstatus Indians and Métis people, by comparison, are often seen as being "detribalized" (even if they are part of a specific Métis community), as coming from untraceable roots and therefore having lost their heritage.

A third function of having Indian status in urban settings appears to be the ability of a status card to confirm, on basic levels, that one has Indian blood. Even the darker-skinned nonstatus or Métis individuals I interviewed spoke of times when they have encountered suspicions about their Nativeness because of their lack of Indian status. Meanwhile, for those individuals who are light-skinned or otherwise white-looking, their Indian card openly functions as an official stamp of Indianness for them, certifying Indian blood. This is particularly the case for individuals from eastern Canada, where, for years, extensive but officially unrecognized intermarriage has taken place in many reserve communities while identity legislation in the Indian Act virtually decoupled Indian status from Indian blood. For individuals from these communities, having Indian status enables individuals to ignore their mixed-bloodedness. One dark-skinned western Métis woman described how this worked in her marriage to a light-skinned status Indian:

When I met my husband, and we started going out together, I think the thing that first attracted me to him was that he was light. I could tell he was part Indian and part white by looking at him, and I felt a kinship to him because I could see that there was a mixture in his background. But as soon as I got to know him a bit, I realized that even though he was a lot lighter and more European-looking than I was, he was full Indian as far as he was concerned. He would never admit that he wasn't full Indian. And if anything came up about his appearance, he would shoot you if you tried to say that he was anything BUT full Indian.

It appears that, in urban settings in eastern Canada, Indian status provides an "official seal of Indianness" for urban status Indians, despite their frequent disclaimers that "status is really irrelevant." Having Indian status secures for an urban individual certified Indian blood (even if the individual is very mixed-race), a verification of concrete connections to land and community (even if these connections do not reflect the individual's family history), and an intangible sense that one is in full possession of one's heritage (even if one does not speak their language and has been taught relatively little about their culture). By defining certain urban Native people as official Indians, status also automatically deprives nonstatus Indians and Métis of a sense of entitlement as Native people. Meanwhile, in actual fact, the lives of urban status Indians, particularly as rights for off-reserve status Indians continue to be withdrawn by the federal government, are actually drawing closer to those of nonstatus Indians and the Métis, than to their cousins on-reserve.

While fluctuations in the colonial regulation of Native identity continue to demonstrate its artificiality and its uses in dividing Native people, the fact remains that Indian status has real implications for the day-to-day lives of many Native people. A few individuals discussed the considerable material benefits that status had brought them, including an education (one woman, who acknowledged the exceptionality of her experience, was nevertheless completing her Ph.D., entirely funded by her band). Others were more doubtful about the actual benefits that status would bring them, because of the gradual erosion of benefits for off-reserve status Indians and the amount of work it takes to actually claim treaty rights because of the tremendous racism that is generated when individuals pull out their Indian card for tax exemption. Meanwhile a few individuals relished the fact that they were able to work in the United States.

Beyond all economic benefits, however, is the meaning that Indian status holds within Canadian society, as virtually the only concrete indicator of the special relationship that exists between Aboriginal peoples and the Canadian government. Several of the participants spoke about how Indian status is the only remnant that remains of Canada's recognition of the First Nations—that since all the treaties have been violated, it is important for status Indians to assert themselves and defend their rights to have status. Status here is often conflated with treaty rights:

Status is important because Natives are . . . we're all human be-
ings, but we're not all the same. Native peoples made treaties
with non-Natives a long time ago. And the treaties were made
because we shared things with them, with the promise that we
would have certain securities. And in the old days, when they made
the treaties, the whites were willing to listen to us, because they
were outnumbered—they were always ready to listen. But as soon
as they outnumbered us, then they broke the treaties. That's what
the elders say. And now, we have to fight for all the little things
that we get, and we have to even fight for our recognition as Native people. So there're people today that are saying, "We're all the
same." Well that's not true. We're Native people, and this is our
homeland. Our ancestors signed treaties to give us a future, and
that's what we have to hang on to. To me, status means that I am
recognized. My ancestors fought for these treaties. And that's what
they are. All we have to do as Native people is to be adamant about
what our rights are and know who we are.

It is important to be clear that while status is currently being used
to promote Native heritage and defend treaty rights, *status is not "heritage" and it is not the same thing as treaty rights.* The imposition
of the category "Indian," as articulated through the Indian Act, in
fact was Canada's way to preempt the rights of Indigenous nations to
govern themselves, a signifier that the colonizer, not Native people,
controlled Native destinies. Having Indian status means having your
identity regulated by the federal government; there can be no greater
violation of the nation-to-nation relationship specified implicitly in
the treaties, when Indigenous citizenship in every sense of the word
is currently defined by a body of colonial legislation. Moreover, every Native person currently without treaty rights would also have
been the recipient of treaty rights had not legislation been enacted by
Canada excluding so-called half-breeds. This legislation denied status
to twenty-five thousand women and their descendants and refused to
recognize eastern Native people who did not sign treaties. Indian status, then, is a central means through which treaty rights to nonstatus
Native people are denied.
A number of participants were also unequivocal that the government acknowledgment of the special nature of Indian status is far
outweighed by its divisive effects among Native people. They all acknowledged that having had Indian status and band membership has

served a protective function for First Nation communities, enabling them to maintain a land base and maintain a stronger Native identity, and that in this respect, Indian status has real meaning. Nevertheless, they also asserted that despite the rhetoric from status Indian organizations about status being linked to the treaties, the fact that the organizations representing First Nations, off-reserve Indians, nonstatus Indians, and the Métis are all competing against one another for federal monies made the status Indians' assertions that status gave them some sort of unique sovereignty claim over and above those of other Native groups quite meaningless:

> Status is a crock of shit. No, really, it is. The point is that it's a government definition. And I respect that I'm not a status Indian and maybe not what most people would think of as an Aboriginal person. I'll accept that. But what I won't accept is the notion that "You're a nonstatus Indian, and this person is a status Indian, and you're a Métis, and . . ." I mean, we've already got so much difficulty, and we're always scrambling to meet those definitions. I just have a problem with them. I also have a problem with people who only have some distant blood in there, and they're playing at being Indian—that's not respectful, to me. But those people are few and far between, and they're nut cases, and everyone knows it.
>
> Why are people identifying as Métis all of a sudden? Well—there're bucks in it. Why did people sell their status [enfranchise]? So they could join the army, or get a job, or vote, or go into a bar, or get married and live in the city, or what have you. Why are they going back now? So they can get money. These categories are all government-defined. It's nonsense.

Other individuals concurred that money was at the root of many of the divisions between status Indians and all other nonstatus Native people:

> What it comes down to is usually fighting over dollars, the bones that are chucked to us from the government. There's always a big fight over where the money's going to be spent. It gets divided up between the on-reserve and the off-reserve, with the on-reserve feeling that the off-reserve shouldn't be getting the money, because they're the REAL Indians. Like "They should give US the money and we'll look after our people." Well, of course, off-reserve peo-

ple know that—THEY DON'T, right? So there are power struggles between the on- and off-reserve people. At different times I've sat on different sides of the policy tables, fighting for dollars for one side or the other. That's a lot of what it's about. There's lots of stuff you'll hear around the table at First Nations organizations—stuff about, "Aw, the Métis, those people don't even have status—you know, who are they?" . . . or, "Well, off-reserve people have access to most services in the city, so they don't need any money. They don't need anything." There's a real sense, I think, that "We're the real Indians—we deserve all the rights and all the services." Right? But with the urban organizations, there's a much greater sense that everybody's accepted.

From this perspective, individuals who assert the importance of status and then say at the same time, "but that doesn't mean status Indians are any more Indian than nonstatus people," are simply refusing to look clearly at the issues of power and privilege *between* Native people.

Native people, of course, did not choose this conundrum, and in a sense, as long as they continue to rely on government regulation of Native identity to set the boundaries of Indianness, they will face this problem. The reality is that *the only way that Indian status can continue to maintain its "clout" as an indicator of a special relationship with the government is precisely by maintaining its power to exclude.* The primary function of Indian status is as a boundary marker—a clear indicator of who is Indian and who is not, and it is only by retaining this power to include some and exclude others that Indian status has any meaning.[1]

A few of the participants, looking toward the future, have pointed out the problems they see occurring with the next generation of urban Native people when large numbers of people lose their status, or retain their status but find that all benefits for off-reserve Indians have been removed. They talk about the impoverishment that will result when individuals find themselves no longer eligible for education or employment programs, and how difficult it will be for these people when they get older and do not have treaty health benefits. Widespread loss of status will, according to them, turn the tide against Native empowerment in the cities, drying up the benefits that Native people have begun to experience because of a generation of access to education and to jobs in the urban or on-reserve Native communities and truncating the rebirth in cultural pride that an empowered community can work toward. These individuals point out that this is the first generation of status Indians to really enjoy access to the education that had been expressly specified in many of the treaties, and it is these benefits that have helped to create a strong, growing urban Native middle class who are proud of their heritage and working at cultural promotion. All of this is threatened by the government attacks on status rights for urban Indians and by the second-generation cut-off in Bill C-31. In this respect, retaining status *is* tied to retaining heritage, at present, in the cities.

However, in view of the fact that large numbers of the next generation of urban Indians will be ineligible for status, it might be wise for individuals to begin to strategize how Native empowerment can be brought about without status—or how more nonstatus Native people can be brought into the status relationship. Both are risky concepts. Many individuals are aware that the strength of Native people has been in their access to land and to a distinctive relationship with the government—that without these strengths, which at present accrue only through Indian status, Native people could conceivably be further reduced to powerless, impoverished "visible minorities" drifting through the urban mainstream. This, in fact, is clearly Canada's goal. Whether fighting for status rights for a relatively small percentage of the urban population is the key to avoiding this fate—or building for other forms of empowerment—is difficult to say. Again this points to a need for different ways of conceptualizing citizenship in Indigenous nations, one where being Onkwehonwe, or Anishinaabe—that is, members of specific nations—is the goal and where Indianness, as a signifier that one is a member of an oppressed and colonized minority who must fight for federal patronage, ceases to exist.

12

Mixed-Blood Urban Native People and the Rebuilding of Indigenous Nations

This work has focused on the broad range of issues that have shaped the identities of urban mixed-blood Native people. One emphasis has been descriptive, focusing on the family histories of the participants, their struggle to recoup knowledge of culture and history despite profound silencing, and their efforts to create a community for themselves in an urban environment. Another focus, however, has been analytical, attempting to understand how a legacy of legal restrictions and racial apartheid has positioned the participants—in a sense *creating* them as urban mixed-race Native people. Over and over, these analytical efforts to understand the intricate web of historical and contemporary forces shaping urban mixed-blood Native identity keep returning to two central issues—urbanity and Indian status—which in one way or another continuously impact on the participants' lives. These issues reinforce and, in a sense, are mutually constitutive of one another.

Government regulation of Native identity has created a complex array of categories of Nativeness that have been reflected in the very distinct sets of experiences recounted to me by participants who are status Indians (with full or partial status), Bill C-31 Indians (with or without band membership), nonstatus Indians, or Métis. On another level, however, are the differences in perspectives between those who grew up on-reserve, and came to the city as adults, and those who grew up urban—differences created by the genocidal policies of residential schooling, the sixties scoop, and a century of gender and racial discrimination in the Indian Act.

GENOCIDE, HEGEMONY, AND NATIVE IDENTITY

> You know, when you start to really analyze it—that's the way the colonizers work. The beauty of what they do as colonizers is, after they have come and instituted their ways among a critical mass of people over a certain period of time, then they establish that that is now going to be the norm. And so the colonizers have now left a group of the colonized who continue to oppress their own people. They're the ones who are oppressing their own people. And that's what everything that has happened in Canada has been about—the residential schools, and the churches, and everything else. So that it's us doing it to ourselves.

The impact of hegemonic images and definitions of Indianness on urban mixed-blood Native peoples' sense of their own identities has been considerable. At the same time, it is obvious that the urban Native community in general is continually engaging in ways of subverting or actively resisting these ways of thinking about Indianness, with greater or lesser degrees of success. One of the greatest difficulties individuals face in attempting to work their way through these hegemonic ways of thinking is the fact that these constructs have power precisely because of their ability to reflect reality in common-sense ways. Appearance *does* make a difference to Indianness. Having status *has* shaped the realities of status Indians in ways that are highly distinctive. Being reserve-based *has* provided for a stronger collective identity for band members than is typically the case for urban Indians. And yet, as the participants' family and individual experiences have demonstrated, none of these descriptors—appearance, status, or a reserve background—are ultimate signifiers of a Native identity.

For Native people, appearance has been one of the obvious ways in which boundaries have been maintained between members of Indigenous societies and a hostile colonizing society. And yet a crucial way in which the cultural distinctiveness—and the nationhood—of Indigenous societies has been denied within the colonizing society has been to reduce cultural identity to race, therefore reducing Nativeness to appearance, with its implicit connection to "purity" of blood.

In the urban community, a critical response to this colonial obsession with appearance has been the attempt to uncouple Indianness from looking Indian, to ignore colonial divisions among Native people and assert that anybody of Native heritage is a Native person, regardless of appearance. These urban attempts to exercise a strategic flexibility about appearance, intermarriage, and Indian blood, however, are directly opposite to the approaches taken by different First Nations communities, where in some contexts, blood quantum membership restrictions are being implemented to replace Indian status as a determinant of membership. These approaches diverge broadly, and it may be helpful to see them less as philosophical positions than as responses to the significantly different circumstances facing urban and reserve-based Native peoples. In particular, urban communities have had to wrestle with the almost inevitably higher rates of intermarriage with non-Natives than reserve communities typically face. Meanwhile the pressure on reserve communities to maintain their land base and a measure of cultural and racial distinctiveness, in a context where the reserves are the only sites in Canada where Indian land is legally recognized, has created a need to maintain fairly rigid boundaries about Indianness. It is telling, however, that some reserve communities are bringing in blood-quantum standards largely because of the perception that allowing the children of those who lost their status to become band members must be tightly controlled. The sovereignty violation that forcible loss of status represented for over a century, particularly with respect to gender discrimination, remains virtually a non-issue for these communities for whom asserting sovereignty now primarily means exercising the power to externalize certain groups of Native people from band membership.

Indian status, above all, is a system that enabled Canada to deny and bypass Indigenous sovereignty, by replacing "the Nation" with "the Indian." As the experiences of the participants' families have demonstrated, Canada has been able to use Indian status to define who can be considered Indian in ways that have alienated whole communities from any access to a land base and permanently fragmented Native identity through an extremely patriarchal and racist system that has torn large holes in the fabric of Native societies. Indian status has also been an extremely effective way to control access to Native territory, through legislation that for years has stipulated that only those recognized by Canada as status Indians can live on the reserves supposedly set aside for all Native people.

The fact that the participants were able in a relatively straight-forward manner to reject hegemonic concepts of Indianness as deter-mined by appearance or being reserve-based, but continued to wrestle with the implications of Indian status, indicates the profound power of the state to regulate identity. In many respects, the participants' opinions about status were entirely reflective of whether or not they actually possessed Indian status. While the status Indian participants all saw status as crucial to protecting Native people from extinction, virtually all of the nonstatus people saw Indian status as so ultimately divisive that it represented a significant weakness to Native empow-erment. What both groups held in common was an avowed belief that status was irrelevant to Nativeness, combined with a generally deeply held, almost instinctive reaction that the only *real* Indians are those who have Indian status. This is the problem when legislation is intro-duced that controls a group's identity—once created and established, it cannot simply be undone. You cannot put the genie back in the bottle again—you have to deal with it. It is one thing to recognize that Indian Act categories are artificial—or even that they have been internalized—as if these divisions can be overcome simply by deny-ing their importance. Legal categories, however, shape peoples' lives. They set the terms that individuals and communities must utilize, even in resisting these categories.

Legal restrictions on Indianness, primarily on the basis of gender in eastern Canada, and through gender and supposed blood purity in western Canada, have created a legacy of *experiential* differences between status Indians, confined to reserves, and most other Aborigi-nal people. These differences—*between* communities, as manifested in conflicts between on-reserve status Indians and all other groups— urban Indians, the Métis, and nonstatus Indians—and *within* commu-nities, as manifested in conflicts over reinstating band membership for Bill C-31 Indians, are the most divisive issues that Native people face in Canada today. Government-created differences have now been naturalized as inherent differences, to the extent that Canada has been successful in tying treaty rights and a nation-to-nation relationship to Indian status (and increasingly now to reserve residence)—a process that has created a large (and ever-growing) group of disenfranchised Native people. Meanwhile those who fit the government's notion of who a "real Indian" is—on-reserve status Indians—continue to argue that they alone are uniquely entitled to the rights and benefits of Aboriginality.

For the participants, what complicated their opinions about Indian status was the fact that it is tied so closely to access to Native land. Meanwhile, because of conflicting ways in which the Indian Act externalized some mixed-blood Native people and allowed others to stay (on the basis of gender) for over a century means that Indian status has also become inextricably connected both to issues of appearance and to gender.

Regardless of the opinions of the participants, however, in some respects the cities represent a space where status has *already* been uncoupled from the position it occupies in reserve settings as a crucial signifier of Indianness. In urban settings, where a significant proportion of the Native population is the product of loss of status (or never had it in the first place), status Indians and nonstatus Native people work side by side at different agencies and are involved in the same cultural activities in ways that simply cannot happen in reserve settings, where funding for any sort of activity or process is linked to status and where nonstatus people cannot live on reserve land (except through leasing it in the same way as non-Natives do); in any case, regardless of where they live, they cannot participate in the life of the community).

Urban centers, in fact, increasingly represent spaces where boundaries between Native people and the dominant society are maintained neither by appearance nor Indian status but primarily by cultural orientation. In this respect they represent a unique place to observe what happens to Native people who lack legal protection of their rights as Indians and who are flexible about the racial boundaries of Indianness. It is worth considering, however, that urban Native people are able to maintain this flexibility precisely because they have no collective land base, which, in addition to loss of language, is the most problematic aspect of urban Native identity.

The participants were extremely clear-headed about how being urban affected their identities as Native people. While some individuals wrestled with the hegemonic logic that links Native people to images of "living on the land like an Indian," most of the participants were relatively clear that reserve-based individuals did have a stronger sense of their identities as Native people simply because they had grown up in places where Native people were the majority. These individuals, however, were also aware that the boundaries between urban and reserve culture are neither as distinctive nor as fixed as individuals believe—that considerable cross-fertilization continues to happen between urban centers and adjacent reserves.

The participants' experiences of having band membership reinstated were, on the whole, quite positive. It was obvious, however, that despite their individual experiences of acceptance, everything depended on the individual proving his or her fitness to be reinstated. There is no unconditional acceptance as redress for past wrongs—individuals are only accepted back if their circumstances fit current band criteria, and those who do not fit remain externalized. For those individuals who are not accepted back, and for the majority of urban mixed-bloods who cannot get their status back, there is no "going back" to a Native identity (or community) that their ancestors were alienated from. These individuals are attempting to build identities as urban Native people in Toronto. It is clear, however, that their experiences as urban Native people would be extremely enriched by having some form of mutually agreed upon, structured access to land-based communities.

Throughout their interviews, a number of the participants indicated that in general, urban Native people need stronger connections to reserve communities—the so-called homelands of Native culture in Canada. They pointed to the stronger sense of an autonomous Native identity that on-reserve Native people demonstrate, as well as the fact that some reserves represent sites where at least some traditional values have been retained. Most important, however, is the fact that language use, while declining on many reserves, is still in evidence, while very few urban Native people speak their Indigenous language at all. It is obvious, then, that many urban Native people feel that they are in some ways diminished by their relative distance from reserve communities.

On the other hand, a few of the participants pointed out that on-reserve Native people may also have something to gain from stronger connections with urban Native people. When urban Native people appropriate urban spaces as Native spaces, the sovereignty movement from the reserves is inevitably strengthened. In more concrete ways, we can also see that the heterogeneity of urban Native experience might provide a valuable exposure to diversity for the closed worlds of many reserve environments, especially in the face of the fundamentalist Christianity that continues to colonize many reserve communities. In such contexts, the occasional presence of urban people, who take for granted the more secular spaces of urban life, might be helpful in counterbalancing the influence of Christianity in many reserve communities.

This suggests that urban Native people and the First Nations need ways of conceptualizing alliances—or nationhood—strategically, in ways that do not involve individual bands having to endlessly open their membership rolls to those who grew up alienated from community life, *or* urban Indians having to continuously engage in fruitless attempts to recreate themselves in identities that their families left behind.

Kenn Richard, a Métis involved in social services provision in Toronto, has pointed out that with the growing urbanization of Aboriginal Canada, urban communities cannot continue for much longer to rely on the reserves to "maintain the culture" for them. From this perspective, the growing numbers of urban Native people relative to reserve-based populations could mean that urban Native peoples within a few years might be bearing the brunt of cultural preservation. According to Richard, the most immediate priority should be a focus on developing vehicles for language regeneration and a collective urban land base (Richard 1994). In this respect, it appears that urban Native people, who lack a "critical mass" of language speakers and who are therefore somewhat deadlocked in their attempts to teach the languages in urban settings, need to approach First Nations organizations at an institutional level, to find some way of resource-sharing that would maintain and further the use of Indigenous languages. In many ways, it appears crucial that urban and on-reserve Native people begin to address common problems.

On a deeper level, another important issue is how urban Native people, particularly those who are mixed-race, might be involved in struggles for self-determination. How can the sovereignty goals of contemporary First Nations, and the desires and aspirations of urban individuals who consider themselves to be members of Indigenous nations "in the abstract," be brought together? In this chapter, I will be presenting the participants' thoughts on what roles urban mixed-race Native people might play in the rebuilding of their Indigenous nations. The close of this chapter will focus, in a preliminary manner, on the forms of nation-building that might subvert the history of divisions imposed on Native people by government regulation of Indianness and that could make urban and on-reserve alliances possible.

MIXED-BLOOD URBAN NATIVE PEOPLE AND THE FIRST NATIONS

A number of individuals spoke about what urban mixed-bloods are currently doing to strengthen Aboriginal presence within the cities. They referred to the daily grind of urban life that newcomers to the cities face and saw their roles as working with such individuals toward strengthening them, so they could return to their communities as empowered individuals.

> I don't see our roles as any different in an urban setting, or in an Indian community, or up in the north. I've made a very clear commitment to be part of the healing of our nation. And that's going to happen in all different ways and shapes and forms, whether it's in the city, whether it's in the bush, whether it's in an isolated community. My role, as a two-spirited Anishinaabe Kwe is to continue my own healing so I can help other people to heal. That will ultimately heal our communities and our families. There are so many tools for doing that. Like the Outward Bound program for Native people, where you take urban people into the bush and help them reconnect with the land. That's one tool. There are the treatment centers, the health and education efforts, getting our languages into the schools, addressing family violence . . . there are just so many different areas that our people are working on. That's our role. There is no other role for us, but to continue to educate people and break down stereotypes, to do cross-cultural education, and to never give up. We have to work from where we are, with what we've been given.

There was a general consensus that in some respects urban Native people have roles to play for which we are uniquely positioned. Several people referred to the greater awareness of power dynamics in the larger society that urban people have. One individual, for example, spoke of the manner in which reserve communities tend to ignore the presence of people of color and act as if Canada still consisted only of Native people and white people. She noted that one role of urban Native people must be to ensure that newer immigrant agendas did not marginalize those of Native people. Another individual, however, suggested that urban Native people are also positioned to address forms of alliances between peoples of color and Aboriginal peoples, which might be useful in challenging racism within the dominant society.

One individual felt that urban mixed-bloods, as individuals who have had to viscerally wrestle with dominant culture images of Indianness, might have a handle on challenging stereotypes about what Indianness is that do not often get challenged on reserves:

> The first thing that pops into my head is that because we've been outside of the communities, we might have a better handle on identifying what really is Native. So when people have been habituated to think that poverty is Native—and so your macaroni soup and your poor diet is Native—we can maybe clear that up. We can maybe try to sort that out, because we've had to do that for ourselves.

Another participant pointed out the importance of having urban Aboriginal people creating Native spaces in the city that reserve people can utilize when they come there, and that as a result of this considerable interaction is already happening between urban centers and nearby reserves:

> A lot of the stuff that's working really progressively is happening in the cities. People come from the reserves to Toronto to go to drum class, and stuff like that, and then they bring those things back to their communities. The kind of progress that we're making is already being taken back to the reserves. And that brings a breath of fresh air to some of the communities where the politics are so bad, where people are being really oppressed by certain powerful families that dominate the community, so there's no ability to, for instance, challenge the Indian Act, or really be critical about it. The cities can provide some space for reserve people to try to envision different alternatives.

Several individuals spoke to the increasing importance that strong urban Aboriginal communities will be playing in the future:

> Urban Indians might also be the cutting edge of moving on to whatever god-forsaken place we are heading to, here. You know—the

technology and the restructuring of Canadian society. We've got to get some economic and political strength in these places.

One individual cautioned that the urban Native community, while it has taken strong first steps in creating a viable urban culture and is beginning to create urban self-government organizations, will not ultimately be sustainable unless a considerable investment in language teaching and acquiring some sort of urban land base becomes a priority:

> The foundation of Aboriginal culture is language. Language maintenance has to be our top priority. Thoughts don't form language, language forms thoughts. And I've heard it enough from bilingual Indian people who say, "I think in Indian." Well, if that's the case, then those of us who are English speakers are thinking pretty mainstream, eh? So . . . I'm a little nervous there. I know there are Ojibway classes. But you know what? People go and they learn a few words, some animal names, how to introduce themselves and their clan—it's not day—to-day at all. We have to do something about language. And we have to find some kind of land base, [a way] to conduct ourselves, and start living more closely together, so we'll have the day-to-day relations that Aboriginal culture depends upon.

This individual pointed out that this is not only an urban problem—that reserves are also plagued by the fact that those who are trained to acquire power and therefore exercise the leadership are often those who are the most removed from rural traditional Native culture:

> Those reserves that are doing quite well—places like Six Nations—they're the ones that have a lot more say in directing policy than Attawapiskat ever can, or Davis Inlet, or anywhere where you have the people living a much more traditional, land-based life. It's totally ironic that those people who are most estranged from culture seem to be those that have most impact on furthering Aboriginal agendas off-reserve as well. And that's a little scary. I mean—in a sense I'm one of those people! I've made a point of learning about where I come from and about First Nations issues and culture—all those things that I didn't get as a child. I've certainly tried to follow a spiritual path. But not everybody does. And so a lot of these peo-

ple who are estranged from their backgrounds end up getting into positions of authority. I don't think you get Indian responses from those people—you just get good strategic responses, in working the system. Is that Indian? Does that do something in the long run to maintain Aboriginal Canada? Maybe—or maybe not. But it has to be looked at. You can't take these things for granted. It's a little scary, the way that those who are most estranged are most influential . . . But then the beautiful thing about Aboriginal Canada today is it can't be packaged very neatly. It's all negotiable, and I think that's partially its strength.

Another individual suggested that Native communities, urban and on-reserve, had to explore their own complicity in colonial processes—how their desires for mainstream living are hamstringing their efforts at cultural regeneration:

Even though we're in southern Ontario, in the city—if we were on a reserve in southern Ontario, I would say that some of the same pressures exist. The urbanization of reserves is happening. So how do we deal with that? And is it really just about mainstream pressures coming in from the outside? I think we have to recognize the ways in which we welcome those mainstream ways, too. We buy into them. We have to recognize that.

Coming to the heart of the problem, one individual pointed out that reserve-based people need to stop thinking of their tiny "postage stamp" bits of land as their entire nation—and that until Indigenous sovereignty is conceived in larger and more inclusive terms, the divisions between Native people cannot help but multiply.

There is so much need for positive thinking and ways of helping people to think beyond their little postage stamp piece of land as their whole identity as a nation. To me, that's number one.

Another individual pointed out that Native people as a whole have to reconceptualize what is meant by nationhood, to provide a broad diversity of approaches to rebuilding our nations:

I think First Nations have to take over their own memberships, entirely—and do it in a way that the membership is comfortable with and that basically speaks for its members. Now does that mean that some people will be shut out? Probably. But does that mean that they cannot come back in through some other means? I think that we have to rethink this whole thing. How can we adopt people? How can we welcome people back into our nation that are not blood related—through adoption? How can we anticipate problems that will arise and that will come to our door? The whole thing that is really important is cultural integrity. And how do we maintain our culture, our history? This whole question has huge political, social, and economic ramifications. The whole understanding of nationhood, today in the latter part of the twentieth century, is something that really needs to be thought out carefully.

One individual felt that the contemporary generation has not managed to overcome the divisions and weaknesses created by colonial regimes; however, he has hopes that the next generation will be much stronger and see their way more clearly:

My feeling is that nation rebuilding has to come from a very strong grounding in what I think of as a Native value system—and applying it and respecting it. Having something to offer to other communities and other peoples other than just "Can we have our money now?" I don't see it happening in my generation—but maybe in the next generation. It's not like I'm an old person, you know. But I don't see it happening from people in our age group—maybe from our kids who are being born now. I've just seen too much. Politically and relationship-wise, there's still too much damage and corruption and pain. I'd like to think that we would be able to, increasingly, bring the good things into the way we think and live and work—and begin to share that in how we relate to other nations, in a city like Toronto. But I haven't seen any projects that have lasted more than a few months or years. I mean, you build something up, and the good stuff is there, but something happens.

There's a lot of dysfunctional management. The whole agenda is driven by government, and they divide people with money. "You guys get this much, and you guys get this much, and . . . we'll see how you do, and then we'll carve it up differently." I don't see it happening in this generation very much, but maybe it's starting to happen, where we'll be able to articulate Aboriginal values. So that we can approach the problems that are facing us and say, "Well, no, we don't agree that we should just be evaluated on your terms. We have certain needs and distinct values that we feel could be addressed in the services we develop. This is how we want to do it."

RECONCEPTUALIZING INDIGENOUS NATIONHOOD

While the participants have contributed a considerable level of clarification toward the subject of urban mixed-blood Native people and nation-rebuilding, most were stymied by the fundamental impasse that the federal government has created—the presence, across Canada, of over six hundred tiny, almost landless individual entities known as the First Nations, the only Native communities recognized as legally existing according to the Indian Act. These scattered communities, occupying only fragments of their original land base, exist alongside an ever-growing body of urban, dispossessed individuals with no land base at all, whose ties to their communities of origin have been weakened and in some cases obscured. This growing body of urban Native people, instead of having some mode of working from their own strengths toward common goals with the First Nations, are shut out of formal sovereignty processes and instead placed in the role of being in direct competition with reserve communities for federal dollars in the interests of their own separate survival. In such a context, it is important to consider the ancient political systems that Native communities are attempting to revive and how urban mixed-bloods might be able to find a place in such nation-building efforts.

Taiaiake Alfred has suggested that nationalist efforts being made by communities such as Kahnawake derive their power from the existence of a traditional institutional framework, the Iroquois Confederacy—albeit in modified contemporary form—which has provided the Iroquois communities with an alternative framework for nation-building that has powerful cultural and spiritual resonance. Alfred asserts that other Native communities in Canada have remained fixed at what he terms a "latent nationalism" phase, because they have lacked viable political alternatives to the settler-state framework in which they exist only as individual communities, affiliated through territorial organizations that mirror the logic of the Indian Act (Alfred 1995, 184–85). For nations other than the six nations of the Iroquois Confederacy, then, reviving the political confederacies that existed at the time of colonization—as well as creating new ones as a response to specific conditions created *by* colonization—is probably the most effective means for Native communities to overcome many of the weaknesses imposed by the Indian Act system. With respect to urban Native people, it also represents one of the only possible means by which truly effective political alliances can be created between on-reserve and off-reserve communities, in that the ancient confederacies are built on older ways of understanding Native identity that preceded the Indian Act system and the maze of divisions between Native peoples that it has created.

Probably the only confederacy that has existed in an almost unbroken state since precolonial times is the Iroquois Confederacy. While this confederacy, which spans both sides of the Canadian-U.S. border, continuously opposes the imposition of Indian Act governance (in Canada), as an institution adapted to the realities of the twenty-first century, it no longer embraces a precolonial framework of membership. With minor exceptions, such as Kanatsiohareke, a community consisting of Longhouse people who returned to the Mohawk valley in 1993 to create a new community, its membership is primarily restricted to the citizens of existing territories; that is, the band or tribal members of existing communities. Other ancient confederacies, however, can provide a mode of rupturing Indian Act membership codes. Like the Iroquois Confederacy, they are also the repository of historical, cultural, and spiritual practices, providing forms of continuity to peoples whose pasts have been, effectively, stolen by colonization.

The Wabanaki Confederacy, for example, comprising the Mi'kmaq, Maliseet, and Abenaki peoples in Canada, and the Passamaquoddy and Penobscot peoples in the United States, have in recent years been having annual gatherings. Among other issues, they focus on the problem of U.S.-Canadian border crossings. Together with the Wampanoag, Pennacook, Wappinger, Powhattan, Nanticook, and Leanape Confederacies (Boyd 1998, 6), which between them represent the thirteen surviving Indigenous nations and tribes along the eastern seaboard, they have asserted their sovereignty over the entire Maritime and New England regions of Canada and the United States ("Wabanaki Confederacy" 1998, 3). These confederacies, which all predate European colonization, were responsible for the almost continuous warfare that the British faced in one region or another for a century prior to 1750. These continuous wars of resistance were instrumental in forcing the British crown to recognize a nation-to-nation relationship with Indigenous nations, in the Royal Proclamation of 1763.

The growing movement of East Coast Native peoples who are beginning to accept the authority of the Wabanaki Confederacy has already resulted in renewed sovereignty assertions, particularly around Aboriginal harvesting.[1] Other formerly powerful groups, such as the Blackfoot Confederacy, are also on the move, declaring their sovereignty and meeting to discuss reunifying the former confederacy member governments in southern Alberta and the northern United States. They are also asserting, in a preliminary manner, that Treaty 7 should not be considered valid because of the lack of representation of member governments during the signing (McKinley 1998b, 1).

The difference between the ancient confederacies and current nationhood assertions through provincial territorial organizations, such as the Nishnawbe-Aski Nation, or the Anishinabek Nation, is that those organizations are groupings primarily organized around specific territorial treaties, which in most instances follow the logic of the colonizer with respect to who was included or excluded in the process. The ancient confederacies reference older realities, where individuals who are currently classified as nonstatus Indians or Métis, could potentially be entitled to citizenship outside of Indian Act categories. In a similar manner, there is little inherent potential for discrimination between those who grew up in the cities and those who grew up on reserves, as far as citizenship in the confederacies would be concerned, in that the confederacies are premised on the notion that the entire traditional land base, not just the reserve, is Native land.

The possibility exists, however, that the individuals who are currently reviving these confederacies could "imprint" these revived frameworks with the same divisions as the Indian Act has created, whereby status Indians, and communities designated as reserves, are privileged over all other groups. An interesting development, in this respect, is the effort to create a Cree Confederacy, with member communities from Quebec to British Columbia, as well as the United States (McKinley 1998a, 1). While such a geopolitical unit could potentially be truly counterhegemonic, as a confederacy spanning six provinces, any notion of such an entity immediately cuts to the heart of one of the biggest divisions created by the Indian Act—the question of the inclusion or exclusion of Cree Métis communities in such a confederacy. Will Cree First Nations consider including as members the Cree Métis communities that dot the northern prairies (assuming

that the Métis communities wish to do so), or will they simply replicate contemporary treaty Indian–Métis divisions, disregarding common cultural heritage and language?

The confederacies represent a way out of the deadlock of fragmentation and divisions that Native people have been sealed into by the
Indian Act for two reasons—they not only present the possibility of
renegotiating the boundaries that have currently been erected around
different categories of Indigeneity, but they envision a potentially sufficient land base to do so. While Bill C-31 Indians may struggle for
the right to be members in their mothers' communities, the fact remains that the generations of individuals excluded from Indianness
by gender and racial discrimination within the Indian Act will not all
be able to rediscover "home" within the approximately six hundred
existing postage-stamp-sized communities that are currently called
"First Nations." The only really viable way in which urban Native
people would be able to have access to Native land is through the
prospect of being citizens of the original Indigenous territories—the
lands that correspond to those that were held by the different Indigenous nations at the time of contact. We must be clear, though,
that if First Nations genuinely want an end to the divisiveness of the
current system, they cannot create new national entities that simply replicate its logic. First Nations have to be genuinely willing to
work with groups that at present they ignore or disdain—the Métis,
nonstatus Indians, and urban Native people in general—based on the
needs of all of these groups, in ways that are premised on providing all
future citizens of Indigenous nations with the kind of privileges and
rights that at present only status Indians enjoy. This does not mean
denying the differences between the different groups that the Indian
Act has created—but it means finding the connections that a history
of colonial regulation has sought to obscure or destroy.

For mixed-blood urban Native people, the confederacies could be
sites where urban Native communities affiliate *as* urban communities—where urban mixed-bloods do not have to fruitlessly struggle
to remake themselves as "full-blood traditionalists" in order to be
considered members of Indigenous nations, and where struggles over
entitlement framed as who is a "real" Indian and who is not become
meaningless.

We should be clear that Aboriginal peoples in Canada continue to
face ongoing and recently accelerating actions by Canada not only to
erode or openly attack the hard-won Aboriginal rights framed in the

Constitution and acknowledged in court decisions, but to entirely undermine the ability of First Nations governments to individually or collectively resist ongoing loss of land or to acquire a resource base and economic viability.[2] These attacks are in most cases spearheaded by ongoing attempts to change the Indian Act in ways that weaken any protections it provides to First Nations land. An important example is the First Nations Governance Act (FNGA), a suite of nine pieces of legislation currently being pushed through the various levels of parliament despite massive and ongoing protest by Native organizations and Native people across Canada. While the government has provided few details about each piece of legislation, a central element of the FNGA is the First Nations Fiscal and Statistical Management Act, touted as bringing about "fiscal responsibility" in Native communities. This act successfully divided the Assembly of First Nations for a number of months in resisting the act because some of the BC chiefs, who have a small land base and no treaties, see aspects of the fiscal bill, which allows for the creation of financial institutions that serve member First Nations and enable taxation, as useful to them (Barnsley 2003c, 1, 3).

The fiscal relations act codifies a practice that Indian Affairs has already been following for several years—(illegally) imposing third party management on any First Nations government in debt or where allegations of mismanagement have been made (Barnsley 2003g, 3). It should be noted that the standards for financial mismanagement for First Nations are far more rigorous than those faced by any municipality in Canada. Under third party management, the minister of Indian Affairs orders all financial operations on specific First Nations to be controlled by appointed firms, effectively removing control from the band. The bill, in pushing the notion of imposing First Nations accountability, ignores the fact that governments can scarcely be held accountable for programs they do not design. Furthermore, while chiefs of First Nations must be answerable first of all to Indian Affairs (who provides them with the funding), they are expected to be accountable as well to their own people, when in fact they lack any form of control over their own revenues that would give them the necessary authority (Barnsley 2003a, 1, 2). The bill forces a form of limited and federally defined self-government on Native communities while continuing to limit their control over their own affairs.

First Nations fear, among other things, that the legislation will infringe on existing treaty rights and force upon them the status of municipalities. The minister of Indian Affairs has entirely refused any discussion with members of the Assembly of First Nations, has withdrawn funds from treaty organizations that oppose the FNGA, has openly stated that he will not listen to Native protestors, and has devoted $10 million (of money designated for Aboriginal peoples) into selling the bill to the Canadian public. He also states that he has no authority to address treaty issues and that the FNGA has nothing to do with treaty rights.[3]

Attacks on Aboriginal rights are also coming from a number of other directions. A recent example is Bill C-5, designed to protect wildlife species at risk in Canada, but which does not include a nonderogation clause. Furthermore, the attorney general of Canada has recently asserted that nonderogation clauses will no longer be included in any new Canadian legislation. Nonderogation clauses have generally been a part of Canadian legislation since the 1982 Constitution Act, to ensure that new legislation does not infringe on the Aboriginal rights recognized in Section 35. These clauses are considered necessary because most legislation incorporates "gray areas," where the government can put its own interests ahead of Aboriginal or treaty rights for reasons of "public need." Without a nonderogation clause, courts could decide that such infringements were valid. Instead, the nonderogation clause ensures that the Aboriginal or treaty rights protected by Section 35 cannot be violated (Barnsley 2003e, 1, 14).

What these attacks represent is a response to the massive number of direct challenges by different Native communities to the colonial status quo in Canada today. Putting aside the huge volume of residential school cases and the two hundred ongoing court cases addressing the defects and mismanagement of the Indian Act, there are upward of one thousand court cases dealing with Aboriginal and treaty rights currently moving through the justice system.[4]

For these reasons, it is clear that existing organizations of Aboriginal people must continue to struggle to defend existing political and legal rights and to fight for restitution because of colonial policies that have robbed them of land and resources. At the same time, since Native resistance to these ongoing attacks is seriously weakened by the various ways in which we are divided *by* the Indian Act and other legislation, it is apparent that unless there is some attempt to reintroduce traditional forms of governance, it will be more and more difficult to stand up to ongoing colonial assault. Part of this embracing of traditional governments *has* to involve rethinking who is Indian and who is Métis; it involves questioning the meanings of divisions among those with status, those without status, and Bill C-31 Indians. It also has to involve significantly challenging the restrictions to our former land bases, to render meaningless the current divisions between those who live on-reserve and those who are urban.

The day when significant areas of what was formerly Canada have been renegotiated along the lines of sovereign Native confederacies will not be reached during our lifetimes. However, transforming how we think about Native identity does not have to wait until the designation as "citizen of an Indigenous Nation" becomes a reality for most of us. Numerous interim processes could be tried that would provide individuals who lack Indian status or band membership with legal rights and entitlement to at least some of the existing benefits of Indian status. All of these attempts would rupture or bypass some aspect of the Indian Act, and, as result, all of them have the potential to destabilize common-sense ways of understanding Native identity. In this respect, of course, all of these suggestions represent huge, difficult transitions, which in themselves would require extensive long-term struggle—not the least with a federal government which is firmly—and in a sense violently—determined to maintain existing divisions between Native peoples as central to our subordination.

With respect to a movement that is already at hand, in terms of renegotiating the numbered treaties, a move that would tremendously challenge colonialism is for communities to demand that the descendants of individuals who received half-breed scrip should be admitted into treaty. These individuals could then be considered "treaty Métis" and could thus begin to negotiate sovereignty issues in conjunction with treaty Indian groups—in particular, the acquisition of a land base. This approach has the strength of undermining the central role of the Indian Act—of empowering (in a relative way) some Native people in order to disempower the rest. While there would still be numbers of nonstatus Indians (particularly in eastern Canada and in the cities) who were not eligible for Indian status, by challenging the historic exclusion of half-breeds, an estimated six hundred thousand individuals would be brought into fiduciary relationship with the federal government in ways that significantly challenge colonial divisions.

Another approach would be for status Indian organizations to formally challenge, in a concerted way, the limitations to Indian status in Section 6.2 of Bill C-31, so that the second-generation cut-off, and the continued bleeding off of individuals from Indian status if their parents of either gender intermarry with non-Natives, would be stopped. At least a hundred thousand more individuals would therefore be eligible for reinstatement as Indians.

A third direction is to work toward promoting Canada's fiduciary obligation toward whole communities of nonstatus people in eastern Canada who were excluded from the treaty-making process (such as the Algonquin in Ontario and Quebec, and the Mi'kmaq and Innu of Newfoundland) and are asserting themselves as First Nations without recognition by the federal government.

A diversity of forms of affiliation—and of nation-rebuilding—could be taken up, which fit the diverse circumstances that Aboriginal peoples face across the continent. The important point is that these forms of affiliation are concrete ways of addressing the divisions that have been created by the Indian Act, divisions that are not going to go away simply by our labeling them as "colonial divisions" or attempting to disregard them. They are ways of bringing together the very different strengths that urban and reserve-based Native people have developed out of their different circumstances, in the interests of our mutual empowerment.

Appendix 1
Eligibility for Status and Band Membership under Bill C-31 (From Holmes 1987)

Those eligible to be reinstated under Section 6(1) of the revised Indian Act include:

> Women who lost status because they married a man without Indian status, and any children enfranchised along with them;

> Children born outside of marriage to a status Indian woman, whose registration was protested because the alleged father was not a status Indian;

> Women and men who lost status because both their mother and paternal grandmother gained status through marriage;

> Women and men who were enfranchised upon application or under various sections of pre-1951 Indian Acts.

Those eligible under Section 6(2): Any child, one of whose parents is eligible to be registered under any of the subsections of 6(1), above. Those not eligible include:

> The descendants of people who accepted half-breed land or money scrip, unless entitled under another provision;

> Descendants of families or entire bands that were left off band lists or were never registered;

Some women who gained status through marriage and then lost it, for example, by marrying and then divorcing a status man and remarrying a nonstatus man;

Many of the grandchildren of people who lost their status, commonly referred to as the second-generation cut-off. The grandchildren of persons who lost their status and are reinstated under Bill C-31 can be registered as Indians only if both parents have status under Section 6(1) or 6(2), or if one parent has status under Section 6(1) (in other words, who never lost their status).

The following are automatically and immediately entitled to be band members:
Section 11(1)

Anyone who was on a band list or entitled to be on a band list before Bill C-31 came into effect;

Anyone who is a member of a band that was newly created or recognized by the government, either before or after Bill C-31 came out;

Anyone who lost status through:

Section 12(1)(b)—marriage to a man without Indian status;

Section 12(1)(a)(iii) and Section 109(2)—involuntary enfranchisement of a woman upon marriage to a man without Indian status and the enfranchisement of any of her children born before her marriage;

Section 12(1)(a)(iv)—the double-mother clause—loss of status upon reaching the age of twenty-one, if mother and paternal grandmother gained status through marriage;

Section 12(2)—children born to Indian women who lost status upon protest because the alleged father was not a status Indian;

Any children born after Bill C-31 came into effect, *both* of whose parents are members of the same band.

The following categories of people are granted conditional membership. If a band left control of its membership with Indian or Northern Affairs, these people become band members. If a band took control of

its membership, the band's membership code may exclude people in these categories:
Section 11(2)

Anyone enfranchised under Section 12(1)(a)(iii) and Section 109(1);

The voluntary enfranchisement of an Indian man along with his wife and minor unmarried children;

Or under Section 13 of the Indian Act of 1927 (in effect from 1880 to 1951)—residency outside of Canada for more than five years, without the consent of the superintendent or Indian agent;

Or under Section 111 of the Indian Act of 1906 (in effect from 1867 to 1920)—upon receiving a university degree or becoming a doctor, lawyer, or clergyman;

A child whose parents belong to different bands, or only one of whose parents belongs to or was entitled to belong to a band. This will include children born to Indian women who married non-Indian men, i.e., women who lost status under Section 12(1)(b).

Appendix 2
Issues in Conducting
Indigenous Research

For this study, interviews were conducted, over the space of one year, with thirty individuals who identify as Native and who are active in some capacity within the Toronto Native community. The overall focus of the work significantly influenced the organization of this study. For example, in seeking to interview mixed-blood Native people, I was faced with the problem of how I would define "Native" for the purpose of the study. I decided to rely on an individual's self-designation as being of Native heritage, coupled with their playing some role in the Toronto Native community, as a sufficient definition of Nativeness for this context. My desire to capture a sense of the broad range of experiences of Nativeness was at the root of this decision. In any case, to rely on other definitions of Nativeness—for example, Indian status or blood quantum—was to use the same colonial logic as the Canadian or American governments.

In looking at whom I accepted as Native, and the extent to which this reflects the actual composition of the Toronto Native community, it is important to consider the contested nature of Nativeness in urban settings such as Toronto (where those who are "certifiably Indian" by virtue of a status card, regularly share space with nonstatus individuals who are suspected of being "wannabees," especially if they are white-looking). It is therefore crucial to acknowledge the background of relative ambiguity about Native identity in which this study took shape and, accordingly, the care that I had to take in evaluating the identity claims of the participants—to be both respectful of individual circumstances and mindful of my responsibilities to the group as a whole.

Because of this, after interviewing one participant I decided not to include her within this study. As a white-looking adopted individual with only an extremely tenuous claim to a Native identity, based primarily on "ancestral memory," I felt that her identity claims were not adequate for the purpose of this study and have therefore declined to include data from her interview in this work. In all detailing of statistics, throughout this study, I refer only to the twenty-nine individuals who were accepted as participants, although thirty individuals were actually interviewed.

About a third of the participants were immediate acquaintances, colleagues, and friends, located in different circles within the Native community. The other individuals were solicited *by* these participants; almost everybody knew somebody who was eager to talk about this subject. For ethical reasons, I wanted to interview people to whom I had some kind of relationship; this would ensure that in writing about their lives I felt a personal obligation to present the stories in the sense that they had been told to me—not to make their life stories simply "grist for an academic mill." And in a sense, it seemed pointless to deliberately seek out strangers to interview, while bypassing my own community networks. Nevertheless, my own relationship to the participants, and to the area studied, raises an important question. What happens when Aboriginal people conduct research in their own communities, among people they know? Is objectivity compromised? Is objectivity even a desirable goal?

THE INDIGENOUS RESEARCHER IN HER OWN COMMUNITY

In some respects, Aboriginal researchers face circumstances similar to anybody conducting "insider" research. Research methodology in general is shaped by the assumption that the researcher is an outsider, able to observe without being implicated in the scene, capable therefore of neutrality and objectivity. Indeed, what is considered "good" research, within the positivist tradition, demands an assumption of objectivity.

Critiques of positivism, notably within feminist and Indigenous research, question the value of this framework of "objectivity." They have argued for the importance of insider research within a qualitative framework and suggest that researchers must above all engage in reflexivity—they must have ways of thinking critically about their processes, their relationships, and the quality and richness of their data and analysis (Tuhiwai Smith 1999, 137).

For example, one problem I struggled with on a daily basis, which I described in the preface to this book, was the intense effect of this work on my own sense of identity. Another problem I wrestled with was the fact that for the two years in which I was engaged in researching and writing the thesis that became this book, my mind was immersed in the massive amounts of very personal information about the people I had interviewed, most of whom were living around me, had either personal or professional relationships with me, and in some instances were rivals with one another, or at the very least had considerable professional and personal dealings with one another. The implications of what might happen if I accidentally let something slip in a relaxed moment about one person to another made the usually abstract ethical concerns about participants' privacy a full-blown nightmare. Among other things, it meant that for two years I could not fully relax around the people who were my participants. Nor was I comfortable during the occasional instances when my analyses of their words differed from the participants' own perspectives.

Insiders conducting research in their own communities need ways of defining closure and need to develop the skills to say "no," or to say "continue," even when the results might be difficult (Tuhiwai Smith 1999, 137). They may encounter information about individuals and families that they would rather not be privy to, or find uncomfortable things out about friends. For example, at times I discovered that certain individuals carried anger toward individuals with light-skinned privilege, which suddenly put my relationships with them in a different light. Finding the strength to say "continue," and not to shrink away from the anger in their words, was difficult. Still more difficult was negotiating the discomfort that many Native people feel when differences among us are broached, a process that at times threatened to swamp old friendships and hijack new ones.

On a deeper level, as Maori academic Linda Tuhiwai Smith suggests, there is more at stake for Aboriginal researchers when they conduct research. A central issue they face is that both they and their communities will have to forever live with the consequences of their actions (Tuhiwai Smith 1999, 137). Aboriginal researchers are engaged in an activity that has frequently been harmful to Native communities. Tuhiwai Smith has documented some of the many ways in which research represents a colonial project for Aboriginal peoples, disempowering them through studying them (Tuhiwai Smith 1999, 58–106). Accordingly, each Indigenous researcher carries a strong obligation not only to frame her research in ways that strengthen her community, or at the very least does no damage, but also to ensure that in the larger context, it will not in some way reframe colonialism in new ways. And we are doing this for the most part on our own. Unlike feminist researchers, who generally can find a network of mentors and peers with whom to discuss their work, most Aboriginal academics function for long periods as the only Aboriginal person in their department, with neither mentors nor peers.

The issues I faced were compounded by the fact that urban Aboriginal communities such as the Toronto community are unique in their decentralized condition. There is no band council to accept or reject the research or impose conditions on it, and there are a wide range of elders and traditional leaders, none of whom claim to speak for the entire community. This means that there is no representative group of Aboriginal people to guide the researcher's concerns into paths that are beneficial to the community as a whole. In such a context, the Indigenous researcher must rely on those individual elders that she has some form of relationship with, combined with the informed consent of individuals. I attempted to adhere to every form of traditional guidance I could find, in such circumstances. Given the range of leaders and teachers in the community, I could hope for no more than that.

In this relative isolation, how is the Indigenous researcher in an urban Native community to evaluate the effect of revealing the pain of her subjects' experiences, in a culture that, as Emma LaRoque notes, feeds on personal accounts of Native suffering (LaRoque 1993)? Should she address her subjects' battles with alcoholism, with abusive parents, or with corrupt community leaders—issues that will only feed dominant culture stereotypes about Native people? How is she to evaluate the effect of opening up the whole subject of Native identity at all, in a colonizing culture where "primordiality" is demanded of the Indigenous person, in a university environment almost entirely devoid of Native people? "Expert" reviewers, in this context, who are almost unanimously non-Native, offer no guidance here—and in fact, often force dominant culture interpretations on the work. As I prepare this manuscript for publication, ongoing questions continue to be raised as to my responsibility to the community that was central in creating this work, particularly as the final product will be considered almost solely as a product of my own expertise; the collective voices who informed it so deeply will become invisible—and unrewarded.

THE INTERVIEW PROCESS

In organizing the research, I began with the notion that mixed-blood Native identity is rooted in experiences of urbanity, as it has been primarily in the cities that Native people meet and marry non-Natives and create mixed-blood families. A starting point of inquiry, then, was to understand why large numbers of Native people have left their communities and to seek possible connections between their experiences. I therefore began the interviews with the request that participants talk about the terms under which their families had left their communities. In some cases, most of the interview consisted of family history. Considerable space was also made within the interview for discussions about Indigenous sovereignty, about how the participants saw their relationship to their community of origin, and about the role that community activism played within their lives. The interviews were therefore in-depth—most took two hours, while on a number of occasions the interviews lasted for an entire evening. The interviews were completely transcribed and returned to each participant for their commentary and clarification. As I knew many of the participants, previous conversations informed the interview process, and subsequent discussions amplified them, not only throughout the interview process, but through the entire writing of this work.

The decision was made early in the study to focus primarily on individuals of Native-white ancestry. The reason for this was that these are the individuals for whom family life has been an arena where a kind of warfare on Native identity has been waged and where light-skinned privilege, Eurocentric teaching, and/or pressures to assimilate have all made Native identity highly contradictory. The participants are not *exclusively* Native-white people—I interviewed two triracial women, who had either African or Asian ancestry as well as white and Native heritages; however, the rest of the participants were biracial Native and white.

On the other hand, because many people in the Toronto Native community are from South or Central America as well as the United States, I chose to include as participants Native people from any part of the Americas. While most of the participants are from Native nations whose homelands are occupied by Canada, some are from territories occupied by the United States or different Latin American countries. In deliberately choosing to include individuals who were triracial or from Latin America, I was also interested in challenging the "closing down" against diversity that is sometimes evidenced in the Native community toward mixed-bloods whose non-Native identity is too different from the Anglo-Canadian norm—such as black or Latin American. The majority of participants, however, are the products of first-generation intermarriages between Native people and whites in English Canada.

For many of the participants, the fact that they are the product of one generation of intermarriage (usually combined with some degree of ancestral intermarriage during the fur trade, too far back in the family to significantly affect their contemporary identities as Native people) is often portrayed as an accidental "blip" on the screen of an otherwise Native identity, where the whiteness of one parent can simply be ignored and the person asserts herself as unproblematically Native. For some of these individuals, particularly those who look Native or were raised within Native culture, this is an adequate and probably appropriate strategy, although this study also highlights the actual dynamics of living in mixed-race families. Trying to bypass the fact of intermarriage is not, however, an adequate strategy for those who are the product of more than one generation of intermarriage, for whom the reality of cultural and racial hybridity cannot be ignored. The complex identities of mixed-race Native people who have learned to see themselves as Latin American, or of those whose black or Asian ancestors joined up with and intermarried with Native peoples while trying to escape from slavery or indentured labor or other forms of racial discrimination, such as black Indians (especially in the United States), or Asian/Aboriginal people (in western Canada), cannot easily be collapsed into a relatively narrow view of Native identity. Putting it another way, the participants who are proud to be both Aboriginal and black, or Japanese and Aboriginal—as well as those for whom a Latin American identity have shaped their Indianness—all face some difficulty in reducing issues of their identity simply to whether they are "Indian or not" (in Toronto terms), even as they make decisions to "come out" as unequivocally Native.

And this is a dilemma that will not be going away—the reality of large-scale contemporary intermarriage in the Toronto region between African or Asian peoples and Native people, means that mixed-blood Native identity in the future will increasingly be conceptualized in terms of multiple levels of cultural hybridity. While this study does not do adequate justice to the stories of black Indians, or Asian-Aboriginal people, or Mestizos/Mestizas, it is undertaken with an awareness that these narratives are an integral part of the full range of mixed-blood identity that exists in the Americas. My interviews merely touch on these narratives, and they are only taken up as they affect the people in this study.

THE PARTICIPANTS

Twenty-one of the participants are female and eight are male. Twelve are status Indians through their own lineage; however, seven others are nonstatus Native people who have some connection, parental or through their grandparents, to specific reserves (including one Métis woman whose grandmother had lost status for marrying a Métis man, but who had regained Indian status through her marriage to a status Indian prior to 1985). Ten participants are from families that have never held Indian status (including four whose Indigenous nations are not from territories currently occupied by Canada). Two individuals grew up on reserves, and one grew up in a northern Métis community. Two other participants had regular intervals of staying on their reserves throughout their childhood, even though their mothers had lost status through marrying non-Natives. Two individuals had had very occasional visits to their reserves as children; the rest had grown up entirely urban-based.

The participants also varied with respect to their appearance. This is a highly subjective standard; however, as I saw it, six of the participants looked entirely white, with nothing visual to link them to Nativeness at all. A handful of others were very ambiguous in appearance (at times they could be said to be white-looking, while at other times they were noticed as nonwhite). Ten individuals looked distinctly nonwhite—some had Native features and light skin, or dark skin and "less Native" features, some merely looked "different" or "exotic." They were usually seen as nonwhite, but not necessarily as Native, by other people. And finally, eight individuals looked unequivocally Native, under any light and at any time (by my own subjective standard). Interestingly, the individuals' sense of their own appearance did not concur with how I saw them. A number of individuals saw themselves

as darker or more Native-looking than I thought of them—others saw
themselves as capable of passing for white in circumstances where I
never would have thought this possible. It is, of course, impossible to
discuss the issue of appearance without referring to the strength of
hegemonic standards of Indianness, which in fact became a recurring
issue in this study.

The oldest participant was sixty-two and the youngest twenty-four;
however, only four other individuals were in their twenties. Thirteen
people were in their thirties, while seven people were in their forties
and three were in their fifties. The average age of the participants was
thirty-eight; the median age was thirty-five. Older subjects were chosen deliberately, in that it generally takes an individual a few years
to learn about, understand, and even care about identity issues; inevitably, the youngest participants had the least to say about their
own family backgrounds.

The individuals were far more highly educated than is perhaps the
norm for Aboriginal people. While one-third of the individuals lacked
extensive education (four of them had not completed high school, one
had graduated from high school, and four had the equivalent of college certificates), another one-third had undergraduate degrees, while
fully a third of them had postgraduate degrees, including one with
a law degree. The lowest level of education among the participants
was one individual with a grade six education; at the other end of
the scale were three individuals working on their Ph.D.'s. This was a
result both of the selection process—where individuals in the education system refer to other individuals with education—and of the age
level of the participants. A number of the individuals had gone back to
school later in life (as I did myself). The higher-than-average age level
was another reason why the education level among the participants
was so high. Because of this, high education level did not necessarily
correspond with a high-class background among the participants; like
me, many of the people I interviewed had had significant adult experiences of being considered unskilled and/or undereducated, before
they finally entered university.

INTERPRETING THE PARTICIPANTS' STORIES

Throughout the interview process, I played a double role—first, as
an individual who is of mixed Native-white heritage herself, who
interviewed individuals on the basis of friendship or a perception of

common experience, but who then proceeded to take on the role of evaluating these narratives, inevitably through a personal process, but also through an academic lens, and producing a text. Two related issues arose. To what extent does my own framework of concerns, relative to my own circumstances, shape this work? And how do I interpret the participants' words?

The first issue relates to social location. Within the world of mixed-race Native identity, my concerns center around the fact that I do not look very Native, that my Native heritage has been devalued in my family for one generation already and that, as a result, our knowledge of our ancestry is far from complete. Further concerns relate to the fact that I have never lived in Mi'kmaq territory, that I am nonstatus, and that as far as I can tell I am only "one-quarter" Native. I am also a woman whose childhood and adulthood has involved poverty and considerable experiences of abuse, whose choices have been affected in a number of ways by sexism, whose sexuality has ranged from heterosexual to lesbian and back again, who is childless, and who for almost two decades now has been breathing the rarified air of academia. All of these things influence how I see mixed-race Native identity—my concern that Native circles be inclusive of racial and sexual "difference" and that gender and class dynamics not be "swept under the carpet," my conviction that the relationship between Nativeness and Indian status needs to be deconstructed, and above all my sense that the survival of urban mixed-race Native people *as* Native people hinges on their ability to reintegrate their lives into the lives of their nations in ways that are beneficial both to urban and on-reserve people. Despite considerable effort on my part to be aware of and compensate for my own biases, the fact remains that a writer whose experiences of mixed-race Native identity were different than mine might perhaps tell a different story from the same data.

The second issue, concerning interpretations of stories, involves what knowledge I draw on to understand the participants' words. This question arose most prominently around the issue of the silence that was a constant feature of the narratives. The participants spoke of silence from their parents and grandparents about the past. They described stories wrested reluctantly from aunties and uncles after years of silence. Finally, in some cases their own stories contained spaces of silence and incidents described flatly, without detail.

Paying close attention to the silences and flat descriptions in the narratives proved immensely fruitful in a number of ways. The most crucial discovery happened when I began to add up the numbers of the participants who mentioned casually, without further articulation, that their grandmothers had lost status for marrying Métis men, as well as the numbers of the participants whose mothers had lost status or who themselves had lost it, for marrying non-Natives. The apparently minor issue of a history of sexism in the Indian Act suddenly began to represent an immense rupture in the family histories of the participants, as I realized that out of the nineteen participants whose ancestors had held Indian status, a total of thirteen had been alienated from their communities of origin by loss of status under Section 12(1)(b) of the Indian Act. With Bill C-31, twelve of the nineteen now have status; however, only five of these individuals will be able to pass their status on to their descendants in perpetuity. Recognizing the scale of loss that this represented led to an exploration of the relationship between the "bleeding off" of successive generations of Native women, and their descendants, from their communities of origin and cultural genocide.

Other silences remain, however. How do we interpret the almost deafening silence about the past that participant after participant described from parents and grandparents? In this silence, those of us who share this heritage have certain strengths—our knowledge provides us with a lens through which we can read certain things. We know that some individuals may be silent because they carry the burden of unimaginable trauma, as children who grew up in the prison environment of the residential schools. Others may have been gradually rendered silent by lifetimes of social isolation that they faced as Native women, having left their communities forever when they married white men and finding themselves surrounded, in their homes and neighborhoods, by racism and sexism and massive cultural incomprehension. Still other individuals were taught to maintain silence about Indianness as children, as a strategy for survival in hostile environments—the muting effects of a legacy of racial terror, or through learning to associate Nativeness with poverty, degradation, and shame. But those of us who live with these histories can also see the silences whereby our parents refused to conform to assimilation pressures, as well as the messages of affirmation of Indianness that in some contexts were confirmed by silence. We can read our parents' resistance in their silence, because it is equally obvious, through the multiple and sometimes devious roads that led the participants almost inexorably to reclaim a Native identity, that silence about Nativeness was not all that our parents passed down to us.

As the previous passage demonstrates, in interpreting the details spoken so baldly to me, I have relied on my own knowledge of the events in question, which has come from a variety of sources, including my limited knowledge of my own family's history. Published accounts of people's stories have been useful—for example, a recent book by Blair Stonechild and Bill Waiser, which for the first time documents, from elders, the Cree version of the events surrounding the Northwest Rebellion of 1885 (Stonechild and Waiser 1997). After reading this book, where Cree elders spoke of the hangings, persecution, and policies of deliberate starvation that Cree communities endured in the wake of the 1885 Rebellion, the comments by several participants—that their Cree grandparents had suddenly moved to the United States in the late 1880s and spent several decades moving around Montana and North Dakota before venturing back to Saskatchewan or Alberta in the early years of the twentieth century—became visible as part of a larger context and were therefore interpreted as such. In a similar manner, when East Coast participants spoke of the decimation of their nations, my understanding was increased by stories I had been told by Mi'kmaq elders, as well as through books by Mi'kmaq writers such as Daniel Paul (2000), that document the bitter histories of East Coast Native people. The ongoing revelations and discussions about the pervasive effects of residential schooling, which are happening in Native settings everywhere across Canada, also informed my sense of the bigger picture that included the stories of these participants—the multigenerational effects of residential schooling on Native families.

REPRESENTATIVENESS OF THIS STUDY

The participants—representing a cross-section of the urban Native community but nevertheless a cross-section skewed by gender, age, and education level—should not be viewed as a representative sample of the urban mixed-blood Toronto community. What this study *is* most representative of, however, is the on-going dialogue that has been taking place at all levels of the Toronto urban Native community over the past few years, concerning mixed-bloodedness, Indian status, band membership, the nature of the urban community, and the future of Native people in Canada. The participants occupy most of the different niches in the community, from those who have been homeless and who rely on the Native social service agencies, to those who are front-line workers, to those who run the agencies, and those who work at the governmental level on policy issues. In this respect, they have articulated most of the community's recent concerns about mixed-blood Native identity.

Appendix 3
Narratives of
Encounters with Genocide

In keeping with the notion that it is important for Native people to tell their stories with their own words, for this section I have selected a handful of accounts from different individuals describing their family histories and gathered them here. Most of the stories are anonymous, although some individuals have chosen to sign their names afterward. Together, they illustrate some aspects of the range and complexity of the experiences of mixed-blood urban Native peoples with colonization and resistance. Cross-border experiences of colonization in more than one country, multi-racial Native identity, the complexities of Métis existence, and the lived experiences of residential school, of loss of status, and of adoption, are delineated in the words of the people I interviewed.

ROSE'S STORY

In the United States, I'm a member of the Passamaquoddy Tribe of Maine. But here in Canada, where our people come from, I'm non-status. Our people once lived in what is now New Brunswick and welcomed the Loyalists. But then they drove us off our territory to a little island in the middle of Passamaquoddy Bay. But even that was, I guess, still a little too close for the Loyalists. So my people were driven to the other side of the bay, in what is now the United States.

My great-great grandfather was allowed to stay on his land in New Brunswick because he was a guide. You can see the reserve from our property.

The Passamaquoddy people almost went extinct. They were decimated by the Loyalists—they out-and-out killed them. North American Indians were massacred, and most of it was done intentionally. And that's really well documented, too, if people choose to read about it and think. When the Tribe decided that they had to protect their heritage and find the language again—we're talking the seventies, or even later—I think they were down to fifty-six people. The whole Passamaquoddy language was almost lost. So they sort of brought back some of the rituals, like Indian Day—it's a powwow; they have it once a year. And there're some young people who are drumming—but when my uncle died a year and a half ago, nobody was prepared well enough yet to chant for him.

It comes down to survival. Indians were so decimated that they knew if they didn't assimilate they weren't going to survive. I think our parents probably very consciously didn't want us connected to our culture, because they knew that we would only survive if we integrated. "You're gonna be white or you're not going to survive." Until you had some brave soul who said, "Hey, wait a minute." It was probably some old person who could sit back and reflect and say, "We aren't living in the same time anymore." Or maybe they reached a time where they didn't have very much to lose any more. You know, they're going to die soon—so they sit back and say, "Hey, we've lost our heritage." And so they're trying to get it back.

And then, for our family, we didn't have a lot of association with our relatives on the reserve. My father didn't usually come with us when we would visit, because we had to cross the border to get there, and he was Japanese, and it was the postwar era—you know, the forties into the fifties. And so we'd go down with my mother, in the daytime. But we'd never stay past dark. And I'm still like that. When my uncle died, I stayed overnight on the reserve, and it's the first time in my whole life that I'd ever stayed overnight. And it was almost the first time that I stayed after dark. It was just that—you went home before dark. Because you'd go down on a Sunday, and you'd hear about who got stabbed the night before. It was my mother in particular who was very selective about which families we could visit. And some families we could visit as a group. For safety, basically. Although we were probably just as safe there as on the other side. But it was just the liquor. She was death on the liquor.

For a long time, people believed that the reserve—it wasn't really a reserve then—was on the Canadian side. It wasn't until it became clarified that the international border was the St. Croix River that we got into the whole thing of, "Oh gosh, you have to check in at the border, because you're now American and we're Canadian." They would come over from the reserve in canoes, or whatever, and catch porpoise. But then there came a time when the customs officials realized what they were doing. Then they decided that people from the reserve had to check in at the wharf and that they couldn't take the porpoise back, because the porpoise might have been swimming at the Canadian side of the water! I wasn't even aware of all that as a kid. It was just very exciting. These Indians would arrive, to fish and to visit.

We never really did have a deed to the land, here in Canada. According to the oral history, one hundred acres on the point was to be reserved for Natives. The deal was supposedly done by handshake. Two of my cousins visited the family who made the handshake, in England, during the war. And it's written up in a couple of books, too. But certainly my grandfather, and other members of my family, believed that there was a deed.

My mother literally fought off the town, because they had made more than one attempt to move us out. There had always been a path there, or maybe a dirt road. But in the fifties, I remember, the town decided to asphalt the road, to make it easier for the lobster plant. My mother decided that they shouldn't be doing that, so she literally put up a barricade and wouldn't let them pass. Eventually a man . . . I don't know what his title was—the town sheriff? He certainly was in charge of the town trucks. He came along with the mayor at the time—who also owned a grocery store in town. I remember the two of them, walking very cautiously, past the barricade to meet with my mother. She seemed to get along a little bit better with the sheriff; he was a bit more open-minded. And so they convinced her that with all those kids it would be better for her to have a road there.

It was a kind of double jeopardy with my family, because we were in a white, Anglo-Saxon, Loyalist town, and we were the only Natives and the only visible minority family. Not only did we have that Native influence and were bringing "those Indians" onto good white land— but my father was Japanese, and so of course, just after the Second

World War, there was a lot of racism against both sides of my family—
and against my father, after my mother died. For example, I don't
remember him ever getting invited to anybody's house for dinner,
that sort of thing.

Because of my father's experience as a Japanese person, he believed
you had to integrate, in order to survive. He only became confronta-
tional when they decided, after my mother had died, that we couldn't
stay on the land, because he had no right to it, even though we did. And
here he was, with eight kids! He said, "You are right. I have no right
to the land—but my eight children do, you know. They have a blood-
line." They had foster families picked out for each of us, the town
council. They had places picked out for all of us! But he fought it. He
did as much investigation as he could—he was virtually uneducated.
But he wrote to everybody—we had a letter from Diefenbaker; he was
in office at the time. And then there was A. M. A. McLean who owned
Connors Brothers—and he was a member of parliament. He wrote to
all these people about us being removed from our land, and he had
responses. He tried to get some help, or find out how he could get a
deed for the land for his kids. Jimmy Kitpu—he was a Mi'kmaq who
helped him a lot. He used to visit us all the time. But I remember, my
father didn't want us mixed in with the "Mickymacs"—he had quite
an accent, and that's how he pronounced it. It's just that he thought
we'd have to integrate to survive.

I'm a good example of that. Since I got all the recessive genes, and
am so white-looking, when I finished high school, my father took me
to a justice of the peace in town to get my name changed. Interestingly enough, he was going to change my name from his Japanese
name to our Passamaquoddy family name—which of course is really
Anglicized. He never discussed it—he wasn't somebody who chatted
about things at all. But I refused. Otherwise, I think he would have
done it. He just said, "Look—you're white. Life can be a lot easier
for you with your mother's name." Because even though it was our
Passamaquoddy name, I could get by with that name and not be questioned. Plus it maintained the family tie. Like, he didn't try to change
it to Smith or something. I think he was really smart—he knew at
some point there would be a need to challenge our right to the land
again. So to keep that name going, and to make it easier for me to pass
as white, he tried to change my name.

He was successful, finally, at letting us stay on the land. He went to
the town council, and they backed right off, and we stayed. But then,

when my father died, the town decided that he didn't have a will, so the land was theirs. So we spent seventeen years in court. We have a deed, now, for five acres, out of the original hundred. But the claim we put in was just for usage—and we did put in for twelve acres. I felt clearly that we had used ten of the acres. My great-great grandfather is on the census, on that piece of land. They never said we weren't there originally. They just said we'd only started out with 1.7 acres. That's why we ended up in court.

Rose Cunha

ZAINAB'S STORY

In my particular case, my ancestors came together during slavery. Both my Cherokee and African great-grandparents were enslaved on the same plantation. It was the Reynolds tobacco plantation—you know that Reynolds magnate that just had his house burned down and everything? I thought—it's about bloody time! But in that respect I'm very proud of the history of Africans and Native people when they have come together. They did some amazing things. That's as far as we know where we came from. I had a Cherokee great-grandmother, who was, I think, about fourteen when Emancipation came. And she married an African man, and they built their house together in Staunton, Virginia. This is my father's mother's mother, who was Cherokee. My father's father's mother is also Native, but I don't know what nation she came from. The only reason that we know that she exists is that there was a portrait over the mantle piece of a couple of these elderly lesbian aunts that I have in Staunton, Virginia, and they said that this was their mother, and there wasn't a lot of information that got handed down about her background, because they were all enslaved together.

My father lost his parents when he was very young, so he was raised by his Cherokee grandmother. But because of the Jim Crow laws in the South, which is the U.S. equivalent of apartheid, everybody was defined as "Negro" and had to live in the Negro sections of town and take the Negro jobs and that sort of stuff. So we couldn't participate in the censuses, which are usually used to determine whether you are Cherokee or not, because we were in the Negro section of town. So we were always listed on the census as "Negro" and not Cherokee. It doesn't matter—I don't need their laws to tell me who I am, anyway.

My father was into his Native identity when he was around, you know—but then again he was also poor and couldn't afford to travel or anything, to learn more about it. So we were quite unconnected. His grandmother was fourteen when Emancipation came, and she married right away. I've seen pictures of her—she was a very tiny woman, which suggests to me that she had physically been through a lot in her life. She probably lived a hell of a life—malnutrition and that sort of thing, you know, brutalized and everything. So I doubt she was educated. She'd grown up in slavery.

All of my uncles married African American women, many of them mixed-race Native and African, but people who identified primarily as African Americans, right? It was an African American community. And again, it's not that they weren't aware of their Native heritage— and there was a lot of pride when they talked about it—but in terms of being connected and living that way, no. It's not like they had a choice in those days. It was clearly defined by the law who you were.

Zainab Amadahy

A MÉTIS STORY

My mom's family came from Turtle Mountain, North Dakota, but they had never really lived there. I think my grandmother was born in North Dakota, but they lived in Montana as well, when she was very young, and then they moved back to Saskatchewan. My mom said that her family had lived in Saskatchewan before the Riel Rebellion, but afterward they moved down to the States. They came back up around the turn of the century, around 1902 or 1903, I think. I'm still trying to piece together the whole story.

When they moved back to Saskatchewan, my grandmother went to LeBret Residential School. It's only a couple of years ago that my cousin, who is a lawyer, tracked down this information and decided to do his homework on it. He found that my grandmother's name, the name of her parents, was changed by the school records. When she went in, her parents were listed under a certain name, but when she came out, the school record had changed the names of her parents. And when she went in, she was registered with Muskowegan Reserve in Saskatchewan. When she came out, there was no such record. My cousin, who got his law degree, was freaking out when he read all this, because he's trying to understand, "Am I Native or not?" When you try to track it back to say, "Well, who are we?" it just goes on and on.

My mother's cousin played a strong leadership role in the Saskatchewan Indian First Nations, in the 1960s, and she didn't even know it. When he was alive and I met him, I didn't know that I was related to him—I didn't find out until much later. He was so interested in politics, and he kept talking to me and my husband about all the stuff that he knew. My mother didn't even know that her mother was registered with the Muskowegan Band. My grandmother lived in Saskatoon after coming out of residential school, anyway. She never really lived on the reserve, as far as my mom knows.

My grandpa was born on a ranch or in the bush near Lewiston, Montana, and they lived a Métis kind of a life. They had an old shack that I saw a picture of one time, and they hunted and trapped quite a bit. But they also had horses. My grandpa's family was considered Métis, but they lived off the land, and they spoke their language consistently. In fact, they also spoke the Sioux language as well as Cree, because they knew a lot of Lakota people. They lived such a traditional lifestyle, but they never considered that they were Indians, because they weren't from the reserve. But they were still treated the same way as all the other Indians were. That's where it was a double whammy for them; they really suffered a lot of racism.

My grandpa, his brothers, and sisters grew up doing anything to survive, anything. Some of them joined the circus. They would go bone-picking. They'd go out on the prairie and pick buffalo bones, any kind of animal bones, but mainly buffalo. They'd collect them by the ton on an old stone boat and haul them back in to Saskatoon, where they would be paid, because the pharmaceutical companies used them for different drugs, the calcium or whatever, I don't know. They would dig different roots at certain times of the year, to sell. My grandpa would ride the rails to find jobs. And when he married my grandmother, they were both kind of young. When my grandmother came out of residential school at the age of eighteen, all she had was a grade three education. Because by the time she was eleven or twelve, she was big and strong, and so they had put her out to work for farm families instead of letting her stay in school and learn. And she had wanted to go to school, so she could get an education. But she married my grandfather when she was very young, and they had children right away.

The way my mom remembers growing up . . . sometimes she runs into somebody that she remembers, from forty or fifty years ago, who tells her, "Oh, I remember when I spent the winter with you and your family in the tent." She doesn't even remember how many winters they spent living in a tent, out on the land. But then, sometimes, for two or three months of the year, when the snow was very high, they'd rent a house in Saskatoon. So they traveled a lot. And she remembers a lot of hunger and eating a lot of wild meats. She taught my youngest girl how to make a snare. There are so many things that she knows that I never learned from her. But I'm glad that we're close, because this way she can teach my girls these things—because I never have time.

My mother is kind of schizophrenic about her identity. I would say she has about 5 percent non-Indian blood, and yet she says she's "just a little Indian." A huge conflict comes up around that. She can't say, with calm peace, "Yes, I am a Native person." There's no acceptance. But I feel sorry, because she's turning seventy-two, and I don't think she'll ever really come to think of herself as a Cree woman, or an Indian. It's always been that way—and there's not too many left in the family, now. There's only her and her sister left of the immediate family. And my aunt had a stroke almost a year ago and is very, very ill. I just feel that something is really disappearing, in my family, and that they've never had a chance to claim it. My mom says, "We're not REAL Indians." But I don't know if they had a name for themselves. I asked her, one time, "What did you call yourselves?" And she said, "Sometimes we would just say 'breeds.'"

Anonymous

LORRAINE'S STORY

Well, my mother, Emily Donald, was born in Moose Factory and was probably orphaned at around five or six years old. She was transported down to the Anglican residential school at Chapleau—that would have meant a canoe trip in those days. She grew up there, totally without any contact with family. My mother was very bitter about her experiences there, because she had no family, no visits, and she was never taken out to go home. While living at St. John's Anglican School, she would go into the town of Chapleau to attend high school and return to the school at night. Upon graduating from high school she attended Teachers College, known as Normal School in those days, in North Bay. So the residential school was her home and her family. Her role model was one of the residential school teachers, a woman originally from England. I think she was one of the people my mum was closest to—she used to tease her and call her "my little mother"; they had quite a close relationship.

My mother had a younger brother who was sent to the residential school on Moose Factory Island. I don't think they stayed in touch after that. Her mother's sister had also been taken away, probably at the age of five or six, and sent to an industrial training school in Manitoba. That aunt stayed in *that* school until she was eighteen, and then when she got out, she stayed in the town near that residential school, because *she* had an aunt there.

My father's family claimed to be white, but I'm beginning to find out that his parents have this connection to a Métis community in Saskatchewan. They believed themselves to be white, though. I remember my father did say that, growing up in town, he had it a little hard because he was somewhat dark. There's a reference in this little newsletter, from the Carlisle Indian School in the United States, about his mother being a Chippewa Indian, a graduate of Carlisle Indian School. I know that some of his maternal uncles attended the Haskell Indian College.

I remember my aunt—my father's sister—telling me on the telephone, "I don't remember my parents ever holding me and telling me they loved me." I think I wrote to her and said, "There's a reason for that and we'll talk about it some day." [It was] because they were at Carlisle. But she didn't know that. I'm thinking, "No wonder they wouldn't have that affection—they both grew up at residential school." And yet it's so cute, because my aunt said, "They were affectionate to each other. I remember one day when I was a kid, seeing him carrying her down the stairs, and they were giggling." I thought, "What a view of them." I never thought of my grandparents that way.

The only time I remember my mother returning to Moose Factory was about a year before she died, at the age of sixty-five. Both her and my dad traveled to Moose Factory for a couple of days. I think that she was trying to find some identification, to apply for her old-age pension. That's the only time I ever knew her to go back there or even to speak of it.

Somebody once sent me a little card my mother had made, and she'd done a little drawing of a Native woman, with a caption something like, "Always be proud you're an Indian." Yet for me, she totally denied any connection with being Native. She never said to me, "I am a Native person." I had asked her what our background was. I guess I had to be around ten years old, and because I was kind of dark, I asked her, "What am I, anyway?" And she said, "You are what your father is." She wouldn't elaborate on it. I didn't find out what she meant until later—that if your father is white, then you are white. Because he identified as white, he always admonished me to "stay the hell away from those goddamned Indians!"

When I was growing up, all I ever heard were English nursery rhymes that my mother would read to me. She was fluent in Cree—people who knew her in Toronto told me that after she died—but I never heard her speak it. She was out to mold me into a Shirley Temple, making this doll out of me! My mother was fairer than I am. My father would get dark in the summer, but he was light too, you know. So I'm the recessive gene, I guess, darker than both of them. The bad seed . . . .

My mother always wanted to be a nurse, but they had told her at the residential school that she was too fragile, too small and tiny—that she wouldn't be strong enough. So they told her, "No, you'll be a teacher." The Indian agent really tried to control her. She was probably one of the few people that were considered successful. Because she looked white, they figured it would be so easy to mold this person and make a white person out of her—especially having grown up in this school all her life, with teachers who taught her to be white. She was very polite and seemed to be easy-going—but she was not a person you could push around. But between the Indian agent and the residential school, it was decided that she would be a teacher, rather than a nurse. They had control over lots of kids. What a wide net they cast, between the two of them!

So my mother became a teacher in Indian schools. I think that was the only place that would hire her. I was born in Parry Sound while my mother was the elementary school teacher at the Parry Island reserve near there. I think we lived in town at that point. And then, when I was about six months old, we moved to Toronto. We lived in the city for a couple of years, and then when my Dad returned from World War II in 1945, we bought a farm north of Bracebridge. So we moved up there when I was about four years old. That lasted about a year, and then my mother took another teaching position at the Gull Bay reserve, on the northwest shore of Lake Nipigon. We're talking a remote, wilderness, fly-in community, with only a battery radio for contact with the outside world. They traveled by dog team. Most of the village was tarpaper shacks, maybe some little squat log cabins, very crowded, and sometimes only an oilcan for a stove. I remember a lot of deaths. I remember going to a burial for a baby; we all trooped out to the graveyard, and it was all frozen and deep snow. You know, people died—there was a lot of tuberculosis there. If you were lucky, they got a plane to come in, to bring in a doctor, and a dentist, and x-ray equipment, once or twice a year.

We were there together for the first year, but then for the second year, she put me in a Catholic convent in Thunder Bay, where I did grade one. I remember being sick, with earaches, and there was no medication. She had to deal with me being sick, alone. I suppose if you were seriously ill, they would call the plane. I think, though, because she was concerned about my health, that's the reason they put me in the convent.

There was a school, close by the church, and there was a little "teacherage" attached to the school. It had a small kitchen, a little living room, and a small bedroom upstairs. That's where we lived, the first year. The only people we visited would be a Scottish couple who ran the Hudson's Bay post. They had a daughter. We would go and stay there on the weekends with them, and they would play cards, and the girl and I were of the same age, so we played. And that was our weekend.

She didn't want me in the school with the Cree kids. So for the first year I did kindergarten by correspondence course. I wasn't in the classroom—I sat in the teacherage, while she was in the classroom. But she'd stand in the doorway, seeing what the hell I was up to, because I'd get snoopy and into all sorts of things. I think I did sit in the classroom in the beginning, but things must have happened, and I think she must have separated me then. I don't remember, because I was only five. She went in there like a white teacher, I suppose. She was teaching the white system. I remember walking with her, one day, and the kids were playing in a sandpit there, and they were looking over and laughing and calling things in Cree. And she said, "Come on," and hustled me off. She probably knew what they were saying.

But her love was always nursing. And sometime in the 1950s, she finally did it—she went back to school and graduated as a registered nursing assistant. And then she worked at both St. Joseph's Hospital and the Queen Elizabeth Hospital, in Toronto.

Lorraine Le Camp

A "C-31" STORY

What does being Native really mean? What does being mixed-race mean? What does "not Indian enough" mean? All of those things have always affected me because, more often than not, Native people will say that about me, or other people. And I wonder about this when I catch myself doing it. What is it about my insecurities, about my own culture and background, when I pull that on someone else?

My mom grew up in Rama, and my father grew up in a little town just forty minutes away from Rama, called Norland. He was back home visiting his father, on his summer vacation—my father was mining gold in northern Ontario at the time. He came down south to visit his father, and he went to a dance on the reserve; there was a dance hall. This was back in the early fifties. I guess that was the thing people did then. He met my mother, and they spent a lot of time together during his vacation, and on his last day he asked her to marry him, and she said yes. This was at the end of the summer, and they were married at the end of October. And she left the only home she ever knew, a Native community, to move to a gold-mining town in northern Ontario, Kirkland Lake.

I think there was an attitude or an atmosphere, especially toward my mother, with the people that my father chummed around with, or worked with, that "she wasn't like the rest of them"—she was a "civilized savage." So she was accepted—she could run a home, and all of those things, which was just amazing to them, I'm sure!

She worked all over the place. Her last job was as a counselor for the Ministry of Natural Resources. She helped Native kids decide what they wanted to do after they finished high school—whether they wanted to go to college and do forestry, or whatever. Before that, she worked in a variety of places. She worked for the Children's Aid Society, as a Native liaison worker. She also worked as an interpreter for the Supreme Court; it was a circuit court. Wherever they lived, she got work as an interpreter. She could speak Swampy Cree, and Cree, as well as Ojibway.

My mom got her status back, and mine, with Bill C-31. Indian status was something that was taken away because of a misogynous law—so it's only fair that all the women who lost their status receive it back. My parents were married for forty-four years, and my father passed away two and a half years ago. But at that point, it had been so long from the time my mother left. Her mother had already passed away, and she wasn't close to her one remaining sister, who didn't live on the reserve anyway. She goes back every now and then. Her niece has ties with the reserve, so they go back and visit certain people—she only lives forty minutes from the reserve, in Norland.

My mother's cousin owns a shop on the reserve, so we go and visit her every now and then. I was up at the reserve recently, and I went to see her. And she gave me a really big hug. I think it was a turning point for me. It was almost like receiving a message—"It's okay, you can come back. You're part of this family now." Maybe I always was—but this was an acknowledgment of it. It felt really nice.

Anonymous

AN ADOPTEE'S STORY

My sister and I were taken away from my mom when I was two years old. My sister was only a year old, and my mom was not married. We were placed in a foster home, and when I was three, my sister was fostered by one family, and I was adopted out to another. I grew up with a Dutch family. They were immigrants from Holland, who came over after the war. I had two older brothers who had been adopted as babies as well, but they were both non-Native. I lived with that family until I was sixteen, and then I moved out and have been on my own ever since.

We moved around a lot. I grew up in Edmonton, but we lived in Montreal for four years. We went to France for two years, when I was eleven, and came back to Canada, to Toronto, when I was thirteen. We were in Toronto for a year, and then we went back to Edmonton.

I was one hundred percent immersed in the non-Native community. The word "Indian" never came up in my home, although I always knew I was different, because I was dark. When I was young, the stuff that I dealt with were things like, "How come my brothers are so light and I'm so dark?" But then as I got older, into high school, it was other people that reminded me that I was different. I remember in art class in high school, hearing somebody say, "You fucking squaw!" I was just blown away. I didn't even know, really. I did not have an identity.

I've come to understand this today, but I didn't understand it back then, when I started to lead a really self-destructive life—that my spirit was broken. And my only way to deal with it was to drink. I was very, very angry, really enraged. I almost died from alcohol. And I was really self-abusive, before that. I would do stuff like punch my eyes in, you know, and really hurt myself a lot, because I didn't know who I was and I was really angry. I was hanging out a lot in the bars in Edmonton, and these wild things would start happening. I'd be walking down the street, and Indian men would say "Tansi" to me. They totally recognized me, right? Indian people always know I'm one of them. But I would just say, "What?" I didn't know how to react, because I had no experience in the Native community. I was pretty scared. I didn't have any Indian friends. I was very disassociated from who I was.

It's only been recently that I suddenly realized, "Holy shit, I never even thought that people would see me as a drunk Indian." Because that's truly what I was—I was a drunk. I only made the connection recently that I was a drunk Indian—in Edmonton, of all places.

When I moved to Nova Scotia, and my drinking was getting really bad, every time I got really drunk I'd start having these breakdowns around wanting to know who my Indian mum was. It was so important to me. But I got sober first, and then I started looking for my family. I'm really, really grateful that I got sober first. That's when I connected with the Mi'kmaq Child and Family Services in Nova Scotia, and they started writing letters back and forth to Alberta. Because they know who to write to. That's when my uncle came forward—he traveled three or four hours to get to Edmonton to clearly identify that I was his sister's daughter.

That's when I found out that my mom had died. She died in her early thirties from a drug and alcohol overdose. And I've just recently been reunited with my sister. That has been the hardest relationship I've ever had to deal with. It just hasn't been good. She didn't even know she was Indian! It's just been really, really difficult.

There was no mention about either of my parents being Indian on the documents they gave to my foster mother, which provide a bit of background about the birth parents. They put my mother's racial origin as Irish and Scottish and my father's racial origin as French. When I joined the postadoption registry, the agency in Alberta sent me what they call more identifiable information. They gave me a little bit more information about my mom and about my dad, the time that I was born, and the hospital I was born in. At that point, they put "mother's racial origin" as "Indian." But for my father, they put "French." But my dad is Métis. He came from a huge family of twelve kids. I found that out later.

I will never, ever forget the call from my uncle, from Alberta. He was the kindest, nicest person. For some reason, we got on right off. It was great, hearing him say, "This is Tom——, and I'm your uncle, and it's so great to talk to you. Your voice even sounds like our family." Then I asked him, "What kind of Indian are we?" And he told me, "We're Cree and Saulteaux." He was a medicine man, and because he had those gifts, he had gone into the sweat lodge and put flags up, and asked the spirits about me. So on the phone, in our first conversation, he was able to tell me, "You're going to be all right. You've had a very difficult life. You've led a life of a lot of self-destruction, but things are going to get better." I went home that night, and I looked in the mirror, and for the first time in my life—and I was wearing purple, I'll never forget this—I looked in the mirror, and I thought, "You DO look Indian!" It was the first connection I ever had. And I really believed from that day on that I was really an Indian.

And then my life started to change. All of my life, I wanted to belong, and then all of a sudden, I was belonging, and people were recognizing that. My own people were welcoming me home. That's what happened.

But with my family, there's lots I still don't know. My mother's father is from Montana—there's a group of landless Indians there that he comes from. My mother's grandmother is from Cold Lake First Nation. I know that my mom came from a family of twelve kids, and they were all orphaned at a really young age. And so all of my mum's brothers and sisters are dispersed all over Alberta. My uncle was living at Saddle Lake First Nation. I think my mother spent a lot of time at Enoch, just outside of Edmonton, which is another reserve. My sense is that none of these people were necessarily band members, but the bands would let them live there. I know nothing about their schooling. I'm sure my Uncle Joe and Uncle Tom went to residential school, but I'm not sure about my mom.

I met my Uncle Tom before he died. And then I met my Uncle Joe, who's seventy-two, who lives in Saddle Lake now, too. I met my aunt—there's just one living aunt now, on my mom's side, who lives in Edmonton. But I didn't really connect much with her. There are family members that I've met that I really want to stay connected with and other people that I didn't want to have anything to do with, because they are still using drugs or alcohol and not really healthy. I didn't want that in my circle. So that was an interesting process.

But you know, I still feel kind of disconnected, sometimes, around who I am. Because when I really put it in perspective, coming from an Indian family—there's not one person in my family that has not been affected by some kind of violence. I have cousins in prison. I have people who have killed themselves. I have alcoholism and residential school. This is my blood family, but I still feel pretty disconnected from all of those experiences. It's hard to explain, because genocide touched me in a different way.

Anonymous

Notes

PREFACE

1. The issues that arose during the interview process, including methodological concerns about conducting "insider" research, details about the individuals I interviewed, and the parameter of the study itself, are all described in appendix 2.

INTRODUCTION

1. In Canada, similar attacks on the viability of Indigenous cultures based on a hegemonic demand for Native authenticity have been made by individuals such as Tom Flanagan, in his recent work *First Nations? Second Thoughts*.

2. Throughout the trial, a significant problem for the people of Mashpee was the fact that they no longer spoke the Massachusett language, that many of them looked black, or white, rather than Native, and that they spoke with broad New England accents. More subtle indications of cultural cohesion and maintenance of collective identity were invisible to white eyes who demanded the trappings of Indianness before they would recognize a group as Native. See Clifford (1988, 277–346).

3. For example, G. Reginald Daniel, in writing about the so-called triracial isolate communities scattered throughout the eastern United States, is openly dismissive of these communities' claims to Indianness (despite the fact that other Native people consider them Native), asserting that they do not know enough about their culture and instead should be considered either as whites

seeking the exoticism of an Indian identity or as blacks seeking to escape blackness (Daniel 1992, 99–101).

4. As one Native woman summed it up: "I have had the awful feeling that when we are finished dealing with the courts and our land claims, we will then have to battle the environmentalists and they will not understand why" (Wilson, in Plant 1989, 212).

5. The Aboriginal population in Canada, generally estimated at about 1.5 million people, is roughly equal in size to the American Indian population. However, as Jill St. Germain notes, the land base of all Canadian Indian reserves combined constitute less than one-half of the land base of the Navajo reservation in Arizona alone (St. Germain 2001, xix).

6. Sherene Razack, exploring the relationship between bodies, space, and justice, has noted that zones inhabited by racial Others are considered to be "domains of illegality" outside of universality, where racialized Others are evacuated from the category "human" and are denied the equality so fundamental to liberal society (Razack 2000, 116–17).

7. Bill C-31, and other aspects of Indian Act identity legislation, will be explored in chapter 3.

8. This is from a passage in the novel *Lucy* by Jamaica Kincaid, in which the white North American employer of a Caribbean au pair proudly relates how she has "Indian blood." The au pair asks herself how it is possible that her privileged white employer, in claiming "Indian blood," has managed "to be the sort of victor who can claim to be the vanquished also?" Quoted in Strong and Van Winkle (1995, 552).

9. From a speech given at Queen's University, 18 January 2002.

1. FROM SOVEREIGN NATIONS TO "A VANISHING RACE"

1. Distinct Métis identities did arise during the development of the fur trade. And yet it is the contention of this author that these identities were artificially "frozen," by government regulation, as a defining characteristic indelibly separating Métisness from Indianness. This issue is further explored in chapter 4.

2. The exclusive use of the male pronoun is deliberate, as most enfranchisement efforts were directed toward Indian men; in any case, until 1951, their wives and children were involuntarily enfranchised along with them.

3. One example is the case of Fred Loft—a Mohawk from the Six Nations reserve who, after returning from World War I, became a leader and spokesperson for the League of Indians of Canada, a political organization lobbying for Indian rights. For his activism, Loft was targeted for enfranchisement; how-

ever, with the repeal of compulsory enfranchisement in 1922, this was never carried out (RCAP 1996, 1:288).

4. *An Act for the Better Protection of Lands and Property of the Indians in Lower Canada*, s.c. 1850, c. 42.

5. *An Act for the Protection of the Indians in Upper Canada from Imposition and the Property Occupied or Enjoyed by Them from Trespass and Injury*, s.c. 1850, c. 75.

6. *An Act for the Gradual Enfranchisement of Indians, the Better Management of Indian Affairs, and to Extend the Provisions of the Act 31st Victoria, Chapter 42*, s.c. 1869, c. 6.

7. *Indian Act*, 1876, s.c. 1876, c. 18.

8. European race ideology, after all, could only be imposed on those peoples who were sufficiently under the control of the colonizing power to be forced to live according to its dictates. It is only when Native people can no longer live by hunting, fishing, or traditional agriculture, or when they have been restricted from living on most of their former land base in any manner, that they are forced to live on the colonizer's terms and accept the legal dismemberment of their identities.

9. While the manner in which gender has been utilized to regulate Native identity in Canada will be explored in chapter 2, a continuous problem faced by women who lost Indian status in the past but have now been reinstated, is that a number of bands refuse to accept them as members, claiming that gender discrimination is "cultural" in their communities—claims that are hotly disputed by the women affected. It is impossible to explore how First Nations have negotiated changes to gendered identity legislation without recognizing how, in a sense, gendered identity legislation has been "naturalized" as cultural in many First Nations communities.

2. REGULATING NATIVE IDENTITY BY GENDER

1. A number of European French families attempted to challenge the inheritance of Quebec fortunes by Native wives and children, and some were successful. Meanwhile, in 1735, an edict was passed that required the consent of the governor or commanding officer for all mixed marriages in New France to be considered legal, while another edict restricted the rights of Native women to inherit their French husband's property (Dickason 1985, 28).

2. Recent research has documented the presence of mixed-blood communities at no fewer than fifty-three locations in the Great Lakes region between 1763 and 1830 (RCAP 1996, 1:150).

3. In 1803 John Connolly began a customary marriage, *a la façon du pays*, with a Native woman known only as Suzanne. In 1832 he married a wealthy white Montreal woman, Julia Woolrich, while his Native wife Suzanne was still alive. In the court case that followed, several fur traders gave testimony that customary marriages were usually monogamous, undertaken freely by both parties, and of long duration. The court at that point upheld the rights of the customary marriage over the church marriage (*Johnstone et al. v Connolly*, Court of Appeal, 7 December 1869, cited in *La revue legale* 1:253–400).

4. For example, in 1899, the Supreme Court of the Northwest Territories ruled that the two sons of Awatoyakew, also known as Mary Brown, a Peigan woman, and Nicholas Sheran, the founder of a lucrative coal mine in the Lethbridge area, were not entitled to a share of their father's estate. On Sheran's death, his sister took the children, placed them in a St. Albert orphanage, and paid a hundred dollars a year each for their care; neither child, however, ever received any direct returns from their father's mine (Carter 1997, 191–92).

5. In the Northwest Territories, the Real Property Act of 1886 abolished the right of a wife to dower (a lifetime interest in one-third of her husband's property upon widowhood). A further Disability Act was passed in the early years of the twentieth century that removed the rights of wives to any share of their husband's estate (Carter 1997, 193).

6. These figures include both those individuals who were enfranchised and those who lost their status because of gender discrimination in the Indian Act. However the numbers of individuals who lost status due to enfranchisement only reached significant levels for a few years during the 1920s and 1930s, and the policy was ended for everybody but women marrying non-Natives in 1951. By comparison, for over a century, the majority of individuals who lost status were Indian women who married out.

7. *R. v Drybones*, 6 CNOR 273 SCC (1969).

8. In April 1985 the Charter of Rights and Freedoms came into effect. The identity legislation within the 1951 Indian Act was in violation of Section 15(1), which prohibited discrimination on the basis of race and gender, as well as other particularities. Because of this, when Bill C-31 came into effect on 28 June 1985, its amendments to the 1951 act came into legal effect retroactively back to 17 April 1985, the date that the charter came into effect (Gilbert 1996, 129).

9. At the time of *Lavell and Bedard*, there were no women on the National Indian Brotherhood executive council; and the Association of Iroquois and Allied Indians, who first enlisted the help of the solicitor general and turned the tide against Lavell, represented twenty thousand Indian men (Jamieson 1978, 91).

10. The American Indian Movement, with long experience in defending traditional and grassroots Native people against "puppet" Indian governments, offered their assistance to the Tobique women. The women declined, however, for fear that the situation would escalate still further if AIM entered the reserve to support them (Silman 1987, 129–30).

11. Factum of Isaac et al., 58–67, 74, in *Lavell and Bedard.*

12. According to Jamieson, the government debate about this legislation focused on fears raised by white men, for example, citizens of Chateauguay who resided on the Caughnawa reserve (Kahnawake), that they would be forced to leave the community. The repeated response of administrators was that the only white men who would be forced to leave Native communities were those found to be selling liquor or robbing the Indians of their timber. Those white men already resident at Kahnawake—twenty-eight at the time of the legislation—were permitted to stay there and in fact received licenses to do so (Jamieson 1978, 32).

13. In 1872 the Grand Council of Ontario and Quebec Indians sent a strong letter to the minister at Ottawa, protesting Section 6 of the 1869 Act, noting that Native women should have the privilege of marrying whom they pleased without suffering exclusion or expulsion from their tribe and consequent loss of property and rights. Other protests from the Six Nations and from the Caughnawaga band (Kahnawake) also challenged the notion that Indian women should be externalized for marrying non-Indians (Jamieson 1978, 36).

3. RECONFIGURING COLONIAL GENDER RELATIONS UNDER BILL C-31

1. Prior to the passing of Bill C-31, women who married status Indian men gained Indian status. While this usually resulted in numbers of white women gaining Indian status, it also provided a vehicle whereby nonstatus and Métis women could redress past injustices by gaining Indian status through marriage. Since passage of Bill C-31, however, it has been impossible for *anybody* to gain status through marrying a status Indian.

2. Larry Gilbert has noted that for the registrar to follow these regulations concerning illegitimacy also violates the rights of individuals under Section 15 of the Charter of Rights and Freedoms, which holds that it is unconstitutional to deprive a person of the right to inherit property on the basis of illegitimacy. He also notes that whether an individual's father is a status Indian should be ascertained only by the word of the mother, on the basis that any other person's word would be hearsay (Gilbert 1996, 32).

3. *Santa Clara Pueblo v Martinez*, 436 U.S. 49, 56 (1978).

4. The Indian register had two parts: the band list, which contained the names of status Indians who were members of a First Nation; and the General List, which contained the names of status Indians without bands. This list, prior to 1985, primarily contained the names of status Indians who had lost band membership because they had lived outside of Canada for more than five years without permission from the superintendent of Indian Affairs (Gilbert 1996, 131).

5. For example, Maurice Switzer has equated Bill C-31 with Nazi Germany's racial purity guidelines and the color classifications of South African apartheid (Switzer 1997, 2). And yet he neglects to make any comment at all about how women bore the brunt of such restrictions for over a century—or indeed about any of the incredibly demeaning and continuously narrowing racist and sexist restrictions on Indianness that have been contained in virtually every piece of legislation pertaining to Indians since 1857.

6. Justice Muldoon's decision included comments such as "Indians lost their societies upon the coming of Europeans" and experienced "false, puppet chiefs." His response to the bands' appeal to tradition was that Aboriginal oral history was unreliable, "fictitious revisionism," amounting to "skewed propaganda without objective verity," and that the elders' testimonies were "ancestor worship . . . one of the most counter-productive, racist, hateful, and backward-looking of all human characteristics." By comparison, Muldoon considered the government's documents to be "the authentic historical record" ("Bill C-31" 1996, 7).

7. The three Alberta bands have argued that they are not opposed to individuals being given back status, only to their being given band membership. They also distinguish between the women who were reinstated and other C-31 status Indians, stating that "the women returning to membership represent only a tiny fraction of the totally new membership population of 118,000 being forced onto the bands by the government" (thus externalizing the mixed-race children of these women who by far make up the majority of those who gained status under Bill C-31) ("Bill C-31" 1996, 7).

8. U.S. Dept. of the Interior, *Federal Indian Law*, 4.

9. For example, in *United States v Rogers*, the Supreme Court recognized that a white man adopted into an Indian tribe at a mature age was entitled to certain privileges in accordance with tribal membership; however, he could not be considered to be Indian—Indianness in this case was determined by race (Cohen 1942, 3). With respect to mixed bloods, tribal status appears to have been a decisive factor in determining their legal status. For example in *United States v Higgins*, the judgment was that "half-breeds" were to be treated as Indians, so long as they retain their tribal relations." Numerous

treaties as well as statutes, from 1817 to 1908, have recognized individuals with mixed blood as Indians on this basis (Cohen 1942, 3).

10. In the 1780s, white Virginians began to agitate for the termination of the Gingaskin Indian Reservation in Northampton County. The reserve was described as an "asylum for free negroes," where Aboriginal people had become "nearly extinct . . . there being at this time not more than 3 or 4 genuine Indians at most." By 1812 it was argued that "the place is now inhabited by as many Black men as Indians . . . the real Indians [are few]." The reserve was allotted in 1813; by 1832 whites had acquired most of the land. A similar attack took place upon the Pamunkey-Mattaponi in 1843 (which failed) and against the Nottoway from 1830 to 1878 (which succeeded—the landless descendants being described by 1878 as "all being Negroes and very poor") (Forbes 1988, 88).

11. In 1825 the treaty negotiated with the Great and Little Osage tribes, as well as that negotiated with the Kansas Nation, involved setting aside reservations for "half-breeds," while the 1826 treaty with the Chippewa Tribe also provided for allotments for half-breeds (Cohen 1942, 207). In 1830, a reservation was set aside for Omaha, Iowa, and Otoe half-breeds (Taylor 1984, 17).

12. Roosevelt's First Annual Message to Congress, 3 December 1901, quoted in Clark (1994, 2).

13. Act of 30 June 1919, sec. 1, 41 Stat. 3, 9, 25 U.S.C. 163, quoted in U.S. Dept. of the Interior, 90.

14. In early 1990, the town of Oka, situated next door to the Mohawk community of Kahnesatake, in Quebec, attempted to expand its golf course onto a Mohawk traditional burial ground. Because Mohawk communities have refused to recognize Quebec sovereignty, relations between the local police and Quebec Mohawks were already generally negative. For several months the community barred access to the burial grounds and continued to conduct ceremonies there. Finally, a dawn raid on a sunrise ceremony was organized by the Quebec provincial police force. The Mohawks were unarmed, but one policeman was caught in the cross fire and killed. The Mohawks immediately erected barricades around their community to protect themselves and sent out an appeal for assistance. Native people from other communities traveled to Kahnesatake to support them, and the Mohawks of nearby Kahnewake threw up a barricade on the Mercier Bridge, which crossed their territory. In doing this, they blocked a major artery for daily commuters to Montreal from the South Shore and drew immediate national attention to the plight of the people of Kahnesatake.

While the Quebec minister of Indian Affairs agreed to enter into negotiations with the Mohawk traditionalists and the leadership of the Iroquois

Confederacy, Canada refused to take part, instead labeling the Mohawks as terrorists and criminals. As the standoff grew more tense, the Canadian army was sent in. For three months, as international peace observers and Native people around the country converged on Kahnesatake to act as witnesses, the community was subject to an intense military campaign to pressure them to drop the barricades. The community ultimately surrendered, and many were imprisoned for their actions. However, the Oka crisis ultimately drew international attention (including the United Nations) toward Canada's treatment of Indigenous peoples.

15. Alfred, in Barnsley 2000.

4. MÉTIS IDENTITY, THE INDIAN ACT, AND THE NUMBERED TREATIES

1. The mixed-blood buffalo hunters, who hunted and prepared the buffalo, turned it into pemmican, a combination of ground dried meat, berries, and fat, which supplied a continent-wide network of trade canoes with food.

2. Some sources (Jamieson 1978; Gilbert 1996; Reddekopp and Bartko 2000; Bartko 2000) have emphasized that individuals were offered choices as to whether they would enter treaty as Indians or take scrip as half-breeds. Whether individuals could actual choose between categories or not is beside the point—it is the imposition of the categories themselves, which changed how Native peoples saw themselves, and irrevocably divided their people in the process, which is problematic.

3. Other work, which either deconstructs Métisness or upholds it as an unproblematic concept, supports or challenges this assertion. For example, Nicks and Morgan, in arguing against "Red River myopia," have asserted, through examining scrip applications, that in northern Alberta, those now designated Métis are not of Red River heritage but are simply local mixed-bloods who are indigenous to the region (Nicks and Morgan 1985, 173–75). This argument, however, is refuted by Gerhard Ems who, in *his* study of scrip applications, unequivocally labels 1899 mixed-bloods as Métis by asserting that at least some of them are of Red River heritage (Ems 2000, 235). Meanwhile, recent work by Reddekopp and Bartko (2000) and Bartko (2000), upholds Coates and Morrison's tendency to deconstruct Métisness and Indianness by noting how mutably these categories have been lived on the ground.

4. List of half-breeds who have withdrawn from treaty, 1 June 1888. PAC, RG 10, vol. 10038. Virtually all the members of the Bobtail (Hobbema) and Peyasis (Lac la Biche) Bands discharged from treaty and applied for scrip, as did a large majority of the Papasschase (South Edmonton) Band. The few individuals who remained were transferred to the Samson/Ermineskin, Bigstone, and Enoch

Bands, respectively. The annuity paylists for all of these entities are in the Genealogical Research Unit of Indian Affairs (Reddekopp and Bartko 2000, 215).

5. Native people in Newfoundland and Labrador were not brought under federal jurisdiction in 1949 when Newfoundland joined Confederation, but remained under the jurisdiction of the Newfoundland government. While the government of Canada, which observes a distinction between the Inuit and all other Indigenous people, has assumed fiduciary responsibility for the Inuit through a regulatory agreement with the Labrador Inuit Association, the Innu and Mi'kmaq have, in theory, been administered to by the provincial government. Under a provincial-federal Native agreement signed in the 1960s, Canada pays for 90 percent of the costs, but the communities lack access to most of the benefits of having reserve status. The Innu Nation in Labrador has been struggling to be placed under the Indian Act primarily to limit their interactions with the hostile provincial government. Meanwhile, eleven of the twelve Mi'kmaq communities in Newfoundland are still struggling to be recognized as reserves, almost twenty years after one community—Conne River—gained reserve status in 1984 (McKinley 1998, 9).

6. The only legally recognized land bases for Métis people exist in Alberta, where eight Métis settlements were created under provincial legislation; in Saskatchewan, where several parcels of land have been designated as Métis farms; and in northwestern Ontario, where, because Métis people were included in Treaty 3, part of the Métis population of Rainy River were allocated reserve land and have been recognized as Indians under the Indian Act. In parts of the Northwest Territories, the Métis are negotiating land claims (Normand 1996, 12).

5. KILLING THE INDIAN TO SAVE THE CHILD

1. In Canada, where her family has always lived (and where her tribe originally comes from, until they were pushed off their land into what is now the United States), she is nonstatus. Her family is currently making a case for their right to have Indian status and band recognition in Canada.

2. For two intervals, from 1920 to 1922 and again from 1933 until 1951, compulsory enfranchisement, at the discretion of a board of examiners and with two years' notice, was instituted. The participant's mother first lost her status after she left the reserve to work during World War II, a process initiated through the Indian agent for her reserve.

3. For example, in British Columbia, in 1978, 3.5 percent of all children were status Indians, but Native children made up 44.5 percent of all children

in foster homes. In Saskatchewan in 1978, 8.3 percent of all children were status Indians, but Native children made up 65 percent of all Native children in care (Johnston 1983, 27, 39, 55). In 1981, in northern Ontario, where the proportion of Native people in the province is the highest, an estimated 85 percent of children in the Kenora-Patricia agency were Aboriginal (RCAP 1996, 3:25).

7. NEGOTIATING AN URBAN MIXED-BLOOD NATIVE IDENTITY

1. See note 14 of chapter 3 concerning the Oka crisis.

8. MAINTAINING AN URBAN NATIVE COMMUNITY

1. The notion of being "two-spirited" is a concept that many Native gays and lesbians have adopted, not only as a means of conceptualizing homosexuality, but to make connections with traditional Indigenous ways of understanding the qualities of maleness and femaleness and the flexible manner in which these qualities can fit different bodies, across gender.

11. INDIAN STATUS AND ENTITLEMENT

1. Just prior to the passing of Bill C-31, certain individuals proposed Bill C-47, which would have amended the Indian Act to reinstate everybody with any historic claim to Indianness. These individuals would all be on a general band list, and then chiefs and councils would indicate who could be accepted back as band members. This was strenuously resisted by the women who were struggling to have their status reinstated, on the grounds that it would mean that "anybody could be an Indian" and that the "general band list" would simply be a meaningless bureaucratic item to be filed away in Ottawa, leaving Native people more powerless than before (Silman 1987, 202–4). In this view, rather than the government abolishing status, as they attempted with the White Paper, the government would render status meaningless by opening up the category of Indianness to anybody with any claim to Native ancestry. Status, then, is only effective as a means of protecting the rights of some Indians insofar as it can exclude others from Indianness.

12. MIXED-BLOOD URBAN NATIVE PEOPLE
AND THE REBUILDING OF INDIGENOUS NATIONS

1. In July 1998, for example, the hereditary chief of Gespegawaq, one of the seven regions traditionally governed by the Mi'kmaq Grand Council, a member government of the Wabanaki Confederacy, asserted their rights to

log so-called Crown land, resulting in a direct confrontation with the band council of Listuguj, whose chief, Ronald Jacques, refuses to recognize the authority of the Mi'kmaq Grand Council (Dow 1998, 1).

2. Section 35 of the Canadian Constitution, developed from the British North America Act of 1867 and repatriated from Britain in 1982, recognized and affirmed existing Aboriginal and treaty rights. This means that these rights are recognized as already existing at the time of colonization—they are not delegated, and do not flow from the Crown, and therefore are acknowledged as inherent rights.

With respect to court decisions, Patricia Monture-Angus, in her 1999 work *Journeying Forward: Dreaming First Nations Independence,* has extensively examined the history of Supreme Court cases and their effects on Aboriginal rights. She has concluded that between the 1990 *Sparrow* decision, which first ruled on the terms by which Aboriginal rights could be said to be extinguished, and the *Delgamuukw* decision of the late 1990s, which ruled on the extent to which section 35 could protect Aboriginal title to land, the Supreme Court of Canada has used its opportunities to define section 35 as a means to water down the protections it is intended to afford and to therefore limit the content and exercise of Aboriginal Rights protected by the Constitution.

3. Taiaiake Alfred, in *Peace, Power, and Righteousness,* describes how Canada administers "self-government" by divesting of any responsibility toward rectifying centuries of colonialism, while holding tight to the land base and resources, and by further entrenching in law and practice the real basis of its power, while maintaining basic policies of assimilation and destruction unchanged. The First Nations Governance Act should be seen in such a light.

4. The implications for crown liability are enormous (Barnsley 2003e, 14–25). Most notably, the case *Victor Buffalo v the Queen* involves a lawsuit by the Samson Cree Band against the federal government for mismanagement of $1.5 billion in oil and gas trust monies. The lawyer for the Samson Cree Band, veteran James O'Reilly, is subpoenaing Prime Minister Jean Cretien and Minister of Indian Affairs Robert Nault to testify (Barnsley 2003f, 9).

Bibliography

Acoose, Janice. 1995. *Neither Indian Princesses nor Easy Squaws.* Toronto: Women's Press.

Alfred, Gerald R. (Taiaiake). 1995. *Heeding the Voices of Our Ancestors: Kahnawake Mohawk Politics and the Rise of Native Nationalism.* Don Mills ON: Oxford University Press.

———. 1999. *Peace, Power,and Righteousness: An Indigenous Manifesto.* Don Mills ON: Oxford University Press.

Anderson, Benedict. 1991. *Imagined Communities: Reflections on the Origin and Spread of Nationalism.* New York: Verso.

Anderson, Kim. 2000. *A Recognition of Being: Reconstructing Native Womanhood.* Toronto: Second Story Press.

Armstrong, Jeannette C. 1998. Land Speaking. In *Speaking for the Generations: Native Writers on Writing,* edited by Simon J. Ortiz. Tucson: University of Arizona Press.

Assembly of First Nations. 1999. *Annual General Assembly Resolution 10/99, Vancouver, on Adoption and Repatriation Services to First Nations People of Canada.*

Barnsley, Paul. 2000. Membership Issues Illustrate Cultural Differences. *Windspeaker* (February): 6–7.

———. 2003. Minister Accused of Abuse of Power. *Windspeaker* (January): 3, 9.

————. 2003a. Harvard Study Group Finds Fault with FNGA. *Windspeaker* (February): 1, 2.

————. 2003b. New National Métis Organization Forming. *Windspeaker* (February): 15.

————. 2003c. Assault on Rights Alleged. *Windspeaker* (March): 1, 14.

————. 2003d. Cracks Begin to Show in AFN. *Windspeaker* (March): 1, 3.

————. 2003e. White Paper Revisited? *Windspeaker* (March): 14, 25.

————. 2003f. Compelled and Compelling. *Windspeaker* (April): 9.

————. 2003g. "Same old tricks, lawyer." *Windspeaker* (April): 8.

Barsh, Russell, and James Youngblood Henderson. 1980. *The Road: Indian Tribes and Political Liberty*. Berkeley: University of California Press.

Bartko, Patricia. 2000. Lesser Slave Lake Aboriginal Population Circa 1899—The Community Quandary—Choosing Between Treaty & Scrip. In *Treaty 8 Revisited: Selected Papers on the 1999 Centennial Conference*, edited by Duff Crerar and Jaroslav Petryshyn. Grande Prairie: Grande Prairie Regional College.

Beyefsky, Anne F. 1982. The Human Rights Committee and the Case of Sandra Lovelace. In *The Canadian Yearbook of International Law*. Vol. 20.

Bill C-31: The Challenge. 1996. Classroom Edition. *Windspeaker* (March): 7.

Boyd, Gail. 1998. Struggle for Aboriginal Mobility Rights Continues. *The First Perspective* (March): 8.

Caldwell, E. K. 1999. *Dreaming the Dawn: Conversations with Native Artists and Activists*. Lincoln and London: University of Nebraska Press.

Carter, Sarah. 1997. *Capturing Women: The Manipulation of Cultural Imagery in Canada's Prairie West*. Kingston and Montreal: McGill-Queen's University Press.

Chrisjohn, Roland, and Sherri Young, with Michael Maraun. 1997. *The Circle Game: Shadows and Substance in the Indian Residential School Experience in Canada*. Penticton BC: Theytus Books.

Churchill, Ward. 1994. *Indians Are Us? Culture and Genocide in Native North America*. Toronto: Between the Lines.

Clark, Blue. 1994. *Lone Wolf v Hitchcock: Treaty Rights and Indian Law at the End of the Nineteenth Century*. Lincoln and London: University of Nebraska Press.

Clifford, James. 1988. *The Predicament of Culture: Twentieth Century Ethnography, Literature, and Art.* Cambridge: Harvard University Press.

Clinton, Robert N., Nell Jessup Newton, and Monroe E. Price. 1973. *American Indian Law: Cases and Materials.* 3d ed. Charlottesville va: Michie Company.

Coates, K. S., and W. R. Morrison. 1986. More Than a Matter of Blood: The Federal Government, the Churches, and the Mixed Blood Population of the Yukon and the Mackenzie River Valley, 1890–1950. In *1885 and After: Native Society in Transition,* edited by Laurie Barron and James B. Waldram. Regina sk: University of Regina, Canadian Plains Research Centre.

Cohen, Felix S. 1942. *Handbook of Federal Indian Law.* Reprinted: American Indian Law Centre: University of New Mexico, Albuquerque, New Mexico.

Cook-Lynn, Elizabeth. 1996. *Why I Can't Read Wallace Stegner and Other Essays: A Tribal Voice.* Madison: University of Wisconsin Press.

———. 1998. Intellectualism and the New Indian Story. In *Natives and Academics: Research and Writing about American Indians,* edited by Devon A. Mihesuah. Lincoln and London: University of Nebraska Press.

Daniel, G. Reginald. 1992. Passers and Pluralists: Subverting the Racial Divide. In *Racially Mixed People in America,* edited by Maria P. P. Root. Newbury Park ca: Sage Publications.

Deloria, Vine Jr. 1998. Comfortable Fictions and the Struggle for Turf: An Essay Review of *The Invented Indian: Cultural Fictions and Government Policies.* In *Natives and Academics: Research and Writing about American Indians,* edited by Devon A. Mihesuah. Lincoln and London: University of Nebraska Press.

Deloria, Vine, Jr., and Clifford Lytle. 1984. *The Nations Within: The Past and Future of American Indian Sovereignty.* Austin: University of Texas Press.

Deloria, Philip J. 1998. *Playing Indian.* New Haven and London: Yale University Press.

Dickason, Olive Patricia. 1985. From "One Nation" in the Northeast to "New Nation" in the Northwest: A Look at the Emergence of the Métis. In *The New Peoples: Being and Becoming Métis in North America,* edited by Jacqueline Peterson and Jennifer S. H. Brown. Winnipeg: University of Manitoba Press.

————. 1992. *Canada's First Nations: A History of Founding Peoples from Earliest Times.* Toronto: Oxford University Press.

Dion Stout, Madeleine. 1994. Fundamental Changes Needed to End Violence. *Windspeaker* (November): 7.

Dow, Cynthia. 1998. Listuguj Protestors Won't Back Down. *Micmac-Maliseet Nations News* (August): 1.

Dumont, Linda, and Tara De Ryk. 1997. C-31 Women Protest. *Alberta Sweetgrass* (July): 15.

Ems, Gerhard J. 2000. Taking Treaty 8 Scrip, 1899–1900: A Quantitative Portrait of Northern Alberta Métis Communities. In *Treaty 8 Revisited: Selected Papers on the 1999 Centennial Conference,* edited by Duff Crerar and Jaroslav Petryshyn. Grande Prairie: Grande Prairie Regional College.

Flanagan, Thomas. 2000. *First Nations? Second Thoughts.* Kingston and Montreal: McGill-Queen's University Press.

Forbes, Jack. 1987. Shouting Back to the Geese. In *I Tell You Now: Autobiograpical Essays by Native American Writers,* edited by Brian Swann and Arnold Krupat. Lincoln and London: University of Nebraska Press.

————. 1988. *Black Africans and Native Americans: Color, Race, and Caste in the Evolution of Red-Black Peoples.* Oxford: Basil Blackwell.

Gilbert, Larry. 1996. *Entitlement to Indian Status and Membership Codes in Canada.* Toronto: Thompson Canada Ltd.

Gilroy, Paul. 1993. *The Black Atlantic: Modernity and Double Consciousness.* Cambridge: Harvard University Press.

Gould, Jeffrey L. 1998. *To Die in This Way: Nicaraguan Indians and the Myth of Mestizaje, 1880–1965.* Durham and London: Duke University Press.

Grant, Agnes. 1996. *No End of Grief: Indian Residential Schools in Canada.* Winnipeg: Pemmican Publications.

Harring, Sidney L. 1994. *Crow Dog's Case: American Indian Sovereignty, Tribal Law, and United States Law in the Nineteenth Century.* Cambridge: Cambridge University Press.

Hatt, Ken. 1986. The North-West Rebellion Scrip Commissions, 1885–1889. In *1885 and After: Native Society in Transition,* edited by Laurie Barron and James B. Waldram. Regina SK: University of Regina, Canadian Plains Research Centre.

Hirschfelder, Arlene, and Martha Kreipe de Montano. 1993. *The Native American Almanac: A Portrait of Native America Today*. New York: Simon & Schuster.

Holmes, Joan. 1987. *Bill C-31—Equality or Disparity? The Effects of the New Indian Act on Native Women*. Background Paper. Canadian Advisory Council on the Status of Women.

How Indian Is Indian? 1996. Classroom Edition. *Windspeaker* (September): 12.

Huntley, Audrey, and Fay Blaney, with the assistance of Rain Daniels, Lizabeth Hall, and Jennifer Dysart. 1999. *Bill C-31: Its Impacts, Implications, and Recommendations for Change in British Columbia—Final Report*. Aboriginal Women's Action Network and Vancouver Status of Women.

Jamieson, Kathleen. 1978. *Indian Women and the Law in Canada: Citizens Minus*. Canadian Advisory Council on the Status of Women and Indian Rights for Indian Women.

———. 1979. Multiple Jeopardy: The Evolution of a Native Women's Movement. *Atlantis* 4, no. 2:157–76.

Johnston, Patrick. 1983. *Native Children and the Child Welfare System*. Toronto: Canadian Council on Social Development in association with James Lorimer & Company.

Kahnawake Excludes Students on Basis of Blood Content. 1995. *Windspeaker* (May): 1.

Le Camp, Lorraine. 1998. *Terra Nullius/Theoria Nullius—Empty Lands/Empty Theory: A Literature Review of Critical Theory from an Aboriginal Perspective*. Unpublished manuscript. Department of Sociology and Equity Studies, Ontario Institute for Studies in Education.

LaRoque, Emma. 1993. Preface—or "Here are Our Voices—Who Will Hear?" In *Writing the Circle: Native Women of Western Canada*, edited by Jeanne Perreault and Sylvia Vance. Edmonton: NeWest Publishers.

Lemkin, Raphael. 1944. *Axis Rule in Occupied Europe*. Concord NH: Carnegie Endowment for International Peace and Rumford Press.

Leonard, David, and Beverly Whalen, eds. 1999. *On the North Trail: The Treaty 8 Diary of O. C. Edwards*. Vol. 12. Alberta Records Publication Board, Historical Society of Alberta.

Long, John S. 1978. *Treaty No. 9: The Halfbreed Question, 1902–1910*. Cobalt ON: Highway Book Shop.

———. 1985. Treaty No. 9 and Fur Trade Company Families: North-eastern Ontario's Halfbreeds, Indians, Petitioners and Métis. In *The New Peoples: Being and Becoming Métis in North America*, edited by Jacqueline Peterson and Jennifer S. H. Brown. Winnipeg: University of Manitoba Press.

Loomba, Ania. 1998. *Colonialism/Postcolonialism*. London: Routledge.

Mahmud, Tayyab. 1999. Colonialism and Modern Constructions of Race: A Preliminary Inquiry. *University of Miami Law Review* 53, no. 4:1219–46.

Mainville, Robert. 2001. *An Overview of Aboriginal and Treaty Rights and Compensation for Their Breach*. Saskatoon SK: Purich Publishing.

Mair, Charles. 1908. *Through the Mackenzie Basin—A Narrative of the Athabasca and Peace River Treaty Expedition of 1899*. Toronto: William Brigg.

McKinley, Rob. 1997. C-31 Appeal Decision Overturned. *Windspeaker* (July): 1, 4.

———. 1997a. C-31 Court Case Can Continue without Twinn. *Windspeaker* (December): 2.

———. 1998. Human Rights Commission Defends Status Claim. *Micmac-Maliseet Nations News* (February): 9.

———. 1998a. Gathering Looks at Cree Confederacy. *Alberta Sweetgrass* (May): 1.

———. 1998b. Push Is On for Re-creation of Blackfoot Confederacy. *Alberta Sweetgrass* (June): 1.

———. 1998c. Inuit Ancestry Lost with the Stroke of a Pen. *Windspeaker* (October): 9.

Miller, J. R. 1989. *Skyscrapers Hide the Heavens: A History of Indian-White Relations in Canada*. Toronto: University of Toronto Press.

———. 1996. *Shingwauk's Vision: A History of Native Residential Schools*. Toronto: University of Toronto Press.

Monet, Don, and Skanu'u (Ardythe Wilson). 1992. *Colonialism on Trial: Indigenous Land Rights and the Gitksan and Wet'suwe'en Sovereignty Case*. Philadelphia: New Society Publishers.

Monture-Angus, Patricia. 1999. *Journeying Forward: Dreaming First Nations Independence*. Halifax: Fernwood Publishing.

Moraga, Cherrie. 1996. The Breakdown of the Bicultural Mind. In *Names We Call Home: Autobiography on Racial Identity*, edited by Becky Thompson and Sangeeta Tyagi. New York: Routledge.

Morris, Alexander. 1880. *The Treaties of Canada with the Indians of Manitoba and the North-West Territories*. Toronto: Belfords, Clark.

Native Child and Family Services of Toronto, Janet Budgell, and Sevenato & Associates. 1999. *Our Way Home: A Report to the Aboriginal Healing and Wellness Strategy on the Repatriation of Aboriginal People Removed by the Child Welfare System*. Joint Management Committee of the Aboriginal Healing and Wellness Strategy.

Nicks, Trudy, and Kenneth Morgan. 1985. Grande Cache: The Historic Development of an Indigenous Alberta Métis Population. In *The New Peoples: Being and Becoming Métis in North America*, edited by Jacqueline Peterson and Jennifer S. H. Brown. Winnipeg: University of Manitoba Press.

Normand, Josee. 1996. *A Profile of the Métis*. Ottawa: Statistics Canada.

Paul, Daniel. 2000. *We Were Not the Savages: A Mi'kmaq Perspective on the Collision between European and Native American Civilizations*. Twenty-first Century edition. Halifax: Fernwood Press.

Paul, Johnny. 1997. To Treaty Descendants of Papasschase. Letters to the Editor, *Alberta Sweetgrass* (September): 4.

Penn, William S. 1997. Tradition and the Individual Imitation. In *As We Are Now: Mixblood Essays on Race and Identity*, edited by William S. Penn. Berkeley and Los Angeles: University of California Press.

Peterson, Jacqueline, and Jennifer S. H. Brown. 1985. Introduction to *The New Peoples: Being and Becoming Métis in North America*, edited by Jacqueline Peterson and Jennifer S. H. Brown. Winnipeg: University of Manitoba Press.

Plant, Judith. 1989. Wings of the Eagle: Interview with Marie Wilson. In *Healing the Wounds: The Promise of Ecofeminism*, edited by Judith Plant. Toronto: Between the Lines.

Plaskow, Judith. 1990. *Standing Again at Sinai*. San Francisco: Harper and Row.

Razack, Sherene. 2000. Gendered Racial Violence and Spatialized Justice: The Murder of Pamela George. *Canadian Journal of Law and Society* 15:2.

Reddekopp, Neil G., and Patricia Bartko. 2000. Distinction without a Difference? Treaty and Scrip in 1899. In *Treaty 8 Revisited: Selected Papers on the 1999 Centennial Conference*, edited by Duff

Crerar and Jaroslav Petryshyn. Grande Prairie: Grande Prairie Regional College.

Richard, Kenn. 1994. The Urbanization of Aboriginal Canada. *Perception* 17, no. 4:4.

Roseberry, William. 1994. The Language of Contention. In *Everyday Forms of State Formation: Revolution and the Negotiation of Rule in Modern Mexico,* edited by Gilbert Joseph and Donald Nugent. Durham NC: Duke University Press.

Royal Commission on Aboriginal Peoples (RCAP). 1996. *For Seven Generations: Report of the Royal Commission on Aboriginal Peoples.* Vols. 1–5. Ottawa: Government of Canada.

Schmalz, Peter S. 1991. *The Ojibwa of Southern Ontario.* Toronto: University of Toronto Press.

School Board and Mohawk Council Clash over "Blood Quantum": Council Checks Heritage of Children for Racial Purity. 1995. *The First Perspective* (June): 1, 4.

Scott, Duncan Campbell. 1914. Indian Affairs, 1867–1912. Edited by A. Shortt and A. G. Doughty. Vol. 7 of *Canada and Its Provinces.* Toronto: Glasgow, Brook.

Sifton, Clifford. 1898. Superintendent General of Indian Affairs to His Excellence the Governor General in Council, June 18, 1898. In *Treaty Negotiations between the Indian Affairs Department and the Native People, 1891–1899.* NAC, RG-10, Vol. 3848, File 75236-1.

Silko, Leslie Marmon. 1998. Interior and Exterior Landscapes: The Pueblo Migration Stories. In *Speaking for the Generations: Native Writers on Writing,* edited by Simon J. Ortiz. Tucson: University of Arizona Press.

Silman, Janet. 1987. *Enough Is Enough: Aboriginal Women Speak Out,* as told to Janet Silman. Toronto: The Women's Press.

Sioui, Georges. 1997. Why We Should Have Inclusivity and Why We Cannot Have It. *Ayaangwaamizin: The International Journal of Indigenous Philosophy* 1, no. 2 (Winter):51–62

St. Germain, Jill. 2001. *Indian Treaty-Making Policy in the United States and Canada, 1867–1877.* Toronto: University of Toronto Press.

Stoler, Ann. 1991. Carnal Knowledge and Imperial Power: Gender, Race, and Morality in Colonial Asia. In *Gender at the Crossroads: Feminist Anthropology in the Post-Modern Era,* edited by Micaela di Leonardo. Berkeley: University of California Press.

Stonechild, Blair, and Bill Waiser. 1997. *Loyal till Death: Indians and the North-West Rebellion*. Calgary: Fifth House Limited.

Strong, Pauline Turner, and Barrik Van Winkle. 1995. "Indian Blood": Reflections on the Reckoning and Refiguring of Native North American Identity. *Cultural Anthropology* 11, no. 4:547–76.

Switzer, Maurice. 1997. Time to Stand Up and Be Counted. *The First Perspective* (December): 2.

Taylor, Drew Hayden. 2003. Life as a Native Is Often Just Too Interesting. *Windspeaker* (February): 5.

Taylor, Theodore W. 1984. *The Bureau of Indian Affairs*. Boulder co: Westview Press.

Thomas, David Hurst. 2000. *Skull Wars: Kennewick Man, Archaeology, and the Battle for Native American Identity*. New York: Basic Books.

Treaty 7 Elders and Tribal Council, with Walter Hildebrandt, Sarah Carter, and Dorothy First Rider. 1997. *The True Spirit and Original Intent of Treaty 7*. Kingston and Montreal: McGill-Queen's University Press.

Tribunal Upholds Couple's Rights as Mohawks. 1998. *The First Perspective* (April): 2.

Tuhiwai Smith, Linda. 1999. *Decolonizing Methodologies: Research and Indigenous Peoples*. London and New York: Zed Books.

United States Department of the Interior. 1958. *Federal Indian Law*. 1966. Reprint, Dobbs Ferry ny: Oceana Publications.

Wabanaki Confederacy Conference at Odenak—1998. 1998. *Micmac-Maliseet Nations News* (August): 3.

Waldram, James. 1986. The "Other Side": Ethnostatus Distinctions in Western Subarctic Native Communities. In *1885 and After: Native Society in Transition*, edited by Laurie Barron and James B. Waldram. Regina sk: University of Regina, Canadian Plains Research Centre.

Warren, Kay. 1992. Transforming Memories and Histories: The Meanings of Ethnic Resurgence for Mayan Indians. In *Americas: New Interpretive Essays*, edited by Alfred Stepan. New York: Oxford University Press.

Weaver, Jace. 1997. *That the People Might Live: Native American Literatures and Native American Community*. New York: Oxford University Press.

———. 1998. Preface to *Native American Religious Identity: Unforgotten Gods*, edited by Jace Weaver. Maryknoll ny: Orbis Books.

Wilson, Terry P. 1992. Blood Quantum: Native American Mixed Bloods, In *Racially Mixed People in America*, edited by Maria P. P. Root. Newbury Park CA: Sage Publications.

Womack, Craig. 1997. Howling at the Moon: The Queer But True Story of My Life as a Hank Williams Song. In *As We Are Now: Mixblood Essays on Race and Identity*, edited by William S. Penn. Berkeley and Los Angeles: University of California Press.

Woody, Elizabeth. 1998. Voice of the Land: Giving the Good Word. In *Speaking for the Generations: Native Writers on Writing*, edited by Simon Ortiz. Tucson: University of Arizona Press.

Yellow Bird, Pemina, and Kathryn Milun. 1994. Interrupted Journeys: The Cultural Politics of Indian Reburial. In *Displacements: Cultural Identities in Question*, edited by Angelika Bammer. Bloomington and Indianapolis: Indiana University Press.

Ziervogel, Kim. 1996. South Edmonton Claimed by Pahpahstayo First Nation. *Windspeaker* (August): 8.

Index

Aboriginal rights, 3–5, 70, 71, 242–44, 289n2

Aboriginal sovereignty, 2, 11, 28–30, 33, 62–63, 69, 74, 195, 237–46. *See also* Native identity (mixed-blood): and nationhood

Aboriginal title, 4–5, 244–45, 289n2

Alfred, Taiaiake, 5, 58, 289n3

allotment, 16, 28, 39, 74–75

appearance, xi, 13, 76, 257–58, 266; and alienation from Native identity, 145–46, 147–51, 173, 176, 179–81; importance of, 154, 156, 173–76, 177, 179–80, 214, 228–29; and resisting hegemonic values, 174–75, 187–90, 229

Assembly of First Nations (AFN), 58

assimilation, 31, 130–31, 138, 152–53; policies of, 31, 105–7, 111–12, 119, 120

Association of Iroquois and Allied Nations (AIAI), 58, 282n9

authenticity, 89, 135–36, 168

band membership, 64, 67–73, 74, 77–81, 191–97, 237–38; entitlement to, 194–

96, 248–49; importance of, 192–94, 196–97, 275

Bill C-31, 56, 57, 64, 67–73, 77, 101, 114, 192, 274–75, 282n8, 283n1, 288n1

blood memory, 6, 11, 198–201

blood quantum, 15–16, 18, 28–29, 39–41, 68, 69, 73–77, 78–80, 153–56, 175, 185–87, 285n10. *See also* Indian Act: and blood quantum

Cherokee Nation v. Georgia, 28

child welfare, 37, 105, 112–19; and Native identity, 146–47, 203–4, 275–78, 287n3. *See also* "sixties scoop"

colonization, 107; and identity regulation, 7, 16–18, 27–30, 39–44, 74–77, 229–31, 284n9, 287n5; and land theft, 28, 46–47, 74–75, 77, 229–30, 280n5, 287n6. *See also* Indian Act: and identity legislation; Native identity: regulation of

cross-border issues, 111, 113, 218–19, 263–65, 268, 271, 277, 287n1

Delgamuukw, 4, 289n2